PRAISE FOR
THE NOVELS OF PATIENCE GRIFFIN

Meet Me in Scotland

"A captivating story of four friends, two madcap romances, an idyllic Scottish town, and its endearingly stubborn but loyal inhabitants. Add scones, quilts, and kilts? Griffin sews this one up. Witty, warmhearted, and totally charming!"
—Shelley Noble, *New York Times* bestselling
author of *Breakwater Bay*

To Scotland with Love

"Griffin's lyrical and moving debut marks her as a most talented newcomer to the romance genre."
—*Publishers Weekly* (starred review)

"A magnificent triple-hankie debut written straight from the heart, by turns tender, funny, heart-wrenching, and wise. Prepare to smile through your tears at this deft, brave, and deeply gratifying love story."
—Grace Burrowes, *New York Times* bestselling author
of the Lonely Lords and the Windham series

"Griffin has quilted together a wonderful, heartwarming story that will convince you of the power of love."
—Janet Chapman, *New York Times* bestselling author
of *The Highlander Next Door*

"Griffin's .... able as a cherished he.............

.... *mes* bestselling
.... l, Texas Novels

"A life-a.. edemption. Patience G...................................... ng characters, a spectacular setting, and a poignant romance into a story as warm and beautiful as an heirloom quilt. Both heartrending and heartwarming, *To Scotland with Love* is a mustread romance and so much more. The story will touch your soul with its depth, engage you with its cast of endearing characters, ..."
—Di.. y series

Also by Patience Griffin

Some Like It Scottish
Meet Me in Scotland
To Scotland with Love

The Accidental Scot

A Kilts and Quilts Novel

Patience Griffin

A SIGNET ECLIPSE BOOK

SIGNET ECLIPSE
Published by New American Library,
an imprint of Penguin Random House LLC
375 Hudson Street, New York, New York 10014

This book is an original publication of New American Library.

First Printing, December 2015

For more information about Penguin Random House, visit penguin.com

ISBN 978-0-451-47638-8

33614056447419

Printed in the United States of America
10 9 8 7 6 5 4 3 2 1

Penguin
Random
House

Acknowledgments

Thank you to my wonderful and loving PhD, who answered the question when I asked what story should I write next. What other husband would've provided so many textbooks and detailed research . . . but that's my guy. This book, my dear man, is for you.

For my son, Mitch, who makes me laugh and is a constant source of joy. Thank you for being you.

Many thanks to Deborah Chabrian for her continuing amazing artistic talent on the Kilts and Quilts book covers. They make my heart smile.

PRONUNCIATION GUIDE

Aileen (AY-leen)
Ailsa (AIL-sa)
Bethia (BEE-thee-a)
Cait (kate)
Deydie (DI-dee)
Fairge (fah-[d]RAYK-yuh)—sea, ocean
Lios (lis)—garden
Lochie (LAW-kee)
Macleod (muh-KLOUD)
Moira (MOY-ra)
Taog (took)

DEFINITIONS

bampot—a crazy person
céilidh (KAY-lee)—a party/dance
CNC machine—a machine used in manufacturing to increase the accuracy and efficiency of metal parts by utilizing a computer to control machining tools
English paper piecing—A quilting technique used to piece small shapes with precision, in which fabric is basted over paper templates, then whip-stitched together
kirk—church
mo chroí (muh khree)—my heart
postie—postman
reive—to rob
skiver—a person who avoids work or duty
Tha gaol agam ort—I love you

Quilters of Gandiegow

Rule #3
The most important piece stitched into a quilt is love.

Chapter One

Pippa McDonnell adjusted her winter coat, tightening the belt around her waist. She did her best to shut out Father Andrew's words during the graveside service. She tried to distract herself by thinking of different ways to solve the high-pressure test problem at the North Sea Valve Company—her da's company. Her tactic didn't work. Her emotions threatened to overtake her as the service concluded and the villagers processed down the narrow path from the cemetery. Pippa followed them, focusing on the scenery—the familiar rooftops of Gandiegow below, the choppy sea on the horizon, and the crunch of the snow beneath her boots. But all pretense of *not feeling* fell away once the women made their way into Deydie's cottage. Deydie was the head quilter, the town matriarch, the bossiest woman Pippa had ever known. That's when and where reality sank in.

Pippa's father, the McDonnell, could end up like Kenneth Campbell . . . dead.

She had come home the second week in July, when her father had his accident, and taken his place running the North Sea Valve Company. It was now almost December, and NSV still wasn't standing on its own legs. Neither was her da.

Each woman pulled out a chair and sat around Deydie's worn dining table, devoid of the sewing machines that had always been there when Pippa was a girl. Now all the machines resided at Quilting Central, where the women gathered regularly. The usual crew was here, the quilters.

Pippa wasn't one of them, though the older women had tried their damnedest to mold her into a quilter when she was knee-high to a midge. But she was a part of them, shared a commonality with the village women, closer than a lot of blood relations. She just couldn't remember it ever being this quiet in Deydie's cottage.

Pippa glanced over at Moira, the reason they were all here. Moira was painfully shy, but the pain on her face today had nothing to do with being bashful. Kenneth Campbell, her father, had been laid to rest only an hour ago. Normally, the town would've gathered to support her at the kirk or at Quilting Central or at her house, but Moira needed only the quilting ladies . . . and of course, Pippa.

Laid to rest seemed fitting. Pippa sure hoped God would let Kenneth Campbell rest after all this time. The big Scot had spent many years trying to recover from a fishing accident. In pain, miserable, and lingering, but he'd never complained. Moira had taken diligent care of him for years, but Kenneth never got better, never overcame.

The words that Da's doctor had spoken to Pippa only yesterday—in hushed tones—fell over her again like the quiet enormity that rested around the table now. *Your father's not healing as expected. He's not recovering like we'd hoped.* Pippa's da was everything to her. He had been her whole life. What if his fate was Kenneth's fate? What if his broken bones never mended? What if he was *laid to rest* in the cemetery as well?

But Pippa wouldn't sit by and wait to see what would happen next. She stood and paced the floor. Deydie was the only one who seemed to notice her movement. Pippa had always been a woman of action. She would find a way to pay for the private care the doctor suggested. She couldn't stand by and wait until a slot came open for a specialist. Her father needed help now.

Deydie pushed the teapot closer. "Pippa, pour Moira a cup of tea."

Freda jumped to her feet, too, pulling down mugs from the cabinet. Pippa filled while Freda placed. When tea was poured—and ignored—Pippa resumed her pacing.

Bethia, Deydie's oldest friend, grabbed Pippa's hand. "Sit, dear. Please?"

Begrudgingly, Pippa took her chair. Her heart went out to Moira, who'd been through the wringer this past month. Her father's decline, her young cousin Glenna coming to live with her as her own parents had perished, and then three days ago, the inevitable . . . Moira's da died.

Pippa shouldn't draw parallels, but was Moira's future to be her future, too? Moira had completely withdrawn, shutting out a good number of them, but none so much as Andrew, her beau and Gandiegow's Episcopal priest.

Cait, Deydie's granddaughter, touched Moira's arm. "Come stay with us tonight at the big house. Mattie can keep Glenna company."

Moira shook her head *no* without looking up.

Cait was dealing with her own loss, two miscarriages. And leaving soon. With a book about her famous husband Graham coming out shortly, they'd decided to escape Scotland to avoid the media frenzy. Everyone in the world would learn that this was Graham's hometown.

Pippa was the opposite of Graham. He'd never wanted to leave Gandiegow, while she hadn't been done with school two minutes before taking off and planting herself in Edinburgh. Her plans and dreams had been too big for this village to hold. They still were. But nothing could change how she felt about Gandiegow's people. They were pure gold.

Cait gazed up at her kindly. "Why don't you go on home and check on yere da." She'd misread Pippa's restlessness.

Pippa didn't correct her, but took the out. "Aye. Da should be ready for his pills."

Freda jumped up, too, always willing to help. Something Pippa both resented and appreciated. She held up her hand to stop the woman who had been a fixture in Pippa's life forever. "No. I've got it."

Pippa laid a hand on Moira's shoulder as she passed by. Too much more and Moira would've been escaping for home. But no one would be there. Pippa grabbed her coat off Deydie's quilt-laden bed. As she slipped it on, she glanced at the wall, seeing something new.

"What's this?" Pippa stepped closer, pulling it from a nail.

"What do ye mean?" Deydie acted as if she wanted to call her a *ninny* but seemed to hold her tongue out of respect for Moira and Kenneth. "Haven't you ever seen a calendar before?"

Pippa flipped the top page over. It was indeed a calendar, but it featured handsome men dressed in kilts: *Men of the Clan*. When she realized all the quilters were staring at her, she hung it back in its place. "I better get home to take care of my da." But then she wanted to kick herself. Hadn't she heard Moira say that same phrase a hundred times?

Pippa quickly slipped out the door. The temperature had dropped as the days grew shorter. Her brain, though, barely registered the cold weather.

A pang of guilt hit her. She had left Gandiegow to escape everyone trying to marry her off. Sure, she'd been back to visit, but stayed only as long as the weekend or a bank holiday. But she hadn't been here when the Mc-Donnell had needed her most, when he'd almost killed himself doing something incredibly stupid and dangerous. Who in his right mind puts a pallet on a forklift, then a ladder on the pallet, then climbs to the top of the ladder to change a lightbulb? A pigheaded old Scot, who wouldn't dream of asking for help, that's who.

But guilt and lecturing the McDonnell wasn't going to fix the problem at hand. She needed to find a way to afford private health care. Possibly get Da to the U.S. to see a specialist there. But NSV wasn't making it either. Everything was falling apart. She'd have to work on all three problems at once . . . Repair NSV's finances, find cash for Da's medical care, and keep everyone from pressuring her into marrying Ross now that she was home.

Only last year MTech had made an offer for NSV when they'd gotten wind of Da's new subsea shutoff valve design. Da told them flat-out *no, North Sea Valve is not for sale*. But whether her da liked it or not, she'd let

MTech or any other outside investor come in and she'd listen to what they had to say. Scots weren't known for taking charity, but she'd entertain the foreigners as long as they brought an infusion of cash to the table—and scads of it.

Her other problem would take some thought. She hoofed it toward home to get Da his painkillers. Later, she'd head back to the factory to do paperwork.

Deydie's calendar flitted through her mind. Maybe she could do something similar. Not a calendar with half-naked men but something to raise money. Women were suckers when it came to a few muscles and a bit of swagger.

Pippa arrived home to find her father asleep in his wheelchair. She didn't have the heart to wake him, so she laid two painkillers beside his glass of water for when he woke up. As she walked out of the cottage, her eye caught the photo of her mother and father on their first date. Da had bid on her mother at a charity auction at university. Their beaming faces belied the fact that her mother would be gone four years later when Pippa was only a week old.

She glanced once more down the hallway. "I'll be back in one hour." There was no one awake to hear her words, but she said it anyway—their old habit. Just to reassure herself.

She walked to the parking lot, thinking of her parents' picture and how the auction had brought them together. She drove up and over the bluff to the factory a mile away. Once in her office, she pulled out a pad of engineering paper and began jotting down ideas, as if she were designing a piece of equipment. As she wrote, a grand idea started to take shape.

Outside her door, the factory floor came alive. She'd

given everyone the day off for the funeral, but apparently they were as restless as she was—needing something to take their minds off losing one of the long-standing members of the community and the nicest man they'd ever known.

Ross and his brother Ramsay stood outside her door. Ross leaned into her office. "Can we talk to you a minute?"

She'd grown up with these two hulking Scots and considered them like family. Ramsay, the youngest of the Armstrong brothers, wore the same easy smile he'd had on his face since marrying the matchmaker Kit Woodhouse, now Armstrong. Ross, on the other hand, didn't look so happy to see Pippa. He shoved his hands in his pockets, looking uncomfortable, things weird between them. She had long been expected to marry Ross, and now that she was home, the pressure was on. He must be feeling it, too. But she refused to think about all that now.

She joined them outside her office. "Can ye both take a look at conveyor three? There's something hanging it up."

They gazed down at her, expectantly, but it was Ross who spoke up first. "We want to know what the doctor had to say yesterday when ye were in Aberdeen. We're worried about the McDonnell."

Hell. Couldn't she have a little more time to process the news herself? "I really don't want to talk about it."

More of the workers made their way over and gathered around.

Ross motioned to the group. "We have a right to know."

Many of the men had invested not only their time into her father's vision, but what little money that they had. Ross included.

"He's not healing." Taog, the factory's ancient machinist, seemed to have read her mind. "What a rotten herring. 'Tis bad enough the McDonnell took a spill."

"'Twas more than a spill," Murdoch interrupted, running his fingers through his beard. He was the other machinist. He and Taog were always together, and more times than not, were at each other's throat. "I saw the bone sticking out of his leg meself. Jagged, it was. Och, blood was everywhere."

"Quiet," Ross commanded.

"Don't worry, lass." Taog dug in his pocket and produced his wallet. "Somehow, we'll get him the medical treatment he needs. We'll pass around a bucket to collect for private care."

"It won't be enough. We could ask Graham." Ramsay looked embarrassed to have said it.

"Nay. The McDonnell wouldn't want it." Pippa had to do this on her own. "No one better bother Graham and Cait. They have enough worries." She pointed at Taog. "Grab the notepad off my desk."

Taog lumbered past her to get it.

"But we want to help." Murdoch nodded his head, his beard bouncing.

"I know you do. And most of ye will." Pippa took the pad from Taog. "Here's how we're going to raise money." She thanked the Almighty for the clues and ideas that he'd dropped in her lap today—Deydie's calendar, her father buying her mother at auction, and her engineer's calculating brain. "There's no need to call anyone. We have all we need right here." She looked around at the ruggedly handsome men of the village, *the single handsome men*. She sent up another thank-you for that, too.

"We'll have an auction. We're going to sell off our bachelors."

Ramsay's face uncharacteristically clouded over, a storm coming. "And who's going to tell my wife that ye're horning in on her business with this plan of yeres? It won't be me."

Pippa laughed and it felt good after so much sadness. "No worries. It shouldn't interfere with Kit's serious matchmaking. It's just a bit of fun for one evening."

Ramsay grinned. "Then I'm sure you can count on us to assist you with it."

Pippa looked into the eyes of each single, bonny Scotsman standing there. "Ye'll all help with the auction?"

"Aye, Pippa," they all agreed one by one.

The whole lot of them were like brothers to her and she could get away with talking to them like a bossy sister. "Each of you will be shaved, showered, and kilted. And there better not be the stink of bluidy fish on any one of you. Do ye hear?"

"What'd'ya have in mind?" Taog, being an old married man, had nothing to worry about.

"Here's the plan," Pippa said. "We'll round up every rich lonely female in Scotland. We'll even reach out to London if we have to. We'll entice them to come to Gandiegow with their purses stuffed with money. And after we've filled them with our best single malt whisky, we'll sell off you lads for an evening of debauchery to the highest bidders."

Miranda Weymouth read the e-mail from Roger Gibbons, MTech's president, concerning NSV's patents for the subsea shutoff valve. *Send Max McKinley. Have him convince Lachlan McDonnell to sign. Tell McKinley to put his honest face to good use. Don't share the details with him.*

But NSV had been her deal . . . though one small miscalculation on her part had ended the negotiations early. Since then Roger's confidence in her had waned.

Miranda typed back to Roger. *North Sea Valve is my project. I'll go. I know Lachlan McDonnell.*

No sooner had she hit the SEND button than Roger had written back. *No. McKinley will go. You'll be his backup, but only if he fails.*

She closed her laptop, knowing what rested on this deal. Max, the golden boy, better not screw this up.

Max McKinley was jarred awake from his nightmare as the plane touched down in Scotland. *The same damn dream every time.* The real live nightmare he'd lived through at fifteen. He wiped the cold sweat from his forehead and tried to put the tragedy out of his mind. It always got worse this time of year. God, he hated Christmas.

He grabbed his carry-on and rushed off the plane. The first order of business was to call Mom and let her know the news—he wouldn't be home for the holidays. She would have a cow. Maybe he should've called before he left. But hell, he'd barely had enough time to pack before MTech pushed him out the door. It still puzzled him. Max was the new guy. The technical asset. Brand-new in the acquisitions department. Why send him?

Before he went in search of his rental car, he pulled out his phone and delivered the bad news.

"You're what?" His mom came close to blowing a gasket.

"Not coming home for the holidays," Max repeated.

"Or *won't*? How did you arrange it this time?" There was severity in her mom-knows-all Texas twang.

He cringed for the truth in her words. But he was thirty-four, for chrissakes. He was entitled to do what he thought was best. He loved his mom and her heart was in the right place, but she was ruthless when it came to the holidays.

"Come for at least the day," she said.

Max was tired from traveling, and tired of the same old argument, so without cushioning the blow he released the second bombshell. "I can't. I'm in Scotland."

"You're where?"

"Scotland. For work. Please don't give me a guilt-trip over it." Max sighed heavily into his cell, making sure his mother heard him all the way back in Houston.

She lit into him anyway. "You volunteered for it, didn't you? Found the perfect excuse to get out of Christmas this year."

"Mom—" he tried.

"You're not the only one who's suffered. Your father would've wanted you to move beyond this. And your brother . . . Well, at least we bought him a wheelchair instead of a casket."

Max ran a hand through his hair. "I know."

"You still blame yourself for Jake's accident, but—"

He cut her off. "Enough, okay? This trip has nothing to do with the past. It's work." But both nightmares still felt fresh. A fifteen-year-old boy should not be awakened on Christmas morning and given the news that his dad was dead. For the whole day, the television had re-played the oil rig explosion over and over again. Max had made it through some rough Christmases since. Then Jake's accident . . .

Mom was the one who sighed heavily this time. "Why couldn't they send someone else?" She could be such a pit bull when it came to family. And Christmas. "Why you?"

Exactly the question he'd asked himself. "I guess MTech wants me to cut my teeth on this deal." Even though he had no experience, as yet, in the acquisitions department. It must be trial by fire. But maybe it was be-cause he was such a damned good engineer. MTech had made him the youngest lead engineer in the history of their company, and now they'd given him a new challenge.

"Well, I hope at least you packed some warm clothes," Mom said begrudgingly.

"Love you, Mom." He meant it. "Tell Bitsy and Jake I'll call on Christmas Day." There'd be hell to pay if he didn't talk to his siblings then.

After a few more good-byes, he hung up. He got his rental car and started the trek to Gandiegow. It was only five o'clock in the afternoon, but the sky was dark, no moon in sight. The northeast coast of Scotland at the beginning of December would take some getting used to. With only the hum of the car to keep him company, the question niggled again. Why did MTech send him?

Max understood the importance of the new technol-ogy he was to evaluate. He was also here to close the deal. Miranda and the rest of the acquisitions depart-ment must have some pretty big Christmas plans to ship

Max out alone. The whole thing was crazy, but he hadn't questioned his superiors. *Anything to get out of Christmas.*

Yes, this trip came at exactly the right time. A nice cold visit to Scotland *by himself* would be an excellent way to spend the holidays. It would be the best damn Christmas he'd had in a long time.

The drive took longer than expected, given the icy, curvy roads. Not to mention that his GPS had not calculated how a herd of languorous hairy cows, dawdling in the thoroughfare, would slow him down.

When Max finally arrived in the village, he parked his rental car in the lot on the edge of town, knowing that no vehicles were allowed within the actual city limits. The walking paths were only wide enough for the small carts or wheelbarrows that rested here and there in front of the doorways. He'd read about this and many other quirks of the community in the MTech file.

He pulled out his American Tourister, locked his rental car, and rolled his bag toward the sparse civilization of stone cottages. He wasn't in Texas anymore.

The small village of Gandiegow hugged the coastline in an arc with a smattering of houses and buildings. The town looked as if an artist had painted it there to add visual interest to the snow-dusted bluffs rising out of the North Sea. Besides the valve factory, Gandiegow was known for two things: its commercial fishing and its international quilt retreats—*Kilts and Quilts*, they called it.

Max wheeled his bag over the snow-covered cobblestones until he reached his destination, The Fisherman. After getting a look at the town, he understood better why there was no hotel. It was a small community and ancient. He should be happy there was at least a space for him to rent—the room over the pub.

For a moment, he stood peering down the narrow walkway that expanded to the other end of town. This strip of concrete was the only thing separating the ocean from the village. He really should go inside the pub—he was freezing his ass off—but he couldn't get over it. One strong wave and the town could be washed away; the sixty-three houses and various establishments pulled out to sea. Who in their right mind would live near such danger looming outside their door?

He stepped inside the mayhem of the crowded pub and made his way to the bar with his bag in tow. He'd considered staying in Lios or Fairge at one of their bed and breakfasts, but he needed to be close to the factory, and it wouldn't hurt to embed himself in this community. He had only a month to win these people over and convince Lachlan McDonnell and his son to make the deal with MTech.

It would be a hell of a partnership. NSV's new subsea shutoff valve had the capability of shutting down an oil rig leak in seconds and preventing a catastrophic event. *Like the one that killed my father and many others over the years.*

If Max did his job right, the valve would be perfected in MTech's state-of-the-art research facility and in full production by the end of next quarter. He knew MTech saw dollar signs when they drew up this deal, but Max saw only how the valve would save lives.

As soon as he sat on the barstool, a strawberry blonde—tall, lean, and tempting—materialized. She glanced at his luggage and then peered at him.

"What can I get for ye, Yank?" She had a thick Scottish burr and the most incredible sea-blue eyes.

Before he could answer, an inebriated lug pushed Max aside and got in the bartender's face.

"Give us a kiss, Pippa," the man slurred. "Just one kiss before I have to go home to me wife."

"Och, ye're stinking drunk, Coby. Back off with ye. Can't you see we have an important guest in our midst? An American."

"American?" Coby telescoped his head back and forth, likely trying to get Max in focus.

Max caught him as he fell forward.

"Don't muss the pretty Yank." She motioned to the group at the end of the bar. "Taog, Murdoch, get Coby home, will ye?"

Max transferred Coby to the others and waited until they were out of earshot. "So I'm pretty, huh?"

"Aye and you damn well know it." She gave him a sardonic once-over as if *real* men were honed during barroom brawls and covered in scars from wrestling with sharks. She plunked a shot glass in front of him and filled it, though he hadn't ordered. "Here's yere drink, *sir*." She cocked a mocking eyebrow at him.

He didn't let her less than warm welcome bother him. He'd expected some resistance, especially since MTech had tried before to buy NSV outright. Instead, he smiled and thought about how her spirited name suited her . . . *Pippa*. He'd grown up around sassy women—his tough mother, grandmother, and firecracker of a little sister. He wasn't in the least put off by this Scottish lass and her sharp tongue. Actually it was quite the opposite. Her long curly hair and perfect curves made this Texas-born man want to know more about this intriguing woman.

But he wasn't here to hook up with the local barmaid. He was here to make a deal, which would prove himself to the higher-ups at MTech. Max needed to earn the trust of the Gandiegowans or he'd go home empty-handed.

"Thanks." He picked up the mystery drink and eyed the caramel-colored liquid before knocking it back. It didn't taste like the scotch back in the States. It was smoky and burned smooth. He pulled out money for another, enjoying the shocked expression on Pippa's face.

She leaned on the bar and he couldn't help but notice the tease of her cleavage in her tight green sweater.

"So ye can handle your whisky?" There was an air of respect in her tone and perhaps admiration shining in her sea-blue eyes.

"Aye," he said teasingly.

"But here in Scotland, we sip our drinks." A reprimand as she poured him another one.

Before taking the dram, he stuck out his hand. "I'm Max McKinley."

She eyed his hand but didn't take it. "We know who you are." She motioned to the room, but no one else paid attention. She leaned in again. "You may have been invited here, but beware. We know ye've come to rob us blind—take our factory and its jobs away from our people."

Her words doused him as if she'd thrown ice water in his face.

"Whoa, there." He scooted back, putting his hands up. "I haven't come to steal anything."

"Are you not with the big American company who was sniffing around before?" She stood tall and straight. "The mangy dogs."

"Yes, but that doesn't mean—"

"Just because our little factory needs a bit of help, you Yanks think it's a fine time to swoop in and swallow us whole, then spit out the leftover bits."

He frowned. He didn't agree with all of MTech's business practices. Yes, many times they bought a company for one of their products, only to dismantle the rest, letting thousands of employees go in the process. He had to keep telling himself *business was business, it wasn't personal.*

Besides, the deal he brought to the table was different this time. MTech wouldn't get run out of town with a buy-out offer like before. MTech was willing to do a partnership. *And I didn't come here to discuss it at the local pub over a shot of whisky.* He was here to speak with Alistair McDonnell, the chief engineer, and his father, Lachlan McDonnell, the owner of the North Sea Valve Company.

"You needn't say a word. It's plainly written on your face." She gave him a dismissive glower.

Maybe it was the exhaustion, or jet lag, or the scotch. But he'd had enough.

"For a bartender," he snapped, "you certainly act like you have some say in the matter."

She didn't flinch but surprisingly backed down. "Aye, you're right. 'Tis not my fight. It's up to the McDonnell." She dropped her eyes with a submissive shake to her gorgeous head. "I've no say. I should remember my place."

She wandered off and he downed his shot, regretting

what he'd done. He couldn't afford to get on the wrong side of even one villager. The stakes were too high.

"Miss?" he called out to her, motioning for her to come back. When she sauntered toward him, he saw the disguised shrewdness playing in her eyes. She wasn't the demure pussycat who'd backed down a moment ago. She was a cunning panther, ready to pounce.

She stopped in front of him and smiled sweetly. "Yes?"

"Sorry for being rude. Please forgive me. Can I buy you a drink to make it up to you?"

She *tsk*ed at him. "Da says never to drink at the trough with the swine."

He winced. "Ouch."

"Besides, us working girls can't afford to imbibe on the job and get fired. How long are you planning on being here, Yank?"

"As long as it takes. The New Year? Maybe longer." Max knew these deals took time.

"That long, huh?" She looked at him as if taking his measurements, then sashayed away.

She hadn't forgiven him, and he hated being in this position—the perceived bad guy. He squeezed his empty glass. But he was the one who'd put in for the promotion, trying to stretch his skill set. He wasn't just an engineer anymore. He was a *closer*. And by God, he would close this deal if it was the last thing he did.

Chapter Two

The next morning Max woke to a text message from Alistair McDonnell. He'd moved the appointment up, which was fine with Max. Over the last twenty-four hours, the two of them had exchanged many messages, and Alistair seemed like a decent, knowledgeable guy. Max knew Alistair was the one responsible for calling MTech back to the table. From the project file, the McDonnell—as others referred to Lachlan McDonnell—would never have opened the door to MTech and another meeting.

Max stretched and gazed out the small window of his room. During the night, the snow had quietly tiptoed in. White covered everything, which was a real treat. Living in Houston, he'd seen snow only when he went to Vail or Durango to ski.

After a quick shower, Max trudged to the parking lot in a business suit, tie, and dress shoes. By the time he arrived at his car, his dress shoes were soaked and his feet had turned into ice blocks.

Thankfully, the steep road that led in and out of town had been scraped, but he wasn't taking any chances with any slick spots beneath the wheels. Slowly and carefully, he drove back up and over the rounded bluff to where NSV sat about a mile away from Gandiegow. Just as the factory came into view, the sun peeked through the clouds, giving Max hope that all would go well here today with Alistair and the McDonnell.

NSV, made of ancient stone, had none of the glitz or size of the mega-factories in the U.S. But it did have character—an old warrior, worn-out from many years of battling time and the elements. He knew the building had stood empty for many years until eighteen months ago, when the McDonnell had reopened the factory doors. His son, Alistair, had recently joined him, stepping in as chief engineer.

Max pulled into the lot and turned off the car. No one was outside except one guy shoveling snow from the sidewalk leading to the front entrance.

As he got closer, two things struck him at once. It wasn't a man clearing the walk at all. It was a woman in men's coveralls. Secondly, this wasn't any woman. It was the tall barmaid from last night. *Pippa.*

"Mornin'," she said, as chipper as the sunlight above.

"Good morning to you, too." He was glad she'd let bygones be bygones. He pointed to her shovel. "Your day job?"

She smiled brightly. "Aye. Here in Gandiegow, a lass needs to hold several positions to make ends meet. Ye'll never know where I might turn up."

"Where else do you work?" And because he was a guy, and hadn't had the bandwidth to date lately, the word *positions* got kind of caught in his mind, rolling around. And not in an innocent way either.

"Ye'll see me here and there." She smiled evasively and scraped the last bit of snow from the walk. "Come. I'll point you in the right direction." She leaned her shovel against the building and took the lead.

Inside, the lobby was the strangest he'd ever seen. No contemporary plush furniture or end tables with trendy magazines. This place was barebones. Three kitchen chairs, one folding, and one dilapidated Queen Anne rested against the wall. A crest and a sword hung above the seats. In the corner sat the grand prize, a damned Douglas fir, decorated with loads of Christmas cheer. The magnificent tree didn't fit with the rest of the substandard decor.

A brunette came from behind a worn receptionist desk with a *hungry-for-men* smile and a mug in her hand. "I saw you pull up and poured you a cup of tea. In case you needed warming up. I'm Bonnie, by the way." She seemed to stick out her chest, flaunting her very large breasts in his direction.

But Max wasn't half as interested in her as he was in the strawberry blonde who'd put him in his place last night. He took his tea and thanked the receptionist just the same.

Pippa unzipped her coveralls and slipped her arms out, letting the top dangle down. He was stunned to see that underneath, she sported an old, form-fitting Tau Beta Pi T-shirt.

Tau Beta Pi? The Engineering Honor Society?

If he could've put together words, he might've asked where she got it. But he couldn't stop staring at her nipples. *God help him!* He jerked his eyes away, and in the process, spilled tea all over his suit from his chest to his knees.

"Damn."

"Not to worry." Pippa leaned over and whispered to the brunette who had resumed her position behind the desk. The only word he made out from the exchange was *auction*. From a nearby closet, Bonnie retrieved two items—a kilt clipped to a hanger, and a brown shopping bag. She handed them to Pippa.

Pippa presented the clothing to him. "Here, put this on. We'll take care of yere suit."

He frowned at the man skirt. "Thank you, no. I'll be fine."

"It's company policy to be dressed in a kilt." Amusement danced in her eyes, in addition to a fair dose of determination. "Everyone has to wear one for their company badge. For plant security."

That seemed highly unlikely. He glanced at her chest; she wore no badge.

He tore his eyes away. "Don't you have a guest badge?" *Like a normal factory?*

"A guest badge is only good for the day. Ye said you plan to be here the month." She planted her hands on her hips. "It's company—"

"Policy?" he finished for her.

"You catch on quick, Mr. McKinley."

"That's what they tell me." He grimaced at the kilt again.

She spun him toward a small door. "I'll be the one taking yere picture when you come out."

"Another one of your jobs?"

"Aye. Now change in there."

He marched into the small restroom and closed the door behind him. The brown bag held a white flowing shirt, black hiking boots, and thick, cream-colored knee-high socks.

"Don't be long, Yank," she hollered through the door. "I've work to do."

He quickly dressed, surprised the clothes and boots fit pretty well, considering. He left his wet things over the towel rack and went back out.

The brunette rose, giving him a low whistle. "Aye, Pippa, you were right about the Yank in a kilt."

Pippa nodded appreciatively at his legs. She grabbed a tartan and threw it over his shoulder. When she bent to fasten it by his hip, he couldn't help but let his mind wander to places it shouldn't. She smelled like fresh snow and woman. He felt both turned on and a little like Rob Roy.

She dragged him to the Christmas tree, positioning him in front of it.

"What are you doing?" he asked.

"Just smile for the birdie."

He didn't.

She snapped several photos anyway.

"Bonnie, pull the Queen Anne chair over to the tree and I'll take a few more."

He folded his arms across his chest. "What's really going on here?"

Pippa gave him an innocent *I've-no-idea-what-you're-talking-about* smile. "Are you sure ye're not Scottish, Mr. McKinley? You have the name for it. And the stubborn attitude. A veritable Scottish warrior through and through."

"Stop buttering me up." He narrowed his eyes at her. "You're up to something."

"Don't be a prig, Mr. McKinley." Pippa readjusted the

sash on his shoulder. "Americans love to claim to be Scottish."

The receptionist slipped from behind the desk.

He frowned at both of them and moved the Queen Anne chair himself.

The way Bonnie sauntered up to him, there was no denying she was out to stake her claim. "So what are you doing later? How about we grab a few drinks and have some laughs at the pub?"

Pippa put her hands on her hips. "Back off, Bonnie. He's here on business. Not to be handled by the likes of you."

He felt like a spectator at a tennis match, looking from one to the other.

Bonnie smiled, no offense taken to Pippa's harsh words. "A lass can try, can't she?" She slunk off, leaving them alone.

"Can I change back into my clothes yet?"

"Nay. We have to make sure you look right. For the badge and all." Pippa snapped a few more shots. One with him standing by the Queen Anne chair. Another with him seated like the frigging king of Scotland or something. She even had the audacity to point the camera at his legs and take two more, mumbling, "Good, good," to his shins.

"So do all the employees have their legs on their badges?" he drawled.

"Oh, aye, absolutely." Pippa looked as if she could barely hold back from laughing. "Leg shots are imperative for security. *Especially if someone is running from the building with our top-secret designs.*" She gave him a pointed look, as if that was why he was here. Her own words had a sobering effect. "I think we're done here."

She brushed her long curls out of the way as if being the photographer had worn her out. Or was that relief he saw on her face?

"Go change now, Mr. McKinley," Pippa ordered. Without a backward glance, she walked through the double doors leading into the plant with the camera swinging at her side.

He stood all alone in the lobby; Bonnie was gone, too.

Max looked again at the double doors Pippa had gone through. He wondered if her other jobs included sweeping the factory floor or cleaning the toilets. She perplexed him and he didn't know why. He forced her from his mind and went into the bathroom to put his clothes back on.

"What the hell?"

His tea-soaked pants weren't where he'd left them. Or his jacket. Or his dress shirt. He marched back out and found Bonnie had returned.

"Where are my clothes?"

Bonnie smiled helpfully. "Soaking in a bucket in the break room. Tea can be a bitch to get out."

He stared at her slack-jawed. "What am I supposed to wear?"

Bonnie eyed him like her favorite box of Christmas candy. "The kilt, of course."

"I can't go around like this."

"Och. It's Scotland. Ye'll be grand."

He peered down at his outfit, wishing to be anywhere else, and then tried to look at the bright side. At least the boots were warm. He approached her desk. "I assume Alistair McDonnell knows that I'm here?"

Bonnie stilled. For a moment, he wondered if maybe she'd misunderstood. She seemed genuinely confused.

He tried again. "Alistair McDonnell? We have an appointment." He lifted his mug and drained the remaining dribbles of his now-cold tea.

She frowned at him, picked up the phone, and put it to her ear. "The American says to tell ye he's here." She glanced up at him as if he'd been short-changed upstairs. "Go ahead and take a seat."

He wandered over to the coat of arms and studied it. After a few minutes, he chose a chair as far away from the Christmas tree as he could and checked his messages.

One from his mom. One from his sister. One from his brother.

And crap, Miranda wanted him to check in. He texted back quickly that he'd arrived, was staying in the room over the pub, and was about to meet with NSV's chief engineer.

As he hit SEND, the doors swung open and a professionally dressed woman came through. He stood. She had on a well-fitted navy suit with a tantalizing slit up the left side of her calf-length skirt. The way her heels clicked as she walked toward him sounded like a command—the same heels that made her almost as tall as him. Her loose hair from earlier had been stretched into a knot at the back of her head. However, it was her sea-blue eyes that shocked him.

Pippa was also *secretary to the owner?*

She stuck out her hand. "Alistair Philippa McDonnell. It's nice to meet you." She gave him a firm handshake.

He fumbled with the mug. If there'd been any tea left in it, he would've doused his kilt and been forced to tour the factory buck-naked.

She smiled, her professional aloofness daring him to acknowledge the switch-up. "Well, then," she finally said. "Should we have a look around?"

He seldom backed down from a challenge. "But last night—" he started.

"Let's not ruin last night by talking about it," she purred.

Bonnie's head shot up.

Pippa—*no, Alistair*—gave a throaty laugh and sashayed away, not seeming to give a damn about her reputation.

Max trailed behind her through the double doors like her lowly servant. They went down a long corridor as a million questions rolled through his baffled brain. He'd been given a data sheet on the McDonnell with as much personal information as could be attained. How had he not known that Alistair McDonnell was female? He certainly knew now by the shapely derriere in front of him. Max's only explanation for his file not being complete— privacy laws in Europe were much stricter than in the U.S.

He didn't let the subject drop. "Hold up. What should I call you?"

She stopped and turned to him, the epitome of seriousness. "How about *Yere Excellency*?"

"Alistair or Pippa?" he clarified.

"Since we're in Gandiegow, you can call me *Pippa*."

"Where's the McDonnell? Is he waiting for me in his office?"

Her eyebrows stitched together and she looked away, not meeting his eye. "Da took the day off."

Max frowned at her. "He knew I was coming, didn't he?"

She didn't answer but pushed open another set of

double doors. They stepped into a room filled with industrial sewing machines and bolts of canvas. In the corner stood . . . *another Christmas tree?*

"What the devil?" Max said. Nothing was typical in this factory.

"We rent this space to Agnes Bowie. She makes custom sails to sell on the Internet. Agnes needed a spot for her shop and we made room for her."

Apparently Pippa took umbrage to his shock. She scooped aside a sail as she walked by—much like a cat swishing her tail. And like a cat, her irritation was evident. He hadn't been criticizing NSV or the sail shop, but it was too late to say so. She was already gone.

Through the next set of doors was a machine shop, the place finally looking more like a manufacturing plant. However, the machines were ancient and antiquated, some held together with bits of wire and duct tape. *Another* Christmas tree, this one decorated with plaid bows, sat proudly in the middle of the room. Two old codgers, the same two from the pub last night, stood by a drill press, a flurry of heated words flying between them. They stopped at once.

The bearded one bobbed. "We'll be getting back to work now, Pippa." He eyed Max's kilt but didn't act as if it was out of place.

"Aye," said the other one, nodding at the kilt as well.

"You run a tight ship," Max muttered, trying not to feel uncomfortable about his attire.

She nodded. "I keep them on task. Taog, I told you to move the CNC machine in here yesterday." She had the command of a drill sergeant. "Why haven't ye?"

Taog turned red. "The CNC's too pretty to use."

The bearded one laughed. "And Taog's uglier than his own arse."

"Murdoch," Pippa said in warning. "We've discussed this before. No more insulting Taog or cursing on the job. I'll not be having it."

"Aye, lass," Murdoch said, rubbing his beard. "About the damned CNC machine. Taog keeps it polished up just fine. Not a speck of dust on it."

Max was impressed a small operation could afford such an expensive piece of equipment. "Can I take a look at it?"

Pippa turned to him, seeming irritated. "It's at the back of the building. I'll show you."

She handed him a hard hat and a pair of earplugs. "Ye'll need these." She donned her own hard hat, making it look at home on her head. A funny thought hit him. *She is the sexiest chief engineer I've ever seen.* She pushed through another set of doors.

Max was glad for the ear protection. Conveyor belts clapped, horns blew, and pneumatic drills hissed. Most people would find it annoying, but a wave of nostalgia washed over him. He missed working for the factory and being close to the end product. Now that he'd been promoted, he was a long way from actually making anything, except maybe a deal.

He scanned the room and once again encountered the bizarre. In one corner sat three pleasure boats on blocks.

Pippa's eyes followed to where he looked. "Winter storage rentals," she hollered over the noise.

That explains the boats but doesn't explain the farm's worth of Christmas trees scattered throughout the factory floor.

Max focused his energy on the assembly line. He immediately saw ways to streamline their process and make the plant more efficient, just by rearranging things. While she explained the different valves and their applications, he flipped open his notebook and jotted down his recommendations.

"Ye better not be stealing our designs," she warned.

"Wouldn't dream of it." When they had a quiet moment, Max would share his ideas with her. "And the subsea shutoff valves? Where are they being made?"

She frowned at him and he knew it was because he'd asked after their Golden Goose. Every oil and gas company in the free world wanted to get a good look at the McDonnell's design. Perhaps others were being invited here as well. The fact that Pippa had let Max in the front door must mean MTech was in the running. Her glare in his direction, though, said she wasn't pleased with him or MTech right now.

She stood tall. "Mock-ups are in my office. Do you want to see the CNC machine or not?" Without giving him a chance to answer, she walked away at a clip.

Sure enough, in the far corner of the factory sat a very large CNC machine.

Max gave an appreciative whistle. "What a beaut." CNC machines were used to build parts with efficiency and accuracy in manufacturing. He did his best to ignore what they'd done to the poor thing. The CNC was decorated like a damn Christmas tree as well: Garland was swagged around the circumference and an angel was crowning the top.

"If you don't mind me asking, how did NSV afford this machine?"

She cocked an eyebrow as if she did mind, but then deflated as if to say, *what the hell.* "It's a gift from Corbie Engineering. Right before they went bankrupt."

Her eyebrows furrowed as if she understood all too well what was at stake. North Sea Valve could very well be the next to go into bankruptcy court.

"There's no need to worry," he assured her. "I can help."

Her shoulders went back and she sucked in a breath before shouting over the racket of the machinery. "I'm concerned about MTech's definition of help. I know I called yere company back to the table, Mr. McKinley, but the last time MTech was here, they tried to rob NSV blind."

This is going to be an uphill battle.

He patted his notebook. "I'm not talking about the MTech proposal. I'm talking about reconfiguring your operations, moving things around. Things you can do right away to save money, and it won't cost you a penny."

She sized him up but looked too stubborn to acquiesce.

"Can we talk about it in your office where it's quieter?"

She glared at him for a moment before turning on her heel. "Follow me." She marched in the opposite direction.

Damn she was prickly. Why did she think the worst of him?

For his whole life he'd assumed, by the easy trust others placed in him, that his honesty shone through. But to come to Scotland and be treated like a common thief felt . . . foreign.

He wasn't a shyster. He was a stand-up guy. Was it too

much to ask for them to put a little faith in him? Were all Scots this distrustful? All he wanted was to make sure their subsea shutoff valve came to fruition. Preferably with MTech, so he could keep his job. He opened his mouth to try to convince her that his motives were pure. But hell, pleading wouldn't do a damn bit of good. Everyone knew actions spoke louder than words.

He focused his attention on her lovely backside as she paraded away from him, and unabashedly let the spectacle outshine his injured pride. The view also helped him to ignore how the workers were staring at his bare legs.

She opened the office door and went in. He followed and his first thought was — *Hoarders work here.*

She glanced around, too. "Organized chaos."

Bookcases packed with technical tomes filled the small room. Piles of manila folders sat on the desk and floor. Stray valves here and there acted as paperweights. In the middle of the desk was that damn camera of hers from earlier.

She flipped over what looked like a stack of photos before removing her hard hat. Her hair had come undone and a disarray of strawberry blond curls fell around her face. She shook them out as if she didn't know how distracting it was. From another kitchen chair, she moved a mountain of papers for him to sit.

She waved to the accumulation in the room. "My system is organic. I'm still coming up to speed on the factory."

He understood digesting a lot of information in a short period of time. Like this project, which he'd had only days to prepare for. "Don't apologize."

"I wasn't." She settled herself behind the desk. "Now what ideas do you have for me?" she asked skeptically.

His gaze alighted on the one area of the room that seemed well put together—the wall behind her. Three diplomas hung in perfect order. It was an impressive display—bachelor's, master's, and doctorate in mechanical engineering.

She followed to where his eye had landed. "Da insisted that Taog and Murdoch hang my diplomas." Interestingly, her cheeks tinged red.

"Don't be embarrassed by your intelligence and accomplishments."

"Are you always this cheeky with strangers?" She held his stare.

"I'm impressed, is all."

She shot him a stern frown that spoke volumes ... *I'm not impressed with you.*

He ignored it. "What's that?" Beside the diplomas, a strange plaque hung, near enough for her to easily reach out and touch while seated at her desk.

"A healthy dose of humility" was all she said.

It was an honest-to-goodness cross-wise section of a valve with a hole blown through it. He leaned forward to read the inscription ...

PROOF THAT

THEORY ≠ REALITY

AND REALITY CAN BITE YOU IN THE ARSE

CONFIRMED BY ALISTAIR MCDONNELL AND

HER DESIGN TEAM

"Wrong size valve for that particular high-pressure line," she admitted candidly. "I keep it close to remind me that if I don't do my job correctly, I could cost some-one their life."

His mouth went dry and he couldn't speak. What could he say? That he understood her? His dad and a multitude of others had died in industrial accidents. Max was in the same business as Pippa was in—preserving lives.

She cleared her throat. "I haven't received anything in writing from MTech yet. Did you bring the proposal with you?"

"No. I understand they'll e-mail it soon. We have time," he reassured her.

She shook her head as if they didn't.

He'd been given only a few selling points. *Straight-forward,* Miranda had said. Max's job was to check out their facility, review the specs on the valve—make sure the valve was viable—and then get NSV to partner with MTech.

He told Pippa what he knew about the deal. "The crux of it is, MTech would supply the research facility for testing the subsea shutoff valve. In return, MTech would receive a small percentage of the profits when the prod-uct goes live. Easy."

"Nothing is ever *easy*, Mr. McKinley. When the con-tract is ready, the McDonnell and myself will go over it with a fine-tooth comb."

"I understand." If he was in their position, he would, too. "We're hoping your father will make a decision by Christmas or by the latest, the New Year."

"About my father . . ." The phone rang.

She pointed to it. "Do you mind? I'm expecting a call."

"Not at all." He turned to his notes.

She listened for a moment, and then her brows crashed together. "Hold on a second."

She placed her hand over the receiver and spoke to Max. "We're going to have to cut this short, Mr. McKinley." As an afterthought she added, "Come to dinner tonight, six o'clock. It's time you met the McDonnell. You can share your ideas with both of us then. We're the house nearest the postbox—red roof, green door. Can you find your way out?"

"Sure." He shut his notebook and headed for the door. On the other side, he found Taog standing by the CNC machine, sizing it up.

"Do you need any help?" Max asked.

"Murdoch is retrieving the front loader." Taog walked to the corner and looked at it from that side. "Just trying to figure at what angle to go about it."

"I'll give you a hand." Max was pleased to set his notebook aside and get his hands dirty.

They spent the rest of the morning maneuvering the CNC into the machine shop, while Max took the opportunity to learn more about their processes and procedures. The fact that he was accruing brownie points with the natives wasn't lost on him.

When the machine had been situated in its new home, Taog and Murdoch offered to buy Max a drink that night at the pub. Max accepted, wondering if Pippa would be behind the bar again. In the lobby, he grabbed his damp suit hanging by the door and headed out. That's when he remembered his dinner date at the house with the red roof and the green door.

Ugh, their house sounded like Christmas. Max wasn't

sure he could stand any more decorated trees and holiday cheer.

Pippa stared at the camera, feeling letdown and desperate. The bachelor auction was their only hope. She'd hit
another brick wall with the National Health Service.

*Were they sure there was no money in the budget for
her father to see the specialist sooner?* They were sure.

*If her father relocated to her apartment in Edinburgh,
could he at least get his initial workup?* No.

*If she promised to give blood once a week for the rest
of her life would the NHS rethink their position?* No.

She'd been lucky the NHS had even called her back,
but her last hope of their help had been dashed. The
Strapping Lads in Plaid auction had better be enough.
Because if not, it felt like her da was a goner.

Chapter Three

As Max exited the factory, the wind kicked up and with it, his kilt. He would literally freeze his ass off if he didn't get warmer clothing, especially if he was forced to wear one of these skirts again. The boots Pippa had given him, however, were a vast improvement over his dress shoes. If he caught her in a good mood, he'd ask if he could hang on to them for the duration of his stay. He got in his car and headed back to the village. Snow-drifts had partially hidden the road but he made it safely to the town's parking lot.

Outside his home-away-from-home, he glanced down the boardwalk and noticed an old woman wrestling a long piece of garland in the gale-force wind. His empty stomach urged him to take the last few steps into the pub where a bowl of potato soup was waiting for him. Despite his fluttering kilt and his growling stomach, his Southern boy upbringing had him bracing into the wind to assist the old woman.

"Hey there," he hollered over the crashing waves and the roar of the wind. "Can I give you a hand?"

At first, he thought she wouldn't answer. She eyed his

kilt and raised an eyebrow, then finally spoke. "It's you. Ye might as well help. Ye're dressed for it." The woman was as old as the ocean. Every line on her face was a testament to her time living here on the dangerous edge of Scotland. But he could tell she was as strong as an ox. Between the two of them, they positioned the garland securely to the building next to the patchwork sign that read QUILTING CENTRAL.

"Would you like to come in for some lunch?" She frowned at her own offer as if she had no choice in it. She opened the door to the large building and the most delicious smell of beef stew drifted out.

His mouth watered and he smiled. "That would be great."

She ushered him in with a scowl. "After you eat, I expect ye to get that old Douglas fir positioned in the tree stand in the back corner." She pointed out the spot with a gnarled hand.

"You sure know how to bribe a guy. The stew smells wonderful." He would remain upbeat and friendly, no matter how much the townsfolk disliked him. Besides, he could put up with a little attitude in exchange for food.

She waddled over to the kitchen area. "Go sit yereself by the fire. I'll bring ye a bowl."

He walked farther into the large open room with I-beam supports strategically placed to hold up the roof. All the women who worked there stopped simultaneously and stared at him. And his kilt. The old woman shooed them back to arranging chairs and tables.

The smell of sizing and fabric reached his nose, too, reminding him of his mom's sewing room. On one side of the huge room, rows of sewing machines were positioned with ironing boards nearby. Not too far away, mats and rotary cutters waited. One wall had been dedicated to bolts of fabrics, another for design. Toward the back, three longarm quilting machines sat quiet.

The old woman returned with a bowl and spoon, laying it on the coffee table in front of where he stood.

"Thanks." He smiled at her and the surroundings. "My mom and my sister, Bitsy, would love it here. They're both quilters, too."

The old woman bobbed her head. "It's an honest way to spend yere days."

"Yes, it is." He thought about all the work his mom had put into the Texas Star quilt draped across his bed in his apartment. "By the way, I'm Max McKinley." He held out his hand to her.

"We know who you are." She crossed her arms over her large chest.

He read the subtext well enough. *Gandiegow doesn't warm to strangers easily.*

She moved her ham-sized hands to her hips. "Now, I'll feed you because you're hungry and because you're going to help us, but that's all. Best get to eating that stew." She started to walk away but stopped. "I'm Deydie Mc-Cracken," she added, begrudgingly.

She left him and went to bark at a group of women who were apparently hanging a Christmas quilt all wrong on the far wall. The women spared a glance at him while doing as Deydie bid, seeming to take her gruffness in stride. He decided he would, too.

He made himself comfortable on the oversized sofa and took a bite of stew. It was rich, hearty, and hit the spot.

Deydie hollered to him from across the room. "Hurry up there. We're having a quilting retreat this weekend. The last one before Christmas. We need the lights on that tree before the needles fall off. And before I grow another year older."

He grinned at her.

A woman in her mid-thirties made her way over to him. "Hi. I'm Cait Buchanan. Sorry about Deydie. She's my gran . . . and a handful." Her accent wasn't quite Scottish, more a mixture between a brogue and his own American English.

He put down his spoon and stuck out his hand. "Max McKinley. And don't worry about Deydie. I like her. She reminds me of my own grandmother."

"Good. Because she seems to have taken to you, too."

"Really?" That's *taken to*?

"Aye. She's a funny ole bird." Cait pointed to a young redheaded boy. "Mattie, come here."

The kid, maybe eight years old or so, dropped his backpack at the door.

Cait smiled as he made his way over and put her hand on his shoulder as he stood near. "Mattie, this is Mr. McKinley. He's come to do some work at the North Sea Valve Company. Say hello to him."

The kid seemed to regard Max for a long moment, making him wonder if the kid would say anything at all. Finally, he extended his small hand. "Hello." His voice was quiet.

Max took his hand and shook. "You're a reserved young man."

Mattie tilted his face up to Cait. For a flash, she looked upset, but she pulled it together and smiled down at him.

"Aye. A good trait. Sometimes it's best to think a wee bit before we speak."

What did I say? He should've wiped his feet, because apparently he'd stepped in it this time.

But just like that, Cait must've forgiven him—her genuine smile returned. "We're all glad ye're in town. I'll let you get back to your lunch. I only wanted to introduce myself."

He said good-bye and watched them walk away.

As he took another bite of stew, another young woman, who'd been standing close enough to have heard the exchange, glided over to him. He wasn't sure if she meant to speak to him because she kept her gaze plastered to the ground.

Finally, she glanced up. "That wasn't yere fault." Her voice was soft, and he could tell she was painfully shy. "Ye couldn't have known about Mattie and the accident."

He felt like a heel. "Mattie was in an accident?"

"Nay. He witnessed a boatful of men drowning."

Crap!

The woman hesitated and then continued. "He's had trouble speaking ever since. But he's come a long way."

"Thanks for filling me in." He'd have to apologize to Cait and Mattie for any pain he caused. He didn't seem to be making friends fast in Scotland. "I'm Max, by the way."

"I'm Moira." She nodded and left him alone.

He ate the rest of his stew without making any more faux pas. The rest of the afternoon flew by as he helped out at Quilting Central. He learned the names of many more of the women and a few of the men who'd been wrangled into lending a hand, too. Everyone was polite, if not warm, and he hoped his efforts would build some bridges between himself and Gandiegow. As he readied to leave, Amy, who'd told him she ran the General Store, brought him a bundle—a down coat, a god-awful Christmas sweater, thick gloves, and a nice wool plaid scarf.

"It's the McKinley tartan," Amy explained. "And the sweater, my auntie made."

He took the provisions from her. "This is so generous of you."

"Nay. Stop by the store tomorrow to settle up. I'll have your bill ready." She said it sweetly, but firmly.

He nodded. "Fair enough. I'm grateful all the same."

He shrugged on the down coat and headed back to the pub. The day had passed quickly and he barely had time to prepare for his dinner at Pippa's. He slipped out of the kilt and into a warm pair of jeans. Feeling a little chilled, he decided to don the ugly sweater with the green and red baubles scattered across the front, complete with sewn-on tinkling bells. When Max got downstairs, Taog and Murdoch were waiting for him.

"Come here, lad." Taog pounded him on the back. "We owe you that drink. Pippa was quite pleased when she saw the CNC in the machine shop."

"Sorry, fellows," Max said. "I can't stay."

"But you promised," Taog complained.

"Promised," Murdoch said in affirmation.

"Yes, but if I show up stinking drunk at the McDonnell's for dinner, what do you think would happen?"

"Pippa would cut yere balls off and feed them to the sharkies." Murdoch shook his head as though he'd heard accounts of such a tale.

Taog only frowned sympathetically. "Aye. 'Tis a dilemma. Ye best be getting on to supper. And to Pippa."

Murdoch suddenly looked wise. "Watch yereself with Pippa, Yank."

Max gave a noncommittal nod, wondering who Murdoch had meant to protect. Pippa or Max?

"Where's the postbox?" Max asked.

Taog sipped his drink. "North of the General Store."

Max bundled up in his new coat, gloves, and scarf, and set off for Pippa's. It was a cold walk, but he found the house with the red roof and green door easily enough. Given the overkill at the factory, he wasn't surprised to find multicolored lights and decorations overpowering the outside of the cottage from one end to the other.

As he stepped onto the porch, the door swung open and there she stood, wearing a long red sweater with gray leggings underneath. She had just enough cleavage showing to make him want to see more.

"Come, get out of the cold." She grabbed his arm and pulled him in.

She smelled good. Like gingerbread.

And God help him, he wanted to lean closer and inhale her scent a moment longer. That's when he realized he was in trouble.

Pippa couldn't keep from laughing as the Yank shrugged out of his coat.

"How on Earth did Amy talk ye into buying that atrocity? It's been at the store for ages." She shook her head. "No self-respecting Scot would be caught dead in such a thing."

He looked down and flicked one of the puffy baubles. "It's warmer than anything I brought with me."

It was endearing that he'd wear the ridiculous sweater. Also, she noticed, it didn't take anything away from his broad shoulders and captivating smile. "Christmas must really be your holiday."

"God, no. Not by a long shot." A crease formed on his forehead and he crossed his arms. In the process, the bells on his sweater jingled. He rolled his eyes and seemed to struggle with regaining his composure. "Amy mentioned her auntie had made the thing." He shrugged and the sweater jingled another *tinkle, tinkle*. "I didn't want to hurt her feelings by not wearing it."

"Very giving. We should call you *Mr. Christmas*." Pippa waved him farther into the house. Up to this point, she'd done pretty well feigning her indifference, but Max was so genuinely nice that it was getting harder and harder for her not to like him. And so good-looking, too. But how could she be drawn to the man who might rob NSV of her da's patents for the subsea shutoff valve?

Pippa couldn't help but inhale Max as he walked by. No trace of dead fish on this one. Nothing but *clean, attractive man*. It was disarming.

Back in Edinburgh as *Alistair*, she'd made sure from the beginning her colleagues saw her as a serious engineer and just one of the guys. No one could get through her armor. But here in Gandiegow, she was *Pippa*. The fishermen's sons still remembered her at eight when she sobbed at the death of the beached baby whale at their water's edge. To her credit, she'd toughened up. She'd made sure those boys regretted their ruthless taunts. She could swear with the best of them now and knew how to gut each and every one of them—not with a knife but with her wicked tongue.

Damn Max McKinley. He made her five-ten frame feel delicate. But she had bigger worries than some fleeting attraction.

She focused at the spot just beyond his shoulder. "Stop for a second. There's something I must tell you before you meet my da."

The doorbell rang. Impatiently, Pippa turned and answered it.

Freda Douglas stood in the entryway with a sheepish smile on her face, holding one of her pots of soup. Freda was as interesting as the worn wallpaper in the hall, but had been a part of Pippa's life for as long as she could remember.

"'Tis for you and the McDonnell." Freda started to step in.

Pippa stopped her by taking the soup tureen. "I'd ask you to stay but we're busy right now." She rolled her eyes in the direction of the Yank behind her.

"Aye. Tell yere da I'll call on him tomorrow."

"Thanks for the soup." Pippa closed the door, feeling a smidge bad for the look on Freda's disappointed face, but she had bigger fish to fry right now.

She set the tureen on the foyer table and turned back to Max.

"As I was saying"—she chewed on her lower lip—"there's something you need to know. My father isn't well. He's had an accident." She wouldn't tell Max everything—there was no need.

His eyebrows cinched in concern. There was also a hint of *why wasn't I told before* written across his face. "What kind of accident?"

It was none of his damn business. She glowered at him. "Don't say anything to upset my da, do you hear?" She picked up the soup and marched away toward the parlor. She didn't give a crank that she hadn't informed MTech beforehand about the McDonnell, and that she was running NSV now. If they'd known, the vultures would've sent ten executives to pick away at her father's carcass instead of just one.

Max grasped her arm. "Hold on a second."

Pippa stopped and glared at him.

"What's going on? Am I here under false pretenses? Does NSV want a partnership or not?"

She wanted him to unhand her. His touch was unnerving and it sent a warning sensation down to her very bones. She had to be careful with this one. She needed to keep MTech interested without NSV appearing weak. She couldn't let on that they were the only firm willing to work fast . . . fast enough to save the factory. All the other potential investors wanted to wait until after next quarter.

"Everything's fine," she said. If only it were.

"Is your father still the decision maker?"

"He's perfectly in his right mind. Now come along and don't keep him waiting."

Pippa stepped into the parlor. Her da seemed a bit better this evening. He rested in his wheelchair in front of the fireplace, one foot and one arm in casts with metal pins surgically placed in both appendages. Ribs had been cracked and his back messed up during the accident, too.

A can of oxygen sat in the corner but her father refused to use it.

"Crusty ole bastard." Pippa walked over and kissed the top of her da's head before laying a protective hand on his shoulder.

The McDonnell peered over his glasses. "Is this him?" He motioned to Max. "Come closer so I can get a good look at ye."

Get a good read on him was more like it. Max McKinley would be toast then.

The McDonnell had the gift—he could discover a person's character within the blink of a gannet's eye. It didn't matter that her father was injured, he could still recognize a bullshitter from a kilometer off. Da would get to the bottom of things.

"Sit here beside me." The McDonnell motioned to the love seat next to his wheelchair.

Confidently, Max walked over, acting as if he had nothing to hide.

He stuck out his hand. "It's nice to meet you." And the two shook.

At one time, Pippa had been sure she had the gift, too. But that was before she'd had any real dealings with the opposite sex in the romance department. As it stood, her track record was horrendous at best, and she no longer trusted herself when it came to choosing men. Heck, she no longer trusted men, as a rule. Except her da.

For a long moment, the McDonnell gazed into Max's eyes. He finished with a satisfied nod.

"Well?" Pippa asked.

"Your fears are unfounded, daughter. He'll do nothing to hurt us." Da gave her a look of finality like there would be no more said on the matter.

"Fine." She felt dismissed and looked up to see Max frowning at her as though he understood her depth of mistrust.

Her father held out his design notebook for the Yank. "Take a look at what I've been working on. It's an idea I had this afternoon for a new control valve. Tell me what you think."

Pippa blocked Max as he reached for it. "Don't, Da." She glared at her father. The American was the wolf in sheep's clothing, no matter what her father might have seen in his heart.

Max tilted his head toward her. "She's right. If your chief engineer isn't comfortable with me seeing your designs, then I don't want to see them either. Besides, I came here tonight to show *you* something—just some little improvements—things you could implement now at your plant to increase your efficiency."

Her da nodded, satisfied with the interaction, and set his notebook on the side table. Max didn't even glance toward it, which must've taken a Herculean dose of self-control. Everyone knew the McDonnell had vision when it came to engineering innovation.

"I'll get you both something to drink if you promise, Da, not to give away the farm before I return."

"Don't worry, daughter."

Before she left altogether, she addressed their guest. "And you, Mr. McKinley, don't start talking about those plant improvements without me."

Max smiled at her and she felt discombobulated and a wee bit uncomfortable. She made her way to the kitchen to pour them all a soft drink. For the hundredth time today, it hit her that maybe inviting the American to dinner wasn't such a good idea.

During their meal, she did a better job of keeping an emotional distance from the Yank. While they sipped tea afterward, Max laid out his ideas—booting up the offline conveyor to move parts from one side of the factory to the other, revamping how they pressure-tested their valves, and installing a few radio frequency transmitters to remotely track their whole process. She hated to admit it, but she was impressed. Scots were world-renowned engineers and it irked that an American had swooped in and shown them a thing or two.

She noticed her father was looking peaked and uncomfortable. He fumbled while putting down his teacup and he had gray circles under his eyes. The evening had drained him.

She laid a gentle hand on his arm. "It's time for your medicine, don't you think? One painkiller or two?"

"Just one. Maybe bring my oxygen into the den as well?" He shifted toward Max. "I sleep in the den. Can't manage the stairs with my banged-up body."

She stood but Max beat her to it, positioning himself behind the wheelchair.

"You point the way, sir. I promise to give you a smooth ride."

She put her hands on her hips. "I'm perfectly capable of taking care of my da by myself."

Max raised an eyebrow. "But apparently not capable of taking help from others."

Her father chuckled. "He's got yere number, daughter. I believe ye've finally met your match."

Max balked at the words, but recovered quickly, grabbing the oxygen can and tucking it under his arm as he began rolling her da toward the doorway.

"Suck-up," Pippa muttered, making sure the Yank heard her.

He had the audacity to grin.

Her da turned his head slightly to address her. "The lad will help with the kitchen before you walk him home. While ye're out, daughter, stop by Bethia's and pick up the herbal tea she's fashioned for me."

Pippa wanted to argue. She didn't need or want any help in the kitchen, and Mr. McKinley certainly didn't need an escort to find his way back to the pub. But she kept quiet. Her father had a tendency to read more into matters than was actually there.

"Fine," she finally said.

"That's my good lass." Her da and the interloper disappeared down the hallway together.

Max helped the McDonnell onto the chaise lounge and propped pillows where the older man directed, putting them behind his head and under his injured arm and leg.

"What else can I do for you?" Max asked.

"Set that glass of water over here next to me on the side table." The McDonnell laid his head back and sighed. "And one more favor."

"Anything."

"Look after Pippa while ye're here. She works too hard and I'm in no condition to help or to stop her." Worry camped in the older man's eyes.

It seemed a strange request. Max had spent enough

time today with the people of Gandiegow to know they were protective as hell when it came to her.

In any case, from what Max had seen, Pippa wasn't the type of woman who would accept assistance. Especially from him. But nevertheless, he answered, "I'll do my best."

"Off with ye now," the McDonnell said gently. "She'll have that kitchen tamed and spotless before you can even get in there."

"Yes, sir." Max left and went to NSV's chief engineer.

She was banging pots and pans around in the sink and muttering loud enough that the neighbors could've heard. "Never needed a man to help before. Why would I need one now?"

Max cleared his throat. "Wash or dry?"

She flinched, and then regained her composure. "Wash," she said firmly. "Ye've no idea where the dishes go."

He pushed up his sleeves, took his place at the sink, and contemplated whether or not to ask about her father's condition. Max waited a full minute for her to say something or at least give an explanation as to why he hadn't been told. When she didn't, he turned to a safe subject instead. "Tomorrow, I could get the offline conveyor up and going. I have plenty of controls experience to give you a hand."

By the stubborn set of her jaw, he didn't think she'd accept his help.

Finally, she turned to him. "Actually, that would be grand. I have an appointment in the morning, but afterward we can discuss further what MTech has in mind."

Max rinsed the platter and handed it to her. "What

about your father? Shouldn't I discuss the deal with him at the same time?"

"Nay. Tomorrow's not good." She gave him no other explanation. As she dried, she seemed to be wrestling with the universe.

Alistair Philippa McDonnell was an interesting creature. She acted as tough as any roughneck on an oil rig but had a vulnerability that made him want to wrap her in his arms and tell her it would be okay. Which was ridiculous on so many levels. He shook the thought away and concentrated on the next dish.

With both of them working, it didn't take long to get the kitchen back in order and the counters wiped clean. Pippa set items out for tea in the morning. The act seemed so domestic and natural that Max uncharacteristically wished he had someone at his apartment to share a cup of coffee or tea with in the morning before heading off to work.

He banished the idea. Marriage and family were for people like his brother or sister, but not for him. He was happily married to his career—liked his independence. And planned to keep his life just as it was.

Pippa held the swinging kitchen door open. "Are you ready?"

"Yes." He made his way down the hall to the front.

She retrieved their coats from the closet. He started to reach out and help her, but she shied away from him, slipping into her parka herself. *Fine. Apparently, chivalry is dead in Scotland.*

He slipped into his down jacket and put on his hat. "So what is this tea your father wants you to pick up?"

Pippa walked onto the porch and waited for him.

"Our Bethia has recently become a certified herbalist — at seventy-five, no less. She's one of the ladies from Quilting Central."

"I met her today," he said as they made their way down the boardwalk. "Deydie's sidekick, right?"

"Aye. Doc MacGregor talked her into it. With Bethia on call, it gives the doc a chance to get away now and then. As we speak, Doc's in Edinburgh with his da, something about minor surgery."

"So what has Bethia prescribed?" he asked.

"She's concocted a remedy for my da that she hopes will help heal his bones. She's done wonders for others in the village." Pippa got this worried look on her face and he wanted to reach over and smooth out the pinched line between her eyebrows.

"Your father, what's going on? How did he get injured? Is he going to be okay?"

She gave an evasive shrug. "I don't want to talk about it." Her voice caught on the end. "It's hard to see Da so . . . so . . . He's the strongest man I know." She seemed to crumple.

He didn't know what to do and was surprised by how deeply he felt her pain. Irrationally, he wanted to hold her. But he couldn't do that — her independent streak was wider than the ocean before them. In the next second, she confirmed it, straightening into a rigid pillar, back to being strong and prickly.

"I'm not normally so—"

"Human?" he said, cutting her off. "It's okay."

She pushed her curls back, glaring at him.

He didn't back down. "You care about your father and there's nothing wrong with needing someone to talk to or to lean on every now and then. I get the feeling you're used to being *the shoulder to lean on* and not having one for yourself."

"Don't pretend you know me, Mr. McKinley. Ye're here to conduct business, not to be my therapist."

She was right. He didn't know her, but for some reason he wanted to. He wouldn't admit he'd spent a major portion of the day thinking about her. *Things that didn't have to do with engineering either.* He wanted to peel back her armor and see what lay beneath. Find just the right spot to touch her and drive her crazy. To have those long legs of hers wrapped around him . . .

He ran a hand through his hair and forgave himself for objectifying this intelligent woman. He was only male, after all, but not caveman enough to act on his basic urges. He was here to negotiate MTech's deal. Not to get her into bed. Or even offer comfort, for that matter. She had a whole town to do that for her. Max had been stupid. "You're right. Sorry. I don't know you."

She seemed satisfied, and then glanced at the house they just passed.

He stopped. "Is that where Bethia lives?"

"Aye," she replied.

"It's getting late. Go ahead and get the tea now."

"Fine." At the rate that she took off up Bethia's walk, he wondered if she might be embarrassed to be seen with him.

After a few moments of knocking, the old woman came to the door. She leaned out and peered at him and then went back to talking to Pippa. A few minutes later, Pippa rejoined him on the sidewalk with a small bag in hand.

"All right then." Max wheeled around in the opposite direction, toward her house with the red roof and the green door.

Pippa grabbed his arm. "What are you doing? That's not the way to the pub."

"I know."

She bristled. "You're a regular cowboy, aren't you? I don't need an escort to make it home. A woman has a weak moment about her da and you think—"

"Stop right there. There's no way in the world that anyone could accuse you of being weak. I want to walk you home, is all." It would make him feel better to know she made it home safe and sound. But he didn't dare voice that out loud.

As she marched ahead of him, she muttered to herself above the crash of the waves and whistle of the wind. "Been handling Gandiegow in the dark my whole life. Even as a wee lass." Her brogue seemed thicker when she was angry.

Max caught up with her and they plodded along in silence. At her door, as he opened his mouth to tell her good night, he sneezed.

"Bless you," she grumbled.

He coughed, not able to stifle it.

"Are you okay?" She wore a troubled frown.

"I'm fine." But he sneezed again.

Her expression deepened into concern, looking much like she had over her dad earlier.

Max reached around and opened the door for her. "Stop worrying. I'll see you in the morning."

"I'm not worried," she snapped. "It's just we have a lot of ground to cover tomorrow."

"I know."

"I'll come by and get you at the pub," she reminded him. "You might as well ride with me to the factory. Save petrol. Save the planet, and all."

He sneezed again. "Sounds good."

"Are you sure you aren't getting sick?"

"I'm great." He stepped off the porch. "See you in the morning."

But, he suddenly realized, he didn't feel great. Burning the candle at both ends this past week, plus jet lag, plus cold wet feet this morning and his breezy kilt, had finally caught up with him. He felt achy. He dragged himself back to the pub and fell into bed. But his sleep was fitful. He just couldn't stop shivering.

The next morning, with extra coffee in hand, Pippa stomped her way up the pub stairs, grumbling. "I can't believe I have to go looking for him. He should be waiting at the front door for me."

Granted, they hadn't agreed to meet on the main level, but she'd assumed she wouldn't have to rouse the Yank from his bed. "Does MTech want to do business with North Sea Valve or not?" She knocked on Max's door.

No answer. She peered down the hallway at the loo, where the door stood wide. "Where is that skiver?" She knocked again, and heard a groan.

Chapter Four

Pippa cracked the door open and saw Max twisted in his blankets with his arm over his eyes. He groaned again.

"Are you ill?" *Stupid question.* Of course, he was sick. Hesitating only a moment, Pippa crossed the threshold, walked to his bed, and laid a hand on Max's forehead, like Freda had done to her when she was a little girl. "You're burning up."

He didn't open his eyes. "I feel bad. . . ."

"I know. Your fever's high."

"No," he croaked. "That I might've infected your father last night. I didn't know I was sick. It came on suddenly."

"Och. Good grief. You mustn't torment yereself." Did Max have the Highland flu? Regardless, she needed to bring his fever down.

"But," he argued, "I could've made things worse for him."

Max was a decent man to worry about her father, especially with the Yank as sick as can be.

She straightened his covers. "It's Da's bones that are

the problem. They aren't healing as they should. Other than that, his constitution is as strong as a Caledonian ox."

"Good." Max sighed and rolled over.

"Listen, Yank. I think you have the Highland flu. Fine one minute, on your back the next."

"Lucky me." He tried to smile but failed.

She grabbed an extra quilt from the cupboard and laid it over him. "I'm going to run to Bethia's to get some medicine. You stay in bed."

He gave a derisive laugh. "Like I could go anywhere."

As Pippa rushed down the stairs and out the door, she rang up the factory. "Bonnie, I'll be late this morning." She thought about Max's pallid coloring and high fever. "Scratch that. Let everyone know I'm out today. If necessary, I can be reached by mobile."

It took her only a few minutes to arrive at Bethia's, get the herbal tincture, and run back to the pub with the covered goblet. She didn't bother to knock this time.

"Max?" She gently shook him awake. "I've something for you to drink." She held it close to his mouth.

"God, no. It smells awful. And I shouldn't be able to smell a thing."

"It's Bethia's version of Tamiflu." Pippa eased the goblet closer. "It really works."

He shied away from it. "Shouldn't I take real Tamiflu? Don't you have a doctor in town?"

"Aye, I told ye we did. But Doc MacGregor is still in Edinburgh with his da."

"Let me lie here and die quietly then," Max moaned.

Pippa gently brushed his hair back from his forehead. "Don't be such a baby. I promise ye'll feel better in the morn. Now drink up."

"You first," he said.

She pinched her nose and pretended to take a sip. "Yummy. Yere turn."

She helped Max sit up. He took the goblet and drank it all, only sputtering twice.

"There." She adjusted his pillow and blankets, settling him as comfortably as she could, considering how lousy the Highland flu can make a body feel.

A few moments after Max lay back down, the furrow between his eyebrows relaxed and he fell into a deep sleep.

The Highland flu had been all but eradicated from these parts by an annual shot. Everyone here took it very seriously. Pippa's own mother had died from the Highland flu the week after Pippa was born, her immune system zapped during the long labor.

Pippa picked up Max's room—his jeans, the god-awful sweater from last night, and a polo. She had no idea what possessed her, but she held his shirt close and inhaled. Even lying there, helpless as a run-over otter, the man was overwhelmingly beautiful. But life had shown her that beautiful men were usually jerks. She stepped into the hallway to call her father about Max before he heard it elsewhere. News, especially bad news, traveled fast in Gandiegow.

When Da picked up, Pippa made sure to speak with a calm, matter-of-fact voice. "Da, Max has come down with the Highland flu."

There was a long silence before her father exhaled. "Did you get the remedy from Bethia?"

"Aye. He's taken the first dose."

"Good." Da sounded concerned but satisfied. "Daughter, ye're not to worry about me today. Freda called and she'll be by to warm my soup."

"Aye." Pippa rolled her eyes. If Freda was known for anything, it was for peddling her soup.

"I shan't expect you back tonight either," Da added. "Stay with the lad and make sure he's comfortable."

"But—"

"I mean it, daughter. Don't leave his side." Even though her da wasn't quite himself, he still had the where-withal to order her about. "We both know how serious the Highland flu can be."

"Yes, Da." Pippa never knew her mother but her father still carried a torch for her . . . even after all these years. It must have been some love that they'd shared.

Her father broke in to her thoughts. "The whole village is watching out for me. I don't want you to worry about our Max McKinley either. He's a strong lad. We've come a long way in treating the illness. Stay with him tonight and he'll be better by morning."

Pippa agreed, hung up, and went in search of a cot for herself to put in Max's room. She found one in the storage area of the basement and dragged it back up the stairs. Max was still sleeping. She set her phone alarm for two hours and pulled out the massive stack of financial papers on NSV.

At some point, Deydie stopped by with a plate of scones and oolong tea.

"I thought ye'd be needing some refreshment. Would you like to stretch yere legs for an hour? I'll sit with him."

Pippa glanced over at Max. "No. I'm good."

"Well, he better get well soon," Deydie said gruffly. "If

he perishes, it might ruin Christmas." She stopped suddenly as if remembering how Pippa's mother had died. She cleared her throat, then diverted her attention to the sick man, regarding him with concern for a long moment. "I'll fresh-kill a chicken for the Yank. My healing stew will be just the thing to get him back on the mend."

"What about the quilters who are coming for the retreat?" Pippa asked.

Deydie shook her head, her wrinkles jiggling. "No need to worry about the lad being contagious, lassie. We're just hosting a quilt guild from Glasgow. They would've all been vaccinated."

"But you'll check all the same?" Pippa asked.

"Aye. I'll call before I wring that chicken's neck."

Deydie said her good-byes and was gone. Pippa ate two of the warm scones and then got back to NSV's financials. Freda stopped by with an extra sweater and Pippa's favorite quilt. Bethia brought more tincture and instructions. When the time came, Pippa woke Max and had him drink another goblet. Then she put away her papers and pulled her chair close to listen to him breathe.

Sometime later, she heard footsteps ascending the stairs. She scooted away and struck a nonchalant pose. Deydie traipsed in with the promised chicken stew, which smelled of vegetables, protein, and goodness. The old woman didn't stay long, whispering she had to get back to the final preparations for the quilting retreat.

Pippa gently woke Max and helped him into a sitting position. He seemed weaker than earlier, but Bethia had warned her to expect that. Pippa fed him his stew. Poor Max seemed too tired to talk.

"Good" was his only word.

"Better than Bethia's medicine?" She reached for the new goblet. "Which brings me to the bad news. It's time to take some more."

He offered her a weak smile and drank all he was given. She had him settled and asleep within minutes.

Just as she sat back in her chair, a phone rang, the sound coming from the armoire. What if his family was checking up on him? Pippa found his coat and dug his mobile from the pocket.

"Max McKinley's mobile," Pippa said.

"Put McKinley on," a woman barked with no salutation.

Pippa agreed with what she'd heard about American women—very abrupt. "Mr. McKinley is indisposed."

"What are you talking about? He won't be too indisposed to talk to me. Who are you?"

"Scullery maid," Pippa snapped. "Who are you?"

"Miranda Weymouth. His boss."

Pippa stopped short. Her women's intuition kicked in. Something in the other woman's voice sounded possessive, making Pippa think that Max and this Miranda might be involved.

I'm such an idiot! Some part of Pippa had been— *what?*—hoping Max was single and interested in her? God, she needed to get a grip.

"I need to talk to McKinley *now*," Miranda commanded. "Where is he?"

"In bed," Pippa purred. Och, she shouldn't have, but the flotsam on the other end of the phone infuriated her.

"Get him up," Miranda demanded. "I need to speak with him immediately!"

"I don't think so." Pippa was as calm as the eye of a

hurricane. "Mr. McKinley is deathly ill. I'll have him call ye in the morning . . . if he lives."

With a huff, the line went dead on the other end.

Pippa leaned back and gazed at her patient—handsome Max McKinley. He was a heartbreaker for sure. All innocence with his boy-next-door charm. How could the Mc-Donnell have gotten it so wrong and think this one could be trusted? Da's injury must've short-circuited his gift. If Max was involved with a woman such as Miranda Weymouth, then that was a huge mark against him.

Darkness fell over Gandiegow with daylight scarce this late in the year and this far north. Pippa expected that any minute a ruckus would break out in the pub below, but it stayed surprisingly subdued—no music, no loud voices. She slipped out of the room to see what might have happened.

Downstairs, there was a fairly large crowd, but they were eerily quiet. Bonnie was behind the bar tonight.

"What's going on?" Pippa asked.

Bonnie tipped her head toward the stairs. "They heard about the Yank."

Taog sat on the barstool. "How is he?"

"Sleeping." Pippa glanced up as if she could see through the floorboards.

Monty cut in, acting defensive. "It's not that we give two shakes about an outsider, it's just we don't need one to die on our watch. It'd be bad business for Gandiegow."

"Och, Monty," Pippa admonished. "Ye calloused ole soul. I'll tell Mary and she'll take a frying pan to your sorry head."

"He's not a bad lad," Murdoch said quietly to the crowd. "He helped Taog and me settle the CNC machine."

Quiet rumbles of conversation rolled across the floor.

"I better get back upstairs to check on him." Pippa turned to go. "Thank ye all for keeping the noise down."

She hiked up the steps and settled herself beside the Yank. Not long afterward, she heard the pub patrons leave and Bonnie close up early for the night.

Pippa roused Max and gave him more of the nasty drink. His color looked better and he seemed a bit stronger. Bethia said she could stretch out the doses now. Pippa retrieved an extra quilt from the armoire for herself and fixed her bed. When he was asleep, she pulled her cot next to him, only so she'd be close if he needed her, of course.

After turning off the lamp, she lay down and stretched out one hand to feel if he was warm enough. She thought Max was out cold—until he grasped her hand and squeezed it. She was stunned. Too stunned to speak. Too stunned to pull her hand away. His touch electrified and warmed her middle. She'd held hands many times in her life, but none of those had been so . . . thrilling.

Even though he was totally out of it, holding hands with Max McKinley felt like coming home to a roaring fire after a chilly day at sea. With their hands entwined, her body relaxed to its very core.

She should've pulled her hand away, because as comforting as his touch was, it made her feel like a traitor to her community—sleeping with the enemy, sort of. Instead, she held on tight. No one need know. Hell, Max didn't even know. Which was perfect. In minutes, she fell asleep, too.

In the morning, she woke slowly, opening her eyes and turning toward Max's bed . . . only to find he was gone! Alarmed, she scrambled off her cot. Just then the door opened and Max stood in the entry with two mugs.

"Why are you out of bed?" she said sternly. She took in his change of clothes and wet hair. "And freshly showered, too?"

"I feel great." He thrust a mug in her direction. "You were right. There's something miraculous about those nasty drinks you forced on me."

She took the warm cup while giving him her best chief engineer glare, under which many a man had buckled. "Back in bed, McKinley."

He cocked his head, as if he took orders from no one. "Normally, I'd be at your service, especially when the request comes from a woman as enticing as you."

Her stomach gave a jolt, melting into a warm and exciting mixture of goo. Apparently, her weaker side liked a man who couldn't be bossed around. Or it could be how he said *service* and *enticing*. No matter. She was a mass of hormones right now.

He held a hand to his forehead. "I'm fine. The fever's gone."

She sucked in a deep breath and squashed down the effect he had on her. She pointed to the bed. "Lie down. Now. You have to be careful with the Highland flu, Max. I mean it. If you don't rest, you'll get worse. Fatally worse." That's what had happened to her mother. "Besides, it's Bethia's orders. If you stay in bed today and keep warm, then tomorrow you may venture out."

He stepped farther in. She could easily see he was feeling better. *And perhaps randy?* His gaze traveled up to meet hers. "I can't tell you how much I appreciate all you did for me."

"'Twas nothing."

He sauntered over, and the closer he came, the more nervous Pippa felt. Suddenly she was nattering away.

"The whole village helped, really. Bethia and her tincture. Deydie killed you a chicken. Taog and Murdoch made sure the pub stayed quiet for ye last night."

He took her hand, sat on the bed, and tugged until she was beside him. "And you watched over me." He gazed at her as if he really liked what he saw. Perhaps he'd contracted that patient-grateful-to-caregiver syndrome.

Well, her sex-starved hormones didn't give a crank about some syndrome. Flames sizzled where he grasped her, causing tingles to zip up her arm. She gulped for air and stared at their linked hands.

Finally, she came to her senses and yanked her hand away. "As I said, 'twas *nothing*. Now, lie down."

He raised his eyebrows at her. Either he was going to call her a liar or he was going to invite her into bed with him.

Before he could say anything, she added, "Miranda called."

That chilled the mood.

He frowned.

"She's a dear, isn't she?" Pippa really wanted to ask about his relationship with his boss, but couldn't work up the nerve. What right did she have, anyway?

"What did she say?" Max said.

"She wanted to speak with you." Pippa moved her cot to the far side of the room.

He rose. "I need to call her back."

Pippa hurried over and blocked his path. "Finish yere tea first. Ye have to drink one more dose of the tincture."

Halting, he screwed up his perfect face. "Seriously?"

She laid two hands on his shoulders, putting on the pressure, until he sat again on the bed. "Aye, now, take yere medicine like the big man that you are. And if you refuse, I'll sic Bethia and Deydie on you." She raised an eyebrow at him. "I know Bethia doesn't seem all that scary, but I assure you Deydie is."

He smiled at her and swallowed his tea. Pippa handed him the goblet and he drank it as well. In a few minutes, his eyes drooped.

"Get further under yere covers." She pulled them up and tucked him in as his eyes drifted shut.

He reached out and took her hand again. "Thank you."

This time he let go and she was grateful.

Pippa had many skills, like sizing and designing control valves, but she had no idea how to squelch the stirrings the Yank caused deep inside her. She grabbed her briefcase and her coat, and headed home to check on her da and get ready for work.

Outside, the wind picked up and twirled fresh snow around her. She stopped at Quilting Central to speak with Bethia.

She found the older woman inside, arranging miniature garland wreaths on the tables.

"How is our patient?" Bethia asked.

Pippa brushed snowflakes from her sleeves. "Max thinks he's ready to take on the world."

Bethia *tsk*ed. "Did you tell him I said to take it easy?"

"Aye. He's back to sleep. I thought it safe to go to the factory for a bit."

Bethia nodded. "Not for too long, though. I want ye to keep an eye on him. Tomorrow he can sit with the

McDonnell for his exercise. For today, though, you need to make sure the Yank stays in bed."

Pippa grinned. "Since when do you advise a single woman to keep a man in bed?"

Bethia blushed, but Deydie, who had clearly over-heard, clomped over, shaking a finger at Pippa. "Ye better keep yere panties on, missy. I'm afraid *that one* could smooth talk a porcupine out of her quills."

Pippa forced a hearty laugh. "Believe me. He has absolutely no effect on me or my undergarments. My panties are quite safe."

Deydie's eyes narrowed and she scoffed. "Ye're a big liar."

Pippa swiveled toward the door before her red face gave her away. "I better get home to Da."

"Don't forget," Bethia called. "Keep Mr. McKinley in bed."

As Pippa walked into the cold, her belly warmed. Wouldn't she just love keeping Max in bed! It'd been such a long time.

But it was a risk she couldn't take. She needed to re-member he wasn't there to be her boyfriend or to be the next man to see her naked. Max McKinley was in Gan-diegow for one reason only: her Da's patents, and maybe to swindle the townsfolk out of their livelihood.

Max roused several times during the day just as someone was leaving. Or at least he thought so. He never saw any-one but a plate of dry toast would appear, or fresh tea, or more hot chicken stew. The fourth time he woke up, it was dark out, and Pippa was sitting in her chair with a pencil behind her ear, examining ledgers.

He propped himself up on his elbows. "Hey." It felt like he'd swallowed concrete dust. "How was work today?"

She glanced up. "Short."

He pushed himself to a sitting position. "I'm sorry . . . was your day short because of me?"

"Don't fash yereself." She held up the reports. "I brought work with me."

The place between her eyebrows was pulled together. Apparently, whatever she'd found in those ledgers hadn't been to her liking.

"You know," he said, trying to lighten her up, "they make accounting software for that."

She wadded a piece of paper. For a second, he wondered if she might pelt him with it. Instead she tossed it into the wastebasket. "Being cheeky with me won't get you anywhere."

"Boy, that's a shame." He let his eyes freely roam over the curves of her snug blue sweater, trying to imagine what was going on underneath. *Yes, I'm definitely feeling better.*

She kept her eyes glued to the page, though her cheeks colored. "Going over things by hand helps me process the information."

Before he could goad her more, there was a knock, and the door opened. Amy, the store clerk, was holding a tray filled with sliced meat, broth, and bread. "Pippa? Yere dinner." She grinned at both of them, before placing the meal on the side table.

"It smells good." A hell of a lot better than Bethia's foul tinctures.

Pippa handed him the mug of steaming broth and took the plate with the sandwich fixings away from him.

"Only broth?"

She set the plate on her chair. "Ye're not well enough for this."

Did he need to remind her that he'd eaten Deydie's stew?

Pippa walked Amy out. Two seconds later, insistent whispering wafted through the crack under the door. When Pippa returned, she had a duffel bag in hand.

She tossed it on the cot, appearing a little put out. "Looks like ye'll have me as a roommate for another night."

He grinned at her, thinking to tease. "I guess I can suffer through." But his thoughts twisted on him. *I want to hold your hand again. I want you watching over me, too.* The gravity of it slammed into his chest. Where had those feelings come from? He did want her there with him. And he shouldn't. He cleared his throat. "You don't have to stay. I'm fine. Really."

"I've been given my orders." She tore off a small piece of bread, frowning at the cot. "As I understand it, the pub is going to keep it to a low roar again for you tonight."

"It's not necessary." His illness had sent a small upheaval through the town and he felt lousy about it. He wanted to endear himself to the villagers and instead he'd been nothing but a pain in the ass. "It's a good bunch of folks who live here, isn't it?"

She offered him a napkin from the tray. "Oh, it's no kindness. They just don't want to be responsible if you meet with an early grave." She walked to the end of his bed, chewing on her lip.

He laughed in midsip. "Good grief, it's only the flu."

She adjusted the quilt at his feet, not meeting his eyes. "It killed my mother."

Her words were a battering ram to his chest. "God, Pippa, I'm sorry. I didn't know. Sometimes I can be an insensitive jerk."

She shrugged. "It's okay. I never knew her. Da, though, still misses her a lot."

Pain sat in her eyes. Max wondered if it had more to do with her father than her mother.

She gazed back at Max. Some other worry seemed to be lingering there. "Can I get you anything else?"

He grimaced at the clear liquid in his mug. "Man cannot live on broth alone."

She shook her head, with a hint of a smile developing at the corner of her mouth. "Drama queen."

"You want me to keep my strength up, don't you?"

She gave him half her sandwich. "Eat. It's getting late and I have an early morning."

"Thanks."

When they finished, she took the tray and dishes downstairs. She returned, but it was only to retrieve her duffel bag and head to the bathroom. Within a few minutes, she was back, wearing green plaid flannel pajamas with her hair pulled into a ponytail.

"Not a word," she said when she caught him ogling her.

He didn't tease her because that down-home-girl thing she had going on was sexy as hell. He really couldn't stop staring.

"That color makes your eyes . . . stand out. Not that your eyes weren't already beautiful, it's . . ."

She blushed, glancing down at herself. "Flattery will get you nowhere."

"That's a shame. But your eyes are stunning."

"Save your bull for the boardroom, Mr. McKinley. It's

time for bed." She turned out the light and lay down on her cot, clear on the other side of the room.

Though he'd been out of it last night, he'd liked having her near.

"You're too far away," he said into the night. "Do you want me to help move your cot closer?"

She snorted. "Like you have the strength."

He could think of several things he had the strength for. One of them was turning the light back on and gazing into her sea-blue eyes while he peeled her out of those pajamas. She was tall and sleek as a jaguar, but downright prickly when it came to him. He'd like to tame her with a kiss, and smooth out her ruffled edges with his hands.

The cot legs scraping the hardwood floor brought him out of his fantasy.

She flopped onto her cot. "Better?"

"Not quite." He reached for her hand. It was warm, slender, and soft. Since it was dark, his thumb braved a caress to her palm.

"Enough," she said huskily.

Damn! What would it be like to have that voice whispering in his ear? All sorts of images flooded him. But he stilled his hand to stop torturing himself and her.

She could've easily unlatched her hand from his, but she held on to him, too. She seemed relaxed. She must like being near him as much as he liked being near her, which gratified the hell out of him.

But not all of his thoughts were as innocent as holding hands. He could think of a hundred different ways he'd like to hold on to Pippa, and they all involved her being naked.

God, it was going to be a long night!

*   *   *

The next morning when Pippa woke, she was startled to find she was being stared at. Max was lying on his side, gazing upon her face.

She should've been incensed—there was something so personal and vulnerable about being watched while she slept—but she was more embarrassed than mad.

"Morning," he said.

"What's the time?"

"Seven, I think," he answered.

She jumped out of bed. "Why'd you let me sleep in?"

"I've been enjoying the view."

"Stop enjoying, and get yere arse up. I need to get ready for work, and I need to get you to my house. Bethia said ye're to keep my father company today."

"But I feel well enough to go to NSV with you."

"Nay, Bethia is calling the shots. Besides, I need to get some things done without worrying if ye'll collapse on the factory floor."

"That's sweet," he deadpanned. "What things?"

"I have a call at nine I can't miss."

"Are you negotiating with other companies to partner with NSV?"

She didn't want to tip her hand, even if her da said they could trust Max.

"Don't worry over what I need to do." It was her last chance to convince the bank that North Sea Valve was good for the quarter-million-pound loan they needed to bring their subsea shutoff valve to market. If approved, they wouldn't need help from MTech or anyone.

Max sprang from the bed. "Give me a minute to get ready." He grabbed some things and blew out the door.

Pippa straightened his bed and propped her cot in the corner, thinking to return it to the basement later. She wasn't happy with the twinge of regret that shivered through her. She had no reason to continue to sleep beside the Yank. He was going to be fine, and she was being absurd. Things had already gotten too cozy between her and her adversary. *Holding hands, indeed!* She needed perspective—and perhaps some distance from Max McKinley.

It didn't take long before he returned, clean-shaven and showered. Another stray thought landed in her belly and spread south—*Will I ever get tired of looking at him?*

"Are you ready to head out?" She glanced toward the door to keep her eyes from giving her away.

He bundled up and grabbed his messenger bag.

As they trekked to her house, she should've kept her eyes straight ahead, but instead she focused on Max, making sure the exercise wasn't too taxing on him. When they arrived, Max went to the parlor and she went upstairs to get ready for work.

She meant to keep Max McKinley from her mind ... she really did. But while she was showering, her subconscious wandered nakedly into his capable arms. Being all relaxed and soaped up was a dangerous combination—all sorts of fantasies playing out in her mind. When she suddenly realized how crazy it was to be dreamy-eyed over MTech's deal closer, she quickly rinsed off and got out of there.

Back in the parlor, she showed great restraint by keeping her eyes averted from their guest as she settled him beside her father. She made sure her dad had the TV remote and a fresh carafe of tea.

Pippa shoved items in her bag as she spoke to them both. "Bethia will be by to check on ye and bring something special for lunch. I expect Freda to stop by, also."

Max wrinkled up his face. "I hope my lunch isn't another of Bethia's smelly goblets. I do believe she drugged me."

"You got better, didn't ye?" Pippa sniped.

"Yes," he agreed. "But I'm tired of sleeping."

"Is there anything else I can get for ye, Da, before I go?" she asked.

Her father pointed. "My design book from the den."

She squatted down, getting eye to eye with the Mc-Donnell. "Listen, ye can't be givin' away all yere secrets to this man."

Max touched her arm. "*This man* is right here."

Her da patted her face. "Trust me. Max has a good heart. Who knows what could happen if Max and I collaborate. We might come up with something that could change the world."

She stood. More likely Max would steal everything and run back to his boss! But she didn't argue. She had to get to the factory and her conference call.

At NSV, Pippa had only a few minutes to organize her employees. She put Bonnie in charge of setting up for the Christmas Roundup tomorrow. Taog and Murdoch were already dragging barriers into place so the children couldn't wander into the dangerous parts of the factory. When Pippa's phone rang, she ran into her office to catch the call from the bank.

The arrogant tossers didn't waste any time delivering their verdict: The bank wouldn't extend their credit any further. She slumped in her chair; it was time to face facts. North Sea Valve was doomed without MTech's influx of cash. But she couldn't just roll over and hand Max the keys. She had to do something.

An idea hit her.

Before going any farther on the MTech deal, she'd make sure Max got to know the people of Gandiegow, those who'd be destroyed when the big corporation stripped NSV of all its value. Pippa would start tomorrow. She'd show the Yank the true meaning of Christmas on the faces of the Gandiegowans, and thus reveal the heart of her clan—one personal encounter at a time.

She returned to her office and practiced what she would say to him. "Business isn't just business in Gandiegow, Mr. McKinley. Business is personal."

Chapter Five

When the front door opened to the McDonnell's house, Max checked his watch, wondering if this time it was Pippa. He'd enjoyed his time with her father and the others who'd stopped by today, but Max was surprisingly anxious to see the chief engineer. Like sunshine, Pippa appeared in the parlor doorway, revitalizing his day. Her face was flushed from the cold wind, exertion, or both. She looked beautiful. More than beautiful.

He couldn't help smiling. "You're back early."

She shrugged out of her coat and kissed the top of her father's head. "I am back early. I did all I could do at the factory. I stopped by the dock to pick up some fresh fish." She held up a white-papered package.

"Halibut?" the McDonnell asked.

"Aye."

"Want some help in the kitchen?" Max assumed she'd turn him down but she didn't.

"Sure. As long as you feel up to it."

"I'm fine."

Her father tapped his design book. "The lad speaks

true. In fact, we came up with several new products to develop."

She shook her head in disbelief. "I should've known."

The McDonnell didn't look repentant in the least. "Besides Bethia, Maggie and her sisters stopped by today."

Max had felt like a rare exhibit at the zoo with the number of women who came to peer at him. He stood and stretched. "Bread is rising in the oven."

"Da, we'll start the meal. Call out if you need anything." Pippa left the parlor and Max followed.

Once in the kitchen, Pippa got down to business and showed him how to clean the fish and fillet it. He pulled seasonings from the cupboard, prepared the pan, and preheated the oven. She tossed the salad and he made the dressing. Together, he thought, they made a pretty good team.

Dinner went well, the McDonnell telling one embarrassing story after another about Pippa as a young tyrant. By the sounds of it, she'd taken no flak from the snotty girls of the village and even less from the fishermen's sons. Max liked that Pippa could hold her own.

But when the McDonnell complained about her never giving the local men a chance, she defended herself. "The lads were all immature. Da would say you have to kiss a few toads to find Prince Charming." Her cheeks tinged red. "From my experience, all men are toads."

"Hey," Max said. "I take objection to that."

She nodded to her father. "Present company excluded." She looked to Max specifically and smiled. "The jury is still out on you."

The McDonnell laid his napkin on the table. "Ross is no toad."

Pippa popped up and grabbed an empty serving dish. "We're not speaking of Ross."

"Ross who?" Max had heard the name whispered at Quilting Central.

"Ross Armstrong," the McDonnell provided. "Maggie—who was here earlier today—is married to Ross's brother, John. Ross is—"

Pippa shoved the dirty dish at Max. "Come, Yank. Help clear the table."

Max followed her into the kitchen. "Why don't you want to talk about Ross?" Who was he to her?

"It's a long story." She acted as if that was the end of it.

"Would you rather tell me or should I go ask your dad about it?" Max took a step like he was going to do just that.

She grabbed his arm. "Start the dishwater and I'll tell you."

He grinned at her as he retrieved the dish soap. "I'm all ears."

She frowned at him as if he was one of the toads she was referring to a minute ago.

"I spent a lot of time with the Armstrong lads while growing up. They're like brothers to me. My father and Alistair, their father, were best mates." She paused as she placed a few dishes in the sink.

"Alistair? You're named after Ross's father?"

"One and the same."

"But that can't be the end of the story," Max said.

She crossed her arms over her chest as though she wasn't saying more.

Max picked up the first plate, washed, and rinsed it. "If that was all, why did you want your dad to drop the subject?"

Her shoulders slumped. She took the dish from him and dried it completely before answering. "Because it isn't worth mentioning."

Max cocked an eyebrow. Once again he acted like he was going to ask her father.

"Fine. My da and Ross's da had the grand scheme to join the two families by marrying me off to Ross."

Max stopped washing. He might have stopped breathing as well. It wasn't only that he'd held her hand . . . she was to marry another man!

He finally found his voice. "I don't know what to say." He wasn't the type of guy to horn in on another man's territory.

Apparently, she didn't know what to say either.

But Max wanted something from her. An explanation might be nice. "So that's the reason for all the whispering at Quilting Central the other day?"

"Aye. The town has nothing better to do than to gossip about when Ross and I are to marry."

Max grabbed the steel wool and scrubbed the hell out of the baking dish. "And when *are* you getting married?"

She sighed. "I said it's what the town and my father wants. I never said it's what I want."

And Ross, what did he want? Max told himself to forget it. He grabbed a dish towel and dried his hands. "I'll get the rest of the dishes."

He stomped to the parlor. *So Pippa is promised to another man.*

"Dishes," he said to the McDonnell in explanation, though he hadn't asked.

"Can ye leave those for a second and help me? I'm ready for a lie-down in the den."

"Sure." Max exhaled and left what he was doing. He stepped behind the wheelchair. "Do you need your oxygen?"

"Not tonight." The older man leaned his head to the side, speaking over his shoulder. "Ye should stay with us. Take my empty bed upstairs. I can't use it. I'm sure the room over the pub isn't comfortable."

Max felt like a prick. Didn't the McDonnell understand that his thoughts about his daughter weren't completely innocent? Max had been imagining doing all sorts of things with Pippa only last night. And this morning. And all day long. Apparently, the McDonnell wasn't as good at reading minds as he thought. And didn't the McDonnell take Ross into account when making the offer of Max sleeping under the same roof as his intended?

Max laid a hand on the older man's shoulder. "Thank you, no. I'm fine at the pub."

"Aye." The McDonnell nodded. "A man needs his space. Now, take me into the den so I can have mine."

Pippa stepped into the hall as Max wheeled him out, a mixture of emotions playing on her face. Was she thinking of Ross? Or had one of those emotions been the same disappointment that Max felt, that he and she would be sleeping in separate rooms tonight with the span of the town between them?

Max got her father settled, but when he returned to the hallway, she was waiting with his coat over her arm.

He took it. "I'm being kicked out before the work is done?"

"Nay." She reached for her coat on the hook behind her. "The dishes are soaking. I thought to walk you back."

"I can make it on my own." He leaned in just close enough to smell the flowery scent of her shampoo.

"We have things to discuss." She shrugged into her coat and slipped on a stocking cap. "We'll have a drink at the pub."

"Surely I shouldn't mix alcohol with Bethia's cure."

She rolled her eyes. "Hot tea, Mr. McKinley. The pub serves hot tea. We can discuss our plans for the next few days."

"Good." Better to discuss business than the details about her wedding with Ross. "I'd like to get right to work. Make up for the time lost while I was sick."

Pippa touched his arm. For a second, he thought it was a show of affection, but it was only to get his attention.

"Your scarf. Bundle up. I don't want you on your back again."

Oh, his libido couldn't help itself . . . On his back was fine as long as she was on top.

They stepped into the cold wind and didn't say a word to each other as they made their way across town.

A crowd had formed at the pub, the noise level closer to what one might expect on a Friday night. Max waited by the bar while Pippa made tea in the kitchen. When she came out with the tray, she motioned for him to follow her up the stairs.

She must've read the surprise on his face. "It'll be quieter up there."

Nearly every eye in the room was on them as he followed Pippa behind the bar to the steps. Bonnie nudged a large Scot sitting at the bar, and he glanced over at them.

"Who's that?" Max asked.

Pippa shrugged uncomfortably. "It's Ross."

The large Scot had a strange look on his face. Surprise? Jealousy? Disappointment? Max couldn't tell which. Hell, maybe it was all of the above.

And shouldn't Pippa care enough about Ross's feelings not to parade Max in front of him like this? He tried to put Ross out of his mind as he followed her up the narrow steps. But Max couldn't help feeling like a heel for lusting after another man's girl. Truthfully, though, she didn't act like an engaged woman. Once again, he recalled their joined hands as they slept.

"What are the townsfolk going to think about you coming up to my room?" *Especially Ross.*

She blushed, but in a bristly sort of way, as she pushed open the door. "Let 'em talk. It's not like I'm going to bed with ye. Besides, it's no one's affair except my own what I do in a man's room."

God, she was sassy, testy, hot. All that lip had him wanting to find out what it would feel like to have her backed up against the door, kissing and—

She gave him a hard glare. "Mind out of the gutter, Mr. McKinley. We've business to attend to."

Max shut the door behind him. "That can wait. I want to talk about Ross."

"Well, I don't."

"That's tough, because we're going to talk about this anyway. If he's your boyfriend, why would you let me hold your hand? Twice." It was best to get it all out in the open, though it embarrassed the hell out of him. He wasn't one to discuss his *feelings*. Or anything approximating feelings. She took her time, setting the tea tray down. He could almost see the wheels spinning in her head. "I'd like to know the truth," Max said. He didn't know why this was so important, but it was.

"This whole notion that I'm promised to Ross—as I told ye—it's not my idea."

Max pulled her chair close to the bed and motioned for her to sit. "Elaborate." She hadn't been completely clear about where *she* stood.

She shrugged off his invitation and paced instead. "To me, it would be absurd for us to get married." She shivered as if the thought chilled her.

Max felt a little appeased. "How does Ross feel about it?" He wasn't sure he wanted to know the truth, but he was going to see this through.

"I believe Ross wants to honor his da's wishes. Alistair died three years ago." Pippa grabbed the handle on the teapot and poured them both a cup. "Ross is a good man. A good friend, too. He's not someone to make waves. He'd marry me just to keep the town happy."

Oh, good Lord. Max had stumbled into a regular Peyton Place. "And what about you, Pippa? Are you going to marry Ross because everyone else wants you to?"

"Heavens, no. I've sidestepped marriage this long, I'm sure I can keep sidestepping it for the rest of my life."

Max breathed easier, knowing he hadn't compromised anything between Pippa and Ross. But he wondered if Ross was completely in the dark about how Pippa felt. Or even worse, was he carrying a torch for her?

Suddenly, it hit Max that he was being ridiculous. His thoughts had gotten turned upside down and twisted sideways since the moment he'd seen her standing behind the bar on his first night here. He wasn't going to get any more tangled up in her affairs than he already had. He was here to make a deal. Nothing else. No more wishful thinking. No more hand-holding. No more dwelling on how Pippa's lips might feel against his own. He had two objectives—make the deal, then go home.

"It's time to get down to business. MTech's proposal," he clarified.

"Not MTech's proposal. Not yet. We need to discuss the Christmas Roundup," she countered.

"The what?"

"The Christmas Roundup. It's what we're doing to-morrow."

"I don't do Christmas." The holidays held only dark memories—things he didn't like dredged up.

"If you're in Gandiegow, ye do."

"Do I dare ask what a Christmas Roundup is?"

"Ye sound like Scrooge." She handed him his cup of tea and finally sat. "It's for the children. All our employ-ees have contributed things from around the house. When the children come to the factory tomorrow, we'll help them upcycle bits and pieces into gifts for their loved ones. A lot of the kids come from poor families. It's a way for North Sea Valve to give back to the community." It sounded as though she'd rehearsed this speech. "And you will be there to help. We need all hands on deck to keep track of the lads and lassies of Gandiegow."

He felt shanghaied. "What about the MTech deal?"

She straightened herself as if the mention of MTech

was the prickly thorn in her backside. "We'll get to it. Right now, Christmas is more important."

He begged to differ. One of the benefits of coming to Scotland was to *skip* Christmas. He stared back, not saying anything.

She surveyed him closely. "I promise I'll listen to what you have to say about yere MTech deal, *and consider it*, if you help me."

"Fine." He guessed doing Christmas crap for one day wouldn't kill him. "But only because you and the others were good to me while I was sick," he groused. "I normally avoid Christmas like the plague."

"And why is that?" she said.

"Too much merrymaking." He was usually a cheerful guy, but Christmas sobered the hell out of him.

Her curiosity appeared piqued. "Oh, do share."

"Nope. It's a long boring story."

She took a sip of her tea. "Perhaps you'll tell me one day."

He dodged her request. "Is this normal, putting your visitors to work like this? Or am I just special?"

Her grin was only part of the answer. The gleam in her eye said she might have something else up her sleeve. "We don't get many visitors here."

What a crock. The town was crawling with the out-of-town quilters for the Kilts and Quilts retreat.

Pippa dabbed at a drip of tea on her lips. The action was innocent, but it hit him as erotic. And just like that, he was off balance and burning up. He tugged at his sweater. "You don't mind, do you?" He didn't wait for her answer, but went ahead and slipped it off, leaving only the polo underneath. "It's getting warm in here."

He must've moved toward her, because she stood abruptly.

Her confidence seemed to have faded. She fumbled to zip her coat. "I better go. Ye need your sleep."

"Not as much as I might need other things." Sure, only a moment ago, he was determined to extinguish this attraction he felt for her, but now the mouse-and-cat game between them felt too powerful. He was on autopilot and stepped closer.

She ducked past him. "Meet me downstairs in the morning. Eight, sharp." She slipped out the door and was gone.

He was satisfied that he'd unnerved her. But a shiver passed through him, a reminder that he better get his head back in the game and quit messing around. Ross may not have a claim on her, but neither did Max. Nor should he.

That night, his sleep was erratic, filled with Pippa. In his dreams she wasn't slipping out the door, but entertaining him . . . in bed. She was teasing, giving, and exciting and . . . she was crazy about him.

But it was only a dream.

When he woke in the morning, his nighttime fantasies had put him in a dark mood. Because none of it had been real. Or ever would be.

As directed, he met Pippa downstairs at eight sharp. He was going to do as she asked, but he wasn't going to do it without a bit of a fight. *Wrangling me into the Christmas Roundup was damned presumptuous of her.*

He ignored how festive she looked in her red-and-white-striped sweater and how cute her hair was braided with plaid ribbon. "I need details about today. How many kids are we talking about?" He might've sounded rude, but he couldn't help it. He really was annoyed.

She eyed him closely. "Ye're grumpy this morning. No one likes a grumpy Father Christmas."

He backed away, putting his hands up. "No. I draw the line right there. No dressing up as Santa. It's bad enough you already got me in a skirt."

She *tsk*ed. "A kilt is only a skirt if ye're wearing something underneath." She raised her eyebrows in question as if she wanted to know. "*Real men* wear kilts."

He'd never tell. "Can we go?" His mood was crappy this morning, but he still mustered up some good Texas boy manners and held the door open for Pippa as she strolled through.

"Maybe thirty," she said.

"Thirty what?"

"Children who are coming to the Christmas Roundup. And I'm sorry you don't like kids." But nothing in her words or body language hinted she would give him a pass on today's activities.

"I like rug rats fine," he answered, "as long as I'm related to them. I have a nephew and a niece."

"What are they like?"

"Loud. Little Max is a handful. My brother, Jake, keeps him riled up, which drives his wife crazy. Bitsy, my little sister, has a girl, Hannah. She's two, and a handful like her mother." He smiled, thinking about the tantrum Hannah had thrown over wearing tights to church the last time he was there. "That little girl knows her own mind. I know better than most that strong women rule the world. There's something powerful about a female who knows what she wants out of life."

He paused for second. *What the hell.* "Like you." He was only telling the truth.

"What makes you think I know what I want out of life?"

"You're as easy to read as a schematic," he said. "You love a challenge. You love figuring things out. You're starting to see that it doesn't matter whether you're in Edinburgh or Gandiegow, that there'll always be things that need to be fixed. Like North Sea Valve."

She stared back at him, horrified, as if he'd used X-ray vision to see clean through to her soul.

"It's okay." He understood why she'd used her given name, Alistair, when dealing with MTech and with him. Engineering, for all its advancements and diversity, was still male-centric. "I'm a pretty intuitive guy. It's one of the reasons MTech wanted me in the Acquisitions Department. I can see things that perhaps others can't."

"Or imagine that ye see." She stared straight ahead. "Ye've got one thing spot-on. Strong women do make the world go round."

"They certainly do." His mother, grandmother, Bitsy, Hannah, and every woman he'd met in Gandiegow were a testament to that.

Relative peace surrounded the two of them as they reached the car lot, but not silence. Waves crashing against the embankment filled the space where conversation had been, reminding him that he wasn't in Texas anymore.

Pippa maneuvered the car up the treacherous slick hill, seemingly in deep thought. He wanted to ask her what was so perplexing that it would stitch her eyebrows together like that. Hopefully, she wasn't worrying over the

MTech proposal. He would do his best to make it advantageous for both parties, as much as was in his power.

At the factory, they were making their way gingerly through the slick parking lot when Pippa slipped on a patch of ice. Max instinctively wrapped his arms around her waist, jerking her toward him.

She smelled so good. No perfume for this Scottish Amazon. Only shampoo, body wash, and something all her own.

Perhaps he held her too close for too long. She tried to dislodge herself from him.

"Nope." He stay attached to her arm, guiding her up the walk. "We're going to hold on to each other to keep the other one from falling."

"Or we're both going down?" she mumbled.

He chuckled, relishing holding her. He liked keeping her safe, though that was only more fantasy. Pippa could take care of herself.

"Do you have salt I can put down before the kids get here?" he asked.

"Aye." Pippa unlocked the building and pointed behind Bonnie's desk. "Utility closet." The same place the kilt and boots had been.

As Max spread the salt on various patches in the parking lot and sidewalk, a van pulled up with factory workers. Taog and Murdoch gave him a hand and soon the walkway was done.

Back inside, Pippa took Max to the factory floor, where a large space had been cleared and tables had been lined up. Household items covered each one—old books, jars, rope, glue, glitter, a cheese shredder, spoons, bowls of rocks . . . all sorts of junk.

"Okay, everybody," Pippa announced. "The children will be here any minute. Look at the list, find yere assignment, and get to your tables."

Max turned to Pippa. "Where will I be?"

"With me at my table." She handed him a red Santa cap.

"What's this for?" He wasn't a frigging elf.

"It's for the children. Now put it on. And a smile, too, or else ye'll scare the wee ones with that frown." She donned a matching cap. "We'll have the six- and seven-year-olds."

"Fine." He pulled his on, feeling as petulant as a seven-year-old himself.

Max remembered Jake at seven. There were almost nine years between them, and back then he had found Jake annoying as hell. The kid followed him everywhere and bugged the crap out of him and his friends. Not until Max had gone to college had he realized how super cool his kid brother was. Now, they were best buds. He'd have to call his brother tonight to see how things were going back home. Hopefully, Jake had calmed Mom down and she wasn't still on the rampage over Max missing Christmas.

"Are you all right?" Concern rested in Pippa's eyes.

"Yeah, just thinking about my brother." And how it sucked that he was stuck in a wheelchair, a young father with an energetic son.

At that moment, a sea of rug rats rushed in, filling the large open area of the factory with laughter and excitement.

Max saw one last chance for a reprieve. He looked to Pippa . . . and faked a cough. "Are you sure I'm not contagious? I'd hate to get the kids sick."

"Pathetic." She shook her head. "I can't believe a big man such as yereself is afraid of a few wee ones."

"Thirty is not a few." Max wasn't looking forward to the hours ahead. But if helping Pippa would get him in her good graces so they could talk about the MTech contract, he'd do it with as little attitude as he could muster.

Behind the children came a flock of adults. "We have backup," Pippa said. "Parents and family."

Max pulled his cap down farther. "Good. I didn't want to be the one responsible in case a kid got lost or something."

"Go sit down and plaster a smile on your face," she said. "Pretend you like Christmas."

That'll never happen.

As the adults corralled the kids and settled them at their tables, Max went to his. Pippa stood in the center of the room and said, "The North Sea Valve Company would like to welcome everyone here today. But before we get started, I want to introduce our honored guest, Mr. Christmas."

Max looked around for who that might be.

Pippa pointed in his direction. "Stand up, Mr. Christmas. Give everyone a big 'HO-HO-HO.'" With a twinkle in her eye, she dared him to refuse.

He cringed. If she'd asked him to be the Easter Bunny, St. Patrick, or the damned turkey at Thanksgiving, he would've willingly obliged. But Mr. Christmas was the last person he wanted to channel.

He didn't budge from his seat.

Pippa speared him with a withering glare. He refrained from returning her look with his own eye roll. She had no idea how much he hated the holiday.

"Come, now," she tried again. "Show us yere Christmas cheer."

To appease her and the others, he stood, super-glued a smile in place, and waved to everyone. "Ho, ho, ho," he said with little enthusiasm.

"Everyone, let's say good morning to Mr. Christmas together."

Pippa raised her arms like a symphony conductor.

"GOOD MORNING, MR. CHRISTMAS," the chorus of children and adults rang out.

He gave another wave and sat down. *Oh, Pippa will pay for this.* When he got hold of her and that saucy little mouth of hers . . . His thoughts were too X-rated to entertain while sitting with a bunch of children.

The vixen glided over and began explaining the project to the kids at their table. Pippa wouldn't meet his eyes, but her less than innocent smile said she was still whooping it up on the inside over putting him on the spot. Max pushed back his cap, tried to stop focusing on her lips, and did his best to listen to the instructions.

Max's table was making welcome mats from small ocean-polished rocks found on the beach. A pile of used floor mats sat at the end of the table, along with glue. A large box of pebbles sat in the middle. Pippa held up an example of what the finished project should look like and the kids stood to get a better look, oohing and aahing. She also had to stop a few hands from reaching into the box while she explained how to make the mat, but soon she was done and the kids dove in.

"I have to go help the other tables." Pippa pointed to his chest. "Mr. Christmas, ye're in charge."

He wanted to complain, but Pippa was gone. Then he

noticed the blond-haired girl at the other end of the table, sitting by herself, looking lost. He glanced around for backup, but Pippa had her hands full now with a four-year-old who was already covered in glitter.

Crap. He peered at the sad-faced girl again. He moved down the table and sat directly across from her.

"Hey," he said.

She turned sad green eyes on him.

"Hi there," he tried again. "What's your name?"

"Glenna," she said, but her voice was quizzical, as if she might be processing his words.

His accent. "I bet you think that I talk funny. I'm from Texas. In America. My name is Max."

"I thought yere name was Mr. Christmas."

"Yes, well, so it is." He motioned to the other adults. "Which one is your mother or father?"

Her eyes welled up with tears, but she didn't cry.

"Mama and Papa have gone to heaven. I live with Cousin Moira and Uncle Kenneth. 'Cept Uncle Kenneth died, too."

Moira was the one who'd clued him in about Mattie. "Is Moira helping with the quilt retreat this weekend?"

Glenna nodded.

Okay. He really had to man up now, whether he wanted to or not. "Since Moira can't be here, can I help you make your welcome mat?"

She gazed up at him with big innocent eyes and nodded again.

"All right then. What do we need to do first?"

"We need one of those." She pointed to where the stack of used mats had diminished considerably.

"Well, Glenna, pick one out for us," he said. "I'll gather some pebbles."

He glanced up and found Pippa staring at him, a look akin to gratitude. He nodded to her and began picking out pebbles. Glenna returned and they got to work, gluing the polished rocks into position.

Thirty minutes passed before Pippa glided over. Was it his imagination, or did her hand brush his hair? An accident or on purpose? Either way, it had a powerful effect on him.

She sat down beside Glenna but directed her comment to Max. "Do you want me to take over here so you can have a break?"

Panic crossed Glenna's face.

He winked at the little girl. "No break. But I believe Miss Glenna and Mr. Christmas need some refreshments. Do you mind getting us some cocoa?"

Glenna smiled at the pebbles she was gluing to the mat.

"Aye." Pippa stood. "Glenna, would you rather have hot cider?"

"Cocoa, miss," Glenna said softly.

A few of the other kids must've noticed the attention being paid to this end of the table. A group of them wandered over and started engaging Glenna in conversation. *Who was her mat for? What did she want for Christmas? Did she want to go sledding later?*

Pippa came back with their drinks. Max took his and stood. The kids scooted closer to Glenna.

"That was a nice thing that you did," Pippa whispered.

Sure, a nice thing letting Glenna believe a little longer

that Christmas was her friend. Because reality would come soon enough. Maybe not as dramatically as it had in his life, but *something* would eventually ruin it for her. There was no way to sustain the magic of Christmas forever.

Pippa eyed him, waiting.

"I didn't do anything," he finally said.

"Humble, too," she said to herself as if she was cataloguing him. The thought made him uncomfortable.

Pippa motioned to Freda to take their place. "Come with me, Max. I need muscle to transport some boxes."

He assumed she meant from the car to the factory. Instead, she led him to her office and held the door open while he walked in. The door shut behind him and the lights went out. He spun around, only to see her hand on the switch. Light through the office windows illuminated the determined look on her face. Before he could say anything, Pippa had wrapped her arms around his neck and was giving him one hell of a kiss.

Chapter Six

Pippa couldn't breathe. This kiss wasn't the warm co-coa kiss she'd expected, tender and sweet. Max's kiss was a shot of whisky, hot and intoxicating. They were revving like a well-oiled machine at top capacity, and she could've gotten lost in it.

"Oh, God," Max groaned, pulling her closer.

Pippa hadn't meant for this to happen. Kissing him was supposed to be only a thank-you for what he'd done for Glenna. Or maybe she'd wanted to kiss him to test the waters, find out if the chemistry between them was real. Perhaps she wanted only to prove to herself—and to the town—that she wasn't promised to anyone. But if she didn't break the kiss soon, she was afraid she'd let him take her right here behind the closed office door . . . inside her da's factory.

"Whoa, Yank." She pulled away, reverting to chief engineer in three seconds flat. *He is the enemy.* The one who'd come here to steal their subsea shutoff valve. She smoothed down her red sweater that he'd pushed up.

He looked as flushed as she felt.

"I just wanted to say thanks for all the help. Now grab

the boxes over there." She was going to be all business now.

He grinned at her, and it was almost more than she could handle.

He stepped forward and kissed her—a short, quick promise that whatever was going on between them wasn't over—not by a long shot. She patted his chest, and then he stepped away and grabbed the largest box.

"This weighs a ton," he complained. "What's in here? Bricks?"

Her branded lips hadn't quite recovered. "C-canned food." *Stuttering?* God, could she be any more of a lightweight? "Take it to the car."

She followed him out, trying to pull herself together. The cold breeze outside helped considerably, making her focus on potential frostbite instead of him.

Afterward, they rejoined the Christmas Roundup, and fortunately the children made excellent chaperones. The kids attacked Max, peppering him with questions as he made his way back to their table. Glenna looked to have acquired several more friends while they were gone. One little boy was smitten with her, which was evident when he helped slide her mat onto a heavy piece of cardboard and insisted he carry it for her.

All the kids looked proud of their upcycled gifts, and thrilled when Pippa handed each of them a goody bag to take home. "Ye wait to eat your sweets until after ye have yere lunch. Do ye hear?"

But some were already breaking into their sacks as the parents and workers walked the kids out to the waiting vans.

Pippa, her workers, and Max cleaned up the factory

floor. There was safety in numbers, keeping her from being alone with the Yank. But it didn't take long to clear the tables from the floor and get everything back in order. Pippa's stomach reeled as the group of them walked to the front entrance together. She wanted to slip out first, but she had to lock up. One by one, she thanked her employees and said good-bye as they left. She wished Taog or Murdoch had offered to take Max back to town with them, but she had no such luck. Suddenly, she and Max were the only two remaining in the factory. She fumbled as she pulled out the keys.

"Ready?"

"Not quite." Max took a page from her book, laying a hand on the light switch. Maintaining eye contact, he flipped it off as he moved in closer. He didn't dive in right away, like she'd done, but gazed into her eyes for a long moment. The mischief resting there transformed into something more serious and meaningful. He backed her against the wall and leaned in.

The kiss was more powerful than before, delivering on the promise the short kiss had made ... and then some. She couldn't stop herself, kissing him back fervently, wrapping a leg around his ankle to anchor herself to where she wanted to be.

"Sweet Jesus," he murmured.

Amen.

But what had she started? She couldn't make out with MTech's minion.

Her hormone-induced fog cleared. She pushed at his chest. "Enough."

She glared at Max's mouth. The Yank was here in Scotland only to make the deal for MTech. She had the sinking feeling that his expert kissing was one of many weapons in his deal-closing arsenal.

And Pippa was an idiot. Once again, she'd fallen for a handsome face and had forgotten how duplicitous men could be.

"You're right." Max was breathing hard. At least she wasn't the only one who was affected.

A distressed flicker rolled across his features as if he was only now realizing what line they'd crossed.

He moved away. "I promised Taog and Murdoch I'd have a drink with them."

"Good." She didn't want him at dinner tonight anyway, all comfortable in her father's house, with her feeling the way she did. It would only muddy the waters further.

He straightened, pulling the Santa's hat from his head and offering it back to her.

"Keep it." Her voice sounded like strangled nerves.

"You better get home. Your father will be waiting."

Had he meant his words to be an ax to split them apart?

She was numb inside as she exited the building. He followed, but an invisible door had slammed shut between them. The loss was palpable.

"Try not to get stinking drunk tonight at the pub," she said flatly. "Ye'll be expected at the kirk first thing in the morn. Everyone attends church, no excuses."

His brows furrowed. "I'll be there."

She felt like a cardboard cutout of herself, not full of life like she'd been in his arms moments ago. "Da will expect you for noon meal tomorrow, though." There was no way around that one.

"Fine." His tone was dead.

Like a couple of strangers, they got in the car and drove the short distance back to town without a word.

She'd done the right thing, putting the fire out between them. More was riding on this deal than stealing a kiss or two.

She had a plan and would stick to it. She would make sure Max got to know the people of Gandiegow through and through. After seeing him with Glenna today, she knew her instincts were right. Max had a soft spot. All she had to do was exploit it.

But when she glanced over at him and saw how the kindness in his eyes from earlier had been replaced with steel, she second-guessed herself. Her plan might not work. But MTech's money was the only way to save the town's economy and her da's dream.

But how much would it cost her?

Pippa squared her jaw. She wasn't a romantic. She was an engineer . . . architect of her own future. She wouldn't let her hormones wreak havoc with her determination. She would keep her eye on the prize—stabilize the factory and get her father well. Then and only then, she might think about having *more*.

Freda Douglas rinsed the last plate and put it in the drainer. It wasn't her kitchen, but she'd washed more dishes here than at her own cottage. She lovingly adjusted the dish towel over the oven handle and stood back to make sure everything was in perfect order.

Pippa hadn't come home for lunch so it had been only her and Lachlan . . . no, *the McDonnell*. Freda had given up calling him Lachlan thirty years ago when he'd returned home after university with Pippa in a swaddling blanket and his new bride dead. Freda had no right to him, then or now. But her heart had never quite gotten the message.

She made her way back into the den and pulled the quilt over the man she loved. He needed a haircut, strands standing up here and there. She'd make sure to bring her clippers tomorrow when she came to sit with him. Because he was asleep and wouldn't know, she reached out and smoothed down the spot.

The front door slammed. Freda dropped her hand and stepped back. She busied herself, straightening the cushions on the love seat and rearranging the magazines on the coffee table.

"Hey," Pippa whispered from the doorway. "Has he been asleep long?"

"Drifted off right after the noonday meal." Freda moved closer. "Can I warm you up some cauliflower and bacon soup?"

"That would be grand. I need to run up and change." Glitter coated Pippa's shirtfront.

"Yere food will be waiting when ye come down." Freda watched as Pippa left the room, fascinated by the determination on her face. With a smile, she wondered what was coming next. When the lass got that look, anything and everything could happen.

Feeling both elated and a bit sad, she gazed over at the McDonnell. The two people she loved most lived in this house, and they had no idea that they were everything to her . . . her whole world.

The next morning, Max's head felt like a front loader had dropped on it. He was sure he hadn't gotten stinking drunk at the pub last night, but the hangover begged to disagree.

Taog and Murdoch had been no help. Those two kept shoving drinks at him until Max lost count. Maybe it was his own fault. He should've eaten more for dinner at the town's restaurant before meeting up with Taog and Murdoch at the pub. But a very pregnant Claire, the co-owner of the restaurant, and her chef-husband, Dominic, insisted on introducing Max to every damned Gandiegowan who came in. Max had wanted time alone to figure out what to do about Pippa, but every villager persisted in bending his ear, especially about the factory. He couldn't get a bite in edgewise. Life here was the opposite of what he knew back in Houston.

The problem of Pippa remained. He couldn't shake her. God, he never should've kissed that woman. Granted, she'd kissed him first. But this wasn't playtime. His career was on the line and he was letting a nice piece of *lass* get in the way of closing the deal.

But Pippa didn't seem like the kind of girl to have a fling with. He envisioned her as a forever kind of woman, the marrying type.

And he wasn't a forever kind of guy.

He had time only for his career. He'd never been in love. Lust, yeah, sure, many times. Max had to remind himself that his attraction to Pippa was only that—attraction. Okay, *explosive chemistry* described it best. But it wasn't love.

Max's phone dinged with a text message from Miranda.

Call me with an update, whether you're well or not.

But he couldn't text Miranda back. What could he tell

her about the deal? That NSV's chief engineer kissed like a veritable love goddess, or that she made him as hard as a concrete pier? How about that he'd spent his time making Christmas presents and drinking with the locals instead of discussing the subsea shutoff valve?

Hell, he was screwed.

He checked the time, nine thirty. He'd better hurry to church, headache or not. Twenty minutes later, he was bundled up and out the door. He didn't know what to expect from an Episcopal church. He'd grown up Methodist. In the last few years, though, he'd spent his Sundays on the job, instead of sitting in a pew. Working 24/7 had paid off with recognition and promotions. The problem was that if he didn't get his brain back to the program and off Pippa soon, or stop cozying up to the locals, his career would be over.

Max sneaked into the church just as the music for the processional started and the congregation rose. Pippa gave him an exasperated glance as she stepped out in the aisle so he could squeeze in. Yes, he'd cut it close. At least she'd saved him a seat. *Barely.* She was too near for comfort. His arm had nowhere to go, save up against hers. He could even smell her damned flowery shampoo! He kept his eyes fixed forward. But out of his peripheral vision, she had no warm smile for him, only a coolness that matched the frigid weather outside.

She elbowed him while handing him a hymnal. "Page seventy-six."

As the choir and the blond-headed priest gravitated toward the altar in time with the music, Max remained determined to ignore the woman beside him and sing along as if he possessed some Christmas cheer.

Pippa leaned up and whispered against him, "That's Father Andrew."

Her breath on Max's ear brought on sensations not normally associated with church.

Max focused on the pastor. Father Andrew seemed to be a few years younger than himself. He bestowed a smile on each of his parishioners, until a worried expression passed over his face as he looked at one woman—Moira, the shy one from Quilting Central and Glenna's guardian. Moira didn't meet Andrew's eye, but kept her face fixed on her hymnal. It was clear that Andrew was in love with Moira; Max knew it instantly. He always caught these kinds of micro-emotions, whether he wanted to or not. He looked one more time at Moira and Andrew, wondering what might be going on between them.

The service was pretty similar to the one at home, except for the kneeling, with Andrew delivering a nice sermon about helping thy neighbor. Back in Houston, Max didn't know his neighbors. With all his time spent at work, he hadn't gotten around to making friends at the apartment complex. He glanced about the church and was struck that he knew the names of more people here in Gandiegow than he did back home, and he'd lived in the same apartment for six years.

At the end of the service, Andrew asked if there were any announcements. Kirsty, the new schoolteacher, stood. She was also one of the people he'd met last night at the restaurant. She was a petite brunette who was into yoga and taking charge of things.

"As most of you know, the set for the Christmas pageant has seen better days. We've gathered together some supplies to build a new one. I'm looking for volunteers to help construct a nativity scene. Is there anyone who could help this afternoon?"

Pippa's hand shot up in the air. "Mr. McKinley and I will help."

His mouth fell open.

She turned to him and shrugged unapologetically. "Ye can't ignore Christmas in Gandiegow."

But ignoring Christmas was better than the alternative.

The last time he trusted in Christmas was three years ago. His mom, everyone, convinced him it was time to give up his grudge against the holidays. But when Max tried to get into the spirit of things and sent Jake on a Christmas errand, his little brother was hit by a car and paralyzed. The holidays had sliced his family's heart in two. Again.

Pippa was looking at him, apparently expecting an answer.

"Fine," he finally whispered back. He didn't mind helping people out. He never had. But Christmas wasn't the only thing that he'd boycotted. The last time he'd used a hammer for more than hanging a picture was before his dad died. He felt too guilty to work with a tool since.

Crap. He hated when he remembered stuff like that. Even to this day, grief could overtake him, making him feel helpless. Automatically, he reached for Pippa's hand, but stopped himself, jerking back.

When she looked at him questioningly, he turned away.

After church, Pippa went to speak with Kirsty, who was not only spearheading the set construction but was also the pageant director. Max wanted to slip outside for some breathing room, but person after person kept stopping him. Father Andrew first, shaking Max's hand and thanking him for volunteering his time to work on the manger scene. Then Bethia to see how he was feeling. Even Amy made a point to ask how the warm clothes were holding up. When Moira nodded in passing, Glenna pulled away and ran over to him. She yanked on his hand as if to pull him down to her level.

"I want to give Mr. Christmas a hug." Glenna's lilting voice tugged at his heart.

He knelt down and hugged her back.

"Talk to Santa Claus for me," she whispered in his ear. "I want Cousin Moira to be happy again."

Max had no words for her, but nodded his head as she looked into his eyes. *Now, how am I going to do that?*

As she ran off, Taog and Murdoch cornered him, wanting to recount the drinks they'd had last night. Max broke away to stop Deydie and thank her for the chicken stew, which he declared was as much responsible for his quick recovery as Bethia's tinctures. Deydie beamed at him with an alarming grin.

The experience of a tight community was almost surreal. He hadn't shared this much conversation since college. Back home, he mostly talked about work, either technical issues or corporate gossip. He'd certainly never had the occasion to thank someone for chicken stew! The villagers reminded him a lot of his own family—a bit nosy, but endearing. How had he developed a strong connection with Gandiegow in such a short period of time?

Pippa returned and grabbed her coat from the rack. "We better hurry to noonday meal with my da. I promised Freda and Kirsty we would be back in an hour to work on the new nativity scene."

Max took her coat from her and held it up so she could slip her arms in. He stopped himself from doing more. He could tell her hackles were already up that he'd played gentleman to her lady.

Lunch was a quick affair of potato soup and fresh bread—provided by Freda. As promised, they were out the door within the hour, leaving the McDonnell to visit with Abraham Clacher, one of the old fishermen.

Back at the church, the manger crew consisted of Father Andrew, a couple of teenagers named Samuel and Robert, Freda, Kirsty, and Ross—Pippa's supposed beau.

As they walked to the rear of the building, Max considered introducing himself to Ross. Not because Pippa was promised to the fisherman; Max needed to befriend *all* the people of Gandiegow if he was to close the deal with the North Sea Valve Company.

But at the doorway of the makeshift workroom, he stopped short. The smell of sawdust and the sight of workhorses and carpentry tools strewn out across the floor knocked the breath from him.

Old memories flooded his senses.

Helping his dad in his workshop, aka the garage, was one of his earliest recollections. It was their special father/son time. So many of his memories of his dad were when they had tools in their hands. Max always felt comfortable telling Dad things when they were alone like that. There were never any lectures in the workshop, only the sharing of wisdom among the claw hammer, the palm sander, and the scraps of wood.

But Max's last memory of the workshop was filled

with regret. He'd bailed on his dad, wanting to hang out with friends instead of the old man. *Go on,* his dad had said. *Have a good time. We can work on this bench later.* If Max had known then it would be his last chance to build something with his father, he would've ditched his friends in a heartbeat. But he hadn't known. All opportunities to make it up to his dad for being selfish had been obliterated when the oil rig exploded.

A warm hand touched his arm. Max shifted his gaze to find Pippa looking at him with concern.

"What's wrong?"

"Nothing." His voice sounded scratchy. "I'm fine." He walked farther into the room to prove to himself that he had overcome those feelings long ago.

Ross picked up two hammers, handing one to Max. "We haven't met yet. I'm Ross Armstrong."

"Max. Max McKinley."

Ross sized him up. "Are ye any good with a hammer?"

"I used to be." Max hefted the tool from one hand to the other.

Kirsty clapped to get their attention as though they were her students. "Here are the plans for the collapsible stable and manger. I printed them off the Internet. If we do it right, the pieces should convert to a food stand for the children to use during the summer months." She handed out their assignments.

Max headed off to a corner to work alone. Between the smell of fresh-cut wood and the buzz of the circular saw, he couldn't think clearly. Why was Pippa torturing him by dredging up old memories? But she couldn't know how painful it was to use tools again, or how much he missed his dad.

He glanced up. Pippa stood there as if he'd conjured her. She grabbed a handful of nails. "Can I help?"

No. He wanted to work alone. "Sure. Can you get me three slats?"

She retrieved them and held them in place while he hammered. "Ye're skilled," she remarked. "Like you've built a manger before?"

Max sat back on his heels. "Yes. My dad taught me. We made the manger for our church when I was twelve." He chuckled, remembering more.

"What?" Pippa said. "Why the smile?"

"That wasn't the only manger we built together. We decided to make another crib, similar to this, one for my little sister to play with." He shook his head.

"And?" Pippa prompted.

"Bitsy, my kid sister, decided, instead of using it for her dolls, she wanted it for herself. Christmas night, my dad called me in to see her sleeping in it. Her legs were hanging over the edge. It's a wonder the thing didn't collapse under her weight."

The warmth of the memory filled him—his dad's hand on his shoulder while the two of them watched Bitsy sleep. He glanced at Pippa now, grateful she'd helped him to remember something good.

They continued to work together, and within the span of three hours, the crèche was done. Max wiped sawdust from his hands. He helped the crew put the room back in order and move the hybrid manger scene/food stand to the far wall. Before they left, Father Andrew thanked each one for donating their time and talent.

Pippa brushed sawdust from Max's arm. "Ye did a fine job."

It was nice having her beside him, but things were getting a little too cozy again. He stepped away from her and retrieved his coat. "I better head back to the pub now."

Pippa put her hands on her hips. "Not so fast, Mr. McKinley. Aye, ye better head back to the pub to clean up, but then we're expected at Quilting Central."

"Why? Am I required to make a quilt next?"

She laughed. "Nay. To Christmas carol. 'Tis a lovely way to send off the quilters at the end of the retreat."

Good God. Was she going to make him take part in *every single Christmas tradition* while he was here in Gandiegow?

He screwed a smile on his face. "Shouldn't I rest? Wasn't I recently in grave danger with the Highland flu?"

"Singing is good for you."

"Says who?"

"Says everyone. Besides, caroling at Quilting Central will help people forget that ye've come here to steal our subsea shutoff valve." She'd said it without missing a beat, as if that sentiment was always first and foremost on her mind.

"Let's get one thing straight, Pippa—"

She cut him off. "We'll have to argue later. Deydie said we better be on time *or else*. The quilters' bus is headed back to Glasgow at six p.m. After that, ye can rail on me all you want."

She was so full of life and determination. Her competency, her drive, was incredibly sexy.

Without warning, all blood in his head rushed southward. He had the urge to grab her and kiss her senseless. He stared at her for a few steamy moments, then finally answered, "Fine." The word was sharp, begrudging—which had little to do with caroling and more to do with how little control he had over himself when he was near her.

She blushed as if she could read his dirty mind. "No dawdling either. I don't have time to come and get you; I need a shower, too."

Not the image I need right now. He ran a hand through his hair. Maybe he should suggest they shower together . . . to save water and time.

She put her hands on her hips. "What are you grinning about?"

"Nothing," he said, imagining all sorts of angles at which to soap her up.

"Well, stop it." She looked at her watch. "And get going."

"I am." But not before he gave her the once-over again. For good measure.

Thirty minutes later, when Max walked into Quilting Central, he was hit with estrogen overload. Four men from the church choir and two fishermen—Ross and his brother, Ramsay—stood at the back wall, a small battalion against an army of women, especially gray-headed women. Max ignored the appreciative female glances as he stalked by them to join the men.

Pippa noticed the women, too, and gave an eye roll, but then she moved on to the business of arranging the carolers. "Stand there, Max. Everyone else gather around."

The makeshift choir did as they were told. Pippa started singing "Hark! The Herald Angels Sing" and they joined in. Max was surprised he remembered the words. The last time he'd sung carols was at a school Christmas concert. Next they sang "Good King Wenceslas." As he looked out at the quilters and their genuine smiles registered, his annoyance at Pippa began to fade. The quilters clapped along with "Jingle Bells," and then the choir finished with "We Wish You a Merry Christmas."

As they disbanded, Pippa touched his arm. "Still angry with me?"

"Not so much."

"Does that smile on your face mean you're not the Grinch you thought you were?" she asked.

"No," he lied. "I can keep my inner Grinch under wraps when I have to."

"Nay. You enjoyed yereself, I think. I told you singing was good for you."

He didn't get to respond as the Glasgow women converged. Pippa had mercy and steered the crowd toward the cookies and hot cocoa.

Max watched her from across the room as she entertained a large group with an animated story. He couldn't hear what she was saying over the noise in the room, but he could tell it was one whopper of a tale. Suddenly, she pointed at him and they all laughed, but instead of getting up in arms over it, he waved back good-naturedly.

Bethia sidled up beside him. "Our Pippa is something special." She examined him closely, chewing her lip in thought.

Max didn't know what Bethia was getting at, so he answered cautiously. "Pippa does have spunk."

Bethia nodded. "Aye. One in a million."

Aye, indeed. There was something magnetic about Pippa McDonnell. But he wouldn't let on that he agreed.

Pippa left her audience and joined him and Bethia, her

face flushed from laughing. "And Mr. McKinley, what are you doing for dinner? Are you coming to my house and feasting with the McDonnell and myself?"

He would like nothing more than to remain near her. But the Highland flu wasn't the only thing he was susceptible to here in Scotland. Wanting to spend more time with Pippa was running rampant through him. And that was not good.

"Thanks for the offer, but I'm bushed," he said. "I'll grab a bite before I go to bed."

The light in her eyes dimmed for a moment but she recovered quick enough. "Aye. You must keep up yere strength."

"Yes, we have a lot of work to do," he reminded her.

"Then I'll wish you good night." She stuck out her hand as if they were only acquaintances. Maybe it was for Bethia's sake.

He took it and had quite the shock. A sizzle pulsed between them.

Hell.

Bethia was too observant. She raised her eyebrows and canted her head in the direction of Ross. *A little reminder?*

As if on cue, Max's cell phone dinged. A text.

Pippa heard it, too, and she let go.

He glanced at the message. *Miranda.* He should've waited to check it, or at least hidden the screen. When Pippa saw who was texting him, her face tensed and she stepped away. But physical space wasn't the only distance she put between them.

"I'll see you in the morning, Mr. McKinley." Her smile

was gone, her tone professional. The warmth between them had turned to frigid air.

"Fine."

Pippa had the right of it. Between now and then, he better regain some perspective. The electric attraction between them was only a distraction. And though she claimed there was nothing there, in Gandiegow's eyes Pippa was promised to Ross.

Chapter Seven

In the morning, Max dressed for business in his suit and tie, but wearing the warm boots Pippa had given him at the factory.

No more Christmas Roundups, no more Christmas carols. No more bullshit. The e-mail from Miranda this morning had been a veiled threat. He should've been more reassuring in his text back to her last night. If Max didn't make headway on this deal soon, she'd send someone who would. In other words, he'd be out of a job. He went downstairs and waited for NSV's chief engineer. She would not derail him today.

Pippa showed up wearing jeans and a blue cable sweater, not the business attire he expected.

She gave him the once-over. "You're certainly not dressed appropriately for today's task."

He glanced down at his dark suit, hoping she meant they were going to get their hands dirty. "I don't mind if we're working on the production lines, but afterward we'll discuss the MTech/NSV partnership, right?"

She screwed up her face. "Not exactly." She held out the last word.

He didn't budge. "How *not exactly*? We're going to work on the production lines, but we're *not* going to discuss the partnership?"

She shook her head, not making anything clear. Surely she didn't expect him to do any more Christmas crap today.

She gestured toward the steps behind the bar. "Hurry and change. Make sure to wear Amy's dreadful sweater."

Max stayed rooted to the floor as a terrible feeling crept over him. "What's this about?" He prided himself on his good manners, but felt close to losing his temper.

She flipped her long curls over her shoulder. "We're running errands today."

"What kind of errands?" Maybe they were heading into Inverness to pick up something for the factory. That would give them plenty of time to discuss the deal. "Did you order some new equipment?"

"Ye're wasting time." She thrust her hands on her hips impatiently. "If ye must know, we're running Christmas errands. We've packages to deliver."

Good grief. Not again.

He was drawing the line here and now. It was one thing for her to have the kids call him Mr. Christmas, but it was a whole other nightmare to impersonate Santa Claus himself.

Max glared at her. "No. No way." He was done playing her game. "No more Christmas activities. I'm here to discuss the MTech deal and nothing else." Or nothing more. He'd already crossed the line and kissed her, but it couldn't happen again.

Her eyebrows lifted. "And that's your final answer?"

"Yes." It felt good to set her straight. No more jacking

around. "Your obsession with Christmas could get me fired!"

She sauntered past him and picked up his gloves from the bar. "It's a shame. I thought we were coming to an *understanding*."

The word coursed through him as she stopped and held his gaze.

Then she shifted and faced the wreath hanging over the bar as if it was the most interesting thing in the world. "Fine. If ye don't care to know the people of Gandiegow, then my father and I will have to bring in another company that will."

Bring in another company? There. The lightbulb went off in his brain. The number one rule when dealing with customers was to figure out what they wanted. Max was no dummy, but since the moment he'd met Pippa, he had been thinking with his *member* instead of his brain. He should've figured this out sooner.

"So that's what this is all about? You've made me take part in all of your Gandiegow Christmas nonsense so I'll take the townsfolk into consideration while we're hammering out this deal?"

"Aye. The reason for the season."

Time to backpedal from his earlier assertion. "I'll need a minute to change my clothes."

She tapped his arm with an index finger. "Ye're a quick learner, Mr. McKinley."

"Not as quick as I should've been. But top of my class at Texas A&M."

Pippa was holding the damned deal hostage and he resented it, and at the same time, he understood. She was just watching out for her town. And for that, he admired her.

He stepped behind the bar, but stopped. "Why the sweater?"

"Ye'll see."

"Tell me now."

"The people we're going to visit today don't have a lot to laugh about. I thought the fact that you bought Amy's sweater, and that a gorgeous man such as yereself would actually wear it, would bring a smile to their faces."

Had she just barbed him and called him gorgeous in the same breath?

When he returned, Pippa had two coffees and a thermos. She gestured to Amy's sweater, softness in her eyes. "Ye're a trouper."

"I can suffer through a few hours of humiliation as long as the deal is made in the end." He gave her a capisce-look, grabbed his coat, and held the door open for them to leave.

Before starting their deliveries, they retrieved the wagon from Quilting Central. He'd assumed most of the packages would be presents, but their load consisted primarily of food and essentials. Their first stop was the small house belonging to the Bruce family. Poor Mrs. Bruce was worn-out, deep lines between her eyebrows. With five sick children at home and her husband the janitor at NSV, she looked to be scarcely hanging on to her sanity. Max stoked the fire while Pippa put the groceries away. He tried not to notice how bare the cupboards were. His mother raised three kids as a widow, but they'd never gone without food like these folks.

The oldest of the Bruce children, a coughing seven-year-old, cornered him. "Play with us."

With a big grin, Max joined three of the kids in front of the fire. The homemade blocks made a racket as he poured them from a basket onto the floor. The kids *shh*ed him because their baby brother was asleep in the crib in the corner.

"Pippa, can I fix you a cup of tea?" Mrs. Bruce looked hopeful for some company.

"Aye."

The women sat at the table and talked quietly.

"Are your shutters in good working order? A big storm is brewing," Pippa finally said.

Max stacked two more blocks on the tower he was building.

"The screws have gone loose on two of them." Mrs. Bruce looked down, embarrassed. "I need to get out there and tighten them. With Calder so tired at the end of the day, I haven't had the heart to ask him to do it."

With a quick apology Max handed off his blocks to the children and got to his feet. "Put me to work, Mrs. Bruce. Do you have tools?"

She pointed to the bed in the corner. "Under there."

Pippa beamed at Max with approval, but he avoided her warm gaze. It was just a couple of screws. He retrieved the tools and his coat. After he secured the storm shutters, he fixed the loose leg on the dining table. When one of the Bruce girls brought Max her doll, he fixed it, too. Pippa's gaze seemed to follow him wherever he went, and he couldn't help liking it, even though he knew he shouldn't.

The little girl's face lit up when he handed the toy back, its arm reattached. "Danks," she chirped, then took the doll and climbed into her mother's lap, sticking a thumb in her mouth.

Mrs. Bruce squeezed her daughter and gave Max a grateful smile. "Thank you, Mr. McKinley."

"My pleasure," he said sincerely.

Pippa bombarded him with another of her tender looks as she handed him his scarf and coat. "We need to be off. We have several more stops to make today."

Mrs. Bruce stood. "Where to next?"

"Mr. Menzies," Pippa said.

"Wait just a minute." Mrs. Bruce wrapped a fresh loaf of bread. "Can ye give this to him from us?"

Max was astounded at her generosity. The Bruces had so little.

Mrs. Bruce and three of her children waved good-bye from the door as he and Pippa made their way down the walk.

Mr. Menzies lived in nothing more than a shack. He had to be in his eighties and was nearly deaf. But he had the gleam in his eyes of a much younger man who loved making merry. He was full of funny stories about Pippa's father, especially the trouble Lachlan had gotten into as a boy, before he'd become the McDonnell. Mr. Menzies seemed to grow livelier the longer they were there, and Pippa sat listening without the slightest show of impatience, even though she'd probably heard the same stories a dozen times.

Then Mr. Menzies mentioned the land NSV sat on, a piece of property that had gone to him after all his family members had passed.

"I never expected to see a dime of rent for the place." Mr. Menzies cleared his throat. Max was afraid the old man might be overcome with emotion. "I'm right grateful to the McDonnell for starting up the factory." He pointed to the new woodstove in the corner. "I'm making some needed improvements around here with the extra cash."

Pippa hugged Mr. Menzies and then wrapped a green-and-gold quilt around his shoulders.

He reached for Pippa's hand. "Thank you, lassie. Ye're a good one."

Max tried to not be affected by the old man's fondness for Pippa, but she seemed to bring it out in people. She brought it out in him!

The more places they stopped, the closer he felt to NSV's chief engineer and Gandiegow's benevolent elf. He found excuses to keep touching her—straightening her scarf, dusting snow from her sleeve, adjusting her hair when she pulled her cap off. He couldn't help himself. His attraction toward her had shifted into something tender, something that made him slightly uncomfortable in his own skin. She seemed to have softened toward him, too. The pull to be together was strong. He used every ounce of his willpower not to kiss her between houses. He focused on the task at hand and began warming up to being an elf right along with her. *But only an elf.* He could have compassion for these people and still hold on to his grudge toward Christmas.

When at last their wagon was empty, he should've been smart and hightailed it to the pub alone. But when it came to Pippa, he was anything but rational.

"Will you come back with me?" He wanted her to himself. "For cocoa?" Something sweet, hot, and satisfying.

"Aye. I'll come with ye."

They'd have an hour, maybe a little longer, before the pub began filling up for the evening, and he wanted to spend every minute of it with her. To hell with keeping his distance.

They didn't talk as they walked through town. They left the wagon outside of Quilting Central, then continued straight on to the pub. Max was on a mission, and it seemed Pippa was, too.

At the pub, they slipped inside and climbed the stairs, the cocoa forgotten. He held the door open as she walked into his room. Before he had time to shut the door fully, Pippa was in his arms, kissing him.

She kissed him because she couldn't be around him another second without having his lips on hers. Why had MTech sent this one? It was bad enough that he was good-looking. But for Max to have a generous heart added insult to injury! Even worse, he didn't *know* he was a good guy.

She'd made him come along to deliver presents to teach him a lesson—that the people of Gandiegow mattered—but what had happened had only drawn them closer together, made her want to know him more thoroughly, made her ache to be in his arms.

Damn him. She could not fall for the Yank.

But she could . . . do other things.

As they kissed, her desire for him increased, need pulsing from the very center of her. As she ran her fingers through his hair, he retaliated by pulling her bum to him intimately. She could *feel* exactly where this was headed.

And she couldn't stop it. She didn't want to.

She pulled at his coat and pushed it to the floor, never breaking their kiss. He did the same to hers. She was a woman who knew how to get things done and her goal was to get to his skin. She pulled Amy's ugly sweater over his head, but didn't quit there. She yanked his red T-shirt off, too, and tossed it.

"My turn." He took the bottom of her sweater, eased it off, and threw it on his bed. He gazed at her appreciatively before pulling her back into his arms. Apparently, his goal was to get to her skin, too. And to kiss her senseless. The heat surrounding them was scorching.

As his hands cupped her breasts through her bra, the door downstairs slammed. They stilled.

A woman hollered. "Max? Max McKinley? Are you up there?"

He froze. Pippa gazed into his hard glare.

"Max?" There was a clicking noise, heels coming up the steps.

"Shit," he growled.

"Who is it? Oh, God! You better not be married!" Pippa jerked away, reaching for the nearest piece of clothing—Max's red T-shirt on the chair. Just as she got it over her head, the door flew open.

A woman sauntered in. Pippa followed her stern gaze to Max, who had grabbed Amy's sweater and was pulling it over his head, the awful thing tinkling away. This woman's skin was more white and flawless than a vampire's. She wore a severe pantsuit under her black cashmere trench coat, and her bobbed black hair was razor-straight. With sharp, intelligent eyes, she scanned the room and digested the situation in an instant.

"Getting cozy with the natives, I see." Her eyes flitted to Pippa's sweater on the bed. Clearly in retaliation, the woman retrieved Max's coat, slung it over her arm, and stroked it as if it were a lion cub.

"What are you doing here, Miranda?" Max's voice held an edge.

Pippa should've known. This could only be the woman she'd spoken with on the phone. Miranda was everything that her voice had suggested—powerful, perfectly coiffed, forty but hiding it. And her actions solidified Pippa's initial thought—she was more to Max than just his boss.

Miranda pointed a bloodred nail at her. "Scullery maid?" She was so cool and put together that on some weird level, Pippa admired her.

Max's mouth flopped open like a damned halibut. "Scullery maid?"

"Aye," Pippa said, directing her comments to Miranda. "And nearly his one-night stand. Thanks for interrupting. You did me a favor." Pippa cocked her eyebrow at Max and he glowered back. *Good, at least he knows I'm still in the room.*

He spun back on Miranda. "You didn't answer the question. Why are you here? I have things under control."

"You certainly do." Pippa grabbed her coat and pulled it on. "I'll leave you two alone." She nodded in Max's direction. "I have to get to the factory," she said flatly.

He frowned at her but she kept walking toward the door. Before she left completely, she had a weak moment and looked back. Part of her hoped Max would— *what?*—kick Miranda out and insist Pippa stay? But his eyes were glued to Miranda. The scullery maid had become invisible.

Pippa found refuge in the lonely hallway. "God, I'm so freaking stupid," she whispered. The way Miranda looked at Max, and the way he acted in return, Pippa knew they were more intimately involved than boss and underling. How could Max be with a woman like Miranda? She was all wrong for him.

Shades of the past wrapped around Pippa, all the asinine mistakes she'd made with men. Starting with Derrick from college—smooth-talking, charismatic, all-the-right-moves Derrick. He'd taken her virginity in his dorm room, making all kinds of promises about their future together. Pippa later found out that he and his girlfriend had been together for four years. Pippa felt awful about being the other woman. Then she'd discovered that she wasn't the first freshman to fall for his line . . . or the last. *Two-timing bastard.* If only he'd been her only lapse in judgment. She'd dated Tony, then Patrick. Neither one had broken her heart, but both had given her further glimpses into the casual dishonesty and vast unfaithfulness of men. She'd given up trusting in the opposite sex then.

But why had she sidelined her beliefs when the Yank walked into Gandiegow? She wanted to bang her head against the wall.

As she quickly descended the steps, she looked on the bright side. Thank God the universe had intervened to keep her from making another monumental mistake. What did she really know about Max McKinley? Nothing. Except he was a helluva kisser.

There was only one man she trusted and he was back at the house in a wheelchair. Pippa hurried home to her da.

The cold air outside made her eyes water; those certainly weren't tears on her cheeks. She wiped her face with her scarf before opening the green door to her house. She hung up her things and went in search of her father. She found him and Freda in the parlor. They both looked over when Pippa entered the room.

Freda shoved her hand-stitching project into her bag. "I better get home. I need to bake some cookies for Mr. Menzies. His nephew is coming to visit in a few days."

"Thanks for sitting with Da."

Freda glanced at the McDonnell first, then she gave Pippa a warm smile and lightly touched her arm as she passed. "It was my pleasure." But then Freda glanced down at the oversize T-shirt that Pippa was wearing. Questions filled her face, but Freda had the decency to keep them to herself. Pippa wanted to hug her.

Da didn't seem to have noticed his daughter's strange attire. "Night, Freda. Will ye be by tomorrow?"

"Aye. I'm making you fish soup."

"My favorite," Da said appreciatively. "And chocolate fudge?"

"That, too." Freda gave Da one of her fond glances before heading toward the door.

"I'll be right back." Pippa slipped upstairs and donned her Edinburgh University sweatshirt, shoving Max's T-shirt under her pillow before returning to her father.

"Daughter?" the McDonnell called out. "Can I have a minute of your time?"

Panic, mixed with guilt, washed over her. Maybe he'd seen Max's T-shirt after all, and her splotchy face.

Pippa stepped into the parlor.

"Sit here by me, where I can see ye." Da seemed a little down, pensive.

Pippa chose the chair next to him instead of the one across.

"Now that ye're home for good"—her father's eyes fell on her, as if he was ready to weigh her reaction to his words—"I think it's time you consider settling down."

Even though she'd known this day was coming, Pippa felt blindsided. Ever since returning home in July, she'd been consumed with getting her da back on his feet, helping to heal his broken body, and getting the factory in the black. No one had expected her to jump right in and seal the deal with Ross, and he'd seemed in no hurry either. But now apparently the reprieve was over.

Da went on. "It would mean so much to me if I could see you wed." He sighed heavily. "I may not be able to walk ye down the aisle, but I could be there and see it with my own eyes. Don't ye think it's time ye took Ross off the shelf and married him? It would be a comfort to me to know that ye're settled."

Pippa didn't answer. She couldn't . . . her throat was too tight. She'd do anything for her da. Anything. But did she have to marry Ross to prove it?

A crazy thought hit her.

What of Max?

If Miranda hadn't shown up when she had, Pippa wouldn't be here right now discussing Ross and the prospect of marriage. Her face flushed. She'd be naked in Max's bed. Ross wouldn't even be an afterthought.

Da took her hand. "I worry about ye. Tell me that ye'll at least think about setting a date."

It broke her heart to know her da was worried he wouldn't be around to see her married. But she couldn't give an answer. Hell, what could she say? She rose and kissed the top of his head, giving a noncommittal grunt instead, before hurrying from the room.

Outside the doorway, she plastered her back against the wall. She didn't want to lie to her father or disappoint him. For as tough as Pippa came off to the rest of the world, deep down, she was still her daddy's little girl and wanted to please him.

But how pleased would her da be that she'd come close to sleeping with MTech's deal maker? Pippa felt her cheeks burn hot again. She ran upstairs to transform herself into NSV's chief engineer, hoping the right clothes would put her in the correct frame of mind. She pulled her most professional skirt from the closet and dressed quickly.

As she hurried across town, she couldn't shake off that her father wanted her to set a date. This time, she wasn't sure she had it in her to be the obedient daughter. That this time, she didn't have the option of running away from what her da and what the town wanted her to do. She squeezed her eyes shut.

This time, she might have to dig her heels in and fight.

When Lachlan McDonnell heard his daughter leave, he exhaled. Pippa was an independent sort, but he had a pretty good idea that she was a lot like him. She just needed the right kind of person to help her settle down. Ross would do that, just as Pippa's mama had done it for him. It'd been a blessing when his Sandra had turned up pregnant. When he'd married her, he finally felt at home in his skin. Though their marriage was brief, he still thought of Sandra often, with her pink cheeks and her brilliant blue eyes. Eyes that Pippa had inherited.

A knock sounded at the front door but Lachlan didn't stir. Everyone in Gandiegow knew to come on in as he could hardly answer the door with his body so banged up.

"Hallo," Bethia called out.

"We're here," Deydie added helpfully.

"I'm in the parlor." Lachlan felt disappointed it wasn't Freda, even though she'd just left. Freda was always so pleasant to sit with. Deydie and Bethia were pleasant enough, they just weren't Freda.

Deydie lumbered through the doorway first, Bethia following with a plate in her hand.

"I brought you some Christmas cookies," Bethia said.

"No new medicinal tea for me?" Lachlan asked, hopeful.

Bethia shook her head.

So she'd run out of things for him to try. The doctors had all but given up on him and now Bethia had, too.

"I'm glad ye're here," he said. "Sit. I need to talk to you. The both of you."

"We need to talk to ye, too." Deydie took the plate from Bethia and snatched a cookie from underneath the plastic before handing it off to him.

"It's about Pippa," Lachlan started. "She's going to need yere help to plan the wedding."

The women looked at each other, shocked.

Deydie clapped her hands. "So it's finally happening."

"They're finally going to tie the knot?" Bethia asked.

"Aye." Lachlan would give his daughter the little nudge she needed. "I need you ladies to plan the wedding of the century."

"It's been a long time coming," Bethia added joyfully. Then she looked a little perplexed. "But only yesterday . . ."

"What are ye jabbering about?" Deydie barked. "We've been waiting years for those two to get hitched."

"But only yesterday"—Bethia seemed determined to try again—"that Max McKinley did something that made me think . . ." She paused for a long second while Deydie glowered at her. "I got the feeling something might be going on between the Yank and Pippa."

"What?" Lachlan said.

"Bethia's imagining it," Deydie assured him. "There's nothing going on between Pippa and that lad. She only has eyes for Ross."

"Are ye sure?" Lachlan was stuck in this damned wheelchair or else he'd find his daughter and ask her himself.

"We're sure," Deydie said with finality. "Pippa belongs to Ross, and he to her. We'll make certain it's the best damned wedding Gandiegow has ever seen. Besides, if the Yank does have his sights set on Pippa, maybe that new woman in town, that American, will keep him busy."

"What woman?" Dread grew in Lachlan's stomach as he started to put it together.

"Another one that works for that company of his. Miriam something."

"Miranda," Bethia corrected. "Dougal met her as he was delivering mail. Pointed out the pub to her."

Deydie leaned closer to Lachlan's chair. "Now let's talk about the wedding."

But he had lost his appetite for conversation. "I'm tired."

"We should make it a Christmas wedding." Deydie acted as if she hadn't heard him.

Bethia, though, looked at him with worry. "Let's go,

Deydie. The McDonnell needs his rest." She patted his shoulder. "Don't worry about a thing. We'll take care of all the preparations. It'll be a wedding for the ages."

They left and he was glad of it.

He'd concentrate on Pippa and Ross's wedding . . . he just hoped he was around to see it. He didn't need a physician to tell him that he was growing weaker by the day.

He did *not* want to think about Miranda and what she might be doing in town. He'd buried his shame and pretended it never happened. But apparently she was back in Scotland. He might have to face what he'd done the last time they'd been together.

Max hurried down the pub's stairs to find Pippa. He sure as hell hadn't made any headway with Miranda. Why did she have to show up and screw with things here? Just when he and Pippa were *finally* coming to some kind of understanding and were going to get to the MTech proposal . . .

But he was only kidding himself. The understanding between them had nothing to do with any valve.

His life had gotten so complicated. He was so conflicted and wanted it both ways—the deal and Pippa in his bed. He marched straight to his rental car, slamming the door when he got in.

The bigger question loomed: Had his past come back to haunt him? Miranda hadn't said anything yet to make him think otherwise, but he had an awful feeling it could.

He glanced one more time in the direction of the pub, but then tore out of the parking lot, the car slipping dangerously toward the edge of the drop-off. An image shot across his mind. Jake, lying in the hospital, paralyzed. A senseless accident. Max took his foot off the accelerator. He didn't care so much what happened to him, but his mother would be devastated. He remembered how she'd trembled in the emergency room as they'd wheeled Jake off to surgery. His strong mother, pale and shaking. Max pushed the images from his mind, and along with it, every Christmas that had caused his family pain. He forced himself to drive slowly the rest of the way up the hill toward the factory, ready to have it out with Pippa once and for all.

Chapter Eight

With the workers now gone for the day, Pippa sat in her quiet office, thankful for the e-mail from MTech with the proposed contract attached. A diversion was good.

She bluidy well needed time away from everyone . . . especially the Yank, and what he was doing to her.

She felt bad for the waste of trees—the contract looked as if it had taken at least two reams' worth of paper to print—especially when she was having so much trouble making out the gist of it. It had purposely been written to be as clear as Muddy Pond.

She wasn't sure, but thought it was saying that if NSV didn't make the agreed-upon numbers, MTech would assume control of her father's factory. Did that mean they could take control of his patents, too? She needed to get fresh eyes on this. If only her da were himself; he'd ferret out the truth of the contract in no time. Maybe she could call Mr. Corbie and see what solicitor he'd used. Or maybe not. Corbie had lost everything; even sold his patents to help pay the legal fees.

She closed her eyes. She couldn't let that happen to

NSV. It would kill Da to lose his company. She was already worried by how *off* he seemed this morning. She didn't know if it was because he wasn't healing, or the stress over what was going to happen to his beloved factory and patents. The only thing that seemed to brighten his day was the thought of her marrying Ross.

But she couldn't think on that now.

Or that her da had been totally wrong about Max.

Pippa rubbed her temples and looked up. Like some terrible magic trick, Max stood in her opened doorway. He looked great—jeans and a dark maroon long-sleeved polo that made the flecks of green stand out in his eyes. If she closed her eyes, would he just as easily disappear?

Parallel frown lines sat between his eyebrows. "May I come in?"

"That depends." Pippa leaned back to peer around him. "Where's Maleficent?"

His frown deepened at her assessment. "I left her at the pub. She's jet-lagged and had to lie down."

"I bet she did. With you on top?"

He took a step forward. Pippa suspected it was to intimidate her. But she wouldn't back down.

She gave a low whistle. "You are some stud. Two women from two continents in one day."

"Pippa—" he said in warning, pulling the door closed behind him.

"It must be some kind of record. Maybe we should call Guinness and get you in the next book." She stood, repositioning her skirt, feeling more than a little self-conscious under his gaze. "What's wrong, McKinley? Are you upset that I pegged you from the beginning?"

"What are you talking about?"

She shrugged as if her chest didn't hurt. "That you thought it would help MTech's cause if you got into my pants." She held her fingers up an inch apart. "Ye were this close. Good job." She dropped the act. "Now, get out."

Max stalked closer. "We have business to discuss."

Her stomach fell. So he didn't come here to make sure she was all right—especially after the embarrassment of Miranda nearly finding her half-naked. Pippa was such an idiot. When would she ever learn?

She flipped the contract closed. "We're not talking until I get this monstrosity examined."

Max's eyes zeroed in on the double stack of paper. "Is that it? The contract?"

"Aye." *Of course* the MTech deal was the only thing he cared about.

"Good, I want to talk about that, too." He ran his hand through his hair. "But first we have to discuss what happened—what's happening between us—"

Pippa couldn't take any more. She was removing herself from the game. "Nothing's happening between us. Seriously, Max. We had a few laughs. The kissing was adequate." A total lie. Them together? Crazy hot. "Now I've got work to do."

"Why are you being this way?" he growled.

She gave a brittle laugh. "I'm not interested in some heartfelt girl talk right now, McKinley. Go back and see if Her Bitchiness wants to be all touchy-feely. I don't."

He turned an inflamed shade of red and was in front of her in a flash, grabbing her arms. His grip didn't hurt but he seemed hell-bent on making sure she couldn't free herself until he'd had his say.

"Drop the *Alistair* act. I'm not some employee you

can boss around. I'm not one of your fisherman buddies either. We've got something . . ." Maybe it was her glare but he faltered and dropped her arms.

Part of her wanted him to finish his sentence. But the smart part of her wasn't interested in his next words. She was pretty sure that pining over the American would only lead to regrets . . . bigger regrets than she'd ever had over Derrick, Tony, or Patrick.

Max seemed to have come to the same conclusion—there couldn't be anything between them. He pointed to the contract. "Do what you have to do. Talk to the Mc-Donnell and then get back to me. My ass is on the line."

Max sat in his rental car, more screwed up than when he'd driven to NSV. Pippa may be something special, but God, she drove him crazy. "She's exactly the reason *why* I'm single!" he snapped.

The woman was a pain in the ass. How could she be so heartless? They had a connection. Why couldn't she see it?

He put the car in gear and drove away from the factory. But, crap. Pippa was right. He was acting like a sappy girl. He didn't need to talk about his feelings. He was a man, dammit. Acknowledging the sick feeling in his chest only made him weak.

He pulled into Gandiegow's parking lot and trudged back through town.

Without realizing where he'd been going, he found himself outside the house with the red roof and the green door.

Merry freaking Christmas.

Max was a man with no place to go. He couldn't go

back to the pub; Miranda was sleeping there. What was he supposed to do? Hell, where was he supposed to stay?

He frowned at the green door. Strange, but being here seemed logical. He rationalized that it couldn't hurt to ingratiate himself with the owner of North Sea Valve. But it was ballsy to come here, especially when Max had come close to ravishing his daughter. But he genuinely liked the big Scot. They'd hit it off from the beginning.

He let himself into the house and found the older man dozing in the den. He started to tiptoe out but the McDonnell called out to him.

"Don't leave. I could use some company."

Max walked into the room and was struck by the thought that the McDonnell had shrunk a little from the last time he'd seen him. "Can I get you anything? Something to drink?"

"I guess whisky's out of the question?" The McDonnell chuckled at his own joke. "Tea would be grand, though. Do you mind?"

"Not at all." Max slipped from the room. When he returned the older man was sitting up straight, looking more awake.

"Do ye know what my daughter is up to? Have ye seen her?" The McDonnell looked worried.

"She's at work." Max hoped his voice sounded casual and that the McDonnell wouldn't ask more. "I'm sure she'll be home soon." Which meant Max couldn't stay long.

For the next half hour, he and the McDonnell had companionable conversation about Gandiegow and how the factory had changed the economics of the village. He should be thinking only about making money for MTech, but it played on his conscience that peoples' livelihoods were at stake.

After he said good-bye and left, Max was once more at loose ends. As soon as Miranda woke up, he'd pack his things, and maybe sleep at NSV, in the machine shop next to the CNC machine. Perhaps there was a cot he could appropriate.

Another cot came to mind. *Pippa's cot.*

She'd been good to him while he was sick—but he wouldn't get all girly over it now. He didn't want to remember how they'd held hands.

Besides, that damn cot wasn't good for anything. It certainly wasn't wide enough or strong enough to hold him and Pippa when they made love.

Holy hell. He had to stop with the fantasies. Wishful thinking wasn't doing him a bit of good, only making things worse.

His cell phone rang. With dread, he put the phone to his ear.

"Where are you?" Miranda's irritation was as clear as her words.

Couldn't she have slept a bit longer?

"Never mind. Let's talk with Lachlan and his son, Alistair, right now."

Lachlan?

"No." Max was firm on this one point at least. "Now isn't a good time." He didn't want to explain about the McDonnell just yet. He should check with Pippa first. "You'll meet with Alistair later."

"Set up the meeting, then. I want to meet his bastard of a son. I want to see for myself why he's dragging his feet."

What could Max say? You've already met? And you royally pissed her off? Or, you're the last person in the world *Alistair* wants to see? Except maybe for Max himself.

Besides, MTech had sent her the contract just today! And he hadn't even seen it!

"We'll talk about it. I'm almost back to the pub."

"Is there a restaurant in town?" Miranda asked.

"I'll pick up something on the way." Max wanted to keep her contained. He was afraid if he didn't, Miranda would go in search of the McDonnell and Alistair without him.

"Get me a kale salad," she ordered.

"I'll try." Max hurried to the restaurant, pretty sure kale couldn't be found this time of year in Gandiegow.

When he arrived, there was a small crowd, and he immediately noticed Ross Armstrong and an old man sitting at the counter, each with a mug in his hand.

Claire motioned to Max. "What can I get for ye?"

The double swinging doors to the kitchen whooshed open, and Dominic joined her, wearing a matching white apron and carrying two plates of food. He held one up in Max's direction and said, "Would you like a plate of lasagna?"

"Yes. And a salad." Max wouldn't mention the kale.

"I'll have it out to you shortly." Dominic set the plates in front of customers, then kissed his wife soundly on the mouth and went back to the kitchen.

"Have a seat. I'll have Moira bring you over a hot cup of tea while you wait."

Andrew was sitting by the window, looking miserable. Max started to leave him in peace with his problems, but he felt bad for the guy, so he moved toward the Episcopal priest.

"Mind if I join you?" Max said.

"Aye. That would be grand." But Andrew's voice didn't sound all that enthused. A moment later, Moira made her way toward them with downcast eyes. She didn't even look up when she placed the hot water and teacup in front of Max.

"Moira?" Longing was evident in Andrew's voice. He looked worse off than Max felt.

Moira moved away quickly without acknowledging the town's pastor.

"Your girl?" Max asked.

Andrew focused his attention back to him. "Aye. Or at least I thought she was."

"Do you want to talk about it?" Max cringed. Pippa was right; he was acting way too touchy-feely. But hell, he was all-in at this point. "What's going on?"

Andrew shrugged. "I don't know. Things changed."

They always do. But Max wouldn't share his pessimistic view about the opposite sex with a man who had clearly gotten the crap knocked out of him by love.

"Did you two have an argument?" Max probed.

"Nothing like that. We were fine, grand really."

"Then what happened?"

"I don't know. I only know after Glenna came to live with Moira, and her father got worse, Moira withdrew."

Yeah, Max could commiserate. Pippa had withdrawn from him, too. But he didn't want to share that with Andrew or anyone, so he changed the subject. "I met Glenna at the Christmas Roundup. She's a sweet girl."

"Aye. She didn't deserve to be orphaned. I find myself

questioning why God would allow such a thing." Andrew pulled at his cleric's collar, looking more miserable. "But my training tells me I shouldn't."

Max felt for him. "I heard about Moira's father, too. It has to be hard on her."

"It's been hard on all of us. Kenneth was a good man; the best. Moira should be leaning on me. Instead, she's completely shut me out since her father passed. Won't talk to me at all."

Max understood. "It's the grief. It has a way of kicking a person in the gut. Give her time. She'll come around."

Moira took that moment to glance over at them. Pain was etched into her face, too, as if it'd been written there with a permanent marker.

"Yank?" Claire called. "Yere food is ready."

Max looked back at Andrew.

"Go. I'll be fine."

"I'd stay if I could, but my boss is here," Max explained.

"I heard another visitor had arrived. I hope she'll be able to come to the Christmas pageant."

"We'll see." Max wasn't making any promises. It was natural for the pastor to welcome all the sheep; he just didn't realize that this particular sheep was a wolf and could bite. He said good-bye and went to the counter to pick up his order and pay Claire. Then he headed outside.

When he opened the front door of the pub, Miranda was standing there in her coat with a Louis Vuitton briefcase looped over her shoulder.

"Where are you going? I told you I was bringing food."

"I got tired of waiting." The aroma of Dominic's lasagna must've hit her nose, because she stopped suddenly, and sniffed. "That doesn't smell like kale salad."

"The pasta's for me. The salad's for you. No kale, though. Come on, sit down. I have questions for you." Max walked farther in and headed toward a booth.

Miranda chose a table instead, looking dignified but clearly feeling indignant. She didn't belong in this joint. This was Pippa's territory. For a brief moment, he thought about that first night at the bar and how Pippa had pulled one over on him. He smiled.

Miranda broke his reverie. "Are you going to stand there all day or give me my food?"

He passed her the salad and took the chair across from her. "Miranda, I haven't seen the complete contract you want the McDonnell to sign. I'll be better equipped to deal with his questions when I have a copy. Did you bring one with you?"

"No," she said firmly, and he knew she was holding out on him. He just didn't understand why.

This must've been her plan all along. Have him come in and butter up the townsfolk and then she would get the signature without Max ever knowing the fine points of the deal.

"I see." He *had* to get ahold of the contract. But the only other person in town who had a copy was the chief engineer. How could he pry it from her hands? Maybe if he kissed her and made her dizzy first . . .

Max stood. "I'll be right back with some napkins." He stepped into the kitchen and pulled out his phone. Joe ought to be able to help. He was the only other person in acquisitions at MTech Max knew well enough to call.

They said their hellos, and then Max got right to it.

"I need you to e-mail me a copy of the North Sea Valve Company contract."

"Sure, no problem. I'll do it right now." He heard Joe typing on the other end. "So how's Scotland?"

"Cold," Max answered, thinking of Pippa's rejection.

"Umm," Joe said. "There's a problem. That contract has been taken offline. Let me do another search on the server."

A few seconds passed. "Yup, I found it. But it's been password-protected. I wonder why?"

Max thanked him for his trouble and hung up.

Shit. Why wasn't the contract available? What was in there that they didn't want Max to know?

When he returned to the dining room, Miranda was pushing her salad away, barely touched. "I'm going back to bed. When I get up, we're going to come up with a plan so we can get out of here as soon as possible. Care to join me?"

And there it was. The proposition. He'd known it was coming.

She eyed him as if he was the meaty lasagna. "You know, McKinley, what happens in Scotland, stays in Scotland." Miranda was as exact as always. Direct. The same way she'd propositioned him before. "I'm a busy woman. I don't have time for games. I'm attracted to you, plain and simple. And we have time on our hands apparently."

Max grabbed his coat and went to the door. "Call me when you wake up." He had no idea what he'd do with her then. Maybe while she slept, he'd come up with a plan. Anything to get himself out of this mess with Miranda, and hopefully get Pippa back in his arms.

*   *   *

Miranda lay on the twin-size bed, exhausted and kicking herself for not coming to Scotland sooner. She should've been more assertive with Roger, MTech's president, and convinced him to see it her way—she should've been the one sent to close the deal.

She slipped off her heels. But Roger didn't know that she was here, and she planned to keep it that way. Roger expected Max to get this deal under his belt all on his own. Max, the golden boy, *Roger's new protégé*. But she'd known to her very core that Max wouldn't be able to do this without her. He didn't have the killer instinct. What she didn't expect was to catch him messing around with one of the locals.

She couldn't throw stones. She'd messed around with a local when she'd come to Scotland, too.

Lachlan. Last year, she'd set up a meeting with Lachlan McDonnell in Edinburgh to discuss selling NSV to MTech. She was surprised when he'd actually met with her. She'd liquored him up—a tactical move—hoping to get him to listen to why NSV would be better off under the MTech umbrella.

Surprisingly though, his charm had gotten through her armor. But he was, after all, an attractive middle-aged man. When they'd ended up in bed together, she'd enjoyed it exceedingly, hoping the affair would continue. But in the morning, Lachlan seemed to regret their love-making. He'd turned MTech down flat and left her alone in her posh Edinburgh hotel room.

Miranda shifted toward the wall and pulled the quilt over her, willing her jet-lagged headache to subside. The only reason she could admit Lachlan's rejection had hurt was because pain was a great teacher. It made her stronger. She was the type of person who learned from every mistake she'd ever made.

The first lesson she'd learned in the business world . . . nice girls finish last.

Not long after graduating from business school, her let's-all-play-fair-and-get-along attitude had been trounced into oblivion. Women needed to hide their soft side, as she had learned to do. Emotions were for losers. It took a few rounds with the big boys, but she learned her lesson. She squashed down her femininity, put her game face on, and had become a ruthless, take-no-prisoners winner, doing whatever it took to get ahead. It was, after all, how successful businessmen became *successful*.

She didn't even recognize her old self anymore—the eager-to-please young woman she'd been while collecting her diploma for her MBA.

She squeezed her eyes shut. She was approaching forty-one and feeling . . . desperate? She had not lost her touch! She had more than a sneaking suspicion she was being scrutinized by MTech's higher-ups. She hadn't been able to get the job done before with NSV, and Roger had lost all confidence in her to get it done this time. In the end, though, Roger would appreciate how she'd stepped in, guided Max, and made the deal happen.

She blocked out everything and focused on the end goal. She was a winner. She just needed to prove it. *One more time.*

Chapter Nine

Pippa left her bag by the door as she stepped into Quilting Central. Normally, she had the concentration of a pit bull when it came to dissecting a problem, but she'd accomplished nothing once Max stormed out of the factory. The MTech monstrosity-of-a-contract bulged out of her bag, nearly spilling on the floor. She shoved it with her foot to prop it better against the wall.

She should've gone home first to check on her da, but the details needed to be hammered out for the Strapping Lads in Plaid bachelor auction. Her to-do list had gotten out of hand and there was no way she could get it all done by herself. She was left with no choice but to ask for help. She prayed Deydie and Bethia might have time to take up the slack, or else her father would be sunk.

She found the two of them at one of the small café tables near the back of the room, their heads down, both writing on pads of paper. Pippa walked over to them, but when they looked up, they each had a goofy expression on their face.

Pippa gestured toward their notebooks. "What's all that?"

Like a pair of synchronized swimmers, the two old women simultaneously overturned their notebooks.

"Nothing," said Bethia.

At the same time, Deydie said, "None of yere damned business."

Pippa had enough worries without wondering what they were fooling around with this time. "Can I speak with you both about the auction? There are a lot of particulars that need to be cleared up so we can move forward."

Deydie pressed herself to her feet, then waddled over to an organized desk and pulled out a folder. "It's all in here."

"What's all in there?" Pippa took the folder and flipped through it. She found that two buses were chartered, one from Inverness, one from Aberdeen. The list of attendees riding each bus was attached.

Bethia pulled another sheet of paper from the folder and laid it on top. "We have a smaller coach coming up from Edinburgh and surprisingly a few from London."

"How did you do all this?" Pippa's words faltered. She felt choked by the love they'd shown her and her da.

"It wasn't hard. Everyone pitched in. Amy sent out e-mails. Moira got the posters sent all over. It's done," Deydie said. "Except one thing. You better get to work on that quilt you started."

"What quilt?" Pippa knew which one. Deydie, Bethia, and all the quilt ladies had forced her to start a quilt when she was a teenager. Pippa never finished it, never intended to. She was good at the craft. She just didn't want to be forced into it.

"It's over there in the tissue paper," Bethia said. "Not a stitch done to it all these years."

Pippa followed behind them as they went to the paper bundle on the long table. Hesitating a moment, she pulled back the wrapping. There it was. Her Gandiegow Hometown quilt.

She sighed. She loved the mixture of tartan fabrics and how the plaid buildings represented each home in town because she'd used their respective clans' colors. The first block she'd made had been their own house in the McDonnell tartan, complete with the red roof and green door. Her eyes burned and then blurred. She'd missed her hometown. She might have run off to Edinburgh to keep from settling down, but Gandiegow had never left her heart.

"We thought it was only fitting you should auction off your quilt with our lads," Deydie said.

"It would be a fitting way to honor your da," Bethia added.

Pippa didn't hesitate. No longer did she feel coerced as she had when she was a girl; this was something she wanted to do. "Ye're right." She hugged both of them. "I'm so glad you kept it all these years."

Bethia took her hand and pulled her over to a sewing machine, while Deydie gathered up the unfinished project.

"Get to it," Deydie said.

Bethia pulled out Pippa's chair. "There's no time like the present. Ye can get the quilt done in time if ye put in the effort."

Pippa smiled up at the bossy, interfering women—

women she dearly loved. She didn't have the heart to tell them that she had too much else to do. Instead, she snatched up the fabric and laid out the next block to sew on the table beside her.

She had just put the first two pieces under the presser foot when the bell above the door jingled. She wheeled around to find Max in the doorway.

Her breath caught. *What kind of homing device did he have that he could find her whenever he wanted?*

Deydie leaned over her. "Close yere mouth, lass. Ye look like a strung-up carp."

God, I'm a fool. He's not for me, and I still want him?

Max's mouth hung open, too, but he shut it quickly enough. His eyes left her and focused on Deydie and Bethia.

"Just the two I wanted to see." His greeting seemed to be filled with forced cheerfulness.

And Pippa wondered—quite unwillingly—didn't he want to see her, too?

Max strode over and stood near. And he was taking up all the oxygen. Pippa worked hard at finding her breath.

Deydie wagged a finger at him. "We wanted to see ye, too." The old woman looked ready to take her broom after Max. "We heard ye had a woman up there in the room over the pub."

He and Pippa shared a glance. *Aye. It could've been the two of us.*

"I believe Deydie's speaking of Miranda," Pippa said. She was hit once again with the bitter taste of rejection.

He nodded, appearing relieved. "Miranda Weymouth is my boss. She's here to help along the MTech deal."

Max didn't look happy about it either, which made Pippa feel infinitesimally better.

"Well, it ain't proper for ye two to share a room." Deydie did reach for her broom then.

Bethia nodded her head in agreement.

"Which is the reason I came here to see the both of you." Max shot them a charming smile that looked more practiced than sincere at the moment. "I was wondering if I could stay at one of the quilting dorms since your retreat is over."

Deydie and Bethia seemed to contemplate this for a long moment. His smile wilted while he waited.

"Nay," Deydie finally answered. She held up her hand when Max looked ready to argue. "The woman will stay in the dorm. It'll be too loud for her at the pub."

Bethia nodded in agreement. "We'll keep an eye on her."

Max looked grateful. "Are you sure?"

"She looks to be a handful," Pippa muttered to her machine as she sewed the next seam.

"Aye, we're sure." Deydie used her broom, sweeping imaginary dirt from the hardwood floor. "Dougal said she was none too kind to him. A whole group of people saw her giving him a tongue-lashing. We'll make sure she doesn't get up to any devilment. We'll take care of her."

Max gave a harsh laugh. "Miranda needs to be handled with kid gloves. Not meat hooks."

"But if the meat hook fits—" Deydie started.

Bethia touched her arm to stop her.

Pippa grabbed another piece of fabric. If anyone could keep Miranda from causing trouble, it was these two women.

Deydie's head shot to the side. "Ailsa! Put those quilt blocks down. Bethia and I were going to use that design wall next."

Pippa focused on her sewing, trying to ignore that Max was still near.

Suddenly he was leaning over her shoulder. "I never expected to find you here." His breath was warm on her cheek. *Minty.* "Especially using a sewing machine."

Pippa gave her own harsh laugh. "It's a requirement. You can't live in Gandiegow and not sew. As babies, instead of rattles, we're given sewing needles to thread."

"Tough Scottish stock?"

"Aye."

"My mom and sister are avid quilters," he said. "They formed their own group back in Texas. First Saturday of every month. Food, Fabric, and Friends is what they call it. I call it Grub, Gossip, and Just-Shoot-Me. Those women know how to talk."

Pippa switched off her machine and gave him her full attention. "Do you know how to sew, too?"

He harrumphed begrudgingly. "Yeah. You'd have to know my mom. She made my brother and me learn whether we wanted to or not. She said real men aren't afraid to hem their own jeans."

"And yere father? What does he think about you knowing your way around a sewing machine?"

Max's smile faded. "My father's dead."

Crap. What a bombshell.

Deydie and Bethia quit talking among themselves and listened in.

Pippa waited a second longer but Max didn't elaborate. "Sorry. I didn't know."

"No worries." His tone had an edge to it as he looked away. "It was a long time ago."

But she could tell it still hurt.

So she and Max had something else in common besides being engineers. They both had lost a parent.

For a long moment, he seemed to be contemplating, but then he reached out and touched her shoulder.

"Pippa, we need to talk." His voice had become conciliatory, kind.

But voices could be deceptive. So could a touch to the shoulder.

"Why are you being nice?" Pippa didn't mean to jump down his throat, but her emotions were everywhere. She felt bad that he'd lost his da. Pippa didn't know what she'd do if she lost hers. And at the same time, she was angry with Max for hurting her. Before Miranda showed up, the two of them had been headed down a certain path—but then he'd stopped everything for *her*.

Deydie and Bethia edged closer, seeming to hang on every word.

Pippa wheeled on the quilting ladies. "Go away."

"Careful, lassie," Deydie warned.

Bethia looped her arm through her friend's. "Let's leave the young ones to chat." She gently pulled Deydie away to their blocks and the design they'd started on the wall.

Freda hurried to Deydie and Bethia. She had to know who the new woman was, the one who had stopped Dougal this morning. Freda had seen the whole interaction. *Such an interesting person.* And she had to know more.

Freda came up beside her two friends. "Hello."

Deydie jumped. "Freda, ye scared the shite out of me. Why can't ye make a little noise when ye walk?"

"What do you need, Freda?" Bethia asked kindly.

Deydie picked up a box and thrust it at her. "We can talk, but ye'll have to sort the fabric kits while we do. It should've been done hours ago. With Cait and Mattie going away soon . . ." Deydie's voice was strained. She covered it with a cough. "There's a damned lot to do. The party for them . . . everything."

Freda took the box, understanding Deydie's pain that her family was leaving for a time. "Why isn't Cait waiting until after Christmas to join Graham in New Zealand?"

Deydie sighed heavily. Not because she was angry with Freda; she mostly sounded sad. "Graham's shooting schedule. He'll return to the U.K. to do a couple of publicity events and then gather Cait and Mattie to take them back with him."

Bethia wrapped an arm around her old friend's shoulders. "Ye'll miss them."

Deydie shook her head. "Caitie asked me to go with them. But my place is here. No one else could run the Kilts and Quilts retreat. Besides, they won't be gone forever." But her voice held doubt as if they would.

Bethia rubbed Deydie's back reassuringly. "Graham said that once his biography comes out, the media won't bother with Gandiegow for too long as he'll be in New Zealand. Things will be back to normal soon."

Freda, for one, would do anything for Deydie. The whole town would gather around her and support her in her time of need.

Bethia confirmed her thought. "It'll be okay, my dear friend. Ye have us to help ye through."

Freda glanced about the room. "Maybe we should have our Christmas Eve dinner here this year. We could ask others to join us." Maybe Abraham Clacher. There had to be other people, too, who were at loose ends at this time of year, the same as Freda had been her whole adult life.

For a second, she wondered if Deydie would take the broom after her for suggesting it.

Instead, Deydie nodded. "'Tis a good idea. We could help the lonely souls this Christmas." Deydie looked at Freda pointedly, the message clear: Freda was the lonely soul and she wasn't. She gestured to the box in Freda's arms. "Ye better get to organizing those damned fabric kits."

Freda sat the box on the table beside the design wall and began pulling out the bags filled with fabric. "Tell me about the new woman in town. I haven't heard yet who she is. No one stopped by while I was cleaning the McDonnell's house this morning, and I've waited all day to find out something." She had Pippa and the McDonnell's dinner in the slow cooker, and their kitchen floor sparkling as if stars had fallen from the sky and lay upon their floor.

"Ye were always a strange one, Freda. A dreamer." Deydie shook her head as though Freda was a bampot. "Always interested in people, even as a girl."

Freda put her eyes back on the kits. She'd learned a long time ago to keep her assessments to herself. In some respects, she liked fading into the woodwork so she was free to study people and not be asked about what she thought. But the problem with fading into the background was that when she wanted to be noticed, she had no idea how.

Freda spoke nonchalantly over her shoulder. "So what's the woman's name?"

"She's another one from that big company. Her name's Miranda something. She's Max McKinley's boss."

"Oh. Do you know anything else about her?"

Deydie stopped messing with the quilt blocks and gave Freda her full attention. "I take it ye saw her then. Go ahead and tell me what you think. What was it about this one?"

But Deydie would laugh at Freda, maybe even scold her, if she told her what she thought.

Freda had clearly seen the vulnerability that lay beneath Miranda's overabundant confidence. A vulnerability that Freda knew well. How had Miranda pulled it off? How had she managed to overcome the same flaw that Freda had—insecurity? A small spark of hope flickered inside of Freda then. If Miranda could display confidence, then maybe Freda could, too.

"She's different, is all." Freda picked through the kits, pulling out all the blue ones, laying them on the table.

"Sort them by size, not color, Freda. I know ye like the different shades, but we need to make an inventory to decide if we need to cut more kits."

"Ye're right," Freda agreed. She did like the shades—in fabric and in people.

"We're keeping Miranda at Thistle Glen Lodge," Bethia provided.

Deydie took over, readjusting the kits into piles. "We could use help, keeping an eye on the woman. That way ye can *study* her further."

Freda pulled more fabric kits from the box. "I'd be happy to help. I could make her a pot of soup to keep in the refrigerator, in case she gets hungry." She decided the name *Miranda* fit her well.

Miranda knew how to be noticed. Her hair was perfect, her clothes crisp and commanding. She looked like a woman who always got what she wanted—men, money . . . men.

But there was only one man that Freda wanted. The McDonnell.

"Freda?" Deydie barked. "Where are ye? I asked ye what ye saw in Miranda."

Bethia cleared her throat. "Don't rush her, Deydie." Clearly, Bethia was curious, too.

Freda stepped back away from the kits and grabbed her coat off the chair. "I just remembered I forgot to take the towels out of the dryer at the McDonnell's."

Bethia touched her arm in encouragement, her eyes imploring.

Freda needed time to think on it a bit more, but she knew one thing. She met both of her friends' eyes and told them the truth. "I saw a lot of things in Miranda. But mostly I saw a scared little girl."

When Pippa was sure that Deydie and Bethia were busy at the design wall and not listening anymore, Pippa stood and turned on Max. "I asked ye why ye're being nice to me. Are you feeling randy again, Mr. McKinley? If so, go charm Miranda Weymouth. I'm not stupid enough to fall for yere line again. *We need to talk,* my arse. I can guarantee ye won't see me near-naked again."

Max's eyes narrowed as he took a step toward her, getting too close. He commanded attention with nothing more than his presence—suffocating and intoxicating, and sexier than anything she'd ever experienced.

His nostrils flared as he leaned close. "I don't need lines or ploys to get women. Secondly, you're way off about me *not* seeing you naked. I expect that'll come about naturally. But it's the contract I'm after now. Miranda has blocked me from getting my hands on it. I need to know what she's hiding. Can't you see I'm trying to help you?"

Pippa moved away. Miranda's name made her want to throw something at his head. A hot iron would do. "I told you MTech played dirty."

"Maybe," he admitted. "So whether you like it or not, we have to work together."

"No." She pushed him away, but not without first feeling how hard his chest was under her hand. She was being stubborn, but dammit, she didn't like being bossed around. "My da and I will work through the contract and get back to ye. And keep Miranda out of my hair. I need peace and quiet. She better leave Da alone, too."

Max looked ready to lose it. He walked two steps away, but then spun back. "Why do you have to be so stubborn? Anything between us is less important than bringing the subsea shutoff valve to fruition. I don't want anyone else to die." He walked out the door.

Two things hit her at once. She wondered what *I don't want anyone else to die* was about. And at the same time, it hurt that he clearly wasn't feeling as drawn to her as she was to him.

And where was he going? Was he heading back to the pub? To Miranda?

A chill came over Pippa.

Like hell he is. She left her quilt pieces where they were and dashed for the door, grabbing her bag with the contract on the way out. But once outside, she slowed.

Maybe she should drop her bag off at home first and change into something more . . . appealing.

Chapter Ten

At home Pippa put on her sexiest outfit—a pair of jeans and a tight scoop-necked sage sweater. With simple gold hoops as earrings, her wavy strawberry blond hair brushed over one shoulder, she was happy with the look. This outfit should get a certain American's attention.

She ran downstairs and found Freda in the kitchen, pulling towels from the dryer.

"Leave those," Pippa said. "I can fold them later."

"Nay. 'Tis no trouble." Freda admired her outfit. "You look very pretty. Ye have a gleam in yere eyes, too."

By Freda's sideways glance, she must have known that Pippa planned to give Max a difficult time tonight. "Is it a date?"

One of the things Pippa loved about Freda was that she never said a word about Ross. Once, she'd even hinted that she didn't agree with the rest of Gandiegow: *A lass needs to make up her own mind over the lad that she wants.*

"Why would ye ask if I have a date? Can't a girl get a wee bit fixed up, now and then?"

"Hmmm." Freda grabbed the next towel and folded it in thirds. "The way ye look suggests a man is involved."

"Perhaps." Pippa leaned over and glanced in at the McDonnell in the den. Da seemed more and more tired these days. She should've come straight home after printing the contract at the factory. Da slept restlessly. "Maybe I should stay in."

"Nay. I'll stay. I brought handwork." Freda motioned to her English paper piecing project sitting on the counter. "I'll watch over the McDonnell."

Freda was such a good soul. Something came over Pippa and she reached out and pulled her in for a hug. A tight one. "Thanks."

Freda stood there motionless for a moment, but then hugged her back, fiercely. Pippa understood. She hadn't hugged Freda in years, not since she was a wee thing.

When Pippa let go, Freda had tears in her eyes, and she felt guilty. Maybe she should've thanked Freda more often over the years. Hell, maybe she should've thanked everyone in Gandiegow, too. She was just beginning to see that maybe she should've been more sensitive to her da and others.

Pippa squeezed Freda's hand. "I mean it. Thank you."

She waited until Freda nodded before Pippa grabbed her coat and left. The second she got outside, worry fell over her again. What were Miranda and Max up to in the room over the pub?

When she got to The Fisherman and looked around the room, Max wasn't there. *Crap.*

She wove her way through the growing crowd and joined Bonnie behind the bar.

"Have ye seen the woman?" Pippa asked. "The American?"

Before Bonnie could answer, Miranda appeared behind her at the bottom of the steps. She had on a slinky, long-sleeved black dress. It wasn't revealing, but it had seduction written all over it.

The dress infuriated Pippa. The hag had worn it for Max! And who in their right mind would wear such a thing to a pub filled with randy Scots? Sure enough, the men's gazes gravitated toward her, the fools slathering over her. Didn't her kinsmen understand women like Miranda were as treacherous as barracudas?

Miranda's eyebrows rose at the sight of Pippa. "My, my, you do get around. Scullery maid and bartender?"

"Aye. Quite the multitasker." Pippa tipped her chin up. "Which will it be? Ale or whisky?"

"Doesn't this country have a decent chardonnay?"

Pippa gripped a crystal tumbler. "No. But we have manners."

"I'll take an ale." Miranda turned and leaned her back against the bar, surveying the men and seeming to find them lacking. "It's good we have a moment to chat. Alone. Woman to woman."

Pippa didn't want to chat. She wanted to run this woman from town.

"You should step aside. For Max's sake. He has a great future at MTech. He needs to focus while he's here." Miranda glanced at her over her shoulder. "Did you know he just received a well-deserved promotion?" She made it sound as if he'd slept with her to get it.

Miranda glanced down at her fingernails. "We're going to make the perfect power couple, Max and me. Unstoppable."

Before Pippa could react—like reach over the bar

and yank out her perfect black hair—the pub door blew open. Taog and Murdoch stepped in, followed by Max.

Pippa watched as Miranda's eyes—and resolve—latched onto the Yank. She swallowed her anger and tried to engage her. "So, what are yere plans, Miranda? How long will ye be in town?" But distracting her from her target didn't work.

Miranda shot a conniving smile at her prey. "I'll stay here until I get what I want."

"What's that?" Pippa was clearly trying to punish herself.

Miranda's tongue slithered out and touched her top lip. "A satisfactory partnership." She pushed away from the bar. "Excuse me."

Pippa grabbed onto her arm. "But yere drink's ready. Bonnie'll take your money."

Pippa slipped from behind the bar and made a beeline for Max, who had camped at a booth with Taog and Murdoch. His eyes were on her, or perhaps her neckline, as she made her way across the room. Was that a hungry expression in his gaze?

"Scoot over," she ordered.

He looked at her questioningly but did as he was told. "I thought you'd stay in with your father tonight and discuss the contract."

"More pressing matters." Even though Taog and Murdoch sat across from them, she laid a possessive hand on Max's thigh under the table.

He jumped.

Mission accomplished. Pippa had his complete attention now. She patted him. *Good boy. Now, stay.*

Miranda slunk across the room, her hips swaying like the headliner of a nightclub. "Don't you have something better to do?" she said to Pippa. "Like man the bar?"

Pippa ran her hand along the inside of Max's thigh. "Working the bar isn't as entertaining as this."

"Go away," Miranda demanded. "Max and I have business to discuss."

Max grabbed Pippa's hand, stilling it under the table. "She's staying. As long as she behaves." He gave Miranda a look that said the same went for her.

Pippa purred, brushing her breast against his arm. "Ye're no fun, darling."

Max rolled his eyes and Pippa smiled at him sweetly.

"While I have you both here," Max started, "you should be properly introduced."

Before he could go any farther, Pippa stuck her free hand out to the current-day Cleopatra. "Hi, I'm Pippa." She made sure to sound like a complete bubblehead.

Miranda sniffed the air but didn't offer her hand back. She turned to Max. "Can we go somewhere more private? It's getting too crowded in here." She gave a pointed glare to Pippa.

Pippa freed her hand from Max's hold and was inching her way up to no-man's-land, *or man's land* as it were.

Max suddenly pushed her from the booth, scooting himself out, too. "We were just leaving. Pippa has to get home. Night, guys. And I'll meet you in the morning, Miranda. For the meeting at the plant?"

"But . . ." Miranda stared gape-mouthed as Max drove Pippa toward the door, grabbing their coats from the hooks on the way. Pippa turned around and smiled victoriously at Miranda—they wouldn't be a power couple tonight!

At the last minute, Max turned back to his boss. "Dey-die said she'll be by to get you. The pub is too loud. The women have set you up in the quilting dorm."

He didn't wait for her response, but pulled Pippa outside. It was freezing. But Max looked steaming mad. Or turned on. She wasn't sure which.

"What the hell was that?" he said as he dragged her along.

"A bit of fun," Pippa said lightly.

"A bit of fun is going to get you and me in a lot of trouble." He pulled her between the church and the General Store, a dark alleyway of sorts, sandwiched out of sight of the path.

She didn't get a chance to ask him what he was up to. He wrapped her in his arms, crushed her body against his, and kissed her. She was a struck match, instantly hot. Fireworks exploded inside her body. Any cold she felt was history. She was so turned on that her middle turned to mush and her legs trembled. *The Yank has skills.*

He broke away, breathing heavily. "You're making this hard on me."

She laughed. "I know." She could feel him intimately against her.

But Max was frowning, looking almost in pain. "We can't do this, Pippa. The deal. Miranda. Your dad. And you're supposed to be with Ross." Max listed them off as if she didn't already know it was a terrible idea for them to take up. But she wanted him desperately.

And she couldn't stand the thought of him with anyone else, especially the American harpy.

Rejected once again. Pippa pulled away. "Fine."

As if the Almighty knew she needed to hurt the Yank as much as he had hurt her, a figure appeared at the end of the dock in their line of sight. *Ross.* He looked in their direction.

She would show Max!

"Ross!" she hollered. "Wait up."

Ross frowned.

She moved away from Max and toward the man her da wanted her to marry. "Can you walk me home? We need to speak with my da. Together." She said it loud enough for Max to hear.

She strutted away without turning back. By the time she reached Ross, his frown had deepened.

She latched onto his arm and started walking toward home, but Ross stopped and spun on her.

"What's going on? Ye've got that look on yere face."

She glanced back to register Max's reaction. He hadn't moved an inch.

"Nothing's going on."

Ross tilted his head in the direction of the Yank. "It didn't look like nothing."

"Then it was business." She reached for his arm again. "Can we just get going?"

Ross finally started walking. "What do we need to speak with the McDonnell about? Is there something you need to tell me?"

Ross was the poster boy for loyalty. She wouldn't tell him how Da wanted them to set a wedding date. She wouldn't tell him that even though he was a good man, she wouldn't marry him. And she wouldn't tell him that she was so damned attracted to the American that she ached.

"No," she finally answered. "Truthfully, I just need you to walk me home."

Ross glanced back in Max's direction one more time and she couldn't help but look back again, too. Max was rooted to the spot, his eyes glaring in their direction, as if he was a man who had a stake in what was going to happen next.

Max was a freaking idiot. It had been a long day, one hellish roller-coaster ride. He kicked the snow and walked away. There were a lot of reasons why he shouldn't be interested in Pippa McDonnell. But the number one reason—no matter what she'd said—was that she belonged to the six-foot-something fisherman walking her home.

What did Ross Armstrong have that Max didn't?

Pippa for one. A common heritage for another. A past. Everything. Plus the backing of the whole damned town!

Max better quit thinking with his groin. Pippa was the McDonnell's daughter and chief engineer and nothing else. He blew out a deep breath. If only he could convince the monster in his chest that she wasn't something special. Hell, he wanted nothing more than to call Ross out and fight for her.

Max couldn't go back to the pub right now, not with Miranda still there. When would Deydie come to collect her? He walked on to the restaurant and hesitated at the door. But he couldn't stand out in the cold all night. He hoped the place was deserted so he could brood alone.

It wasn't.

A crowd sat around a group of tables that had been pushed together. He'd been introduced to them all at one time or another since he'd arrived, but he didn't feel comfortable enough to do more than greet them politely. They were having none of it, however, and immediately waved him over.

He noticed Cait with Mattie. He still wanted to apologize for the remark he'd made to Mattie when they'd been introduced. But now wasn't the time. He'd have to wait until he could catch Cait alone.

"Come and warm yereself," Claire said cheerfully. "We were just stuffing envelopes for the bachelor auction."

Andrew, the only adult male, looked at him imploringly, his eyes begging Max not to leave him alone with them.

Emma, the psychologist from England, confirmed it. "We were just counseling Father Andrew on what to do about Moira. Have a chair."

Kit Armstrong—local matchmaker and sister-in-law to Ross—nodded her head. "Moira and Andrew are having some issues at the moment. We're trying to help."

Max didn't move, not sure whether to sit or bolt for the door.

Cait stood and prodded her son, Mattie. "Fetch Mr. McKinley a mug and a plate so he can have tea and scones with us."

Mattie nodded and left the table.

Cait came to Max and laid a hand on his arm. "I see it on yere face, and I don't want you to worry about before. There are no hard feelings. Ye didn't know."

The rest of the table looked at him questioningly, but thankfully they didn't pry. Apparently they had their hands full with Andrew.

Max nodded to Cait. "All right then."

She dropped her hand and took her place back at the table.

Amy from the store scooted over and made room for Max. "Sit here. We were giving Andrew some ideas of what he could do to repair things with Moira."

Max glanced in Andrew's direction, thinking they should leave the poor bastard alone. He parked himself at the table and nodded to the priest in a show of solidarity.

Mattie appeared at his side with a plate and a teacup. "Here, Mr. McKinley." His voice was as quiet as before, but steady.

Everyone at the table stopped what they were doing and smiled at Mattie affectionately. Max had to hand it to Gandiegow—they sure knew how to support and love one another.

Cait seemed overcome by the moment, too. She grabbed Emma's hand and squeezed. "I'm going to miss you all."

"Going on a trip?" Max asked, only to be friendly.

Everyone looked a bit startled, but Cait recovered quickly.

"My husband is out of town on business. An extended stay. Mattie and I are going to go back with him when he returns."

Emma patted Cait's arm, and then hugged Mattie. "But they're going to call often. Right, Mattie?"

"Aye," he said in his small voice. "And Skype."

"And Skype." Emma smiled at the boy. In the next second, she swiveled toward Max, eyeing him. "You're a man," she said in her London accent. "Would you jump in and fight for the woman you love or would you let love slip away?"

Oh, God. What had he gotten himself into? Was it too late to make a run for it?

The others looked at him expectantly. Stalling, Max cleared his throat. He so wanted to tell them to leave Andrew alone, and himself, but he was no match for this many female Scottish warriors.

Amy shoved envelopes, a sponge, and a ramekin of water at him. "Seal these while you give us yere opinion."

"Go on," Claire encouraged.

"I don't know anything about it," Max said, hoping to get them off the scent.

Emma gazed at him matter-of-factly. "Andrew says otherwise. When we insisted he had to talk to someone, the good Father said he'd discussed his problem with you the other day."

He gave Andrew a *what the hell?* glare. What happened to the bro code?

Claire smiled encouragingly as she poured him a cup of dark, hot liquid from the carafe. Cait put two scones on his plate and pushed it toward him, with an expectant gaze.

Max cleared his throat again. "I think everyone should give Andrew and Moira some space to work things out for themselves."

Kit seemed to take umbrage. "I know from experience that these two need some assistance to get back on track."

"Well, I've tried talking to Moira," Amy said, "but she's being stubborn and won't say a word of what's going on."

Andrew seemed to be hurrying through stuffing his envelopes so he could get the heck out of there.

Max looked down at the stack of flyers in the middle of the table. "Maybe Moira needs a push to make a decision."

Kind of like Pippa had made her decision tonight—she chose Ross over him.

"What do you mean?" Emma asked.

He glanced over at Andrew as if to apologize while picking up the auction flyer absentmindedly. "Maybe Andrew needs to put himself back on the market and let the chips fall as they may." He set the flyer in front of Emma.

Amy whacked Max on the back good-naturedly. "That's a brilliant idea. Absolutely brilliant."

Andrew looked horrified, but finally found his voice. "Ye think I should put myself into the bachelor auction?"

Max held his gaze. "What could it hurt?"

Andrew frowned at him fiercely. "I could get bought by another woman. Then where would we be?"

Max shook his head. "If Moira doesn't at least try for you, well, then, I think she's sending you a strong message, man."

Andrew looked heartsick.

"Well, then, it's settled. Father Andrew is going on the

list." Amy pulled a piece of paper from a pile and wrote the pastor's name at the bottom.

Something caught Max's eye—specifically his name on the list. He took the paper from her, and there it was in black and white—MAX MCKINLEY.

"What the . . ."

Amy laughed. "Ye didn't know?"

"Of course I didn't know."

Claire relieved him of the sheet of paper. "We all thought you looked very sexy in yere kilt, brooding like that."

Pippa. The factory. Her camera. Oh, God!

"When was she going to tell me?" Max didn't expect them to reply. He stood abruptly. "If you'll excuse. I'm off to get some answers." *From Pippa. And have it out with her now!*

Pippa sat at the kitchen table with the box of financial papers that she'd been sorting through for weeks. At every turn, she found more and more evidence that her father hadn't told her the truth. In her hand now she held the note that was the tipping point. Da had mortgaged their house to make payroll for the factory.

She slumped back in her chair. She was finding out that maybe her father wasn't exactly the man she thought he was.

She should've just gone on to bed after Ross walked her home. Or she should've read a book. Anything, except come across this. Another payment on the second mortgage was coming due. How was Pippa going to cover that?

Tears ran down her cheeks, but she was mad as hell.

The pressure was killing her. She couldn't take one more thing going wrong. Not tonight.

There was a light rap at the back door and then it opened. Pippa rose, expecting any one of the Gandie-gowans who came and went from their house. She didn't expect, though, to see Max.

He looked ready to go to war with her, his face hard, his stare dark. But then it seemed as if his brain caught up with what his eyes were seeing, perhaps each one of her tears on her cheeks. She wiped them away.

"Oh, hell." He pulled his wool cap off, crossed the room to her, and gathered her into his arms. "Ross didn't do anything to hurt you, did he?"

She shook her head. "No."

"Good. I'd hate to get into a fistfight here in Scot-land."

She'd cried only a handful of times in her life, and two of those times had been since Max McKinley had arrived in Gandiegow. Did he have this effect on all women, mak-ing them break down into a blubbering mess, or was it only her?

Max held her tight. "Can you tell me what's wrong then?" His voice sounded thick with emotion. He stroked her hair.

She didn't speak, only buried herself deeper in his embrace.

He led them over to a chair. When he sat, he pulled her onto his lap. "Spill it." His words were gentle, but firm.

He seemed to know just the right tone to take with her. She slipped into the chair next to him, but he kept his arm around the back of it, as if to show he was there in case she needed to be held again.

She couldn't tell him everything. Max was still MTech after all. But she could share with him how the pressure was getting to her about her da's medical issues . . . that without her da helping, the weight of the burden fell on her.

"I thought I'd figured it all out. I asked MTech to come back to the table to talk about a partnership. I set up the bachelor auction to pay for a specialist for Da. But as soon as I figure out one thing, another problem pops up."

Max stroked her hand. "So at least you putting me up for auction is for a good cause?"

She faced him, feeling terrible. "I should've talked to you sooner about it. I just hadn't gotten around to breaking the bad news. Ye're not too mad, are you?"

"I'll live."

"Ye don't mind wearing the kilt again?"

"I figured as much."

"And that the ladies will be ogling you like ye're a tasty meat pie?"

He laughed. "Great."

"But ye'll do it for Da?"

He leaned over and brushed his lips across hers. "Only because you asked so nicely."

She slipped back onto his lap, and wrapped her arms around his neck. For a long moment, she gazed into his perfect eyes. She still couldn't be with him, but she could show him how much she appreciated his sacrifice. She leaned down and kissed him.

He tasted as enticing as scones. And he tasted like Max. It was that thought that had her deepening the kiss. Without any effort at all, she was completely wrapped up in him. And nothing could make her pull away from kissing him right now.

"Pippa?" her da called from the den. "Are ye there? I need a pain pill and some more water."

She rested her forehead on Max's. "Aye, I'm here, Da. I'll bring it right in."

Max rubbed noses with her. "I better go."

She didn't want him to. She wanted him to stay so she could kiss him some more. "Aye. I guess ye better." She climbed off his lap and went to tend to her father.

Chapter Eleven

Max woke in the morning with Pippa still on his mind. Holding her last night, comforting her, had affected him even more than the steamy kisses they'd shared before. She was twisting up his insides in ways he never thought possible.

Right now, he had the dreaded job of meeting with Miranda. He quickly readied for the day. If it had been any other job site, Max would've donned his business suit and tie again. He thought about texting Miranda, telling her to dress casual this morning, too, but she was all business all the time.

At the Glen Thistle Lodge quilting dorm, which was nothing more than a bungalow, Max rapped on the door. Miranda opened it right away. She was wearing a relentless navy pantsuit, a high-necked blouse, blood-red lipstick, and a frown.

She pierced him with her gaze. "What took you so long? And what are you wearing?"

He chose to ignore both statements. "I thought we'd go to the restaurant first and discuss our plan of action."

His objective ... getting Miranda to divulge the details of the contract.

She slipped on her trench coat and grabbed her expensive briefcase. "We'll have to eat quickly. I want that meeting with Lachlan McDonnell *today*. He's not answering his cell. Do you have another number for him?"

"No." There was no way that he was letting Miranda near the McDonnell in his current condition.

"Never mind. We're expected at the factory this morning, anyway."

"Expected?" Max said, stunned.

"Yes. I e-mailed Alistair last night and it's all set." She raised her eyebrows and nodded. "When you didn't arrange the meeting, I did. I'm getting a little tired of doing your job for you, Max. What have you been doing since you got here, besides the scullery maid?" She put her hand up. "Never mind. I don't want to know."

She clipped past him and out the door.

Great. He pointed out the direction of the restaurant and they were off. He treaded beside her except in the places where the path was too narrow, where only one person could pass at a time. But he was determined to have a serious talk with Miranda before they went to the factory.

When Max walked into the restaurant, Claire waved hello. "What can I get ye? Two morning specials?"

Miranda ignored her and seated herself.

"Sounds good, Claire." He started over to Miranda, but was called away.

"Yank?" One of three men at the far table motioned to him. Max didn't know his name, but he knew the other two—Ross and Ramsay Armstrong.

"Miranda, I'll be a minute." He left her and went to the men. "Yes?"

"I'm Abraham Clacher. These two—"

"We've met," said Ross.

"Oh, that's right. Ross was the one who told me ye was good with a hammer. Deydie asked me to build a platform or a stage, something for that bachelor auction." The old man chuckled, but then it turned into a cough.

Ramsay pounded the elderly guy on the back.

"What Abraham is wondering," said Ross, "is if you're up to helping us build this thing."

Ross turned a paper napkin toward him, on which was sketched the general shape and dimensions.

"Are you going to be auctioned off as well, Ross?" Hell, Max sounded nosy, and it was none of his business, but he was curious if he'd gotten wrangled into it, too.

Ross's frown deepened. "Aye. I've been enlisted."

Ramsay cuffed him on the arm. "See what happens when you dawdle? Ye should've married Pippa years ago. Now ye're going to end up being some boy-toy for a Glaswegian widow."

"Leave off." Ross looked as though he might punch his brother back, but not in the arm, and not in jest.

"I know how you feel," Max muttered. He picked up the napkin and examined it. He set it back on the table and pulled out a pen, adding height to the stage's drawing and four steps leading up. "What if we do this?"

Claire passed by and tapped him on the shoulder. "Yere food's ready. But more important, yere lady is impatient."

Max spun around. Sure enough, Miranda was cutting

a glare at him that should've cleaved him in two. "We'll have to pick this back up later."

Abraham leaned around Max and nodded. "Aye."

Max joined Miranda.

"What was that all about? You seem awfully cozy here among these people." She made it sound unsavory. "You were sent here to do a job. Or have you forgotten?"

"I haven't forgotten. But how am I supposed to do my job if you preempt me and send over a contract I know nothing about?" There. He'd laid it on the table.

"I don't know why you haven't received your copy, Max."

He didn't believe her. She was stonewalling.

Max would have to make Pippa listen to reason. She had to let him read her copy.

Thinking of Pippa brought the issue of *Alistair* to the forefront. "There's something you need to know before we go to the factory today."

She glanced at his clothing. "What, that you've contracted yourself out as one of their hired hands?"

He wouldn't tell her about the times he'd helped at NSV.

"It's about Alistair." He paused for a second. "You've already met *her*."

"What are you talking about? Alistair isn't a woman."

She most certainly is. Max could still feel her on his lips. "Pippa is Alistair McDonnell. *Alistair Philippa McDonnell*."

Miranda looked horrified. "What?"

"Using the name Alistair makes it easier for her to navigate in the business world. She pulled the same trick on me. I didn't want you to walk in there and be surprised like I was."

Miranda seemed appeased and gave a small shrug of understanding. "You might have told me earlier," she muttered.

"I tried. But now you know." He motioned to her plate. "Your bangers and mash are getting cold."

Miranda rolled her sausage away with her fork, frowning. "I would starve to death if I had to live here. Or I'd gain a hundred pounds." She pushed her plate away, her cinnamon scone barely nibbled.

Max hurriedly ate, paid Claire for the excellent breakfast, and walked Miranda to the car. "I guess I should also prepare you for the factory. It'll be like nothing you've ever seen." As he drove, he told her about the sail-making business, the boat storage, even the workers. He just couldn't bring himself to mention the abundance of Christmas trees, the one thing he couldn't rationalize away.

Once inside the lobby, Miranda glanced around with disdain, but kept her opinions to herself as he asked Bonnie to let Pippa know they were there.

Alistair showed up a few minutes later. This was the same Alistair that he'd met, the one wearing the business suit, but this time her suit was plaid, driving home her heritage. Her hair was pulled back in a severe bun as before, and he itched to pull the pins and let it cascade down over her shoulders. But he knew she had a point to prove. He stood back and let her have at it.

With a fake smile on her face, Pippa stuck out her hand as if she'd never spoken to Miranda in her life. "Welcome. I'm Alistair McDonnell. And ye must be Miranda Weymouth." Pippa's brogue was heavy, as if she was ladling out a thick stew—thick enough to choke Miranda.

Miranda, surprisingly, didn't call Pippa on the carpet, but shook her hand as if nothing was amiss.

Max shrugged apologetically and fessed up. "I told Miranda about your split personality."

"Persona," Miranda corrected. "You wouldn't understand. You're not a woman." She didn't look as if she was ready to play nice with Pippa, just as though she could relate. "And where is Lachlan, your father? I assumed he would be here to greet me."

Pippa glanced at Max first to see if he'd told her about the McDonnell—his injuries, his inability to heal.

He shook his head almost imperceptibly.

Pippa faced Miranda. "My da has other things to tend to today."

"I expect to meet with him soon," Miranda said firmly.

Pippa shot her a glance that conveyed it would be over somebody's dead body. "Shall we get on with it?"

Alistair gave them the grand tour, more professional than the one he'd received on his first day. Miranda seemed to be watching both him and NSV's chief engineer closely as if trying to gauge what was really going on between them. Hell, if she found out, then he'd like to know, too.

After they hit the high points of the factory, Pippa guided them back to her office. The room had been straightened and a small table, looking suspiciously like the café table from Quilting Central, sat in the corner with three kitchen chairs around it. The place was still cluttered, but in better shape than when he'd first seen it.

Pippa gestured for them to sit. "Make yereself comfortable."

Miranda pointed to the stack of papers on her desk. "Is that the contract?"

Pippa straightened. "Aye. I'm still working through it."

"Perhaps I can meet with Lachlan and go over the high points with him." Miranda's offer was met with a stony glare.

"The McDonnell and I have it covered."

Pippa might as well have said it aloud, because Max could plainly see it on her face . . . *I'll get back to ye in my own sweet time.*

Miranda held her ground. "Then I want to see the subsea shutoff valve designs while I'm here."

Taog popped his head in the office. "Pippa, if you've got a minute, I need ye in the machine shop." His face reddened as if he'd only just noticed she had visitors. "Sorry. I didn't mean to interrupt."

Pippa grabbed her hard hat. "We were done here. Max, you know yere way out." She stood at her office entrance and waited for them to pass. Then she pulled her door shut, twisted the knob as if to check that it locked, and left without another word to either of them.

As soon as Pippa was out of sight, Miranda turned on him. "McKinley, you better not have ruined this deal by dicking with the owner's daughter."

"I assure you, the deal is on track." *It has to be.* "But as I said, I need a copy of the contract to make any headway." He peered through the office window at the contract lying on Pippa's desk.

Miranda started walking toward the double doors

they'd come through. "You know all you need to know. Close this deal, or else."

He was angry. Miranda, MTech, or both had sent him into battle without weapons . . . and expected him to be victorious! He stomped to the car.

He drove Miranda back to the town's parking lot, where Ross, Ramsay, and Abraham stood in front of a truck that was at least sixty years old, examining it.

"I've got somewhere to be," Max said. "Are you good on your own?"

"Of course," Miranda snorted.

Max waited while she walked from the parking lot and out of sight before joining the other three. He would like nothing better than to find Pippa right now and get the damned deal settled, but he'd promised to help the men with the stage for the bachelor auction. God, Max hoped Miranda was back in the States before he had to prance across the stage in a skirt and be auctioned off. He wasn't some juicy steak in the supermarket to be bought.

"Sorry I'm late," he said to the men.

Ross nodded his head in the direction Miranda had gone. "Ye looked busy."

"Aye," Abraham added.

"So what is it that we're looking at?" Max said.

Ross sighed impatiently. "It's a truck."

"Are ye sure?" Ramsay teased.

Ross clouted Ramsay on the shoulder. "I'm going to fix it up. I figure if my younger brother can start a new business, then I can, too. Of course, for me, the fishing comes first. But *Armstrong Hauling* has a nice ring to it."

Abraham guffawed. "There's more rust and dents on the truck than McCurdy's boat."

"I'm not sure this heap can handle hauling a feather, the shape she's in." That remark got Ramsay another punch on the shoulder.

"We're going to find out." Ross opened the door. "Who's riding to the mill with me to pick up wood?"

Ramsay took a step back, putting his hand to his ear. "I think I hear my wife calling. I'm coming, Kit!" he hollered back to the wind.

"Chicken shite," Ross complained.

Abraham chuckled, walking away. "I've got to swab the deck of me boat. Looks like ye're stuck with the Yank."

"Get in," Ross said, frowning at the backs of the other two men.

Max guessed the contract could wait another hour . . . if the damned truck didn't break down and delay him further.

Freda hurried up to the porch of Thistle Glen Lodge, knowing this was the bravest thing she'd ever done. She tapped lightly on the door. She'd heard the whispers, people calling Miranda the Queen Shrew. Freda knew otherwise. Miranda was going to be her savior. She tapped harder.

Miranda finally opened the door with her mobile phone in hand, clearly irritated, and frowning. "Yes?"

"I'd like to speak with ye." Freda looked down at her snow-covered boots, feeling more like Moira than herself right now.

Miranda didn't budge with her hand on the door. "Go on."

"May I come in?"

"This better not take long. I have calls to make." Miranda opened the door wide and let Freda pass through. "What's this about?"

While a disapproving Miranda watched, Freda slipped off her boots and left them in the rubber tray to catch the melting snow. Her courage of a moment ago felt as if it was melting away, too.

Oh, dear. Maybe coming here was a mistake. She should leave. Instead she made herself stay rooted to the spot. "I'm Freda Douglas. My cottage is just down the way."

Miranda gave her an impatient nod.

Freda hung her coat on a hook, wishing she was better able to tell people what she needed. She turned back to Miranda. "I want to get some advice from you."

Miranda's impatience seemed to be growing. "About what?"

Freda felt as if a lemon had gotten caught in her throat. But her need was greater than her fear. "How you were able to put your insecurities behind you and become confident."

Miranda's mouth fell open. For a second, Freda thought she might question her on how she knew.

But Miranda took a deep breath and wiped all emotion from her face. "So you want to gain confidence." She paused for a long second, then smirked at her. "What do I get in return?"

That took Freda off guard. Gandiegow wasn't a tit-for-tat community. "I don't know. I don't have anything that ye'd want."

The American lass gave her a sly look. "Not true."

"What do ye think that I have?"

Miranda led her into the living area, pointing for her to sit. "I'll help you, if in return you help me with the town."

"This town? What can you mean? I don't have any . . . clout." People barely noticed her. Most days Freda felt invisible. She'd known the McDonnell for her whole life—fifty-nine years—and not once had he really seen her. Why would anyone listen to what she had to say now?

"You have to help me convince the leaders of Gandie-gow that a partnership with MTech would be good for everyone. A win-win."

"Believe me. I have no influence." Freda felt a little desperate. She'd come here with hope, but now she was going to leave empty-handed.

"Promise me that you'll talk to your clansmen or whatever you call them." Miranda waved irritably like Freda's help was a done deal.

She sat there speechless, not knowing how to correct her or how to fix this.

Miranda studied her, putting a hand on her slender hip. "Is this confidence problem that you're having about a man?" She shook her head. "Never mind. Of course it is. Who is he? A fisherman? A lumberjack? What's his name?"

Freda wanted to crawl from the room. She couldn't tell this woman about her deepest secret. The only person she'd confided in was Emma, and even then, she hadn't given his name.

Miranda shrugged dismissively. "If you won't tell me, then I can't help."

Freda was trapped. But she'd come this far to change

her life. She had to go the rest of the way. "It's the Mc-Donnell. He's the one who owns the factory."

Miranda sneered. "Of course."

"Do you know him?"

"A little." Miranda got a gleam in her eye as she gave Freda the once-over. She didn't seem to approve of even one inch of her. "Your hair is mousy."

Freda reached up to touch her mane. She never gave her hair much thought. She knew the gray was coming in, but she wasn't a spring lamb anymore.

"Stop acting like you might cry. Confidence is all about looking your best. You need a makeover," Miranda said matter-of-factly. "A dye job for sure. A revealing dress. And for goodness' sakes, put on some makeup. After I get done with you, you'll have Lachlan eating out of your hand."

Miranda had said *Lachlan* as if she knew him well . . . really well. Again, Freda had second thoughts about coming.

"But I came here to find out what you did," Freda braved.

Miranda waved her off. "We'll start with your hair. I assume there's some place in town to buy dye. A drugstore, or what do you call it, a chemist?"

"The General Store has them."

Miranda grabbed her purse and dug out a nail file. "You work on your nails while I find a decent color for that mop of yours." She shook her head as though it was hopeless, but then shrugged on her coat and was gone.

Freda felt a little sick. This wasn't what she had wanted. But maybe this was the first step that Miranda had taken to change herself.

Freda settled herself on the love seat and looked at her fingernails. It had to be a process. If filing her nails was going to change her destiny, then she would manicure herself until she was perfect.

Pippa tried concentrating after Max and Miranda left, but her emotions were everywhere. She ate lunch with Murdoch and Taog, but even their bickering couldn't distract her. She worked on the books in the afternoon, but knocked off early. When she got home, Da was asleep in his wheelchair, his lunch tray beside him. Freda was nowhere in sight. She wondered how long Da had been alone.

A rap sounded on the door. Pippa went to answer it. A strange woman with platinum blond hair stood there. It took a good minute for Pippa to realize it was Freda.

Freda with makeup caked on her face.

Freda squeezed into a black wraparound dress, her boobs nearly exposed, and with a trench coat hung over her shoulders.

Freda looking absolutely miserable.

"What the . . ." Pippa was at a loss for words.

Freda trembled, but seemed determined. "I came to see *Lachlan*."

Pippa had never heard Freda call her da by his Christian name.

"Nay. Stay right here."

"But—"

Pippa shut the door. She hated to do it, but there was no way she was letting her da see Freda made up like a tart.

"Who is it?" The McDonnell called out in a scratchy voice. "Has Freda come to sit with me?"

Pippa ran into the room. "Nay, Da." She grabbed the contract and laid it beside her father, a hundred thoughts roiling through her head. "I've got to run. Do you mind taking a look at the contract while I'm gone?"

He looked a little confused, but finally nodded.

She kissed his head, grabbed her coat, and ran back to the door. She found Freda shivering even more.

"Come." Pippa took her arm. "We're going to get you back to your cottage." *Before anyone sees you.*

Pippa steadied Freda while they walked to her house. She wondered if Freda had ever worn heels this high in her life. And she wondered who had lent them to her.

Once inside her small fisherman's cabin, Pippa had a plan. "Go change into something comfortable. We're going to Inverness to get this fixed."

Freda stood there, defeated. "I knew I looked awful . . . but Miranda said I looked irresistible."

"Miranda?" Pippa didn't mean to screech, but it sure came out that way. She had the urge to find Miranda and give *her* a *makeover*! But Pippa wouldn't abandon Freda. "Why would you let her do this to you?"

Freda looked down at her hands. "I don't want to say."

Pippa pulled her over to the couch and sat with her. She grabbed the quilt from the back and wrapped Freda in it. The woman she'd known her whole life, the woman who'd cared for her through everything, looked so small and low now.

Pippa said it for her. "Ye did it to get my da to notice ye, didn't ye?" She wrapped her arm around Freda's shoulders.

Freda let out a sob, then another, and then she let go while Pippa held her.

Freda had been the one Pippa had run to when the baby whale had died on their beach. She'd cried in Freda's arms until she could cry no more. Freda had put bandages on her knees. Hemmed her skirts for the céilidhs. Fed her soup when she was sick. Had been a true constant in her life.

The realization hit Pippa over the head like a falling mast. *Freda has been the mother I never had.*

Pippa was ashamed that she'd never noticed before. Ashamed she'd never told Freda how much she loved her. How much she meant to her. How the world was a better place because she was in it.

Pippa was as bad as her da. She wiped away her own tears and squeezed the woman who had done so much for her. "I love you, Freda. Ye're the best person I know."

Freda cried harder.

"Come now. You and I are going to dry these tears. Ye're going to get that damned makeup off your face. After you've changed, we're going to Inverness and fix the mess that Miranda made of yere hair. We'll buy you some new clothes. And if my da doesn't notice ye then, I'm going to find a harpoon and shoot him in the backside. *Bluidy blind bastard.*"

Freda laughed through her tears. "Really?"

"Hurry now. I'll make a hair appointment while ye change."

Freda slipped off the high heels and stood. "Pippa?" She paused for a moment. "I love you, too, lass. Always have."

Pippa smiled at her. "Go on now, or you might have to live with that hair color forever."

Freda hurried from the room.

"And burn that dress," Pippa hollered, laughing. She fell back on the cushions.

Huh, she was okay with Freda having feelings for her father. Better than okay. Even Kit their local matchmaker couldn't have found her da a better match. And her da better agree, too! The second thing that hit Pippa was that Freda—who had settled her whole life—apparently wanted more. A wave of protectiveness came over Pippa. How could anyone even consider transforming one of the nicest, sweetest people on the planet into a parody of a sexy woman? Miranda should be strung up.

But right now, Pippa had a hair appointment to make. She also called Bethia and asked her to check in on her da.

On the drive into Inverness, Pippa shared with Freda what she'd learned while living in Edinburgh on her own. "Self-confidence is really one of the most attractive assets anyone can have."

"I figured that," Freda said sheepishly. "That was why I went to Miranda in the first place. I could tell she had transformed herself from a scared lamb into a mighty tigress." Pippa didn't know about that, but she kept her opinion to herself. "She said a makeover would give me the self-confidence I needed."

"I think the right clothes can help women with confidence, and the right makeup," Pippa answered. "But what I've learned is that the biggest change comes from knowing your own self-worth. Ye do know how special ye are, don't you?"

Freda bowed her head, but Pippa saw a small smile. "I'm beginning to see it."

So there was hope for her yet.

At the hairdresser's, Freda was converted into a chic

version of herself. With a good cut, a new color, and a few highlights, she looked beautiful. She had a determination in her eyes that Pippa hadn't seen before. Next they went on a shopping spree and found Freda some sharp outfits and flattering makeup, perfect to bring out her best features—her big eyes and nice smile.

Pippa was excited when they returned home to Gandiegow. "I can't wait until Da gets a look at you."

Freda laid a hand on her arm. "It's late, dear. I'm worn-out and I'm sure he's asleep. I've been through so much tonight. And, well, to be honest, I need to sleep on it myself to summon up courage again to see him."

"You promise not to chicken out?"

"I'll be brave. I'll see Lachlan tomorrow."

"Good."

Freda stopped at her door. "Pippa?"

Pippa turned to her and saw the gratitude on her face. "Don't say a word. It's only a small amount to pay ye back for all ye've done for me."

Lachlan shoved the contract away. He didn't understand a word of it. His eyes were failing him, like his health, and he couldn't concentrate worth a damn. He was old, tired, and worn-out. And wasn't healing. Was this what the rest of his miserable life looked like?

He felt like such a failure. He used to be strong. Powerful. A force to be reckoned with. Now he expected little Mattie or seven-year-old Dand could whip his sorry arse.

He'd lied to Pippa time and time again since he'd opened the factory. *Aye, everything is grand.* He'd been stupid, arrogant, and prideful. But not anymore. The finances were in a shambles. He suspected Pippa had already figured out to what extent that he'd failed her, failed them all. He may have been a hell of an engineer, even a visionary once, but he was the worst sort of businessman. What made him think he could run a factory? The town would hate him when MTech took his subsea valve and shut down the factory.

He was too tired to even think about any of it anymore. He picked up the phone beside him and made the call. It was time.

Afterward, Lachlan dozed. Bethia stopped by with a plate, but he wasn't hungry. When he woke up again, Pippa was coming in the front door.

She leaned her head into the dark room, but he pretended to be sleeping. Morning would be soon enough to tell her.

He heard her in the kitchen for a moment and then her feet on the stairs. Even after the house became completely quiet, except for the wind blowing outside and the waves crashing against the retaining wall, he couldn't sleep. Failure robbed him of rest. Defeat encamped in his soul.

Before the sun came up in the morning, he heard the front door open. It would be Freda, come to make his coffee and breakfast. But Lachlan was too ashamed of who he'd become to see her. He wanted to call out to Freda that he didn't need her here today, but he didn't want to wake Pippa either.

In an hour when Pippa woke, would be time enough to shift the load to her . . . turn her life on its end.

The light went on in the kitchen. The frying pan was set on the stove. This was torture for him. Why couldn't he just be left alone?

Freda stepped into the doorway. He could make out only her silhouette. "Lachlan?"

She hadn't called him by his first name since they were children.

"Here," he finally said. Anger flared. Where else did she expect him to be? *As if he could come and go about the house of his own volition.* He was an invalid and a burden.

She came into the room and turned on the small lamp. She was the only sunshine to his disastrous life.

Freda looked very nice and he started to tell her so. A new hairstyle? Was that a new outfit?

"Yere coffee is brewing. I brought you books this morning. They're in the wagon outside." She smiled brightly at him as though he'd tacked her sail into the wind. "I'll go start yere breakfast now unless ye need something from me first."

He wanted her to come sit near him, to tell him that everything was going to be all right. But it would never be again. He wasn't the man that he once was.

And he wouldn't do this to her. She'd come to mean a lot to him over the past several months. His affection for her had blossomed as she spent long hours sitting quietly with him beside his fire. He squashed down his growing feelings. It wasn't fair. She was a good woman. She deserved a *whole* man. One with a future. One who wasn't riddled with broken bones that wouldn't heal.

"I don't want breakfast," he said roughly. "Take the books away. I'll not be needing them either."

"But—" she tried, her face turning red in pain and confusion. "I don't understand."

There was nothing to understand.

"Go home," Lachlan said tiredly. He had to make it stick, no matter how much it hurt him to do it. "I'm not interested in yere bluidy coffee or yere breakfast or yere bluidy books. I want to be left alone."

Freda gasped, clutching at her skirt, as if it could offer support.

He turned his head away but wasn't quick enough. He saw the tears running down her cheeks.

Freda hurried from the room. He heard the door slam and knew that she was gone for good.

A minute later, Pippa came down the stairs and rushed into the den. "Is everything all right? I heard noises."

Lachlan straightened himself, though he felt old and stiff. "We need to talk."

"I thought I heard Freda."

"Never mind about that." Only a weak man would take his woes out on a woman. He shouldn't have raised his voice to the kindest person he knew, his closest friend and ally. Instead, he should've told Freda how lovely she looked today. But now he'd ruined it all. If things were different, if he wasn't so pathetic, he might've asked Freda to dinner. He should've done it long ago but he wouldn't dream of asking her now. Freda deserved so much more than a weak man like him.

Pippa's face deepened with concern. "What's going on, Da?"

"I made a call to the law offices in Aberdeen yesterday."

"What did you do?"

He nodded in the direction of the corner. "The papers are over there on the fax machine. I'll sign them and then the factory is yeres."

"I don't want—"

He lifted his good arm to stop her protest though it pained him. "It would be yours eventually. I'm just safeguarding the future by doing this now." He wouldn't tell her that he'd given up hope.

"No."

"I'm still the head of this family." He didn't have the strength to yell, but he was firm. "Ye're fit to run it; I'm not. At least trust me on this." Those last words completely drained all energy from him. He needed this over with. He didn't want to talk anymore.

Pippa knelt beside him. "What's changed? Do ye need a painkiller?"

"Nay."

The way she looked at him, the pity in her eyes, she knew he was defeated, too.

"Now, get me those papers."

She did as she was told. He retrieved a pen from the side table and signed. For a moment, she acted as if she was going to renew her protest, but then she signed, too.

"Now the power lies with you," he said resolutely.

"You're still going to help with the decisions," she said. "Right, Da? This was just a formality."

"I'm tired now," he said, closing his eyes. "Turn out the lamp on your way out."

She touched his shoulder gently. "Can I fix ye a cup of tea to tide ye over until Freda comes back?"

"No."

*　　*　　*

For the past hour, Pippa sat alone at her kitchen table while her tea got cold. She felt utterly lost. What was she going to do about her da? He'd clearly taken a turn for the worse, but he wouldn't tell her what had happened. She wondered if she should have Emma do a psychological evaluation.

If Pippa had thought the weight of responsibility was heavy before, it was nothing but a pin compared to the two-ton lorry resting on her shoulders now.

Finally she grabbed her coat, deciding to appease the old ladies and make an appearance at Quilting Central. Her brain was on overload. As if the factory wasn't enough to worry about, she couldn't stop thinking about Max McKinley. It was as if her brain had been rewired. Ever since the Yank had stepped into Gandiegow, she'd been an emotional mess. And Alistair McDonnell was never emotional!

She would focus on one thing today. She'd sew. It would be mindless and it would get the old ladies off her back about getting the quilt done for the auction. Deydie insisted that Pippa needed to work on the quilt every day if she was to finish in time. Pippa really did want to honor her father, now more than ever. She just needed to put in the effort.

When she opened the door to Quilting Central, a cold breeze blew in with her.

"Shut the damned door, lassie," called Deydie from the hearth. Then she and Bethia lumbered toward her.

"We're so glad you could come in today." Bethia pointed to the matronly twins across the room. "Ailsa and Aileen have offered to press for you while you sew."

The bouffant twins in their matching red and green plaid outfits waved to Pippa.

"I can't stay too long," Pippa said, making her excuses now. "Da will need his pills soon." She doubted he would be a willing patient today. "Has anyone seen Freda?"

"Nay," Bethia said. "She's not been by."

Maybe Freda could get her da to open up.

Pippa took her place at the sewing machine. She decided to work on Freda's block next, picking out the fabrics to represent her small cottage by the sea. She pulled the Douglas tartan from the stack and cut it to the right size. Then she found a piece of red fabric for Freda's front door and attached it. Because Pippa wanted to do something special for Freda's house, she embroidered a cross on one of the windows. This gave her an idea of what to give Freda for Christmas, though she was crunched for time. This year, instead of another soup cookbook, Pippa would hand make Freda a quilted pillow just like the quilt block.

Pippa almost didn't recognize herself, having feelings that she'd never felt before. First, her crazy feelings for Max. Then feeling like maybe her da wasn't the man she thought him to be. And now, finally noticing Freda for who she was.

Ross and Ramsay Armstrong appeared, followed by Abraham Clacher. And then a fourth person stepped inside Quilting Central, too. Pippa's breath caught. *Max.*

Ross pointed to the far end of the room. "Deydie said we're supposed to build it over there."

The four of them stalked to the back. Max, Pippa noticed, couldn't take his eyes off her either. But it wasn't an ogle; it was more of a determined stare. She wondered what was on his mind, but she really should concentrate on the quilt block she had to finish.

The men measured the back wall, talked, and then split up. Max came straight to her. Ross watched him, frowning, but he left without saying a word to them.

"Pippa?" Max's voice was teeming with determination. "We need to speak with your father together. Right now."

"Why?" Pippa wouldn't bother her da, especially since he wasn't himself today.

Deydie, always the eavesdropper, seemed to have zeroed in on their conversation.

"We have to get down to business," Max added as if to let Deydie know she wasn't needed.

"Fine." Pippa shut off her machine and stacked her two completed blocks.

Deydie let loose with her thoughts as usual. "At the rate that ye're going on that quilt, lassie, ye'll be lucky to get her done by the first snowfall of *next* Christmas."

Pippa frowned at Deydie, not replying to the jab, and grabbed her jacket. She followed Max out.

Once outside, he turned and adjusted her coat, zipping it up. "You're going to catch a cold."

It felt both nice and scary to have him watching out for her; she knew from experience that it didn't pay to count on a man. Not even her da. "I don't need ye to take care of me."

He pulled her hood up, too, his touch seeming to mirror his emotions—determined, matter-of-fact. "None of us are living in this world alone, Pippa. Accept a little help every now and then, and you'll be a blessing to those who want to do good for you."

"Since when are ye the Dalai Lama?"

His sternness dropped away. "Since you don't zip up before going outdoors." He surprised her with a genuine smile.

"So where's yere boss?" she blurted.

His smile faded. "On a conference call. But I'm done talking about her."

Pippa wasn't. "Are ye and Miranda seeing each other?"

Max stopped short and stared at her. "No." He seemed at war with himself for a second. "But if you're asking if we have some history together, then I would have to say yes."

I knew it! "What kind of history?"

Max pulled at his scarf. "I don't want to talk about it."

"Fine." *That should satisfy my stupid lips for wanting to kiss him again.* "Thanks for the heads-up." Pippa turned, ready to stomp off.

Max grabbed her arm and spun her to face him. "I'm not proud of what I did, but at one time, I led Miranda on, and I feel bad about it."

"Aye. Ye and every other man in the world. All of ye are experts on deceiving. Maybe it's a requirement of having a penis." She meant to wound him, but the hurt in his eyes had nothing to do with her. It went deeper than that.

He dropped her arm. "It was three years ago. Right after the accident."

Oh, God. "What accident?" she asked quietly.

"My brother's accident."

Pippa shivered.

Max stared at the sea. "Jake was on a Christmas errand for me. When he came out from the store, he had a flat tire. While he was kneeling down, fixing it, a car barreled into him."

"No," she said.

"He's paralyzed now. His boy was only a year old when it happened. Jake is in a wheelchair and it's my fault. I'm the one who sent him to pick up Mom's present, a Kitchen Aid mixer. I was too busy, so I sent my little brother instead."

"It's not yere fault." Pippa wanted to hug Max until the pain left his face.

"It is. A lot of things are. I led Miranda on. At the time, I would've done anything to keep the guilt at bay for my part in my brother's severed spine." His gaze fell back on her as if she was a priest taking confession. "I invited her out to dinner. Afterward, we went back to her place."

Pippa backed away. "I don't need to hear more."

Max seized her hand. "Nothing happened. I couldn't go to bed with Miranda. I couldn't use her like that."

Pippa was relieved, and at the same time, she could easily see how he might've done it to ease his pain. But he hadn't.

"Max, ye can't beat yereself up over it."

He squeezed her hand. "I was surprised when the promotion came through because I knew that I'd be working for Miranda. I was relieved that she took the high road and had forgiven me."

"But?" Pippa didn't really want to know this either.

"I'm under a lot of scrutiny. We need to quit messing around and get the McDonnell to make a decision. I'll fight to get him the best deal with MTech. I promise. But I may not have a job much longer if I keep screwing around." She heard the subtext *with you* tacked onto the end of his statement.

So spending time with me is screwing around?

It felt like a smack to the face.

"I suppose that's *my* fault?" Pippa said, defensively. They were both hotheads, but she could win the title for the top hothead right now.

He dropped her hand. "Good God, woman. You're the one who's jacked me around with all your damn Christmas schemes." He'd flipped the switch to angry now, too. "Tell the McDonnell it's now or never. I can't hold Miranda off any longer."

Pippa had a vision of her father being trapped in Miranda's net. She slammed her hands on her hips. "Keep Miranda away from my da. I'll not have her upsetting him. *Bluidy she-devil.*"

Max didn't back down either, glaring at her.

She would show him who held all the power now. "And secondly, *Yank*, watch how you speak to me." She stepped into his personal space and gave him her best Alistair stare. "My da has nothing to do with the deal or the factory anymore. I'm the one ye'll be negotiating with from here on out."

That got him looking like a cod with his mouth hanging open.

She delivered the final blow. "I'm *the McDonnell* now."

Chapter Twelve

Max stood there stupidly, trying to process what Pippa had just said. He shoved his hat back on his head. "What do you mean you're the McDonnell?" He shouldn't have been surprised—Pippa was a born leader, a warrior through and through. *Which was sexy as hell.*

He didn't wait for her answer, but nodded in her direction. "If you're the McDonnell, then you're going to have to throw Miranda a bone. Invite her back to the factory. Flash the shutoff valve patents in her face. Promise to make up your damned mind soon about the partnership!"

Pippa glared at him. "Miranda seems to be the only thing on yere mind."

He grabbed Pippa's arms and shook. "Listen. Here's what's going to happen. If you and I don't go over the contract together and hammer out a deal, Miranda or someone worse will take over." Not to mention he'd be fired.

Pippa stared at him as if she hadn't heard.

He needed to make her listen. "I can help you, and the town, but we have to work together—fast."

Pippa undid herself from him. "How do I know I can trust you?"

Max gazed into her eyes, trying to convey the truth. "It's easy. The subsea shutoff valve means the world to me. Everything else is secondary."

She got a funny look on her face, as if his words hurt.

"That's not what I mean." He wasn't sure what he was getting at. "But I promise to make it a good deal, a deal both parties can live with. Your father's valve has to be brought to market."

She glanced in the direction of her cottage. "We'll work at my house."

But at that moment, the guys—Ross, Ramsay, and Abraham—came around the corner, carrying the wood they'd picked up yesterday. Max and Ross had said nothing between them on the ride to and from the mill, only a couple of grunts between men.

"Are ye here to help or not?" Ramsay looked at Max and then at Pippa, as if he might have a clue that something was going on between them. He finally walked toward Quilting Central.

Max turned back to Pippa. "It looks like I can't work on the contract right now." Dammit. He hated this. "But later."

She glared at him. "Make up yere mind, Yank. Either the deal is important, or it isn't."

"I made a commitment. It won't take too long."

"Stop by the house when ye're done then," Pippa said begrudgingly. "We'll get my da to help."

"So not really the new McDonnell then?"

She shot him a hard look. "Make no mistake, I'm the one ye're dealing with."

Max wanted to pull her into his arms and remind her whom she was dealing with, too. He didn't get the chance.

"Today, McKinley." Ross came out of Quilting Central on his way to get more wood.

And Ross was the other subject he wanted to revisit with Pippa. But his phone rang.

Miranda. Her timing was terrible. He shifted away to answer.

Pippa must've guessed, because he caught her eyes rolling heavenward.

"Yes?" he said into his cell.

"Max, I have to fly to London for a few days. When I get back, I expect progress to have been made. Do you understand what I'm saying?"

"Perfectly. Have a safe trip." He hung up.

"Well?" Pippa said.

"It's a reprieve. She'll be gone for a couple of days."

"Do ye need to run and give her a proper send-off?"

Max didn't think. And he didn't check to see if anyone watched either. He slipped his hand around Pippa's neck, pulled her to him and kissed her, hard and thoroughly. It wasn't friendly, but it should send the message loud and clear. "Give it a rest, Pippa."

She looked dazed and he wanted to do it again, just to keep that softness and wonder on her face. He started to lean in for another go, but the guys came back with their next load. He'd almost given them a hell of a show.

Max joined the men. But he couldn't help glancing down the boardwalk while Pippa marched off.

That woman was a handful. And he couldn't wait to wrestle with her again.

By the time they'd unloaded the truck, framed up the

stage, and did another huge list of chores for Deydie, it was late afternoon. So much for telling Pippa he wouldn't be long.

Outside, the wind had picked up, and the sea had turned angrier in the last few hours. Waves splashed violently against the thin retaining wall that also served as the walkway, making the trek to Pippa's house slick and dangerous.

She opened the door immediately when he knocked.

He put his hand up. "Don't lecture. Deydie put us to work. Every time I tried to make a getaway, she threatened me with her broom."

"Let's see Da and get down to business." Pippa grabbed his arm and dragged him to the darkened den.

"Da? Are ye awake?"

"I'm tired, daughter. Let me rest."

Pippa turned on the light. Max thought the McDonnell looked frail and thoroughly exhausted.

"I've brought Max. All three of us are going to work on the contract together."

"Nay. You two do it."

"But, Da, I need yere help. Wouldn't it be better to have two Gandiegowans working on it instead of one?"

Her father waved his hand at her dismissively. "Nay. Max can help ye." The older man seemed spent. "Do it somewhere else. I need my peace and quiet."

"But, Da—"

"Leave me."

Pippa seemed to shrink. "I'll call Freda and have her come over."

The McDonnell jerked. "No!" He was definitely

struggling with tamping down his emotions, but finally did. "I'm not in the mood for company."

Pippa leaned down and kissed his head. "I made yere supper. I'll leave it on the tray here beside ye."

The McDonnell nodded, defeated.

While Max gathered their coats, Pippa delivered the promised tray. He heard a few more words between them, saw the light go out in the den, and then she appeared, a look of pained confusion on her face.

"Is everything all right?" Max helped her on with her coat.

She shook her head, exactly like her father had.

Max wrapped his arm around her shoulders and for a moment, she laid her head on his chest. But it didn't last.

"We better get to work." She grabbed her messenger bag and they headed out.

If he had thought the walkway dangerous before, now it was almost impassable. The sea was brutal, water up to the edge, with waves crashing against the house fronts.

She pulled him behind the cottage. "We'll have to take the back walk."

The path hugged the foot of the bluff. As they trudged past Thistle Glen Lodge, he wondered if Miranda had made it out of town before the storm had gotten so bad. He hoped so. He needed her gone so he and Pippa could hash things out.

"A storm's brewing," Pippa hollered above the wind and the crashing waves. "A nasty one."

"I think it's already here." Max couldn't imagine it getting much worse.

"Hold on to me and we'll get to the pub fine."

"I assumed we were going to the factory."

"Nay. I want to stay close in case Da needs me. Besides, ye never know. We don't want to get iced in or snowed in at the factory."

"But we won't be able to get anything done at the pub. It's too noisy."

"No one will be there. The Fisherman closes during bad weather."

"Really? I pictured Scots gathered around the bar during a hurricane, singing bawdy songs."

"We're a smart people. We've found that rough seas and whisky don't mix."

"I see what you mean." He glanced out at the turbulent water, which looked as if it might devour the village whole. Then Max slipped.

Pippa caught him around the waist. "Och, it's only wee waves now."

"Wee?" he said incredulously, still holding on to her.

"The big ones will come. I plan to be tucked safely in at the pub with a cup of cocoa in my hands by then."

Max thought about the last promise of hot cocoa at the pub—how it had led to kisses and to nearly doing the deed before they were interrupted. Sadly, there was no chance of a repeat this time; they had a contract to negotiate.

Once they made it to The Fisherman, they went to the kitchen to start the kettle. He carried their mugs to a table, expecting they'd work downstairs.

"Nay. We'll stay warmer upstairs in yere room. Smaller space to heat," she explained.

She carried the contract while he transported their tray of drinks. As she spread the contract across the bed, he ran back downstairs and retrieved another chair. The wind howled louder outside as they began to sift through the contract together.

After Max's first read-through, he stood up and paced. "My God. No wonder Miranda didn't want me to see this. The potholes set for NSV are everywhere. One misstep on NSV's part and the patents belong to MTech."

Pippa gave him a pen and they both started marking up the contract. While the wind, sleet, and waves battered the village outside, the two of them were cozy in his room. They combed through the pages, fixing every problem, arguing half the time about the details, and then finally compromising. Every time he looked at her, she was smiling back, both of them reveling in the challenge of making a good deal. He really enjoyed working with her. In the wee hours of the morning, they sat back. They had done all they could do.

Max stacked the pages on the little side table. "Well?"

Pippa stood and hugged him. "Thank you. I couldn't have done this without yere help. NSV can live with this revised contract, and MTech would be bluidy fools not to accept it."

She let go of him, but he pulled her back in for a kiss. The kiss should've been innocent, a small peck for a job well done. But once his lips met hers, hormones flooded his system, and Boy Scout Max had left the building. *To hell with keeping a professional distance.* The Max who wanted Pippa more than life itself was present and accounted for. He took a quick inventory—or the best he could with no blood left in his brain as it had gone south—and he felt confident that they could fool around as long as he didn't take it too far. Everything felt right about this moment. Especially the woman in his arms.

By the way she slipped her hands under his shirt, running them up and down, he knew without a doubt that she wanted him, too.

"God, Pippa," he groaned.

"It is heavenly," she said breathlessly between kisses on his neck.

He wanted her so much. He wrapped his hands in her hair, tugged gently, and maneuvered her lips back to his. He slipped his hands under her sweater and up her back, lingering on her bra clasp. Pippa broke the kiss and surprised him by pulling his shirt over his head.

She leaned back for a moment, examining him. "Ah, Yank, ye are a pretty one." She put a hand on his chest and then kissed it as if his pecs were to be cherished. "I could look at you all day and night except I wouldn't be able to keep my hands off of ye."

"Me neither." He wrapped his arms around her and indulged himself further.

As they kissed, their clothes got in the way—blouse, bra, pants, panties and boxers became scattered casualties at their feet. She was so beautiful. All the while, he convinced himself he would stop before things got out of hand.

She pulled him down on the bed, and all seemed right as he lay on top of her. He kissed her tenderly, lovingly . . . and stretched out like this, he suddenly felt unclear what his resolve had been all about. As she kissed him back, she wrapped her hand around him intimately and guided him in.

It felt so freaking good! At that moment he could've

died a happy man. Then he remembered one important detail. He started to pull out. "Condom."

She gripped his hips and yanked him closer. "If ye stop now, I'll . . . I'll run ye through with my grandda's claymore."

Oh, to hell with it. Just this once . . . and like that, his common sense was history. They made love without reservation on his twin-size bed with the lights on, not worrying about being heard above the storm outside. The way she gazed into his eyes before kissing him, the way they fit perfectly together . . . it was more than he'd ever bargained for in sex. But it was more than sex. It was a coupling and he knew it. The way she loved him back, he was sure that she knew it, too. With all these crazy emotions swirling through him, when he came, it was powerful. And to have her under him, calling out his name when she came undone, made everything perfect in the world.

When it was over, he shifted so she lay in his arms, sprawled across his chest. They were completely content, enjoying the hazy wonderfulness produced by magical sex. He kissed her hair.

"Wow," she said. "I didn't know it could be like that."

"I feel the same," he admitted. He'd had his fair share of good times in the sack, but nothing like Pippa had ever happened to him. She was exquisite. Everything a guy could ever want.

She ran her hand down his chest. "But I think we need another data point to see if that was an anomaly."

He laughed, stroking her hair out of her face. "So what you're saying is that together, we make a fine-tuned machine?"

She lifted her head and batted her eyelashes. "Is that hot or what?"

He nuzzled her neck, getting hard again. "You're such an engineer. And the biggest turn-on." He started to roll on top of her but she stopped him.

"Sorry, mister. I'm driving this time."

She took charge of his body, and he was so consumed that when he came, he didn't care if her kinsmen were downstairs or not.

Afterward, as they lay quietly, he became aware of how the storm had kicked up, the wind's wailing intensifying.

He couldn't stop caressing her, running his hands up and down her arms. "Do you hear that?"

"Aye," she said. "I guess ye're stuck with me until it's over."

"I can think of worse ways to while away the rest of the night." Then a thought hit him. "What about your father? Will he worry?"

"No. I'm sure he's sleeping, and he knows we're working," she added. "Why don't you get yere pretty arse up and warm the shower water for us."

"Oh?" Max said. "This night just keeps getting better and better."

"Aye. Grab some candles from the bedside table while you're at it. In case the lights go out." She smiled impishly. "I want to inspect that gorgeous body of yours from top to bottom." She gave him a wicked grin. "Starting on my knees."

Chapter Thirteen

Pippa woke in the morning with Max wrapped around her, a woman thoroughly spooned, a couple of cozy sardines in the little bed. She was sore in places she'd never been sore before. But in a good way. She'd been well loved last night and in the end, he'd been the one on his knees in the shower, making her see stars. It was the most delicious night of her life.

She should feel guilty about it but there was nothing wrong with indulging herself. Especially since she'd gone into it with her eyes wide-open. She was no longer the naive college freshman. And it'd been forever since she'd gone to bed with someone.

The only thing that did trouble her was the fact that they hadn't gotten around to using protection. During the heat of the moment, it hadn't seemed important. But, now . . .

She put it out of her mind. People had sex all the time and didn't get pregnant. She'd never been careless before and would never be again. No matter how tempting Max was, she would make sure that he was suited up properly whenever they made love for the short time he was here.

A pang hit her chest—something to do with him leaving—but she refused to acknowledge it.

Max kissed the top of her head. "Morning," he said huskily.

"Morning." She stretched, accidentally hitting him in the chin. "As wonderful as this is, I can't laze around all day. I've got to get to the factory."

He nibbled at her neck and pulled her back to him. "Play hooky."

"I can't." She could feel him getting hard and it thrilled her. Longing jolted through her veins, as if her nerve endings had downed a shot of espresso. Maybe she couldn't skip work, but that didn't mean she couldn't make him suffer a little. She rocked her bum against his groin just for fun.

He moaned and rolled on top of her, his arms outstretched so he wouldn't crush her. "You shouldn't mess with the bull unless you want the horn," he teased.

"Sir Bull, I'm sore. And late." She wanted to bask in the playfulness they'd enjoyed all night, but it was the light of day. And she was starting to see things more clearly. "I'm sorry. I have to get out of here."

"I'm sorry, too." He lifted a hand so she could scoot out from underneath him.

When she rolled from the bed and stood, she looked back. A blanket of coolness came over her and she shivered—was it from the lack of his body heat . . . or could it be regret?

A worried frown crossed his face as if he was feeling the same thing. "We both better get ready for work. We should probably take one more look at the contract in the light of day, before it gets faxed off to MTech." He sat up, looking perplexed. He pointed to the space between them. "Are you all right?"

But it seemed that he was really asking if *they* were all right. She couldn't address that right now. Relationships were tricky things, even casual ones like theirs. And her track record for taking up with two-timing scoundrels was uncanny.

"Grand," she finally answered, sounding as enthusiastic as if she was signing off on a new sidewalk for the factory.

He put his feet over the side of the bed and pulled the sheet over his midsection as he reached for his boxers.

Awkwardness like a thick fog rolled in and filled the room. What they'd done for the past six hours was irresponsible. Her emotions were turning rawer by the moment, her feelings too new and close to the surface to be comfortable. She wanted to crawl back into his arms to make it go away.

"I better contact Miranda and let her know what's going on," he said as if to himself.

It was the wrong thing to say. Pippa's anger flared. "Feeling guilty for stepping out on her?"

"Pippa, dammit, you have it all wrong." He pulled on his boxers and reached for her. Maybe to shake her.

She scooted back toward the opposite wall.

"You're being irrational."

Maybe. And she hated that he could think straight at a time like this. She was nothing but crazy emotions. But she found some harsh words to bolster herself up.

"Yank, no need to run and confess to Miranda what ye did last night. We were just passing time until the storm let up."

He stepped nearer. "I won't let you lie to me *or yourself* like that. Last night was . . . was . . ."

She wanted to finish the sentence for him.

Last night was magical.

The best sex I've ever had.

I never want to be another night without you in my bed.

She said none of it. It was stupid to even think. They had been nothing more than a couple of adults having a really good time. She found her underwear and shifted away while she slipped them on. She hadn't been embarrassed by her nudity until now. She grabbed the rest of her clothes—coat, too—and hurried out the door and down the hall to the loo.

She made a plan. She'd head home. She'd dress for work. She would forget that she'd ever had this slipup in the little room over the pub. It wasn't her worst indiscretion, or maybe it was. She shook her head at her stupidity. And also for other things, like blowing off the importance of birth control in the heat of the moment. Max . . . he was the only answer she could come up with. He had a way of making her forget herself.

She opened the loo door and stopped short. Max blocked the doorway with his bare chest, wearing nothing else but his jeans. She had the terrible urge to rub herself up against him like some feline in heat.

He'd just proved her point, and she wouldn't listen to her reckless hormones anymore.

"Move," she said. "I've got to go."

Downstairs the door to the pub opened and slammed shut.

"Yank?" Deydie hollered. "Are ye here? Bethia and I

came by to see if ye'd survived the storm. We've brought yere breakfast."

"God, no," Pippa whispered. "They can't find me here."

Too late.

"Who've ye got up there with ye?" Deydie hollered.

Weren't old people supposed to be hard of hearing?

Max shrugged. "I'll be right down. I'm not decent." He brushed Pippa's hair away from her face. "You do what you want to do."

He pivoted and went back to his room.

Pippa wondered why in the world the upstairs to the pub didn't have a separate entrance. She had no way out.

When Max reappeared, shirted and shoed, he didn't glance in her direction as he made his way down the stairs. "Smells good."

But when he hit the bottom step, Pippa could hear Deydie light into him. "Ye've got that woman, Miranda, up there, don't ye? I thought she left town yesterday, but it seems you stashed her in your little hidey-hole so ye could have yere way with her. It ain't right, Yank. She's all wrong for ye. Ye need to quit listening to yere pecker."

Pippa pushed away from the doorway, grabbed the contract from the room as her prop, and went to do the honorable thing—save Max from the women of Gandie-gow.

Once she got downstairs, Bethia saw her first. "Oh."

Deydie glowered at her. "Och, Pippa, what would Ross say?"

Pippa held up the contract. "We were working on the deal between NSV and MTech. We just finished. We're all done." She gave Max a hard look that said she meant it. *We are done.*

Deydie nodded toward her. "And that love bite on yere neck?"

Bethia touched Deydie's arm to quiet her. "Max, we came by for another reason, besides checking on you. Can ye come to Quilting Central later? We're in need of yere help."

He picked up a scone. "I'll be there shortly."

Pippa avoided eye contact with Max and the two quilting ladies as she slipped on her coat. "I better get going." She held the contract up to accentuate her rush.

She fled for the door. Once outside, she breathed a sigh of relief. Everything was going to be okay. She might have been found out, but she'd gotten off easier than expected.

Max watched Pippa's backside as she hustled out the door. It was a damned sexy backside. He'd loved having it pulled up against him this morning.

Deydie made a guttural noise, but Bethia pulled her toward the door.

"We'll leave ye to eat yere breakfast," Bethia said kindly. "But we'll see you soon?"

"Yes." Hell, he had nothing else to do.

The women left and he was alone. Maybe Pippa believed it was over, but she was mistaken. They were just getting started.

The thought hit him like a freight train. Yes, they were *just getting started*, because they were perfect together. He was as certain of this as the tide coming in.

He left The Fisherman and headed to Quilting Central. The damage from last night's storm was evident up and down the boardwalk. A good portion of the garlands hanging on the cottages and businesses had been ripped down. Funny, while the storm had been raging, he'd been at peace with Pippa in his arms. Now, looking out at the calm, almost glassy ocean, everything was unsettled. Even though he knew Pippa would be back in his bed, she'd been damned bristly this morning. How was he going to get her underneath him again?

Deydie hollered to him from outside Quilting Central. "Max, get your arse over here and help me get this garland back up."

He shook his head as he strolled toward her, remembering his first encounter with the old matriarch. "You really know how to charm a guy." When he reached her, he gave her a formal bow. "At your service, madam."

She gave him a hard stare. "Your devil's tongue won't bewitch *me*. And don't think that I've forgotten about ye having Pippa at the pub either. Now grab the other end of this garland, Mr. Christmas, and put it back in place."

"Good grief," he muttered at his nickname.

She put her ham-sized hands on her hips.

"Yes, ma'am," he intoned.

"That's better. If you mind yere p's and q's, ye can stay for lunch after ye get yere chores done for me and Bethia."

Lucky me. He was going to pay for being alone with Pippa at the pub. But really, he didn't mind. He liked the quilting ladies.

All morning they kept him so busy, he didn't have time to worry over NSV's chief engineer . . . much.

For lunch, Deydie fixed him a plate of chicken and dumplings and brought it to one of the little café tables. "Get over here and eat. Ye need to keep up yere strength."

"More things for me to do later?" he asked.

"We'll see." She gave him a funny look, as if she knew something he didn't.

While Max ate his chicken and dumplings, Deydie slipped out the front door, dragging Bethia with her.

"What is it?" Bethia whispered. "Ye're yanking me old arms from their sockets."

"We're off to see the McDonnell."

Bethia glanced back at Quilting Central. "Were we on the list to get him his lunch? His pills won't be due for another two hours."

"We need to see him while Pippa's still at work," Deydie said.

"What for?"

"You know." Deydie didn't enjoy being the bearer of bad news, but it seemed to fall to her more times than it did to others.

Bethia chewed her lip. "Are ye sure this is a good idea? Some might say we're overstepping our bounds."

"Good Lord, this isn't some metropolis like Inverness where people don't watch out for one another. We're Gandiegow. We take care of our own."

They hurried down the boardwalk to the house with the red roof and the green door. They didn't knock, knowing the McDonnell wouldn't be able to answer anyway.

Unfortunately, they came face-to-face with Pippa.

Deydie put her hands on her hips. "What are you doing home?"

Pippa frowned right back. "Lunch. And I live here. Why are ye here?"

"Don't be cheeky," Bethia chided gently.

"I came home to check on Da," Pippa said. "He hasn't been himself."

Bethia swiveled back to Deydie, her old friend touching her arm. "Maybe this isn't a good time."

"No. We'll talk to the McDonnell." Deydie pointed a hard finger at the lass. "And it won't hurt for ye to hear the truth of it. But not a word from ye."

"What—" Pippa said.

"Not a word."

They walked into the den where the McDonnell sat in his wheelchair. He frowned, looking disappointed, like he expected someone else.

"Has Freda been by?" Pippa asked.

Deydie fumed. She'd told the lass to be quiet.

The McDonnell didn't answer his daughter but looked away.

Deydie nudged Pippa to the side so she could come fully into the room. "I said ye could stay, but we're doing the talking."

"What's this about?" the McDonnell asked.

"It's not exactly a social call," Bethia hedged. "We're here with a suggestion."

"Not exactly a suggestion. More like a warning." Deydie gave Pippa a knowing look. The lass had the good sense to shy away from her hard stare.

The McDonnell's frown grew. "Go on."

"Deydie and I think ye should open your house up to the Yank," Bethia said. She was good at coming up with ways to handle things delicately.

The McDonnell's brows came together. "I asked him before but he declined, said he's happy at the pub."

Deydie barked with derision. "Happy's not the half of it."

The damned girl elbowed her.

Bethia jumped in. Which was best. She could smooth things over better than a hot iron. "We were thinking it would be best if Max stayed here. He could help Pippa with things around the house."

Deydie caught Pippa's eye roll and elbowed her back.

Bethia gave Deydie a look that meant she wanted her to behave herself. After seventy years, Deydie was getting tired of that look. Bethia continued with her reasoning. "Max has proved himself right handy at Quilting Central. Hasn't he, Deydie?"

Deydie raised her eyebrows at the lass. "Pippa thinks he's right handy, too." She wondered if the McDonnell was blind or what. Couldn't he tell that his daughter had lain with the Yank?

"I don't need any help," Pippa complained.

This time Bethia gave her a ye-better-play-along stare.

"Maybe a little," Pippa acquiesced.

Deydie was done pussyfooting around. "That's not the main reason ye need to have the Yank here."

Pippa shook her head *no*. Bethia seemed to have given up.

The McDonnell sighed. "I don't understand. What are ye trying to say?"

"I'm going to speak plainly," Deydie cautioned.

"Don't you always?" the McDonnell said.

"The Yank needs watching."

"Oh, Deydie, Da trusts Max. He took a *reading* on him."

Deydie *tsk*ed. "Reading or no, you better keep that

lad under yere roof so ye can keep an eye on him." She paused to see if she would have to spell it out for him.

Surprisingly, Bethia stepped up. "Gandiegow girls can be a randy lot," she said matter-of-factly. "They get bored during the long winter months."

Deydie plunged back in. "Keeping the Yank here at yere house is the best way to keep Pippa out of his bed."

Pippa gasped and turned as red as Deydie's sugar beets in the heat of summer.

The McDonnell shifted in his wheelchair, turning toward his daughter.

"We don't want any accidents—if ye know what I mean—in case another storm blows in," Deydie finished.

"Ross never needs to know," Bethia added.

The McDonnell went deathly still. "Send Max to me."

"Da, don't—" Pippa cried.

He turned to her with a cold calmness. "Get back to the factory, daughter. My body may be sick and broken but I'll have a word with Max McKinley."

She grabbed her coat and briefcase and stomped out with her face blazing.

Bethia wrung her hands in her apron. "Maybe ye should take a minute to think about this. It can't be good to have yereself so riled."

"Send him to me now!" the McDonnell boomed.

Deydie and Bethia hurried from the house.

Outside, Bethia grabbed Deydie's arm. "Maybe we shouldn't have interfered."

"Nay, it had to be done." But Deydie wasn't exactly happy with how it had gone.

Bethia dropped her arm. "Well, we could've handled it better."

Deydie bobbed her head. "Aye. I should've told him in Gaelic. It might've softened the blow."

Just as Max finished rinsing off his plate, the door to Quilting Central opened and Deydie and Bethia appeared. He hadn't even realized they were gone. The two women came straight for him. Probably with more tasks for him to do. But they looked worried.

"Why the long faces?"

"Ye're needed," Deydie said. "The McDonnell has requested you come to him."

"Sure. Let me get my coat and I'll be off." He turned to leave.

Bethia reached out with a bony hand and held on to his arm. "The McDonnell is known for his temper when he's piqued. Prepare yereself."

"Prepare myself, why?" he asked.

Deydie shot him a hard stare. "He knows about—the storm."

He glanced from one guilty face to another. "What exactly did you two do?" he blurted.

Deydie's sheepish contrition of a moment ago turned to righteous indignation. "Just protecting our own, Yank."

"Ye're in hot water," Bethia confirmed.

"But you two were the ones who put the kettle on to boil." Why would they do this to him? "I thought you liked me. Hell, I've been your free labor since I walked into this godforsaken town."

"Watch yere damned language," Deydie barked.

Max walked out, not feeling like the polite Texas boy he was raised to be.

As he let himself into the McDonnell's house, Max

wondered if the old codger would have a shotgun at the ready. And here they'd been getting along so well.

"Come in the den, Max." The McDonnell sounded as if he had a hell of a lot more energy than when he and Pippa were here yesterday.

An old feeling hit him. As if he'd been caught messing around in the backseat of his ancient Camaro.

He walked in. Perched by the fire, the McDonnell was clearly not well, but he seemed ten feet tall today in his wheelchair.

"Sir?" Max said.

"I'll get right to it. When I asked you to watch after my daughter, I never dreamed you'd do it naked."

Shit.

"What are yere intentions toward Pippa?"

Max flinched at the fastball out of left field. A myriad of answers hit him at once.

My intentions?

How about: It's no one's freaking business.

Or: To wring Deydie's freaking neck.

Even better: Get the freaking MTech contract signed so I can get away from this fishbowl.

My intentions toward Pippa . . . only one: By God, to make her moan again while I'm inside her.

The moment stretched out.

Finally, Max answered, "Respectfully, sir, it's between me and Pippa."

The McDonnell glared at him. "Spoken like a man without a daughter. I will tell you exactly how this is going to play out."

"Play out?"

"First, ye're going to pack your things at the pub."

Was this man running Max out of town?

"Secondly, you'll bring yere things here and move in before Pippa gets home."

What the hell? "Sir?"

"And third, ye will promise to keep your hands off my daughter, or by God . . ."

Max felt dazed. "I don't understand. Why would you want me here?"

"I mean to keep my eye on ye while I make up my mind about what's going to happen next."

That sounded both ominous and intriguing. Max finally nodded to the other man. "All right. I'll stay in your house." He ran a hand through his hair, and couldn't keep from telling the truth. "But I can't promise to stay away from your daughter."

As the door closed behind Max, Lachlan deflated. He'd let Pippa down. He was terrified for his daughter. Look what he'd done to his own Sandra. He'd gotten her in the family way, and not even a year later she was dead, with Pippa only a wee bairn. Now it could happen all over again. He had to put a stop to it. But how?

His inadequacies were adding up.

The factory's financial troubles.

The idiotic accident that left him physically unable to protect his daughter.

The damned bachelor auction. Oh, aye, he'd gotten wind of that, the scheme cooked up by Pippa and the townsfolk to take care of him, because he wasn't man enough to take care of himself. Scots did not take charity, but apparently, he was going to be forced to.

He missed Freda terribly. He was a wretched person

to have yelled at her. And he felt proud of her for staying away. It served him right for being such a bastard. She deserved better than him. She deserved every happiness.

Unfortunately, the thought of Miranda slid in and rattled him more. Had Max seduced Pippa to get a better deal for his company as Miranda had tried to do with him?

And here he'd assured Pippa that Max could be trusted and sent them on their merry way.

Lachlan leaned his head back and closed his eyes. And now, his people-seeing skills were gone, too. He had thought Max was the best of the best.

Lachlan had nothing left. He couldn't even trust himself anymore.

Chapter Fourteen

Max stomped to his rental car, feeling like the rug had been pulled out from under him. He had to talk to Pippa, whether she wanted him to or not. It wouldn't be fair for her to come home from work and find him with his feet propped up, warming himself by the fireplace with a whisky in his hand . . . like he belonged there.

He could've argued with the McDonnell, but it seemed best to have Pippa talk some sense into him.

Max drove straight to the factory and walked in like he owned the place. He didn't greet Bonnie or ask permission to go through the double doors leading into the plant. He just did it.

He ignored the curious looks from the employees as he marched to Pippa's office. Without knocking, he slung the door open and slammed it shut behind him.

Pippa jumped. Her surprised expression transformed into a glare.

The place had been cleared considerably. Pippa had gone on a cleaning jag. Two stacks of files were gone from the floor. She was standing with the third stack at the new filing cabinet by the south wall.

He locked the door. He wanted no interruptions and he wasn't letting Pippa escape this conversation either. He pulled all the shades, too. He wouldn't make it easy for the natives to overhear, though he didn't doubt for a second that everyone in town knew absolutely everything that transpired between them. They certainly all seemed to know about last night. Maybe he should invite them to watch next time!

Pippa dropped her files on the desk. *"Thalla is bheir ort."*

"No," he said firmly "I won't '*get lost.*'"

"How did—"

"Pippa," he cut her off. "I think I know you well enough to have a clue what you're saying. No matter the language." He gave her a pointed look. Half the time while they were making love last night, she'd purred Gaelic approval in his ear. The other half of the time, she issued orders.

"Time for a chat," he said.

"There's nothing to say, Yank. We hooked up. It's over."

"It's not over." A brief thought raced through his mind. *It would never be over between them.*

She got a funny look on her face as though she'd read his thoughts, then washed it off as quickly as it'd come. "I say 'tis over," she hissed.

"Batten down the hatches, lassie, because you're about to be hit with a major storm." He paused, but it wasn't for effect. He was still getting used to the idea himself. "I'm moving into your house for the duration."

She slumped against the cabinet. "My da?" she sighed heavily.

"What?" He stared at her for a long moment. "You knew your father wanted to skin my hide but you didn't have the decency to give me the heads-up? Do you know how humiliating it is to come before the *father tribunal*? I'm not a teenager. I'm thirty-frigging-four!"

"At least you weren't there and witnessed them telling it."

"Deydie and Bethia," they both hissed together.

"Can't you stay in the other quilting dorm?" Apparently Pippa understood that he and she under the same roof would be impossible . . . like putting together lit matches with gasoline and telling them not to ignite.

He raised an eyebrow at her. "That's not the point. Your father is intent on keeping his eye on us. *On me.*"

As if she couldn't help herself, she assessed him from head to toe, glanced at the closed door, then chewed her lip.

"Stop it, Pippa. This is no time for fun and games. We need to figure out how to get out of this mess."

"Oh, I don't know. There might be *some* advantages." Subconsciously, her tongue touched her top lip.

He stepped forward and got in her space. "Don't start anything you're not willing to see through to the end." If she wasn't careful, he'd find interesting ways to use her newly cleaned desk.

She grabbed a manila folder and fanned herself. "I don't know what ye're talking about."

He stepped back, satisfied he'd made his point. "Now, about your dad. Can you convince him to give up this asinine plan?"

Her hackles went up. "Don't speak of my father like that. He's the most levelheaded man I know."

"Then you think it's a good idea for me to sleep in the bedroom next to yours?"

"Of course not."

"Then speak to him. Convince him that if he insists on me staying there, he's basically giving me his blessing to ravish his daughter."

A spark shot through her gaze. It was either satisfaction or desire. Max couldn't tell which. He didn't care. He went on autopilot and took her into his arms. And he didn't wait for permission to kiss the hell out of her.

She pulled him against her and in return, his weight pressed her into the new filing cabinet. It would be so easy to push her skirt up and get some release . . . Next thing he knew, she was unzipping his pants. He couldn't argue with her decisiveness, but . . .

"Tell me what you want, Pippa," he whispered in her ear.

"No," she said breathlessly.

"Say it," he growled.

"Dammit, Max." She pushed desperately at his clothes, trying to get to his skin. Finally, she stilled and looked him square in the face. Her desire was as evident as his hard-on. "I want you," she whispered. "Are you satisfied?"

"Yes." He tugged her back to him, smashing their mouths together while he fumbled to get his wallet out of his back pocket with the condom tucked inside. He was frustrated with her, attracted to her, wanted her . . . and had to have her. He could sense all of the emotions roiling through her as well. She pushed his pants and briefs down, took the condom from him, and suited him up. Without hesitation, she wrapped her legs around him and slid down on him hard. She bit his lip and he groaned, enjoying the delicious pain of it. He hushed her moans with kisses and did his best to keep his own climax from announcing to the factory what was going on behind Pippa's locked door.

When they'd both had their release, he lowered her gently to the floor but held her tight, breathing hard, their foreheads resting together.

He loved the satisfied look still lingering on her face, knowing he was the one who'd put it there. If he stayed at her house, he'd be seeing her like this often.

"We can't seem to control ourselves." He gave a half laugh, but what he was feeling was more serious. "Pippa, I care for—"

She cut him off. "Ye're right, Yank." She pulled her panties up and then pushed down her skirt, all business now. "Something will have to be done. I'll convince my da that you should stay elsewhere."

She had gone aloof on him again, but he understood. Pippa needed to step into Alistair's shoes every now and then to regain the upper hand when she thought she'd lost control.

Max's cell blipped. He checked the text. "Crap."

"What is it?"

"Miranda."

Grenades shot from Pippa's eyes. She pulled away. "She's back already? What does she want? A booty call?"

With his free hand, he cupped Pippa's face and stared into her eyes. "You're the only one I want in my bed. Do you hear me?" It was true. Honest to God true.

She removed his hand.

His cell rang this time.

"Answer it outside. I can't bear to hear you whisper sweet nothings into Miranda's ear."

He righted himself and went to the door, the phone still ringing. "This isn't over, Pippa. Not by a long shot."

As Max walked out, Pippa dropped into her chair. She waited until she knew he was truly gone before letting her head fall on her desk.

"Idiot," she said to herself. Honestly, why couldn't she control herself when she was around Max?

And the jealousy was consuming. Until Max, Pippa had never experienced it before. It felt foreign to be so irrational, so crazy. It left Pippa shaky. But Miranda herself had said she was gunning for them to be a power couple. And Pippa's instincts told her Miranda would use every one of her assets—which were considerable—to get Max.

Pippa sat up. What could she do to keep Miranda away from him? Maybe she should search Google for a flamethrower.

As if the filing cabinet had called out, Pippa's eyes fell on it. A heavenly twirl danced across her stomach and her nethers ached for him again. Damned Yank! What was he doing to her?

Pippa didn't stay long at the factory. She should write herself up for truancy, but she needed to go home and clean up. She grabbed her coat and bag, leaving the building without an explanation to anyone, and headed to her car.

She had to speak with her father alone before Max showed up with his duffel bag and his damned good looks. She'd make her da see reason.

"My father practically forced me into bed with the American," she muttered as snow plastered her face. She got in her vehicle and started it. "If only Da hadn't insisted that I stay in Max's cozy room and care for him while he was sick." Yes, it was all her da's fault.

Carefully, she drove back to town and made her way home. She found her da where she'd left him—in the den. He stared off into space.

"Why aren't you out in the parlor? Didn't Freda show up today?" Pippa was starting to worry. She hadn't seen Freda since their shopping trip.

Da shook his head, the light behind his eyes dimmed.

"Can we talk?" Pippa had so much to say. She needed to talk to him about Max staying here at the house, and how that was impossible. She needed to tell her da about the changes to the contract so he'd stay informed. And maybe, just maybe, Da was finally ready to hear what she had to say on the matter of Ross.

"Nay," her da said. "I'm too tired to talk." He'd been proclaiming that a lot lately.

"May I sit with you for a while?" But she could see the answer before he even said it.

He shook his head. "I need my rest. Turn the light out now."

Tears stung Pippa's eyes. But she did what he asked and left. She hated seeing him like this. His spirit was broken. Pippa was at fault here, but damned Deydie and Bethia should take some of the blame, too. She ran upstairs, cleaned up, and put on jeans and a sweater.

Before she left, she stuck her head in the dark den. "I'm going out for a few minutes."

"Don't be long."

She'd never had a curfew before, but it felt as if at thirty, she had one now. Feeling wrung out, Pippa grabbed her coat and left.

Sure enough, Pippa found Deydie and her minion at Quilting Central. Earlier, she'd been too stunned when the women had ratted her out to her da, but now she was armed with resentment. She went straight to the ladies, cutting to the chase.

"If ye ever tell Da about my comings and goings again, I'll put ye in the factory's metal press and flip the switch."

Bethia frowned, but Deydie cackled.

"Like ye scare us, lassie." Deydie thumped Pippa on the back as though she'd told a bawdy joke. "Ye'd have to catch us first." And she waddled away.

"Well, hell."

Bethia *tsk*ed at her. "We thought we were doing right by ye and Ross."

"And the pickle ye got me in with my da? How was that helping exactly? Max is furious, too." But Pippa couldn't think about him without thinking about the damned filing cabinet, too.

Pippa glanced at Bethia. "Gandiegow needs to leave me in peace and let me handle this thing with Ross by myself."

Bethia wrapped a thin arm around her shoulders. "Nay. Gandiegow is here to guide ye. It's our way." She nodded at the sewing machine Pippa had been using. "While ye're here, lass, ye should put in a little time on yere quilt."

"Aye. The auction." It would be here before she knew it. "I think I will."

Pippa grabbed her project from the cubby and sat at her machine. But instead of working on the quilt, she decided to finish Freda's Christmas present. The pillow wouldn't take long and then she'd get back to the quilt for the auction.

Everything was riding on the auction. Once she fixed her da's health, then she could worry about everything else.

But dread covered Pippa. It might be too late for her father. Until recently, he had remained positive and up-beat. He'd been a pillar of strength for her and for the whole town. But now . . . he looked defeated.

As Freda lay in bed, she stared at her frosted window. She could no more see out than she could make herself get up and get dressed. Since leaving Lachlan a day and a half ago, she hadn't eaten. She'd managed only as far as the loo and then back to bed. Her broken heart left her feeling dull and dead, like the gray of the frost on the window.

She hadn't cried for Lachlan since she was a young girl, but she'd made up for lost time. She was still wearing her new clothes, but now they were twisted around her and rumpled. She grabbed the glass from the little table beside her and drank the last of the water. She crawled out of bed and went into her small bathroom. Unfortunately, she caught a horrible glimpse in the mirror of the person she'd become. Her eyes were a puffy mess. Her mascara made jagged lines down her cheeks and her lip-stick was smeared. Her mother would be ashamed of her if she wasn't dead and buried in the cemetery at the top of the bluff.

Freda had lived her life loving Lachlan McDonnell, sacrificing everything for him, making all her decisions with him in mind. Fifty-nine was pretty late to finally wake up and get a clue. She couldn't go back and change the things she'd done, nor pick up and start over. But she could start living life for herself.

She'd gone to work at NSV as Lachlan's assistant—to be close to him—but along the way she'd fallen in love with the business. And she was good at it. When the stubborn bampot injured himself, she'd left NSV to care for him. But no more. No more putting her own life on hold!

Freda stripped out of her new clothes, upset that she'd allowed her new outfit to be wrinkled on account of a pigheaded man. She would take care of her new clothes. She would take care of herself. And to hell—*her mother wouldn't approve of her swearing either*—with what Lachlan thought.

She suddenly wanted food. She went in the kitchen, pulled out a bannock, and leaned against the counter. Sitting in front of her on the tiny table was the basket that held her English paper piecing project, the quilt she'd started for Pippa long ago. Suddenly she felt the urgent need to get it finished.

But first she would shower. And then she'd start living her life again.

Not the life where she'd devoted herself to Lachlan, like before, but something . . . new.

Max sat in his room over the pub for a long time. No matter where he ended up tonight, he was screwed. He should pack up and relocate to one of the small towns nearby, like Lios or Fairge. But the reality was that Max wanted Pippa in his bed. Whether it was here or there, it made no difference.

Pretty sure he was stuck, he crammed his things in his bag and left. But as he passed Quilting Central, he got a glimpse through the window of Pippa at her sewing machine. NSV's chief engineer had the same effect on him as always—she stole his breath away. He made a detour inside and watched while she worked.

She was focused on chain-stitching pieces together, a technique he'd seen his mother and his sister do.

He sauntered up behind her chair. "What are you working on, roomie?" He was being a smart-ass, but surely she understood why.

She jumped and the not-so-nice-boy-in-him felt satisfied that he'd rattled her.

"What are ye doing here?" she said.

Max took the chair beside hers and pulled it nearer. "I won't just walk into your house and make myself at home. I thought you should be there while I settle into my new residence." And because she was so close, and she was staring at him steadily with her sea-blue eyes, a jet of heat filled his chest. Or maybe it was lower.

He shifted. *No, definitely lower.*

He exhaled. "What do you say? Can you help a cowboy out?"

She barked a laugh. "Ye're as much of a cowboy as I am the quintessential country lass." She turned off her machine. "Aye. I'll help ye get settled." She put her sewing things away and grabbed her coat.

Once he was out of Quilting Central and he had a bit of distance from her, his head cleared a little. "Did you send the contract off to MTech today? Have they responded?"

She cocked her head to the side. "Like ye said, I need to read through our changes one more time. I want to be absolutely sure before we move forward."

"Well, this might hurry you along. Miranda is on her way back. She texted me a while ago. Her business was cut short."

"Can't you tell her to go back to where she came from? That you have this under control?"

"Pippa, that ship has sailed. All the Christmas stuff you involved me in might've been worthwhile, but it took precious time away from working on the deal."

She patted his chest, patronizing him. "Ye should get over whatever qualm ye have with Christmas. It's the most wonderful time of the year."

He stilled her hand, holding it in place over his heart. "You know nothing about it." His tone was dead serious, and captured her attention.

Her eyes implored him. "I can understand anything if ye'd only tell me."

He never talked about it, but suddenly he was talking to *her*.

"I told you about Jake's accident happening on Christmas Eve?"

"Aye."

"But there's more. Much more."

"Go on." She leaned closer as if she really wanted to be there for him.

"When I was fifteen, I still loved the holidays." Max let the words pour from him. He told her about the last time he'd seen his dad, the guilt over blowing him off, and the sense of loss he'd felt ever since.

"I've never told anyone before about how responsible I feel, not even my family, because I was afraid if I talked about it, that I'd relive the pain of losing Dad all over again."

The empathy in her eyes showed such compassion that he knew she understood.

He let go of her hand, feeling spent. "The worst part is, I didn't get a chance to tell my dad I was sorry."

She left her one hand over his heart and wrapped the other arm around his waist. She spoke into his chest. "I can't imagine what you went through. I don't know what I would do without my da." She kissed his chest as though trying to heal the pain in his heart. "Here's what I know. You loved yere da, and I'm sure he knew it. I would bet anything he understood that teenage boys need to hang out with their friends." She rubbed his back. "Yere da, after all, was a boy once himself."

Her words soothed him from the inside out. The weight wasn't completely lifted, but shifted off his chest enough to where he could breathe without it hurting so much.

Before he could thank Pippa, the door to Quilting Central opened. Deydie and Moira walked out and stopped abruptly, as if a selkie sat at the railing where he and Pippa stood. Deydie frowned, and Moira hid the first smile that he'd seen from her.

"What are ye doing there, Pippa?" Deydie barked. "I thought I made myself clear earlier." The old woman glanced at the door of Quilting Central as if she might go back in and get her broom.

Pippa opened her mouth, and Max smiled. He was pretty sure the words that were going to fly weren't going to be pleasant. But Moira latched onto Deydie's arm first.

"We need to hurry to my house. I promised Glenna that you, me, and Mattie were going to make cookies to put in the freezer for the going-away party."

Deydie glowered at Moira and then pointed at Pippa. "Watch yereself, girl."

Pippa pulled away. They waited until Moira and Deydie were out of sight.

He felt jagged, raw, but better. "We should get going."

Back at the house, they peeked in on the McDonnell, but he wasn't awake.

She pointed to the steps. "Take your things upstairs to Da's room. You'll be able to figure out which one."

"The one without stuffed animals?"

"Very cheeky."

As he started up the stairs, the front door opened. Maggie, who was married to Ross's brother John, was standing there with a roasting pan covered in foil. She looked from Max to Pippa, and frowned.

"What is *he* doing here?"

Great. Just what I need. Max came back down to stand with Pippa. "Apparently, I live here for now."

Maggie made a guttural noise and glared at both of them. "Does Ross know?"

Pippa rolled her eyes. "Nay. But I'm sure ye'll fill him in. Neither Max nor I are happy about it, Maggie, so ye can stop with the attitude. The McDonnell decreed it."

But when she said *the McDonnell*, Max knew she was remembering she was the McDonnell now.

From the den, the man in question cleared his throat. "Is something going on?"

Pippa shot Maggie a look, but spoke to her father. "Maggie stopped by with some dinner and was just leaving." Pippa took the pan. "Thank you."

Maggie huffed out. Max figured there'd be hell to pay. He just didn't know who was going to get the brunt of it—Pippa, him, or Ross.

Max took the stairs while Pippa carried the pan into the kitchen. How in the world did he ever get wrangled up in this mess? He certainly hadn't anticipated any of this: getting trapped in Gandiegow's gossip mill, being bossed around by a large Scotsman, but only after being nearly caught wrapped up in the sheets with his beautiful daughter.

At the top of the stairs there were three doors. One led to the bathroom, the second to the McDonnell's room, and the third to Pippa's. He stepped into her room and looked around. She had a tool kit and a half-fixed broken fan on her desk. A black dress hung on a hanger looped over the closet door. And a stack of folded laundry was sitting on the bed with colorful panties lying on top. He picked up one of the lacy bits and examined it. Last night, they'd been in such a hurry to get naked, he hadn't paid attention to what she wore.

"They won't fit ye." She stood in the doorway with one raised eyebrow. "Does this look like my da's room?"

"I got lost," he deadpanned. He picked up another of her panties and held it out to her. "Care to model these for me?"

"Nay. Dinner's waiting for ye in the kitchen."

It was a bad idea to get too domestic. He shook his

head. "I can't. I'm meeting Miranda at the pub. She should be back by now and I'm supposed to give her an update on what we accomplished."

"Simultaneous climax?" Pippa asked. "I didn't think ye were the type of lad to kiss and tell."

Pippa was messing with him and he wasn't having it.

Yes, they'd shared a moment outside Quilting Central and connected on a deeper level, but that didn't change anything. It was a bad idea to set up camp in the bedroom next to hers. A terrible idea. He stared down at her panties still in his hand. He wanted nothing more than to spread her on top of her unmade bed and have her pleading for him to give her more. It took everything in him to drop her underwear back on the pile and walk out.

He opened the other bedroom door and set his bag inside. When he turned around, Pippa still stood in her doorway, pinning him with a glare.

"That's it?" she said. "Ye've got nothing else to say?"

He gave her a determined smile. "Yes. Don't wait up." And he forced himself to walk down the stairs and out the front door.

Pippa stomped downstairs and went to the kitchen. She needed to make a tray for her da. He needed to take his pills. *Then I need to call Emma and have my head examined.*

When she got to the den with her father's dinner, she switched the light on.

"What's all the ruckus about?" her da asked.

"Max moved in."

"Good." Da leaned to look around her, wincing with

the movement. "Where is he now? He's having dinner with us, isn't he?"

Pippa rolled her eyes. "He's off to the pub."

"To see Miranda?" It was the first time her da had actually used her name.

"Aye. I don't trust her, Da." Pippa couldn't tell him, for many reasons, about her crazy jealousy.

The McDonnell assessed her for a long minute and then cleared his throat. "Daughter? Didn't ye say that ye had a shift tonight at the pub?"

"Nay. That's tomorrow night."

"No, I believe it's tonight," he insisted.

Pippa turned toward him. "But—"

"If I were you," he said. "I think I'd show up at the pub anyway. Sooner rather than later."

"Da, are you ordering me to go to the pub tonight?" she asked anxiously.

"I wouldn't dream of telling a grown woman what to do."

She gave him a kiss on the cheek. "You're the best man I know."

He smiled, and for a brief moment, he looked like his old self. "Aye. Now, get on with ye."

Pippa stopped in mid-flee. "Is Freda coming over to play canasta tonight?"

He turned away. "She's busy."

"I'll call her," Pippa said. "I don't want ye left alone."

"I'm a grown man myself. I need my peace and quiet."

"But Freda—"

He shifted his gaze away from Pippa. "Freda won't be back."

"But Da—"

"Leave an old man alone. Go on now. I need ye to watch out for the Yank, because I'm not there to do it."

She knew he was conflicted—a pair of lines wedged between his eyebrows. Sending her to watch out for Max was like having a mouse guard the cheddar.

"If ye're sure."

When he nodded, she grabbed her coat. Da would have to be okay for a few hours. Pippa had one goal tonight. Keep Miranda from getting her hooks in Max again.

Chapter Fifteen

When Pippa got to the pub, she joined Bonnie behind the bar while scanning the room.

Bonnie sidled up beside her. "What are you doing here? Tonight's my night. Did ye forget?"

"Nay. Just came in to keep my eye on things." Pippa located Max at the back booth, alone, with a shot of whisky. "You go on home. I've got this."

Bonnie eyed her and where she was looking. She grabbed a rag and wiped down the bar. "Something tells me I better stay."

Just as Pippa was relaxing, thinking maybe Max had fibbed about meeting with Miranda, *Herself* walked into the pub. Her gaze fell on Max as a slow smile covered her face. It was a scheming smile if Pippa had ever seen one. Instead of Miranda attacking her prey, she headed to the bar first.

"My, my," the woman said. "Here again?"

Pippa wanted to scratch her eyes out. "What can I get for ye? Another ale?" *A pint of poison?*

"For you to stay behind the bar this time. Max and I

have business to discuss and I don't want you horning in like you did last time."

"My da sent me to watch out for him tonight." Pippa didn't know why she'd admitted that, except maybe to warn Miranda off.

Miranda surprised her by laughing. *"Lachlan."* She purred his name. "Your father, my dear girl, is one hell of a man."

Pippa went cold with dread. "What are ye talking about?"

She laughed again heartedly. "Oh, he didn't tell you?" She *tsk*ed. "Maybe it was supposed to be a secret. But alas, I've let the cat out of the bag."

Pippa froze. She didn't want to hear any more.

Miranda had no mercy. "You know, MTech sent me to meet with Lachlan in Edinburgh. I recall that it was after you and he had lunch at a café with a strange name. Oh, now I remember, The Elephant House."

Where Harry Potter was written. Pippa had had lunch with Da there about a year ago, when he was in town on business. She hadn't asked him about it, more interested in telling him how her job was going than what was happening with NSV.

Miranda ran her index finger along the bar. "We had dinner and went back to my room. It was a hell of a night. Your father is a skilled lover. One of the best that I've ever had." She gazed back at Max deliberately as if to telegraph that Max was a skilled lover, too.

But Pippa couldn't wrap her mind around the new information: *My father slept with Miranda?*

Max watched them and looked concerned.

"How do I know ye're not making all this up?"

Miranda laid her money on the bar. "Ask your father. Better yet, take me to him; I'd like to be there when you do."

"No!" Pippa's hand closed around a bottle of whisky and she squeezed. "What do you want? Why are you telling me this?"

"It's just a friendly warning. Max and I do business the same way. We'll do anything to make the deal."

Bam. The punch line. Pippa's heart lost several beats. It was true. The only thing Max cared about was the deal. He'd pretty much said so. He'd do anything to have the subsea shutoff valve.

Looking increasingly concerned, Max stood. Pippa's breath hitched—from pain or from some perverse sexual attraction to the enemy, she didn't know.

He scanned her face. Then his eyes shifted to Miranda. He stalked over to them, but spoke to Pippa. "What's going on here?"

Miranda slid her hand down Max's arm. "Girl talk. You wouldn't understand."

"Pippa, are you all right?" He reached out to her.

But Pippa jerked away, knocking the whisky bottle over. She caught it before it shattered on the floor. "I have to get home. I have to see to my da." She had her coat and was gone before Max could stop her.

Outside, she could no longer hold back the tears. Her da was the best man she knew. Why then would he let himself get caught up in that Delilah's bed? It was the final blow to what Pippa believed her father to be—a man with good sense.

"Are all men idiots?" she hollered to the wind.

She'd thought her father was the one man in the world she could trust. But lately, she'd uncovered evidence of the opposite. The shape of the factory. Mortgaging the house to make payroll. Sleeping with Miranda, who clearly was bankrupt when it came to moral integrity.

All these years Pippa had believed her da extraordinary. But the rose-colored glasses were off. He was an extremely flawed man.

"He really can't read people," she whispered, wiping away the tears.

He said Max wouldn't hurt any of them. Yet Max had used her to get what he wanted.

"I can't believe I had sex with him."

"What?"

Pippa jumped.

Ross was standing right behind her. "Can I talk to you?"

"Now's not a good time. We can talk tomorrow at the factory." Then Pippa remembered what she and Max had done in her office. "Or we could meet at the restaurant in the morning for tea."

"Maggie cornered me tonight at dinner. Said the Yank had moved in with ye." Ross looked troubled.

Surely he wasn't jealous.

"So?" Pippa challenged. "It was Da's idea. Ye know how he can be when he's made his mind up. There's no changing it."

"But McKinley isn't really what I want to talk about."

"Then what?"

"I think we should stop dancing around the issue and stand up to our obligations for our families' sake. It's time we set a date."

Crap! The universe really had it in for her. She could deal with only one crisis at a time. And she was still reeling over what Miranda had said at the pub. But Pippa was way overdue in telling Ross the truth. She took his arm, ready to steer him away for a talk, but was interrupted.

"Pippa?" Max hurried up to them. "Why did you disappear?" He glanced at her hand wrapped around the other man's arm.

Ross patted her. "I'll leave ye to talk to the Yank and tell him how it's going to be." He walked away without a backward glance.

Max reached out and snagged her upper arm. "What did Miranda do to upset you?"

Pippa pulled away. "Give me some space, Max." Unfortunately, it sounded a little like pleading. She hated coming from a place of weakness. She had been weak for Max almost from the beginning. But no more.

"But what about the contract?" he said.

Aye. The only thing he cared about.

He implored her with his eyes. "It has to be sent in. Miranda said time is running out. We can go over it again together tonight if you like."

"Is that code for more sex? Never mind. I'll take care of the contract. Now leave me be."

His brows furrowed deeper. "Talk to me. What's going on?" He seemed to be remembering everything good that they'd shared. Working on the contract together. Making love. Those moments of having a deep connection. And then he said it.

"What about us?"

"There is no *us*, Max." She couldn't do this anymore. This was good-bye as far as she was concerned. She chewed her lip for only a second before deciding to use Ross as her excuse just one more time. She steadied her gaze on Max and delivered the words that would sever her from this man, now and forever.

"You forget yereself, Yank. I'm engaged."

Max stilled, but she could see the fiery anger building in him. "Since when, Pippa?" The words shot out like missiles. "Since this afternoon when you climbed on top of me and came in my arms?"

Numbness consumed her. She wouldn't think about making love to him, how wonderful it'd been, how reckless. "Go back to the pub, Max. Miranda's waiting."

He glared at her for one more moment, then turned and was gone. Which was good. She needed to find Ross.

She spotted him at the Armstrongs' fishing boat, checking the lines, making sure they were secure.

"Hey."

He glanced up. "All done with the Yank? That was fast."

She was done with him all right, but it hurt too much to voice it. "Can we step aboard for a minute?"

"Sure." Ross must've understood the need for privacy, because he went into the wheelhouse and she joined him there. For a long minute, they stood looking out at the sea.

She'd put this off for so long, she didn't know where to start.

"Spit it out, Pippa." He gave her a brotherly frown, like he'd done a million times before.

She slipped into the captain's chair and folded her hands in her lap, not meeting his gaze. "Ye know, don't you, that we can't do this."

She hadn't been clear, but she'd finally said it, and he knew her meaning. The air hung with renewed stillness. She waited.

Ross took the other chair and collapsed into it. "Gawd, Pippa." But he exhaled as if he'd been holding his breath since the day the fathers had agreed on their nuptials. He shook his head. "Can we really let the town down? The McDonnell? Are ye willing to step out on that frigging ledge?"

She exhaled, too. "Aye. Don't you agree that we care too much about each other to get married, especially when we don't love each other? In that way?"

They'd never dated, never kissed. The thought of kissing Ross made her cringe.

He didn't say anything, but looked like he was thinking the same thing.

"Ross, I've missed our easy friendship. I want it back."

"Aye. Me, too. But what else do ye want?" He was digging.

She spun her chair toward him. "Well, I don't want to marry anyone, if that's what ye're asking."

He lifted an eyebrow. "Not even the Yank?"

"Not even the Yank." Her words tasted like a lie.

Ross looked as if he didn't believe her anyway.

"I told him to leave me alone . . . That you and I were engaged."

Ross's eyebrows crashed together. "Ye're making no sense. Five minutes ago we were engaged, but now we're not?"

She shrugged. "Telling Max that we were seemed easiest."

"So what's going on between you and him?"

She spun her chair back to face forward. "Nothing."

They were quiet for a long time. Finally, Ross broke the silence. "So what do we do now?"

"I'm not sure. I'm not ready to tell everyone that the wedding is off. Are ye?" She ran her hand over the controls. "The truth is that I don't have the bandwidth. Do you mind if we keep this to ourselves for now?"

"Fine by me. The uproar this is going to cause will be quite unpleasant."

"I know."

Even though they'd settled the future between them, the wheelhouse felt the slightest bit awkward. She slipped from her chair, walked over to her lifelong friend, and considered clouting him on the shoulder for old time's sake. Instead, she wrapped her arms around him and hugged him tightly. He seemed taken off guard at first, but then put his arms around her, too.

She grinned into his chest. "If I had to choose one person *not* to marry, ye know, I'd choose you every time."

He shook his head, chuckling deeply, and patted her on the back. "And I'd choose ye, too, Pippa, you goofy lass."

Miranda sipped a bit of ale, pleased with herself. She'd done the little Scottish girl a favor by waking her up to the cold hard facts of business. Sometimes a woman got *used*. Pippa would toughen up after this and not get taken again.

As a bonus, Miranda could have Max.

Sure, Miranda had been looking forward to seeing Lachlan again. In some corner of her mind, she may have imagined they could pick back up where they left off. He was a smart, commanding man, both in bed and in real life. But even if they did hook up, she had no intention of making a life *here*. Max was a much more appropriate choice.

The door to the pub opened and frumpy Freda appeared, planting herself near the entrance, next to an old guy who must be one of the fishermen. Freda's platinum blond hair was gone, replaced with highlights and lowlights, and cropped neatly about her face. Miranda had to admit that her hair was attractive that way.

Freda slipped her coat off and Miranda saw that she was dressed differently, too. She had on a colorful, long-sleeved flowing blouse that was age-appropriate and attractive in a retiree sort of way.

What happened to the makeover I gave her?

Miranda turned away and spoke to the much-endowed barmaid, the one who doubled as the receptionist at NSV. "What's your name?"

The woman came closer. "Bonnie."

"Give me a whisky." Miranda wondered when Max was coming back. She was feeling restless.

Bonnie poured her a finger's worth into a tumbler. "How long are ye in town?"

Miranda wasn't in the habit of talking to barkeeps but she'd already made an exception with Pippa tonight. "As long as it takes."

Bonnie leaned on the bar. "Then ye'll be here for the bachelor's auction?"

"What bachelor's auction?"

Bonnie pulled a flyer off the mirror behind the bar and handed it to her. "It's all in good fun. I've been saving my money for one man in particular." Bonnie nodded toward the entrance.

Max had returned, standing next to Freda, but in deep conversation with the old fisherman.

Certainly the barmaid didn't mean the old man. "McKinley's in the auction?"

"Aye." A hungry gleam filled Bonnie's eyes. "He'll be worth every bit of cash I can pull together. Of course, I won't be the only local lass bidding on Max McKinley. I'm pretty sure Pippa will use her last pound to get him." Bonnie sighed. "But I'm going to at least try."

"What makes you so sure that he's going to do it?" Miranda asked.

"I've seen the list myself. And the pictures, too. Hell, I was there when the pictures were taken." She got a satisfied smile on her face. "Take a look at the Kilts and Quilts blog if ye don't believe me."

At the bottom of the flyer was the address: www.KiltsAndQuilts.com.

"I will," Miranda said.

"Max will be in the McKinley tartan, of course. Deydie has Sophie making it; she's one of our local lasses, who recently married a laird."

"The McKinley tartan?" Miranda asked.

"Deydie has everything organized over at Quilting Central. She's letting us locals cheat a bit. She has swatches of every kilt and the name to go with it so we'll know who we're bidding on. The out-of-towners won't have a clue."

"I don't understand. Why wouldn't you know who you're bidding on?" Miranda asked.

Bonnie laughed. "A curtain will be drawn halfway down, so when our lads come on stage, the only things we'll see are their kilts and their legs. It makes for a bit of fun to auction them off that way. Don't ye think?"

Miranda thought it was asinine. "So where are these swatches exactly?"

Bonnie stopped short and chewed on her lip as if she'd said too much. "Ye're not a local. Deydie did, after all, only want us to know."

"Don't worry," Miranda assured her. "I have nothing nefarious up my sleeve. I just wanted to see the different colors of plaid. I think Scotland's system of the clans is very interesting." What a line she was feeding this woman.

"Bonnie?" a man at the end of the bar called. "I need a refill."

Bonnie looked relieved. "Sorry. Gotta go."

"Fine. Go ahead." Miranda swung back around, sipping her whisky, while eyeing her employee. She was clever enough to find out which tartan Max McKinley was going to wear, all on her own.

Pippa lay awake in her bed, listening, hating herself for waiting for Max to come home. He'd turned out to be a bastard like all the other bastards she'd known over the years. She should thank Miranda for clueing her in. But still, Pippa had her ear tuned to the third step from the top, the one that creaked when stepped upon. She pulled the clock over and gazed at the time. One a.m.

Where was he?

Dread was tucked around her as if it were a quilt. Only a quilt didn't make her queasy.

She couldn't take it anymore. She crawled out of bed

and dressed in jeans, a thick sweater, and warm socks. She had to know. She opened her door quietly and made her way down the steps, skipping the third one from the top. At the front door, she quietly slipped into her boots and snuck out into the night.

She knew what she would find at Thistle Glen Lodge, but knowing didn't stop her. She had to see for herself. When she caught Max in Miranda's bed, then Pippa would truly be able to let him go, once and for all.

Keeping to the shadows, she stole across town, though who would be out at this hour and in this cold weather was beyond her. *Only the completely deranged.* Acid churned in Pippa's stomach, but she moved on.

When she got to the quilting dorm, sure enough, the light was on in the back bedroom. She tried looking in the window, but the double-lined curtains were pulled tight. Pippa went around front and quietly opened the front door and tiptoed inside.

She heard Miranda talking. She inched forward.

"Yes, Roger. Of course, I can cut my vacation short and go to France."

Pippa peeked in the room. Miranda's back was to her and she was packing her suitcase. No one else was there.

"I'll leave in the morning." Miranda hung up and laid her phone on her bed, next to her folded slacks.

Relief swept through Pippa, but other emotions nipped on its heels. *Limbo.* She'd both wanted and not wanted Max to be there. If he'd been there, then she could write him off forever. But now?

She sagged and backed away silently, ashamed for coming. She wasn't the kind of lass to lurk outside of bedrooms and spy.

As she made her way home, the question that had kept her awake came back to her full-force. *Where is Max?*

Max woke on Andrew's sofa with a helluva hangover, a crick in his neck, and the smell of coffee in the air. He wondered if he could lie here forever and not rejoin the human race. He should've found a way to get out of this godforsaken town last night instead of finding Andrew and tying one on. The nice thing about his new friend, he hadn't probed, hadn't asked why Max had near poisoned himself with alcohol.

Max tried rolling to his side, but the pounding in his head stopped him. One thing was for sure, he would do whatever it took to avoid Pippa today. Whatever they'd had—a good time or something more serious—was over. *The end.* The thought made his chest ache.

The Episcopal priest wandered into the tidy living room. "Ye look terrible." He set a mug on the coffee table, and went to stand near the fireplace. He pointed at his cup. "God's brew. Drink up."

"Thanks." Max dropped his feet to the floor and made his way upright, cringing. "And thanks for letting me crash here last night." He picked up the mug and took a sip.

Andrew nodded and drank, too. "What's on yere list for today?"

"Tying up loose ends."

Last night after Pippa had dropped the E-bomb—*engagement*—there was no way he could go back to her house . . . sober, anyway. But then when he was drunk, he knew he couldn't go that way either. This morning, he'd make his way to her house and clear his things out. Move back to the pub—the McDonnell or no. "I better get going." Surely Pippa was at the factory by now. He didn't want to go to her house, but he might as well get it over with. He couldn't feel any worse than he did already.

"If ye're hungry, scones are wrapped in foil on the stove. Help yereself. Stay as long as ye like. I have a visit to make first thing this morning."

Max nodded, but he shouldn't have. Pain ripped through his head.

Andrew said good-bye and left him alone. Max finished his coffee, folded the quilt, and put it at the end of the couch. He found his coat in the hall closet and his boots on the rug by the door.

Surprisingly, the crisp air outside soothed his head. At Pippa's door, he hesitated only a moment before going inside. The house was quiet. He started to peek in on the McDonnell in the den when Pippa appeared at the end of the hall.

She stopped short as if he were an apparition.

He put his hand up. "Don't worry. I'm only here to get my things and then I'll be gone."

Panic filled her face and he didn't know why. She didn't care about him. She was Ross's problem now.

But Max couldn't stand to see her upset. "I'm moving, but only back to the pub."

Relief washed the panic away. But then she schooled her emotions. "I see. What about my da?"

Max walked toward her, speaking more softly. "What about him?"

"He wants ye here."

Max was directly in front of her now. God, he loved

the slew of freckles across her nose. He shifted his eyes to hers. "I'll handle your father." He tried not to think about the consequences, how the MTech deal might be affected if he didn't do exactly as the McDonnell wanted. Would he encourage Pippa to call the whole thing off? But Max had to think about himself, too, and how he would be affected if he stayed.

"Then ye better go speak with him. He should be awake."

But before he could head to the den, he received a text. He glanced at his phone. "Miranda's off to France."

"Good." But Pippa didn't seem surprised by the news.

"MTech has its sights set on a small valve company near Paris." Another company to buy and dismantle.

She headed for the stairs. "Ye go talk to my father. I have to change. I'm needed at the factory." She ran up the steps and out of sight.

Max tapped on the den door and peeked in when he didn't get an answer. The McDonnell sat in his wheelchair staring out the window.

He knocked harder and stepped in. "Morning, sir." This conversation was going to be damned awkward, but by God, he could avoid only one McDonnell at a time. And he needed to set the older man straight.

"McKinley." The McDonnell nodded to the doorway. "She's gone then? I got the feeling she wanted to dodge ye at all costs. Did ye two have a row?"

Yes, we had a row! She freaking wants to marry someone else! Max gave a noncommittal grunt instead and then chose the chair directly across from the McDonnell.

"We need to talk." Gone was the McDonnell's anger of yesterday. He seemed more subdued.

Max schooled his features. "Yes, sir, we do."

"Don't call me *sir*. Call me Lachlan."

Max leaned forward with his elbows on his knees and steepled his fingers, not knowing how to start.

The older man began first. "I wanted to thank ye."

Max jerked upright. "For what?" For making love to his daughter? "I haven't done anything that deserves thanks."

"I know about the auction and why it's taking place." The McDonnell picked up his glass of water and gulped. "Abraham let it slip. But it wasn't until last night that I heard ye were in it, too." The McDonnell looked directly into Max's eyes. "And ye, of all people, didn't have to be part of it."

Max felt uncomfortable, wishing for a way to escape.

The McDonnell raised a hand. "That's all I wanted."

Max understood what the words had cost the McDonnell and he had to say something, even if it was a lie. "I'm glad to do it." And suddenly, Max was surprised that he was. He'd come to care for Pippa's father, actually all the people of Gandiegow. He admired their close-knit community. It was only right to band together with them to help this proud man.

The McDonnell tilted his head to the side. "Ye had something to say as well?"

Might as well get it over with. "Yes, sir. I mean, Lachlan, sir." God, he was fumbling over his words like a scared teenager. "I hope you know that I respect you, but sir, I'm not going to stay here at your house. I can't."

For the moment, the McDonnell lifted his eyebrow as if stronger men wouldn't dare go against him.

"I'm moving back to the room over the pub."

The McDonnell deflated. "I guessed ye would."

Pippa walked into the room. She seemed to take in the scene and glared at Max as if he'd caused more injury to her father. "Da, I'm off. I'll take out the garbage on the way. Mr. McKinley?"

Max exhaled. "Fine. I'm leaving. Good-bye, Lachlan."

Pippa's glare intensified.

Max walked from the room. She waited until they were out the front door before railing on him.

"What did ye do to my da? What did ye say?"

Max wanted nothing more than to pull her into his arms and kiss her until she forgot all about Ross and being engaged. Instead, he reached out and carefully wound her scarf around her neck, knowing exactly how she would react. She stilled. Max had thrown her off guard, but only to prove a point.

"Maybe it's time to admit that Ross isn't the right man for you."

Chapter Sixteen

Over the next week or so, Max saw Pippa, but they didn't speak. He was a freaking saint, giving Pippa the space she'd asked for. Seeing her and not being with her was hell. Maybe he should've gone back to Houston while MTech's legal team and Pippa hashed out the final negotiations. But he didn't want to miss being here if he was needed. But if he'd thought sleeping across town would keep him from agonizing over her, he'd been dead wrong.

He'd seen her at the factory while he helped Taog in the machine shop. He'd caught glimpses of her at the restaurant and around town. Pippa had even ruined church for him, the one place that should be a sanctuary from hurt and pain. But at the Christmas pageant, he'd watched as Pippa sat with Ross and his family. It had been pure torture. Max looked for signs, actions, anything, trying to figure out if Pippa was truly meant for Ross. He saw none of it.

Max trudged into Quilting Central with his borrowed tools, ready to meet up with Abraham Clacher to finish up the stage. But as he made his way to the back, he overheard Bethia talking to Deydie.

"I've handed out the assignments for the big wedding."

Ross and Pippa's wedding?

"Which ones?" Deydie asked.

"Claire will bake the cake. Amy is looking into decorations. Maggie is working on an invitation list."

"Good. Good." Deydie patted her dress pocket. "I have a few chores to hand off meself."

This wasn't the first whisper of something big that was about to happen, but it was the most definitive. He needed out of here. There was only so much a man could take. He crouched down, grabbed a nail, set it, and pounded the hell out of it.

The door to Quilting Central opened, and as his lousy luck would have it, Pippa waltzed in. He stopped and watched as she made her way to her sewing machine across the room.

Abraham cleared his throat.

"Fine," Max groused. He picked up another nail, placed it, and whacked it. He just didn't understand himself. Why did her engagement feel like a betrayal? He'd known from the beginning that Pippa and Ross were promised to each other.

But he knew why. *She told me outright she wasn't going to marry him!* Max grabbed another nail and abused the lumber with his hammer, doing his best to ignore her.

He heard his name. When he looked up, Ailsa and Aileen, the twins, were making their way over. Ailsa handed him a slip of paper.

"What's this?" He opened it. There was an address on the inside.

"Deydie asked us to take care of a few things," she said.

Aileen took over. "We wondered if ye'd be willing to run an errand for us . . . to Inverness."

"It'll be ready when you get there. It's just some fabric we need," Ailsa said.

Max wiped the dust from his jeans. A little road trip might be just what he needed. He looked to Abraham, who was listening.

"Go on, Yank. I can finish this up without ye."

Max put the slip of paper in his pocket. "Sure, ladies. I can pick up the fabric. Is it for the next quilting retreat?"

"Nay, we've made up a design, ye see," Aileen said. "Sister and I like to work on new things."

Ailsa clamped onto his arm excitedly. "We ordered it special. It's the fabric for Pippa's wedding dress."

Bethia was talking to her, but Pippa was only half listening. She was more interested in what Ailsa and Aileen were saying to Max that had him red in the face.

"It's time to get serious, Pippa," Bethia said. "The auction is only days away."

Bethia wasn't the only one to have scolded her in the past week.

"I know." Pippa picked up two more pieces of fabric. Didn't these women know she had a factory to run? And didn't they realize that she'd slept little since Max was no longer her life? And it wasn't the good kind of *not* getting sleep either. Pippa cuddled up with his damned red T-shirt every night as if the man himself was in it.

And every morning, she'd shoved it back under her pillow for safekeeping. Ridiculous, aye, but ridiculous was what she'd become.

She glanced up again at Max, but this time he wasn't clear across the room. He was marching her way, his eyes blazing a hole in her middle. She automatically stood.

He took her hand and slapped a piece of paper in it. "Get it yourself."

She was speechless. Those were the first words he'd said to her since he'd adjusted her scarf that night outside her house.

He stomped away, grabbed his coat off the hook, and stormed out.

Before Bethia could answer, Moira sidled up to Pippa, too. "Freda called, looking for you. Ye're needed at the factory."

Pippa reached for her mobile. The screen was dark. She'd forgotten to charge it last night before falling asleep with Max's red T-shirt.

Pippa turned to Bethia apologetically. "Sorry. I'll get the quilt done. I promise. I only have two more blocks to go."

Moira took the fabric that Pippa had clutched in her other hand and smoothed it out. "Don't worry. I'll work on it while ye're gone. I'll get Amy, Ailsa, and Aileen to help piece it together." Moira picked up the engineering pad beside the sewing machine. "I'll make sure to follow yere pattern and use the right tartan on the right house block."

"But—"

Moira laid a hand on her arm. "'Tis the only way. When it's done, I'll get the quilt top on the longarm machine."

"Are ye sure?" Pippa said to Moira.

"Aye. Now, go."

Pippa put on her coat and slipped out with Max's piece of paper still in her hand. She'd have to ask the twins later if they could tell her what it meant.

As she made her way through town and then to the factory, she wondered where Max had gone off to. When she arrived at NSV, she found Freda in Pippa's office at work at the little café table that they'd reived from Quilting Central. Papers were spread all over the floor.

"What's going on? Is there trouble?" Pippa said.

"Aye, trouble." Freda answered. "I've been going through this notebook I found of the McDonnell's where he kept a list of factory expenses. The man is a brilliant engineer but he doesn't know a thing about running a business. I figured out why NSV is having financial problems."

Pippa leaned over her shoulder, staring at the notebook as well. It felt good to know she wasn't the only one trying to work things out. "What did ye find?"

"The damn bastard—excuse my language—made the company cash poor. The number one mistake made by small businesses."

Pippa was a little stunned. She tried to form the right question for Freda.

"Don't look so shocked. I've been reading books on business, accounting, and finance for several years now. In case I could help yere da out. But the bluidy pig-headed Scot never let anyone look at the books." Freda slammed the notebook shut. "It'll take a month of Sundays, but I'll get this worked out."

"Thank God." It was one less thing for Pippa to do.

Freda still hadn't been back to the house, and neither she nor Da was saying why. Pippa was disappointed; she liked the idea of her da having someone, and she wanted Freda to be happy. But whatever had gone wrong, Freda seemed determined to move forward. Pippa only wished she could find that kind of determination. She had a lot to learn from the woman who had taken care of her for her whole life.

Pippa laid a hand on her shoulder. "Ye're a godsend, Freda. Ye know that, don't ye?"

"Aye. But ye won't think me much an angel after ye review the expense sheet I set on yere desk."

"I'll get right on it." Pippa sat down and pulled the sheet to her, but then stared at the new filing cabinet, remembering.

Freda put down her pen. "What's going on? Ye seem distracted."

"Oh." It was all Max's fault.

Freda still looked on expectantly. She loved her, but Pippa couldn't talk about her troubles. Hell, she couldn't even articulate them to herself intelligently. So instead, she came up with an excuse. "The auction is coming up. There's a lot to do."

Freda stared at her matter-of-factly. "Ye're not fooling me. I hope ye're not fooling yereself either. I've heard the whispers around town. Don't waste yere life doing what others expect of ye. Ye've got to find yere own happiness in this world."

Pippa was taken aback. Quiet Freda had learned to roar like a lion.

"I *have* been living by my own rules." At least until Max had come along. Pippa changed the subject and tried again with Freda. "Tell me what happened with you and Da."

"Nay. Just heed my advice, dear one."

"I will." Pippa wasn't up to sharing the truth . . . that the wedding the town thought would take place would never happen. She should feel good that at least she'd worked it out with Ross. But instead, inexplicable sadness filled every corner of her life. In her heart, in her head, and through her eyes . . . specifically in the direction of the south wall, in the vicinity of the filing cabinet.

Max stretched out on the twin bed with his tablet in hand. Tonight, he was sequestering himself in the room over the pub and not showing up at Cait and Mattie's going-away party. Sure, he liked them, but he'd had enough of seeing Pippa with Ross. Max slid his finger across the screen, ready to use his evening to catch up on trade journals.

A knock sounded at the door.

"It's open," Max hollered.

Andrew stepped in. "Aren't ye ready yet?"

"For what?" Max played dumb and tapped to the next screen.

Andrew snatched Max's coat from the back of the chair and tossed it to him. "Here. We don't want to be late."

"I'm not going," Max said.

The priest folded his hands in front as if he was getting ready to pray, though it didn't match the determination on his face. "Was I there for you when ye needed a friend? Did I let ye brood without asking questions? And did I not open my home to you and let ye sleep it off on my sofa?"

"Seminary teach you the art of guilt?"

"Ye owe me." Andrew looked so miserable.

Apparently he needed reinforcements if he had to be around Moira tonight. It seemed the only job the women of Gandiegow excelled at was making the men miserable. At least these two men anyway.

"I guess I have no choice then." Max stood and slipped on his coat. "You sure don't pull any punches."

"I have to be at the party, and ye're expected there as well."

Max didn't care that several people had ordered him to be there. He wasn't in the habit of being bossed around. Except since he'd arrived in Gandiegow.

"Ready?"

"Aye. As ready as I'll ever be."

They walked the few yards to Dominic and Claire's restaurant, climbed the stairs to the grand dining room on the second floor, and found all of Gandiegow in attendance. Christmas had been scattered about the room by way of green and red plaid bows, garland, and decorated trees in every corner.

Max turned to Andrew. "Are those the Christmas trees from North Sea Valve?"

"Aye. I saw Taog and Murdoch delivering them this morning."

"Father."

"Father."

Ailsa and Aileen were calling after the Episcopal priest.

"You're being summoned," Max said. "I'm going to get something to drink." Something strong. But on his way to the table, he saw Mattie looking at the multi-colored cards in his hands.

"Hey, what's that you have there?" Max asked.

"Party cards," the boy said.

"What are party cards?"

Instead of explaining, Mattie handed them over. They were blue, pink, and green, and there seemed to be talking points printed on them.

"Conversation starters?" Max had read an article once about ways to break the ice at cocktail parties with a list of talking points. Mattie's cards were geared toward kids. *What is your favorite subject in school? What's your favorite color? Who's your favorite character in a book?* "Emma made these for you?"

"Aye. For practice."

Max handed them back. "I get that the blue ones are for boys, the pink ones are for girls. What are the green ones for? Gardeners?"

Mattie laughed. "Adults."

Max pointed to the cards. "Fire away then."

The kid pulled out a green card, but didn't seem to be reading it. "Who do you love most in the world? Who do ye want to marry?"

The question took Max off guard. "Let me see that card."

But Mattie held it to his chest. "Who?"

Max's eyes unwittingly traveled around the room until they fell on Pippa. She stood with Ross, Ramsay, Kit, and Maggie. Kit, the matchmaker, was watching him. Had she put Mattie up to asking him this question?

Max turned back to Mattie. "I love Betty Crocker."

Mattie's face screwed up. "Who's that?"

"She makes the best cakes in the world. Now let's go over to the cake table and get some. Okay?"

Mattie shoved the green card back in his deck and followed Max. But halfway there, Cait called for Mattie to join her and the quilting ladies. Deydie was glued to Cait as if she was her other half. The old woman looked miserable, but seemed to be trying to put a good face on it for everyone. But her sadness was as evident as the Christmas decorations around the room.

Max picked up a piece of cake and headed for a chair to eat it in peace. He'd shoveled in only one bite before Glenna ran over to him.

"Can I speak with you, Mr. Christmas?" Her voice was sweet, but a frown crowded her innocent face.

"What is it, peanut?" This girl was something special. He'd bet she'd be a heartbreaker one of these days.

She climbed up in the chair next to his. "Did ye talk to Santa Claus as I asked? Christmas is almost here, but cousin Moira doesn't seem even the wee-est bit happier." Glenna leaned closer. "I'm afraid."

Max put his plate on the floor and gave her his full attention. "What are you afraid of?"

Glenna shrugged. Her eyes misted up, and though it broke his heart, he prayed the girl wouldn't start crying.

He looked around to see if anyone could help. But it was only the two of them. He tried again. "What's going on?"

She stared at her hands. "Sometimes at night, I hear cousin Moira crying in her room. And it's all my fault."

Shit! He wasn't a therapist! He glanced to see if Emma could help, but she was busy talking to Cait and Mattie.

Max dove in, praying he wouldn't regret this, and that he wouldn't do more harm than good. "Can you tell Mr. Christmas what's all your fault, honey?"

She picked at her sleeve. "Everyone said Father Andrew and cousin Moira were going to get married." She glanced over at Moira standing at the rear of the quilting ladies, which was about the farthest point from Andrew as possible. Glenna faced Max again. "But I think they're not getting married now because of me. Because I'm a burden."

Oh, God. Max ran a hand through his hair. He should not have come here tonight.

Her head dropped and she studied her hands as if the answers were written there. Poor little thing. He understood better than most how easy it was for a kid to assume the blame. For the longest time, he felt responsible for his father's death—if he'd done the right thing, he could've prevented the oil rig from exploding. If only he'd stayed home and worked with his dad in the workshop that one last time. Max wished now he hadn't waited nearly twenty years to talk to someone about it. But he was glad Pippa had gotten him on the right track. Maybe he could help Glenna.

Max took her hand. "Honey, it doesn't work that way. Whatever is going on between Father Andrew and your cousin has nothing to do with you."

She shook her head in silent argument.

He squeezed her hand. "I promise."

She looked up at him a little hopeful but still chewing her lip.

"If I'm wrong, I'll eat Deydie's broom."

That got him a little giggle.

"Come on. Let's get you some cake and punch." Max grabbed his plate, and then pulled her to her feet. He had to find Andrew and make sure he and Moira fixed things—one way or the other—so this sweet little girl didn't feel like crap.

Glenna tugged him to a stop and broke into a smile. "I like ye, Mr. Christmas." She flung herself at him and hugged him tight.

His heart melted. "Mr. Christmas likes you too, peanut. Come on."

He took her to the cake table and left her with Amy, Ailsa, and Aileen.

Max should stay out of it, but there was no way he could. Mr. Christmas was honor bound to get involved. Instead, he barreled toward Andrew, who was standing alone, his eyes fixed on Moira across the room.

Andrew's eyebrows pulled together when he saw Max. "Is everything all right?"

Max pointed to an empty corner. "We need to talk. Privately."

"Sure."

While Max took a second, trying to figure out how to start, Andrew nodded in Moira's direction.

"She's ignoring me again," he said pitifully. "I've racked my brain, analyzed my every word, and I can't figure out what went wrong."

Max glanced heavenward, thankful for the divine intervention. God had just broken the ice for him.

"You need to know what Glenna told me. And then I'm out of it. Do you hear me?"

Andrew stared at him, confused.

"Glenna believes she's the reason Moira has shied away from you. She thinks Moira is worried about saddling you with a ready-made family." Max shared nothing about Moira crying in the night. That was Moira's business.

Andrew looked befuddled, as if he'd lost his place while reading his Bible. "How—"

Max cut him off. "I don't care what you and Moira do at this point moving forward. But I do care about that little girl. Moira being happy is the only thing she wants for Christmas." Man, Max was in deep. "You and Moira need to assure Glenna that whatever screwed-up thing that is going on in your relationship, that it has nothing to do with *her*. She's had enough heartache, don't you think?"

Pippa watched Max with Andrew from across the room, wondering what was going on. By the looks of it, Max was giving the Episcopal priest a sermon.

"Pippa, did ye hear me?" Ailsa said.

"We were wondering if you had anything else for me and sister to do for the auction." Aileen chimed in.

Ross was looking at her kind of funny, too.

Pippa returned her complete focus to the little group around her. "Nay. Everything is ready for tomorrow."

"But if ye need us," Aileen started.

"Ye know where to find us," Ailsa finished.

Pippa reached out to both and gave them a quick hug. "Thank you."

The two sisters said good night and wandered off.

"We need to speak of it, too." Ross shifted so his big body blocked Pippa's view, keeping her from seeing more of Max and what was going on.

She leaned over nonchalantly and saw Andrew's face

turning red. In the background the band was setting up for live music. "Speak of what?"

"Gawd, Pippa," Ross said, exasperated. "Pay attention. The auction. Take me out of it."

She frowned up at him. "Ye know I can't. We advertised a picture of you as being one of the *lusty lads in plaid.*"

Ross flinched when she used the catchphrase. "But people are asking why I'm in the auction when I'm not exactly single. The town seems to think we're getting married any day now. I caught Deydie whispering to Maggie about wedding veils. Do ye think they're throwing us a surprise wedding? And is that even a thing?"

Pippa eyed him. "Och, Ross, ye're just trying to get out of being auctioned off with the rest of the lads."

"Aye. Maybe. But if ye want to wait to tell the town that we've called off the engagement, then what am I supposed to say in the meantime?"

"The truth. Tell 'em that ye're doing your part to help out the McDonnell." Pippa saw Max move away from Andrew. The priest wasn't simmering now, but looked ready to boil over. She watched where his gaze landed—on Moira, and she was headed this way with Kit by her side.

Andrew marched their direction, too. Pippa didn't even get to find out what was on Moira's and Kit's minds before the priest had descended upon them.

"Moira?" Andrew's face was the color of the poppies that grew out front in the flowering boxes in summer. "We need to talk."

Kit quickly placed herself between Andrew and Moira. "We've discussed this. You need to give Moira some space. She'll speak to you when she's ready."

Andrew gritted his teeth. "No, Kit. Moira and I are

going to talk now. *About Glenna.*" He didn't seem to care that he had an audience.

Pippa looked around for Glenna and saw her engrossed in conversation with a group of kids near the band. *Good.*

Kit didn't budge, glaring at Andrew as if he was possessed or something. Pippa had never seen him like this either.

"What about Glenna?" Moira moved to face him.

Kit stepped to the side, but not too far away.

Andrew leaned closer, his anger fading. Now that he had the floor, he looked lost as if he wasn't quite sure what to say. "Put me out of my misery."

Moira stared down at her clutched hands. "I'm trying to spare you. Don't ye see?" she murmured. "I don't want to burden ye with my responsibilities." Grief and pain was covering every square inch of her face.

Andrew took her hands, unfurrowing them, and surrounding them with his. "We all have baggage, Moira. We all have pasts. Things we can't change or have no control over." His words were pure earnestness. "But still, people marry, become whole, heal by building lives together, clinging to each other. You know that's exactly what I want to do with you."

Moira stood there frozen, her eyes glued to Andrew's thumb rubbing hers as if it was trying to persuade her to see his viewpoint, too.

"I don't know," Moira finally said.

Pippa thought that wasn't much of an answer. But she shouldn't judge. Andrew's solution seemed like pie in the sky to her, too.

He moved abruptly, dropping her hands. "Fine. Then

at least tell Glenna that this man"—he thumped his chest—"would gladly step in and be her father. That yere uncertainty has nothing to do with her. I love Glenna and I love you. Make a decision. Ye have until tomorrow." He stomped away and out the door.

Tomorrow—the day of the auction.

"Wow," Kit said, breaking the silence.

Moira only frowned down at her hands.

Wow, indeed, Pippa thought. Andrew had it bad for Moira. Pippa's eyes drifted to the Yank standing at the back wall, where he was watching her. She didn't dare wonder if Max had it bad for her, too. She had to keep her head in the game—the MTech deal, the auction, and getting her father well. She didn't have room in her life for a man who would be leaving them soon and going back to his home in America.

The lights went down and the band started playing. Max pushed away from the wall and made his way toward them.

Ross nudged her, making her remember he was still there. "I'm going to say good night to Cait and Mattie, and then head home. John wants to get an early start on the boat in the morn."

She nodded. "Okay." But she couldn't take her eyes off Max.

But it had to be because she was nosy—like the rest of Gandiegow—and not because she wanted to be near him. She wanted to hear what he'd said to prompt Andrew to take a stand.

She walked in Max's direction, meeting him in the middle of the dance floor, which was filling up with townsfolk.

"What was that all about with Andrew?" she hollered above the music.

He surprised her by pulling her into his arms.

To hell with everyone watching. This would be Max's last chance to hold Pippa close. God, she smelled good. He'd missed her body. He'd missed her.

"What are ye doing?" she sounded as breathless as he felt.

"Shhh," he whispered in her ear as he swayed them to the upbeat music. "Don't ruin it."

She relaxed into him for a moment, but then reluctantly pulled away. "This isn't a slow song."

Max held on to her hand, smiling, and twirled her out, doing his version of the swing. Every few steps, he pulled her close again. He could almost forget everything when they were like this. Almost.

But his eyes followed to where a crowd of women were around Moira—a fortress—reminding him of how Gandiegow protected its own.

Pippa glanced in that direction, too. "Tell me then. What did ye say to Andrew to rile him so?"

Max didn't feel it was his place to share Glenna's feelings more than he already had . . . even though he knew he could trust Pippa. He twirled her in a circle, then pulled her near again. "There's only so much yanking around that a man can take. Andrew reached his limit, is all."

Unfortunately, the little voice at the back of his head took that moment to lecture him. *"And you? What's your limit, bonehead?"*

Pippa's eyes seemed to sparkle just for him. But she

was engaged to Ross. Suddenly, Max reached his own limit, too. He dropped her hand and stood still. He'd been fooling himself that he might have her again. He frowned at her, the pain crushing.

Then he manned up and walked away.

Chapter Seventeen

Miranda arrived back in Gandiegow just in time before the auction to poke around the quilting place and figure out what tartan Max's kilt would be. She was determined to bid on Max. Determined to win him.

She stowed her luggage and headed to Quilting Central.

When she walked into the building, it was packed. Damn. She had hoped to have the place to herself. But she guessed with the preparations for the auction, she should've expected this.

Maybe it would work in her favor. She could look through things and no one would notice. But the old woman who ran the place hobbled straight over to her.

"What can we do for ye?" Deydie didn't wait for her answer, but handed her a stack of linens. "Put these on the tables."

"All right. Let me slip my coat off first." Miranda scanned the room, wondering where one might store the swatches Bonnie had told her about.

"Hang it over there," Deydie said. "Tea and coffee is at the back. When ye're done, come find me, I'll give ye something more to do."

As Miranda spread out the linens, she watched the people around her, getting accustomed to their language. There were two older women, twins, who were ridiculous, but reminded her of her great aunts, who had raised her. The matronly twins were at the next table over, bickering about the centerpieces. Old memories flooded Miranda. She'd been so embarrassed by Aunt Flora and Aunt Edna—one of the reasons she'd never brought friends home. Those silly old fools raised her to be sweet and soft, teaching her no skills at all to deal with the real world. Miranda gazed one more time at the twins. It was uncanny.

Maybe Miranda could ask these ladies about the swatches. She made her way to them.

"Ailsa, put the holly in here like this."

"No, sister, the ivy goes in there."

"Excuse me." Miranda decided to play dumb. "What is this bachelor's auction all about?"

Miranda kept her eye out for Deydie, but she was busy bossing around one of the younger women.

The one named Ailsa scooted closer. "We can tell ye all about it. We're raising money for the McDonnell."

Miranda stopped cold. "Lachlan McDonnell?"

"Och, sister," Aileen said. "We don't speak of it!"

"Speak of what?" Miranda asked.

"The accident," Ailsa whispered. "We're raising money to help pay for the specialist."

These women were a treasure trove. Miranda considered whether she should share the news with Roger or not.

"And how will the auction work?" she prodded.

Aileen responded, "We're going to put all of the

young lads up on the stage, but with a curtain so that all you can see is their legs. It will make bidding even more fun to have some mystery to it, ye see."

"Might that lead to disappointment, though?" Miranda prompted.

Ailsa pointed across the room. "Deydie has let all of *our* lasses look at the playbook." She giggled. "If one of them really has her heart set on having a certain lad, she just has to pick the right kilt."

"How fascinating—can you show me?" Miranda only needed one glimpse to find Max's kilt.

"Sure."

Miranda followed the twins to a booklet hanging on the wall. She saw Deydie's head pop up and the other woman, Bethia, look her way, too. Miranda held her breath. Ailsa pulled the booklet from its hook. Aileen flipped through it.

"See? All the lads' tartans are here!"

"What are ye doing there?" Deydie yelled.

Miranda ignored her. "Which one is Max McKinley's?"

Deydie and Bethia both descended on them.

Aileen flipped. "Armstrong, Baird, Craig—"

Ailsa pulled it from her hands. "It's alphabetical." She thumbed through the fabric.

And there it was: McKINLEY, in bold letters.

Deydie reached them and snatched it away. "That's only for the Gandiegow lasses."

"We were just showing her the different tartans."

"Sorry," Miranda apologized sweetly. "I didn't know. I never would've asked otherwise."

Miranda slipped past them and grabbed her coat, smiling to herself. Once outside, she hurried back to the quilting dorm. It had been a most successful day. A most successful day indeed.

Deydie clutched the fabric book to her chest. "What the hell were ye two thinking?" She glared at the dimwit twins. "Oh, get back to work."

Bethia laid a hand on her shoulder. "What are we going to do? I think she's after Max McKinley."

Deydie felt the same way Bethia did. They didn't take well to outsiders, but Max wasn't a bad sort of lad. Actually, he'd been a big help and didn't complain much.

"Ye're right. Max doesn't deserve to be bought by the likes of her."

Bethia shook her head. "We don't have time to have a new kilt made out of a different McKinley tartan."

"Aye. 'Tis too late," Deydie agreed.

"And we won't have enough money to outbid her for him."

"I know that, too. I'm not thickheaded."

"What are we going to do?" Bethia said. "Miranda had a look in her eye that said she wanted him, no matter the cost."

Deydie grinned at Bethia.

Bethia glanced to either side. "I know that look. What are ye thinking?"

Oh, it was wicked. But it was perfect. Deydie pulled Bethia close and whispered in her ear. "I've got a plan. Ye're going to put those herbs of yeres to good use."

The time had finally arrived . . . the moment Max was dreading. Any way he looked at it, it was a helluva way to end his stay in Scotland.

He figured the only positive thing about tonight's auction was the opportunity to win Pippa's quilt. He was determined to have it, so he could take a piece of her back
home with him to Texas. He'd taken a chance and asked
Freda to do the bidding for him. He figured she was the
only one in town who would oblige; everyone else would
have a fit, and insist that Ross should have the quilt. Well,
screw that. Max was getting the consolation prize. While
he would have Pippa's quilt to keep him warm at night,
Ross would have her. The real thing.

God, Max felt ill.

The lights from another bus caught his window, shining
as it made its way down the bluff. *Good grief!* How many
women had Deydie invited to this blasted auction? There
weren't enough of them to go around. Max snatched the
kilt off the bed and donned it. He didn't feel as ridiculous
in it as he had the first time, but damned near.

The sheet of instructions Moira had given him on how
to dress—the socks with the flags in them, the sporran,
and the whole nine yards of McKinley plaid fabric—lay
on the bed next to the items.

With a growl, he crumpled the paper. If he had to
wear a skirt, at least the rest of him would be warm. Max
slipped on thick socks and the army boots he'd nabbed
from Pippa on his first day at the factory. Then he put on
a tan sweater instead of the white dress shirt Deydie had
ordered him to wear.

He checked his watch. Deydie had yelled at them not
to be late, but Max had just enough time to grab some
hard liquor downstairs—artificial courage to face the
evening ahead with some strange woman who would
buy him and half paw him to death.

There was only one woman he wanted. She could paw him anytime, anywhere. And for the thousandth time in the last thirty minutes, naked images of Pippa plowed through his thoughts, whether he wanted them to or not.

He stomped out and marched down the stairs. "I'll get ye a drink," Coll said.

Max guessed it was written all over his face, but then noticed the rest of the room. He wasn't the only bachelor in need of a drink. There were at least ten other be-kilted men sitting at the bar, including Ross.

"Sit, Yank." Ross motioned to the stool beside him. "Have yereself a drink before we're put on the market and sold off like so much Caledonian cattle."

"Sure." What the hell. Why not get schnockered with Pippa's future husband? "I just keep telling myself that it's for the McDonnell."

"A good soul. But a bit misled." Ross sounded as miserable as Max felt.

Coll came over and poured Max a drink and refilled Ross's.

"Thanks." Max waited until Coll left. "Why do you say the McDonnell is misled?"

"In his thinking."

Max waited while Ross took another sip of his whisky and set his glass down.

"The McDonnell certainly has a way of reading people, true, but I believe he's blind where his own daughter is concerned." Ross sounded judgmental.

And Max immediately went on the defensive. "Pippa's a little pigheaded, but that's part of her charm."

Ross shot Max a furtive glance, seeming to register his expression, and then went back to gazing at his drink.

"Aw gawd, Pippa will make a terrible wife. I know it. Ye know it. The whole damned village knows it." He paused as if waiting for Max to reply.

Max gripped his glass. If Ross felt this way, why in the hell would he marry her? If Pippa were Max's wife, he'd cherish her, and be grateful for every waking moment they had together.

Ross gave a derisive laugh. "All these years, the McDonnell has acted as if he's giving me a gift by saddling me with his shrew of a daughter for the rest of my miserable life."

"Enough." Max pushed away and stood. Ross had always seemed like a decent guy, but the whisky was making him a jerk. "Stop. Unless you want me to kick your ass. Nobody is going to speak about Pippa like that."

Ross rose. "So ye'd take me on to defend Pippa's honor?"

Max stepped closer. "Hell, yeah. You and the whole damned town."

Ross dropped the frown and grinned. "It's what I thought." He clapped Max on the back and then sat back down. "Then I'll just have to disappoint the McDonnell."

"What?" Max's adrenaline was still on high alert. "What are you getting at?"

"I love Pippa," Ross said. He held up his hand, either to stop Max from punching him, or to stop him from interrupting. "But ye got to know that I only love her like a sister."

Max collapsed onto his barstool, trying to process what Ross was saying and not quite succeeding. "How could you not be in love with her? She's perfect."

"Well, Yank, I'm not. And she's not in love with me

either. The McDonnell isn't seeing things straight these days or he'd tell ye himself: Pippa fancies you, plain and simple."

"Pippa fancies me?" *As in really likes me?* Could it be true?

"And you, well, ye have it bad for her, too." Ross shook his head. "Poor bastard."

"Is that another slam against Pippa?"

"Relax, Yank." Ross reached over the bar and nabbed the bottle Coll had poured from. "More?" He didn't wait for Max to answer, but poured.

Max didn't drink it though.

Ross took another sip, no longer resembling a jerk. "Ye know we have another problem."

Max had a lot of problems. Pippa had made it clear that she wanted nothing to do with him. He was sick to death of giving her space. He wanted to close the distance between them. He wanted to work with her again. He wanted to touch her. He wanted everything with her. If Ross was right about her fancying him, why had she pushed him away?

Ross continued as if Max wasn't in the middle of a crisis. "I said we have a problem."

"Things could not be worse."

Ross gave Max a pointed look. "I'm not sure what they're up to, but Maggie let it slip that Deydie has let every woman in Gandiegow know who is wearing which kilt. I imagine it's in case they have their sights set on one of us men." He made an exaggerated shiver like a hag might bid on him and win.

"But I thought everyone would know anyway. Every clan has a tartan, right?"

"Nay. Every clan has several different tartans—you know, modern, hunting, and ancient. There are over four thousand tartans registered." Ross pushed his drink away.

Max considered his kilt and wondered which of the townswomen who'd ogled him might have plans to get him alone tonight. And as he did, an idea jolted through his brain . . . or it could just be the whisky working on his inhibitions. "Let's throw a wrench in their plans. Let's switch kilts. We're basically the same size, aren't we?"

Ross grinned. "I guess being sold off to one person can't be any different from being sold off to another." He grabbed his glass and raised it. "Here's to pulling a fast one on the quilting ladies."

Max raised his glass as well. "To outsmarting Deydie and her coven."

Quilting Central was abuzz while Pippa was all nerves. Everything was riding on tonight. She couldn't stop thinking about Kenneth Campbell's death, and standing over his grave at the top of the bluff. This damned auction was the only thing giving her own da a fighting chance.

As if the thought of Kenneth had conjured up his daughter, Moira appeared with little Glenna at her side, and Freda, too. Moira was carrying Pippa's completed quilt in her arms.

"Oh, my goodness!" Pippa felt incredibly guilty. It had been her job to finish the quilt.

"It was a blessing for us to work on it." Moira laid the quilt beside Pippa and took her hand. "Ye're going to have to let us help ye more. Ye're doing too much."

Freda chimed in. "I agree. Pippa, ye've taken on too many roles." She motioned to the room of Gandie-gowans. "We've decided that things will change."

"Go on, Glenna, give the tag to Pippa," Moira encouraged.

Glenna held out the embroidered piece of fabric. "Here, miss."

Pippa took it. The inscription read GANDIEGOW ... SUFFICIENT UNTO THE DAY. She knew what it meant. Many times when the day was over and it was time to call it quits, Freda had recited the verse from the Bible:

Sufficient unto the day is the evil thereof.

"What's it mean?" Glenna asked.

Pippa smiled at her, happy the girl was learning to speak up. "It means live in the present and don't worry about tomorrow."

Glenna frowned at them as if it made no sense. Children had the right of it; they knew how to live in the moment.

"Ye'll understand when ye're older," Moira said.

Pippa smiled at Freda. "It's lovely. Thank you."

"Freda thought it was only fitting to be on yere quilt," Moira said.

"Thank you, ladies." She turned to Glenna. "And thank ye, lass. I'll get some thread and sew this on right now."

From Glenna's other hand, she produced a needle and a spool of blue thread.

Freda patted the little one's shoulder. "Let's see if we can find some hot cocoa and maybe a snack." She ushered them away, leaving Pippa alone.

The out-of-towners were at the restaurant for a bite

or a drink if they wanted it. In an hour, the festivities would begin. There would be three auctions tonight. The public auction of Pippa's Gandiegow Hometown quilt, then a silent auction to win a quilt retreat for two, and finally the bachelor auction.

For the millionth time this evening Pippa thought about Max. She missed him. The last time she'd talked to him was when she'd been in his arms on the dance floor, feeling light, free, and wanting him so much. He had a way of making the world a wonderful place to live and her troubles seem small. He could've twirled her from the room and taken her someplace private . . . she'd been so compliant in his arms, she would've done anything. But he'd suddenly walked away without a word, and she'd been crushed. Since then, she'd been giving herself a stern talking to: She would not bid on the Yank, no matter what! The whole point of this evening was to make money. Let the out-of-towners throw down their cash for Max and the other bachelors; Pippa would sit on her hands during the auction . . . duct-tape them to her chair if she had to when the men came across the stage.

Pippa sewed the tag on in record time, then Moira retrieved the quilt and hung it on the display rack at the front of the room. Freda brought Pippa a plate of venison and homemade bread.

"I thought ye should eat something."

Pippa smiled up at her weakly. "Thank you. But I feel too jumpy to eat anything." She was upset at the prospect of someone else spending the evening with her Yank.

Freda looked at her with understanding. "At least nibble at it. Ye need to keep yere strength up."

"I'll try."

Freda left to serve the others.

Moira came and sat next to Pippa. The closer it came time for the auction, the more unsettled Moira looked. She wrung her hands and kept glancing at the door.

Pippa reached over and stilled her. "So ye know then about Andrew being in the auction?"

"Aye," Moira said. "Amy let it slip. I think on purpose. She has a sneaky streak in her, I've found."

"So what do ye plan to do about our good father? Are ye going to bid on him or are ye going to let some other woman have him?"

Moira stared at her, horrified. "Of course I'm going to bid on him. Deydie made a point to show me which tartan he'll be wearing." She shifted away as if embarrassed, her neck and cheeks creeping with red. She picked at the lint on her nicest dress. "I love him, you know."

Such brave words. Pippa always saw herself as strong, but she was a lightweight compared to Moira.

Her shy friend chewed her lip. "Cait came to visit. She forced me to take an envelope full of cash from her. She said she wanted to contribute to the auction even though she couldn't bid on a bachelor herself. *'Graham wouldn't like it,'* she said." Moira laughed, but sobered quickly. "Cait also said if I didn't take the money she'd give it to Bonnie to help *her* bid." Her eyes drifted to where Bonnie sat.

Pippa smiled at Cait's generosity—and her ingenuity for saying just the right thing.

"What are ye going to do with Andrew when ye win him? Are ye going to continue to keep him at arm's length? Or are ye going to put him *out of his misery*?"

Pippa had used Andrew's words, being blunt, but they'd known each other their whole lives.

Moira didn't hesitate. "I'm going to propose."

That shocked Pippa speechless. And she felt jealous that Moira had the freedom to do exactly as she pleased.

Moira looked off into the distance. "I've been a fool. I was worried about Andrew, about weighing him down with so much responsibility. You know, with my da before he passed." Her voice dropped off to a whisper as if in respect. "And with Glenna, providing for her, parenting, everything. It's a lot to ask of someone else. I didn't think it was fair that Andrew should be stuck with my family if we married. But now I believe he really wants me regardless of anything else. He loves Glenna. He said so. He loves me and wants me. And I want him, too. I'm going to take a risk and choose love."

Pippa never heard Moira say so much. She took her hand. "I'm happy for you." What else could she say? Moira would get her happily-ever-after and Pippa would get the factory, making payroll, and shoveling snow from NSV's sidewalks in the winter. She'd never get her true love like her friend. As soon as MTech faxed the completed contract, Pippa would sign it, and Max would go home. He'd probably never think of her again, though she suspected he would always be on her mind, and in her heart.

Before she could dig in and get the details of when Moira and Andrew might tie the knot or where they might live, Deydie hollered.

"Moira, if ye're done yammering, do ye think ye can get over here and help me center this quilt in front of the table?"

Moira stood. "Aye. I'm coming." Before she left, she turned back to Pippa. "It's going to be a wonderful night."

"Sure." *Grand.* It was all so easy for Moira. Andrew loved her. Everyone was cheering Moira on to be with him. But Gandiegow wanted the opposite for Pippa, for her to marry Ross, come hell or high tide. Love never even played into the equation for her.

Once again, Pippa caught herself looking at the door longingly, as if to make Max magically appear. She wanted the fairy tale. She wanted the knight-in-shining-armor to ride in on his horse and whisk her away.

But she wasn't a wee lass anymore with time on her hands. Wishful thinking was a luxury that had been replaced with hard work and responsibilities.

Besides, she knew better.

Chapter Eighteen

Deydie eyed the door, but Miranda hadn't returned yet to Quilting Central. "When do ye think she'll get here?"

Bethia tapped her on the shoulder and gestured toward Pippa across the room. "Are ye sure about her?"

"Stop badgering. Of course, I'm sure." To Deydie it was always as clear as sunshine, but it usually took Bethia longer to see the truth.

She looked worried. "So do we tell Pippa or not?"

"Nay."

"But this could ruin everything," Bethia said.

"Not if we keep our mouths sewn shut." Deydie gave Bethia a pointed look. She hoped by the time the evening was over that things would be settled irrevocably and she wouldn't have to say a word.

At that moment, Miranda sailed through the door, looking as if she was going on an expensive dinner date instead of spending the evening with some regular small-town Scots.

Deydie pointed in the American woman's direction.

"Come on, Bethia. We need to go talk to her before everything starts."

Miranda was a slick one. She was all polished up in her suit like a black onyx, definitely an odd fish who stuck out here on the northeast coast of Scotland.

Bethia wrung her hands, worrying like one of the old women they'd made fun of in their youth. "I'm not sure what we're doing is right."

Deydie waved to the air between them. "Ye agreed that we should do this." Then she motioned to the goblet sitting on the window ledge. "Ye even made the sleeping draft. Ye're not backing out now. Besides, it's more important to protect the Yank from her clutches than some damnable moral conscience. Would Miranda think twice if she was in our shoes?"

Bethia glanced down at her boots, chewed her lip, and then gazed at the goblet. "Aye. I made the draft, but I don't think I can give it to her."

Deydie took the final steps to the windowsill. "Good thing I have sound reasoning, or poor Max McKinley would be stuck with that hellcat." She motioned to Miranda. "Ye don't want that to happen, now do ye?" She didn't wait for an answer, but laid a napkin over the goblet and left it. "Come on."

Bethia clutched Deydie's arm as they made their way across the room. Deydie conjured up a smile and slapped it across her face.

"Hallo, Miranda."

The woman looked at them a bit surprised, but then cocked her head sideways. "Yes?"

"Did ye have good day?" Deydie smoothed out her voice until it was as congenial as a warm cup of tea.

"Yes. But I was concerned about leaving my things at Thistle Glen Lodge. It looks like the place has been taken over by a bunch of other women."

"Not to worry, dear," Deydie said. "Yere things are safe here with us in Gandiegow."

Bethia acted as if she might roll her eyes, and Deydie knew why; Deydie was spooning it on as thick as blood pudding.

Deydie patted Miranda's arm. "We wanted to speak to ye before our lads are brought out onstage. Has anyone told ye how this works?" She was acting like Miranda's best friend.

"No."

Deydie knew she was lying. Bonnie had already confessed that she'd told her everything. "Well, I'm happy to tell ye the procedure." Deydie went into great detail about how the bidding would work. "Most important, ye pay Amy over there *if* ye win one of our lads."

Miranda's eyes sparkled as if that was a foregone conclusion.

Bethia seemed to want to make a getaway, so Deydie grabbed her arm. "We're also offering, to a few select people, a little something extra."

"Oh?"

Deydie had dangled the bait; now it was time to set the hook. "Aye. Bethia here is a certified herbalist."

Bethia looked down, her face turning red.

"She's shy about it," Deydie lied. She pointed to the windowsill with the goblet. "Anyway, she's made a little love potion, a woman's Viagra as it were. It'll make ye randy as a she-goat in heat."

"Really." Miranda seemed circumspect.

"For a price, that is," Deydie added.

Bethia choked.

Deydie pounded her on the back. "Bethia is just getting over a cold."

The door opened to Quilting Central and the women from out of town were led in by Ailsa and Aileen. The out-of-towners were giddy with anticipation—and liquor.

Deydie pointed again to the goblet. "If ye're not interested, then I'll offer it to some of our guests from Edinburgh."

Miranda looked at them with disdain. She turned back to Deydie and nodded to the windowsill. "Is it safe?"

"I'd be happy to take the first sip," Deydie offered.

"And you?" Miranda pointed to Bethia. "Would you be willing to taste it first, too?"

Bethia nodded.

"Of course she would. She's the one who concocted the love potion." And because Deydie felt ornery sometimes, she added, "I promise 'tis as safe as a sleeping draft."

Bethia choked again.

Deydie let go of her friend's arm. "Ye better get some hot tea for that cough."

Bethia looked as if she didn't want to leave Deydie alone with Miranda.

"Go on now." Deydie gave Bethia a shove in the right direction. "Ye get yere tea while Miz Weymouth and I discuss the cost."

Bethia reluctantly made her way across the room as Kirsty the schoolteacher announced the auction on Pippa's quilt. Deydie frowned. Freda was winding her way to the front. *Why is she up there with the others bidding on that quilt?*

But Deydie had bigger fish to fry ... like a cat shark named Miranda. Deydie smiled and gave the woman her full attention. The sleeping draft was only part of her plan. She had another trick up her sleeve to fleece the American woman who wanted to get her hooks into Max McKinley.

Max and Ross left the room over the pub wearing each other's kilts and went downstairs to join the others. The two of them had formed some kind of weird bond, a couple of comrades-in-arms.

Ross's brothers, John and Ramsay, came into the pub. John had a stack of square pages in his hands, and Ramsay had a single sheet of paper.

"Deydie said we should get ye to Quilting Central," John said. "But first, we're to give you yere number and ye're to pin it to the bottom of the kilt. That way, the women will know which of ye to bid on. Read them off to me, Ramsay."

"Kolby, number one. Wylie, number two." And they continued until only Ross and Max remained.

As John held out Max's number, he gazed down at the switched kilt and raised an eyebrow. "Och, so ye're an Armstrong now? My new brother?"

Max smiled at him. "Only for the evening."

"Good. I need my brother Ross to man the nets in the morning. I doubt I'd get as much work out of ye."

"Because I'm a *Yank*?"

"Nay." John looked puzzled. "Because I hear yere gift is with the hammer."

Max pinned the number sixteen to the bottom of his kilt.

"Are ye ready, lads, for me to herd ye like sheep?" Ramsay chuckled at what he thought was a joke, but the bachelors weren't laughing. Ross looked too miserable to even punch Ramsay in the arm. Most of the bachelors looked as embarrassed as Max felt. Maybe they should have one more shot of whisky before they left. He had to keep reminding himself that he was doing this for Pippa's dad.

Coll put the CLOSED sign on the front door as the men filed out the back. They walked the path behind the buildings in silence with John at the front of the line, Coll walking along at the middle, and Ramsay bringing up the rear. The married men seemed to be enjoying their job as security guards, keeping the bachelors from skipping out now, though they wanted to.

John opened the back door to Quilting Central. "The women have hung curtains so no one can see ye."

There was some comfort in that. This whole ordeal was embarrassing enough. Max was getting a clue what women might go through for beauty pageants. It was excruciating, and Max vowed to never watch another one again without remembering this experience.

Kit, Ramsay's wife and the matchmaker, was waiting for them. "Relax, everyone. This is all in fun. And for a good cause. Tonight's events are only that . . . for tonight. It's not for the rest of your lives! So when you're won, I want everyone to smile." She frowned at them. "None of the sourpuss looks you have right now." She leaned in conspiratorially. "You all look like you're channeling Deydie."

Ramsay put his arm around Kit and kissed her hair. "Don't waste yere breath, wife. They can't hear ye in the state that they're in."

Kit beamed up at Ramsay. "I know. Unmarried men are a miserable lot, aren't they? I bet you're glad you signed on for life with me."

Ramsay smiled at the group of them. "After tonight, come see my wife. She'll find yere true love for you."

Max envied Kit and Ramsay—the love between them, the surety—and it was an odd feeling. He'd never thought he'd want to be married.

Kit let go of her husband. "Okay. Everyone go onto the stage and move on down to the end. Stand on your place; it's marked by the green tape on the floor. When Deydie gives the go-ahead, I'll raise the curtain."

Max couldn't believe that he'd helped to make the damned stage now.

The men moved down to the end and Max found his spot.

"Quiet down," Deydie hollered to Quilting Central. Max imagined her brandishing her broom. The people on the other side of the curtain went quiet. "Pippa, go ahead."

Max's breath hitched.

"Welcome, everyone, to our evening of Strapping Lads in Plaid."

Max rolled his eyes.

"We're so happy that ye've come. We know ye're going to have an evening ye'll never forget."

Ross guffawed beside him. "I wish I could."

There was a grumble of agreement down the line.

"Deydie, I'll hand it over to you to explain the rules."

The stage creaked as Deydie stepped up, the curtain between them and her.

"First, and most important, Amy is manning the cash register, over there at the table. Amy, wave yere hand so they'll know where to pay."

"Hi, everyone," Amy hollered.

Deydie cleared her throat to silence Amy. "Here's the long and the short of it, lasses. Our bachelors are lined up here behind the curtain."

There was an excited *ahh* that ran through the crowd. For a moment, Max worried the horny women might rush them.

"Quiet down, now. We'll never git to the bachelors if ye don't," Deydie said. "Okay then. In a moment, we'll raise the curtain just so."

Kit motioned to her thigh, demonstrating how high she was going to pull the curtain up so the men would know.

"Ye all saw the flyer, so ye know that what we have behind here is a bunch of handsome, rugged bachelors. I promise ye that we haven't switched them out with our ugly folk."

The women laughed nervously in the crowd.

"Ye'll have five minutes to look over the men." Deydie raised her voice then. "We'll do this in an orderly fashion. I'll let ye all come up here when yere table is called and ye can write down the different numbers that ye want to bid on. Ye'll only have a few seconds, so make sure to have yere pen and paper ready. Och, and ye better stay behind the line while ye gaze upon their legs."

"What about the knee-fondling?" one woman shouted from the audience.

The men all looked at one another panic-stricken.

"I'm getting to that," Deydie said. "After everyone gets a chance to see the lads *from behind the tape on the floor*, then we'll have the lads come out here on the stage one by one. For those that want to do a little knee-fondling before ye make a bid, that'll cost ye extra. Ye'll be blindfolded as we don't trust ye to keep from looking up their kilts. Ye'll only have ten seconds with them. And we'll have no handsies higher than the knees, do ye hear?" Deydie paused. "Remember, ye'll have to pay Amy before we'll let ye touch the lads. After the knee-fondling, the bidding will begin on that particular bachelor."

There was a hoot out in the crowd and then another.

"Now mind, ye'll not be allowed to see any of the bachelors until all the lads are auctioned off. And ye won't get to have them for the evening until ye've paid for them. Did I cover everything, Pippa?"

There was a weak "aye" on the other side of the curtain.

"Then let the games begin."

There was loud cheering as the curtain began to rise.

As Pippa sat in her chair in the front row, a wave of nausea came over her. For a second, she hoped it was only the stress of the day and it would pass. But it didn't. She bolted for the restroom and lost what little dinner she'd had. She'd heard from MTech today. They finally agreed to all the terms that she and Max had penned together, in addition to forcing some concessions she wasn't pleased with. But it was done as soon as they faxed the final document and she signed it. MTech might already have let

Max know the deal was reached. And she knew what that meant. Max's work here was over. He was going home. Just in time for Christmas. Pippa ran a wet washcloth over her face and went back out for the auction.

Bethia was waiting and Freda rushed over to her, too. Pippa got only a glimpse as the curtain was going down, but it was enough time to catch the McKinley tartan and the number fifteen pinned to the front.

She scanned the audience wildly and wondered who would be fondling him tonight. With Freda on one side and Bethia on the other, they walked her back to her seat at the front and took the chairs on either side of her.

Deydie returned to the stage. "If there was a knee or two that ye wanted to fondle, I suggest ye go pay Amy now for the privilege." Several women left their seats and went to join the line gathering at Amy's table in the corner. "And ladies, let me remind ye that when the bidding begins, we're going to be civilized Scots. Hold yere paddles up high so our spotters can see them."

Kirsty rose with a clipboard and pencil in hand to act as auctioneer. "I'll call the bachelors out one by one. Let's start with number twelve. Number twelve, step forward."

Pippa recognized the Drummond tartan. So it must be Alan.

Deydie called for the knee-fondling. Three women giggled while they were blindfolded. Pippa's stomach clenched. She ought to leave the building now. She didn't trust herself and what she might do when the randy women wanted to feel up Max's knees. She took deep breaths and watched as each of the three women had their turn at poor Alan's knees.

When it was over, Deydie and three other quilters stood on the stage as spotters.

Kirsty held up her pencil. "Let's start the bidding at twenty-five pounds."

Hands shot up all over the place. Within a few minutes, Alan had been sold for two hundred and ten pounds.

Pippa turned to Freda. "It's going to work, isn't it?" she whispered.

"It's a great start."

One by one, the lads of Gandiegow bravely stepped up and were sold. Pippa was grateful for every last one of them. Loyal lads. Honorable men. She was proud to call them friends.

Because Kirsty and her clipboard were calling them out of order, Pippa had lost count of how many were left. But then Max and his kilt came on stage.

She had the ridiculous urge to tackle him and not let anyone bid on him. Freda laid a hand on her to hold her in place. Ailsa had taken Deydie's position. Deydie came to sit with them in the front row next to Freda.

No less than eight women wanted their shot at touching Max's knees. Pippa felt as if her eyes were on fire. One of the randy women from Glasgow got too adventurous, as her hands tried to go for Max's goods. Pippa broke free and shot out of her seat, but Ailsa and Aileen were right there, pulling the Glaswegian away.

"Let's start the bidding at one hundred pounds, since this one seems like a popular lad."

"One hundred pounds," Miranda said loud and clear.

Pippa spun around and glared at her. She shouldn't be shocked that Miranda would use any means to get her paws on Max.

"Two hundred pounds," Deydie shot out.

Pippa whipped around to Deydie. "What are ye doing?"

"Getting every pound I can for yere da."

Bethia leaned over Pippa and whispered to Deydie. "This is not part of the plan. I thought we had this covered."

Pippa had no idea what these two were up to. But Deydie had a nasty little glint in her eye that Pippa fully approved of.

"I'm not going to make this easy on her," Deydie said.

"So you knew she wanted Max?" Pippa asked incredulously.

Deydie and Bethia looked guilty. Why hadn't the silly old fools told her beforehand?

"Three hundred pounds," Pippa shouted out. There was no way in hell Miranda would win Max.

Bethia grabbed her hand. "No, lass. Ye're promised to Ross."

"Four hundred pounds," Miranda said.

Pippa turned around to see Miranda sneering at her.

"Five hundred pounds," Deydie said clearly.

"Ye don't have that kind of money," Bethia hissed to her friend.

"I don't." Deydie jabbed a thumb in Miranda's direction. "But she does."

"A thousand pounds," Miranda countered, victory lacing her voice.

Bethia dropped her grip from Pippa's hand and sat back. "'Tis done."

Pippa felt sick again. She could do nothing about it.

Max belonged to Miranda now. She glanced sideways at Deydie, who had a satisfied look on her face.

The next bachelor came on stage. It was Andrew's plaid.

"Let's start the bidding at fifty pounds."

"What about the knee-touching?" a woman shouted from the audience. "I've been waiting for this one."

Kirsty double-checked her clipboard and smiled. "It says here that there'll be no knee-fondling on this one. For religious reasons."

Pippa glanced around for Moira. She was standing next to Amy, the smile evident on her face clear across the room.

The bidding began. Moira was careful with her envelope of money, only bidding a few pounds higher than the others had bid, but in the end, Moira got her man. Pippa was happy that at least one of them was getting what they wanted tonight. She saw Moira hand the whole envelope to Amy, keeping none for herself.

"And now for our last bachelor of the evening."

Ross came out in his Armstrong plaid. Eleven blindfolded women wanted to feel his knees. When the bidding began, Pippa was shocked when Bethia bid on him against the women from out of town. She'd looked to Deydie each time for the nod before she upped the bid.

"Now what are you two doing?" Pippa hissed at Deydie.

"Wedding present," Deydie said firmly, giving her a pointed glare.

No! These two women were spending their hard-earned cash on her!

Ross sold for five hundred five pounds.

But Pippa didn't want Ross. She wanted Max.

The curtain came down.

"We have to make sure all the bachelors are paid for before we reveal who ye won."

Deydie rose, motioning to Bethia. "I'll take care of this, while ye get the goblet." Deydie pulled a wallet from the folds of her dress and lumbered over to pay for Ross.

Pippa opened her mouth to give Bethia a piece of her mind, but the old woman held up a hand.

"We did what we believed was right," Bethia said. "Don't worry about the Yank. He won't be ..." She seemed to be choosing her words carefully. "Deydie and I are taking care of it."

"What the hell does that mean?"

But Bethia didn't answer. She left Pippa there to stew about what they had done. Sure, the evening had gone better than planned; more money had been raised than Pippa had dreamed possible. But her heart was heavy. Max was Miranda's, and that was a heartache she wasn't going to get over any time soon.

Chapter Nineteen

Max stood waiting his turn to get a silk rose from Kit, frowning at the absurdity of it all. The roses were wrapped with Christmas ribbon.

Kit handed a rose to Ross. "Remember what I said. Smile for your date when you present her with her rose. We're all doing this for the McDonnell."

"I don't see that ye're doing a whole lot, sister-in-law. Handing us a few roses can't compare with being fondled and sold off."

"Chin up, Ross. It may not be as bad as what you might think." She winked at him. But then she frowned at his kilt as if only now noticing the tartan. Her eyes drifted to Max's kilt. "Oh," she said to herself. "The plot thickens."

Max just wanted to get this evening over with. He wasn't a germ-a-phobe, but he needed hand sanitizer for his knees. One overzealous female had kissed his knee before she was pulled off him. God, he hoped that woman hadn't been the one to win him in the end.

Kirsty stepped behind the curtain. "We're going to call ye out one at a time. When ye hear your number, step out front and be claimed." She left with her clipboard.

One by one, they were called, in numerical order this time, so poor Kolby went first. He looked as stoic as if he was being called off to war. When he stepped out, a roar went up in the crowd along with deafening applause and a lot of catcalls.

"It isn't right," Alan Drummond complained to Max. "This whole thing. Men are supposed to be doing the pursuing . . . not the other way around." Another female hoot came from the other side of the curtain.

Every bachelor was subjected to the same thing. When it was only Max and Ross left, Ross held out his hand. "Good luck tonight."

The two men shook.

Max had this sappy fantasy that Pippa had bid on him, but it was only a dream. Unless of course, she'd disguised her voice, because it was an older woman who made the winning bid. Max didn't want to break the bad news to Ross, but he was fairly certain it was Miranda who had won him in the end.

"Sorry," Max said.

"For what?" Ross looked at him, questioning.

"For the night ahead."

Before Ross could ask more, his number was called.

Deydie hurried over to where Bethia was holding the goblet. "Did ye give it to her?" Kirsty was making pretty swift work of bringing out the bachelors, and Deydie had no way of slowing her down. "How fast does this sleeping draft work?"

"Fairly quickly." Bethia shook her head, looking pale. "But are ye really sure this is—"

Deydie snatched it from her. "We're doing this for

Max's sake. Hasn't the poor lad worked hard enough for this town?"

Deydie made her way toward Miranda and held the goblet out to her.

"Now?"

"Aye. It needs time to work. Ye want it to be in yere system by the time ye claim him, don't ye?"

Miranda eyed her one more time. "Here. Give it to me." She grabbed the cup and drank it down. "This better work or I'll be back for a refund."

Bethia whimpered softly.

Number fifteen was called, and Miranda's attention snapped to the stage.

Deydie leaned into her old friend. "Well, we did all we can do for the lad."

Then Ross came from behind the curtain.

"What?" Deydie and Miranda exclaimed together.

They looked at each other, then back at the stage.

For a moment, Deydie thought old age had finally caught up to her, then she noticed that Ross wasn't wearing the Armstrong tartan. He was wearing the McKinley!

"Those little devils," Deydie said. "Who told them what we were doing?"

"What do you mean?" Miranda said. "And who is that? I've seen him. At the factory, I think."

Deydie felt madder than a hornet. "That's Ross Armstrong. We wanted him for Pippa."

"I want my money back," Miranda said. "I was bidding on McKinley."

"No. Ye was bidding on the McKinley tartan. And that's what ye got."

"Well. Yes." Miranda seemed to realize that she'd

cooked herself in her own stewpot. She wasn't even supposed to know which tartan was which. None of the other outsiders did.

A little red in the face, Miranda shrugged. "He is a fine-looking man." She smiled. "I'm flexible. He'll do for the night." She swayed a little.

Deydie shoved Bethia. "Get Ross. I think we're going to need him."

Deydie put her arm around Miranda's waist. The American lass was definitely swaying now.

Miranda looked at Deydie a little droopy-eyed. "I feel strange. What was in that drink?"

"That's just the first effects of the love potion. Trust me—ye'll begin to feel all soft and in the loving way any moment."

Miranda gave her a lopsided grin. "Okay."

Bethia dragged Ross off the stage and toward them. Deydie could tell she was blabbing to him what they'd done.

When he reached them, Deydie lifted Miranda's arm and transferred her to Ross. "Get her to the dorm." She smiled up at Miranda "Yere night of romance awaits."

Ross grimaced at Deydie and Bethia, then schooled his features as he readjusted Miranda against him. "Come now," he said in a soothing tone. "Let's see if we can find a bed."

"Oh, you're a fast one," Miranda slurred. "I like fast."

Ross led her away, but he turned back and gave the two of them one last glower before leaving.

Deydie had missed the calling of number sixteen but now Pippa was rushing over to them. Her eyes shifted to each one of them accusingly.

"What did ye do?" Pippa growled.

Deydie thought the lass had gone wonky until she nodded toward the stage. There was the Yank — wearing the Armstrong kilt.

"Oh, dear. What are we going to do with him?" said Bethia.

"Aye. What are ye going to do with him?" Pippa asked sarcastically.

Deydie looked to heaven . . . and it all became clear. "It's a sign. The Almighty saw fit to intervene. That means we should tell her. Don't ye think, Bethia?"

"Tell her what?" Pippa asked derisively.

Deydie grabbed Ailsa as she walked by. "Tell the Yank to grab some punch and cake. We'll be with him in a minute."

Ailsa nodded good-naturedly and headed toward the stage.

Deydie and Bethia each took one of Pippa's arms and walked her to the corner for privacy.

"Deydie has some news for ye," Bethia said kindly.

"What? That you two have a hankering for younger men?" Pippa eyed the stage again wearily.

"This has to do with Deydie's powers," Bethia said. "She's been able to tell since she was a wee thing."

"Aye," Deydie said. "It got me in a lot of trouble back then. I've learned to keep it to myself. Best to find out on yere own."

Pippa shook her head impatiently. "What are you two talking about? Have ye been nipping at the Glenfiddich tonight?"

Bethia patted Pippa's arm. "Deydie was the first to see that Amy, Emma, Claire, and Maggie were expecting.

Even me, back in the day. She's better than a pregnancy test."

"Ye two are exasperating." Pippa turned to go.

Deydie yanked her arm to keep her still.

"Ouch." Pippa rubbed the spot.

Deydie was done being nice. "If ye don't listen to me, I'm going to get my broom. We've come to care for the Yank. And he needs to know before he heads back to where he came from."

Pippa frowned at her. "Needs to know what?"

"That he's going to be a da."

"I'm pregnant?" Pippa whispered to herself. She never expected to have a baby. Practically her whole life, she'd been determined to dodge marriage to Ross, and so children.

And how could these two old women know that only yesterday Pippa had missed her period?

Bethia patted her hand. "Deydie's never been wrong. The only time she hasn't been able to see was when Caitie was with child."

"I think it's because she's me granddaughter." Deydie looked sad about the two miscarriages that Cait had gone through in the last year.

Bethia noticed and wrapped her arm around her friend. "She'll give ye a great-grandbairn, just ye wait and see."

Pippa only half listened. *Pregnant?*

She glanced up. Max was making his way toward them. His frown was etched deep into his face.

He reached them. "I don't understand. Ailsa said Bethia won me?"

Deydie sliced the air, gesturing to the kilt Max wore. "Ye and Ross thought ye were being funny, huh?"

Max's expression didn't budge. "Where's Ross?"

"He left with Miranda." Pippa could at least get those words out.

Max looked worried, which made Pippa's anger surface quickly.

"Ross is a big boy," Pippa said. "He can handle *her*."

Max rolled his eyes. "Still jealous? God, Pippa. I thought we were beyond this."

He was right. Pippa was done comparing herself to Miranda, or any other woman. She was happy with who she was. Besides, she couldn't be anyone else. "Sorry."

He nodded, appeased, then turned back to the old ladies. "What is it I'm supposed to do now? Am I free to go back to the pub? Or is one of you claiming my attention for the evening?"

"Not sure what we'll do with ye," Bethia said, chewing her lip.

Pippa took a deep breath. "I'm claiming ye since these two busybodies goofed up. They were, after all, going to give me the bachelor that they won. Come on."

She wasn't sure what she was going to do with Max either. Loneliness came over her.

"Don't forget what we told ye," Deydie said. "This is one thing that can't be left undone."

Pippa wanted to tell her to mind her own business. She ignored the inquisitive look on Max's face, too. She couldn't tell him yet. Hell, what if Deydie was wrong. Pippa needed concrete evidence that she was pregnant, not some wizened old woman's word.

"Come on, Yank. We have things to discuss." She'd let

Deydie think what she wanted, but Pippa was going to talk to Max about business.

Away from this town.

Naked.

And after they'd made love.

In that order, or so help her, she wasn't *the McDonnell.*

Contrary to what Deydie thought, even if Pippa was pregnant, she wouldn't tell Max anything. She wouldn't tie him down with news like that. If Deydie was right—which remained to be seen—Pippa could raise the bairn on her own. Just like her da had done with her.

Pippa grabbed Max's elbow and headed for the door as the music started up. Quilting Central was going to turn into *dance central* at any moment; the quilting ladies had organized a céilidh to give the winners something to do with their recently won prizes . . . and to keep the local bachelors relatively safe from what the randy women wanted to do to them.

Pippa donned her coat, and at the last second, gave a thought to something else besides getting Max alone.

"Wait here," she said. "I have to speak with Freda."

Pippa rushed over to the punch table that Freda was manning with Aileen. Pippa laid a hand on Freda's arm and said, "Can ye do me a favor?"

Freda gave her a warm smile, tipping her head in the direction of Max. "Certainly, love."

"Can ye check on my da for me?"

Freda frowned, and Aileen jumped in. "I'll go check on him right now. But then sister and I are headed to Lios. We're going on a quilt shop hop."

"Thanks, Aileen," Pippa said.

"I'll stop by in the morning," Freda finally agreed, "to

make sure he has some breakfast." She made it sound like it was the Christian thing to do and not because she still fancied the McDonnell.

Pippa gave her a quick hug, for both agreeing and for not making her confess her plan to stay out all night.

"Now, can you do *me* a favor?" Freda asked. "Can you let the Yank know that I'll leave his quilt for him in the room over the pub?"

"What quilt?"

Freda smiled and nodded her head toward the front of the room where Pippa's quilt hung. "He had me win it for him."

Pippa was a little choked up and feeling sappy that Max would want her quilt. She gave Freda another hug. "I'll talk to you tomorrow."

Max was no longer at the door. Pippa went outside and found him staring out at the sea, his kilt blowing in the wind. His hair had grown since he'd been here and it was tossing in the wind as well.

She sidled up to him, feeling subdued. Part of her wanted to ask him about the quilt—why he would want it. But the question felt too intimate to ask. Which was strange, considering what she planned to be doing with Max tonight.

"Ready?" she finally asked.

"I'm all yours." His expression was thoughtful. She wondered if he knew this was good-bye, too.

"Do ye have yere car keys?"

"Yes."

She pulled her keys from her purse. "It's best we take separate cars."

He looked at her quizzically.

"It's less complicated that way." The people of Gandie-gow were no dummies, and Pippa felt the need to be as discreet as possible. But in the next second, she thought about stopping in the General Store for a pregnancy test, to know once and for all. But that was only asking for trouble, as news like that would travel nearly as fast as the speed of light. She would pick one up in Fairge on her way home tomorrow.

They walked side by side to the parking lot.

Max finally spoke when they reached her car. "Where are we going? The factory?"

She shook her head. "To a cabin I know about, on the edge of Spalding Farm. Follow me. It's not far."

Max brushed her arm as she slipped into her seat. "I'll be right behind you." He closed her door.

His deep baritone remained with her, comforting her, as she drove out of the lot. Thirty minutes and several back roads later, they pulled down the lane to Colin Spalding's cabin tucked into the trees. The moon shone down brightly on the little log cabin. Patches of snow on the roof made it look like a gingerbread house with frosting on top.

She parked her car as Max pulled up. He shut off his vehicle and joined her. Without speaking, they walked to the cabin door. She tipped over the cast-iron statue of a sheep and retrieved the key.

She would not be sad. She would be happy that the evening had taken an unexpected turn for the better. She would enjoy this last night with Max, and let tomorrow's sadness and loneliness be tomorrow's worry.

She unlocked the door and switched on the light. When they went inside, she lit the gas fireplace, grateful for the modern convenience. Colin had updated the amenities, but kept the rustic charm. Near the back wall stood the ladder which led to the loft, the only bedroom in the cabin. Pippa pulled the curtain on the picture window, though there was no need, really. No one would bother them. If anyone came to use the cabin, they would turn around when they saw the cars parked out front.

Max took her hand when she went to pass.

"You know we have to talk first." He looked serious.

"About?"

"Ross," he said. "The engagement."

"Oh, aye. The engagement's off. It had never been truly on. In my heart, I've known all along I couldn't go through with it, but it took me a while to face the truth. And I still need to set the town straight. Though the *Deydie and Bethia grapevine* will handle the majority of it."

Max raised his hand and gently stroked her cheek. "Ross hinted as much. He also said you fancied me."

"Aye." Tonight was a night for truth. Pippa stared into Max's eyes, mesmerized. She needed the memory of this night to last a lifetime. But first, she needed to tell him about the contract.

She unzipped his parka. "I heard from yere company. They accepted almost all of our changes. We should break open a bottle of wine and celebrate." She pushed his coat from his shoulders and he shrugged out of it.

He moved a lock of her hair behind her ear. "The only thing I want to drink in right now is you."

She pulled his sweater over his head, exposing his wonderful chest. "Had ye heard about it from Roger or Miranda?"

"My phone is off," he replied. "Now, *shh*. No more talk of business."

She unbuckled his belt and let it fall to the floor. When she went to remove his kilt, he stilled her hands.

"My turn." He unzipped her coat and removed it.

"Wait," she said as he went to hang it over a chair. "I need to retrieve something first." He handed it back. She pulled the condoms out and shoved them in her jeans pocket. "Provisions."

Instead of removing her blouse next, he pulled her to him and kissed her tenderly.

So this was how it was going to be. Neither one of them was going to say it . . . Good-bye.

"How about we take this upstairs?" she asked.

He shook his head. "You're not going to rush this, Pippa." Very slowly, he traced his finger down her face to the V of her blouse, gazing upon her body as if she were a star to wish upon.

He was right. She was being impatient. She wanted to savor this last time with him, too—take mental photos that she could bring to mind while she spent the rest of her life alone.

She laid a hand over his heart and felt the rise and fall of his chest. As she tilted her head back to gaze into his eyes again, he leaned down and kissed her once more. But this time, he scooped her up and carried her to the sofa in front of the fireplace, his lips gently melding with hers.

As if they had all the time in the world, he kissed her for what seemed liked hours. Finally, they climbed the ladder and slowly undressed each other. This wasn't the playful sex they'd had the first time or the wham-bam they'd had in her office. This was all about cherishing each other and being in the moment.

As Max made love to her, he gazed into her eyes, and

Pippa felt treasured, loved. His eyes spoke the deep feelings that words couldn't name, but she heard them inside of her anyway. They were in a melting pot of emotions and she savored the moments. *They* savored the moments, soaking each other up. And at the moment that they met their climax, Pippa wanted to confess her feelings, but instead let her body say it for her. They dozed and roused, then made love again.

Pippa woke before the sun, pretty sure her internal alarm clock was warning her that the time had come to feel the full force of her broken heart. She slowly slipped out of bed, gazing upon Max as she gathered her panties and bra.

Before climbing down the ladder, she whispered into the darkness, *"Tha gaol agam ort."* It was the best she could do for him, the most she'd ever given any man. It would have to be enough.

For the briefest of moments she wanted to crawl back in bed beside Max, wake him with a kiss, and tell him what Deydie had said. But if Pippa did and he stayed, she'd always have doubts about whether he'd remained in Scotland for her or for the babe. Quietly, she went down the ladder and out the door, her heart aching.

And once outside, she willed herself to put it all behind her. She had a pressing errand to run. One that would reveal which direction her future life would take—single mother or confirmed bachelorette. On the way back to Gandiegow, she stopped at the chemist in Fairge to pick up a pregnancy test, ready to find out which life it would be.

Chapter Twenty

A t Thistle Glen Lodge, Ross finished making a cup of coffee and went back down the hall to Miranda's room. She'd been out cold all night. He didn't approve of what Deydie and Bethia had done to this woman. And he would definitely think twice before drinking anything the two quilting ladies offered him in the future.

He slipped back in and pulled up a chair near Miranda's double bed. He'd rested in the twin-size bed across the room, afraid to leave her, not knowing if what they'd given her would make her do something crazy, like sleepwalk, which would be highly dangerous in a village at the water's edge.

He was halfway through his coffee with the sun barely making an appearance when Miranda rolled over and her eyes fluttered open.

"Morning, sleepyhead," he drawled. He took a sip from his mug, not breaking eye contact with her. He'd had a helluva time getting her pantsuit off her last night and slipping her into the silk nightie. He'd done his best not to look; she'd been hoodwinked enough by the townsfolk.

He laid a hand on the end of her bed. "Ye're just as beautiful this morning as ye were last night." A moment of guilt hit him for hinting at a liaison, but his heart was in the right place. She deserved more than she'd gotten.

"Good morning," she said shyly. She reached up and checked her hair, as if worried about how she looked.

"Personally, I like my women a little rumpled. Ye are amazing."

"I'm glad you stayed over," she said hesitantly. "I wasn't sure if you would." The hard lines of her face softened as a tentative smile grew. Ross got a glimpse of a different woman under her tough exterior—a woman who longed for love and affection. He hoped one day she would find those things for herself.

He rose, tucking in his T-shirt and straightening his kilt. "I hate to leave ye, but I have a job to do. Fishermen seldom take a day off."

She sat up, looking a little downcast.

He moved closer and took her hands in his. "Before I go, though, I want to thank ye for last night. Ye're an incredible woman, Miranda. Very special. Any man would be lucky to have ye." He leaned over and kissed her cheek.

She put a finger to where his lips had been.

"Thank you, Ross." She hesitated for a second and gave him a confident smile. "It was a night I'll never forget."

Pippa sat outside the chemist, waiting for it to open. Maybe she should've gone home first and crawled into bed, pretending she'd been under her own quilt all night and not snuggled up with Max in the loft at the cabin.

But fretting here in front of the chemist was what she deserved. She never should've fallen for the Yank. From the moment she'd set eyes on his beautiful face, she should've known she was a goner.

Besides, she had to sit here. She had to know one way or another if Deydie was telling the truth.

At nine the young female pharmacist unlocked the door. Pippa pulled her hood up, feeling slightly ridiculous. She didn't know the woman in the white lab coat, but Fairge wasn't so far away from Gandiegow that rumors couldn't get started.

Pippa hopped from the car and went in. It took only a second to find what she needed. She made her way to the counter with her wallet in hand.

The woman gave her an expectant expression. Pippa wanted to tell her not to judge, but instead she took her change in silence. Once back in the car, Pippa shoved the pregnancy test to the bottom of her purse and laid her wallet on top. All the way back to Gandiegow she worried what the contents of the box would reveal.

As she drove down the winding road off the bluff to the parking lot below, red flashing lights shattered her deep thoughts and panic overtook her. Who in town needed an ambulance? Had one of the fishermen gotten hurt?

She pulled into the lot and quickly parked. The townsfolk were gathered around the back of the ambulance into which a stretcher was being loaded. The only two people who registered with her were Doc MacGregor and Freda before the crowd parted and let her through.

"Da?" Pippa's voice sounded eerie, conveying every bit of panic her brain hadn't quite registered.

"Daughter," Da said weakly. He was pale, his eyebrows pulled together in pain. "Don't worry."

Pippa clutched at Freda, who took her hands. "What's going on?"

"I was a damned fool," her father said from the stretcher.

"He fell out of his wheelchair," Doc MacGregor put in. "Freda found him. A compound fracture to his other leg." He stepped up into the ambulance. "Let's get some pain meds going."

"Freda?" her da called. "Freda? I want Freda with me."

"All right," Doc said. "There's room." He offered his hand to help Freda up to sit next to the paramedic. Doc looked at Pippa. "Are ye okay to follow us? I could get Dominic to drive ye."

"No. I can do it." She gave one more look at her da, then ran back to her car. As she started the engine, she saw the doors to the ambulance shut and the vehicle circle the parking lot. She followed with her flashers on.

All the way to the hospital, thoughts tumbled through her brain. *Please, God, let him be okay!* Her da had always been everything to her, but she hadn't realized how angry with him she'd become in the months since she'd returned to Gandiegow. In her mind, he'd let her down. But the truth of it was, it was her fault. She'd always held him up so high on a pedestal that the most saintly of men would've eventually fallen.

It hit her that Lachlan McDonnell wasn't the superhero she'd made him out to be. He was just a man with flaws like everyone else. Imperfect. But he was her da, and a good one. Her heart swelled with love for her father. She'd wanted him to accept her as she was and not demand she fit into his preferred mold; but she had to do the same for him, too.

At that moment, she recognized how she'd grown since coming back to Gandiegow. She was no longer the McDonnell's little girl. Not an easy task when your small town always wanted things to remain the same. She was a woman now. She could stand in the truth of who she once was and who she'd become. No longer was she the girl promised to Ross.

She was the Gandiegow lass who could now face head-on what had happened . . . She'd fallen in love with Max McKinley. And her heart was breaking.

Lachlan didn't care about the pain or the infernal racket of the blaring sirens. The only thing he cared about was that Freda was with him inside the blasted ambulance. She gave him strength. And purpose. Lachlan reached out to take her hand.

"Hold still," Doc MacGregor said. "Let the paramedic get the IV in, and then ye'll be able to move your arm."

Lachlan wished he could erase the worry from Freda's face. "I'm sorry, Freda."

She reached across and clasped his free hand in hers, smiling down on him. "Shh, quiet now."

But Lachlan had to get this out. It might be his last chance to make amends.

"I was an arse."

He expected her to deny it, but she seemed to be waiting patiently to see if he had more to say.

"I never should've treated ye the way that I did. I'm so sorry. Ye looked beautiful."

Freda blushed.

Lachlan squeezed her hand. "Ye still do. Ye always have. I should've told ye sooner what ye've come to mean to me."

Freda glanced at Doc, but the man had the good sense to look busy with the medical supplies in his bag.

She didn't shy away from his words, but leaned closer. "What have I come to mean to ye?"

Och, he liked this confident Freda. "Ye're everything to me."

She didn't melt and weep all over him. Instead, she looked determined. "And?"

"And if the doctors can get my bones to heal and make me a healthy, whole man again, I'm going to ask ye to marry me."

Freda smiled at him sweetly, but there was something more behind it. She looked resolute, single-minded, and unwavering . . . like the strong Scottish lass she was. She let go and patted his hand. "Indeed, we'll be married, healed bones or no. I've not loved ye all these years to be without ye now."

He grabbed her hand, overcome with emotion, and made his vow. "Aye, Freda, we'll be married. I love ye, lass." It was a strong man indeed who had tears rolling down his cheeks, and he didn't care a whit if the love of his life, or the doc, or any other damned person saw him crying like a babe.

When Max woke, the cabin was empty. Hell, his chest felt empty, too.

Pippa is gone.

He wasn't surprised. So many times last night he'd wanted to tell her how much she meant to him, but then he'd chicken out. Or maybe it was because she'd gotten her point across loud and clear. From the time they'd reached the cabin until the last time that they'd made love, she'd said good-bye to him with her eyes, with her body, with everything. She wasn't engaged anymore, but apparently she didn't want or need a man in her life. Max wanted to offer her everything, but something inside him needed her to *need* him. And Pippa needed no one. Or at least that was the bullshit she was telling herself.

After Max dressed and tidied up the cabin, he wasn't in any hurry to leave. He sat in front of the fireplace for a long time. Finally, he grabbed his coat, locked the door, put the cabin key under the iron sheep guarding the house, and went to his car.

While he waited for it to warm, he turned on his cell phone, and within a minute it rang. As if a switch had been flipped, his heart pounded and his hopes soared.

But when he checked the name, it wasn't Pippa.

It was Roger Gibbons, president of MTech.

"McKinley here," Max said.

"Why in the hell didn't you call me back last night?" Roger's voice cut in and out, the connection terrible. "I sent you an e-mail. I called and I texted."

Oh, crap.

Max glanced at his phone, but it was too late to read the messages. "Sorry. My phone was off."

Roger went on. "I wanted to congratulate you on a job well done. Of course you shouldn't have allowed so many concessions, but we were able to get back the most important one, so there's still a chance we'll get the subsea valve in the end. Legal faxed the final contract to McDonnell last night."

Max's stomach fell. What concession had she made? God, he hoped Pippa hadn't signed anything this morning. He needed to get hold of her!

"There's another matter I want to discuss," Roger continued. "I just got off the phone with Miranda and she agrees with me. Said you orchestrated the whole deal with little input from her."

Max's connection was bad, but had he heard right? Miranda had given him the credit?

"We think you should head up the new department—Technical Acquisitions. It's been in the works for some time now. We were looking at other candidates, but this deal showed that you're a team player."

"I don't know what to say," Max said honestly. His emotions were reeling. It was a lot to take in. Only a few days ago, he was pretty sure Miranda was going to fire him. "Can I call you back, sir? Our connection is horrible." Max needed to process this new development. But more important, he needed to stop Pippa from signing that contract.

Roger chuckled. "Take your time. Call me later today." He hung up.

Everything Max ever wanted was coming true—a valve that could have saved his father's life was close at hand. He had the chance to head up a new engineering department, something he'd worked toward since college. He'd sacrificed everything for his dream, gave up having a family of his own, and had focused solely on his career. But if he was getting everything he ever wanted, shouldn't he be happier?

This damn deal. He knew in his gut if Pippa signed that contract, Gandiegow would lose in the end. He sent her an urgent text to do nothing until he talked to her. He put the car in gear and started down the path that led to the main road. Pippa may have said good-bye with her body last night, but Max was going to intervene one more time. And getting ahold of her was paramount. He called her number, but it went directly to voice mail. Was she avoiding his calls? Was she at home signing the papers right now? Max drove as fast as the slick, curvy roads would allow.

When he arrived in town, he didn't worry about changing out of Ross's kilt and into a pair of jeans. Right now, he didn't give a crap if his clothes told everyone that he'd stayed out all night. He rushed through town, and he couldn't help but notice things were too quiet.

Over the last few weeks, the closer it got to Christmas, the livelier the town had become—more people decorating, more people carrying boxes and bags from house to house, more merrymaking. Gandiegow had been a regular Norman Rockwell painting. But today was Christmas Eve and the town was dead, as if the zombie apocalypse occurred and no one told him.

At the house with the red roof and green door, Max knocked, then walked in without waiting.

"Pippa?"

No answer.

He rushed to the dark den. "Lachlan? Are you awake?"

The place was silent. Max stepped in and turned on the small lamp so as not to disturb the McDonnell.

But Max was alone . . . except for the empty wheelchair.

"Oh, God." What's going on?

His eyes landed on the fax machine in the corner. He

rushed to it. The contract was there. He flipped to the last page. Pippa hadn't signed it yet. *Thank goodness!* He took the page and shoved it in his pocket in case she came back.

But where was she? And where was Lachlan?

Max left the house and ran to Quilting Central for answers. There, too, the building was empty. He hurried to the restaurant and the pub, and found them empty as well.

At Thistle Glen Lodge, he found Miranda in the bedroom, packing.

Max ran a hand through his hair. "I'm so glad you're here. I was beginning to feel like the last man on Earth."

Miranda glanced over her shoulder. "What are you talking about?"

It registered that she was wearing jeans and a casual sweater. Her hair was wet. She didn't have her face painted up as usual. Maybe he had stepped into an alternate universe after all. Miranda didn't look uptight. She didn't look like Miranda at all. He wondered if this was the real Miranda and the old version was just something that she'd cooked up.

"What's going on?" he asked. "I can't find anyone in town."

"What? No one in town? But I was counting on someone to take me to Inverness. I have a flight out tonight and the taxi company said they can't make it out today."

"Have you seen anyone? The village is deserted."

"Ross was here earlier. But he was off to go fishing. Fishermen seldom take a day off is what he said."

So Ross had spent the night with Miranda. Max felt guilty about that.

Miranda zipped her bag. "Did Roger call you?"

"Yes. Thanks for giving me credit for the deal."

She set her bag on the floor. "You deserved it." She seemed less harsh this morning. Softer, feminine. Then she gave him a wry smile. "You should have closed the deal sooner, but it all turned out in the end."

We'll see.

"And the new position," Miranda said. "Did Roger speak with you about it?"

"Yes. I told him I'd call later."

She eyed Max as if seeing more than he did. "You look as if you might turn it down."

He didn't answer. He didn't know. The most important thing was to find Pippa.

Miranda shrugged. "Your priorities have shifted."

"Why would you say that?"

"You're thinking with your heart now instead of your head." She looked out the window wistfully. "Watching you and Pippa . . . I wondered if that was what love looked like."

"What?" He paused for a second, letting the truth sink in. Could it be true that he loved Pippa? He knew it was killing him to be without her, and the ache, the pain, the joy was the most real thing he'd ever felt. Why hadn't he realized sooner that he loved her? "I didn't plan on it." And he hadn't seen it coming.

Miranda turned back to him and smiled. "Pippa is a lucky woman."

No. He was the lucky one. And he was grateful to Miranda for helping him clear the fog and see his future—Pippa. And maybe it wasn't professional, but he did it anyway. He stepped forward and laid a hand on Miranda's arm. "You're going to find that one guy who feels like he's the lucky one to have you."

Miranda laughed, shaking her head. "One of the reasons I like you, McKinley. You're such an optimist. But in this case, I hope you're right."

He squeezed her arm. "Of course I'm right." He stepped away. "But we need to talk about the MTech deal."

"What about the deal? Roger said it's done."

"Pippa hasn't signed yet. And I'm going to encourage her not to." The answer to NSV's immediate problem must've been brewing in the back of his mind, because now the answer came to him fully formed.

"I'm leaving MTech and staying here. I can't let there be any chance NSV will be closed down. These people need the factory. You see how little they have." He motioned to the town outside the walls. He'd grown quite fond of all the quirky characters of Gandiegow.

Miranda frowned, but she didn't lash out as she would've done in the past. "What do you plan to do?"

"Cash in my investments and my 401(k). I'll put everything into making sure the subsea valve makes it to market." He'd strike a deal with his alma mater to do the testing. His money would be just enough to keep them afloat until the revenue from the subsea shutoff valve began coming in. The oil industry had been waiting for this kind of solution for a long time. It would be a hit. "Maybe I'll start my own consulting firm. I'm pretty good at improving processes, figuring out ways to make companies more efficient." He would love to keep other small companies from going under, too. He would never go back to a huge corporation that didn't care about the little guy, who was interested only in the profit-loss spreadsheet and not its workers, or how their products could improve lives. It would be starting all over again but Max was okay with that. He welcomed the challenge

Another thought hit him. "I'm sorry how this will land on you. If there is anything I can do to stop the fallout, I will."

Miranda waved him off. "I'll be okay. I'm moving up in the company. The deal I made in France is on the fast track. It's bigger and will outshine what happened here. NSV will be ancient history before next quarter. My question to you is can you be happy in such a small town?"

"Yes." With the right person by his side. He just needed to convince Pippa to have him. But first, he needed to find her.

"I've got to run," Max said. "But let me get your luggage. Maybe we'll find someone along the way who can take you to Inverness." And to tell him where the rest of the town was.

She gave him a fond smile. "I'll let you. But only because I know it'll make you feel chivalrous." She'd said things like this before, but this time there was no sarcasm, only sincerity.

Max rolled the suitcase out with Miranda following. When they got to the parking lot, he saw Dougal getting into one of the few cars left besides Ross's rusted truck.

"Wait up," Max shouted. With the suitcase in tow, he rushed over to Gandiegow's postman. "Where is everyone?"

Dougal shook his head. "Ye haven't heard? Everyone who can be there is. Didn't ye read the note on the door of the General Store?"

Max was exasperated. "No. Where did the town go?"

"The hospital. The ambulance took the McDonnell away."

Max's stomach fell. "What happened? Is he all right? Where's Pippa?"

"She followed them to the hospital. I had to finish the last of the mail delivery. The word is that the McDonnell broke his other leg."

"Which hospital?" Max asked.

"St. Timothy's," Dougal replied.

Miranda came up behind him, pulling out her phone. "I'll get the directions."

"What about your flight?" Max asked.

"Let's check on Lachlan first."

"Thanks." Max stowed her luggage in the trunk of his car and they started off. While Miranda's phone relayed the directions, he worried about Lachlan and how Pippa was doing. He had to keep reminding himself which side of the road to drive on, especially when they made it into Inverness with its confusing roundabouts.

At the hospital, they were sent to the fourth floor: surgery. Once the elevator opened, he had no trouble finding the people of Gandiegow. He followed the noise and the crowd down the hall to the surgery waiting area.

Everyone, absolutely everyone, stared at his kilt, but he didn't give a shit.

Pippa was sitting in the middle of the overcrowded space with the quilting ladies surrounding her. It looked as if she was crying. So it was bad news then. Max pushed his way into the room.

The second she saw him, she vaulted from her chair and threw herself at him. He held her tight, never wanting to let go. Ever.

"He's okay," she cried. "The doctor said he made it through surgery like the stubborn old Scot that he is."

Max smoothed back her hair so he could see her eyes. "Are you all right?"

She burst into tears again and buried her face in his neck.

"Come with me. There's something I need to tell you." He tucked her under his arm and guided her from the room, the Gandiegowans parting for them to pass.

He pulled her into the hallway, where Miranda was standing awkwardly.

"Lachlan's surgery went fine," he told her.

She nodded. "Thank you for letting me know. I'll catch a ride from here."

"Good luck, Miranda."

"You, too, Max."

To his annoyance, Deydie and Bethia had sneakily followed them into the hallway, but he couldn't tell the two old quilters to leave.

"Oh, it's you," Deydie said to Miranda, with an uncharacteristically sheepish expression on her face.

"This is perfect," Bethia said, latching on to Miranda's arm. "We were hoping to get another chance. Deydie and I have someone ye should meet. It's Kit Armstrong. Our matchmaker. She's just in here and we've been telling her all about ye."

Deydie looked her up and down. "Ye look nice today, lassie."

Miranda seemed shell-shocked at the quilters' on-slaught.

At that moment Freda showed up, too, and smiled at Miranda. "Deydie and Bethia told me their idea. It's brilliant. Kit thinks ye might be perfect for one of her clients, Art MacKay. If not him, she has plenty of others."

Miranda took a deep breath and spoke, "I'm sorry, Freda. I never should've given you that makeover and made you up that way."

"It's of no matter," Freda said. "Water under the stone bridge. But I'm excited about ye meeting Kit. She'll help. We all will."

Miranda colored. "Why would you help me after what I did?"

Freda laid a hand on her arm. "You deserve a chance at true love, too. Everyone does."

Deydie and Bethia dragged Miranda into the crowded waiting room. Freda headed the other way, which left Max and Pippa in the hallway by themselves.

"I need a minute alone with you," he said.

"I can't believe you're here." She smiled up at him. "I'm so happy to see you!"

As he was leaning down, a male voice called out.

John, Ross's older brother, was hurrying down the hallway toward them. Andrew followed with his arm wrapped securely around Moira.

"What's the news?" John looked worried. "Is the Mc-Donnell all right?"

"Aye." Pippa gave them the update. Then she looked around. "Where's Ross?"

"He's parking his truck. I was worried the piece of junk wouldn't get us here."

Max held on to Pippa's hand, looking forward to telling her everything that was on his mind and in his heart. She pointed toward the waiting room and Max was glad the conversation was coming to an end. He couldn't wait to get Pippa alone. But then the elevator doors opened.

Max gaped at who was inside. It was Cait Buchanan and Mattie and . . . *Graham Buchanan!* The movie star had an arm wrapped around both Cait and the boy.

"Is that . . . ?" Max whispered to Pippa.

"Aye. It's a long story."

Cait ran to Pippa and hugged her. "How is your da?"

"Surgery went well. But what are ye doing here? I thought you were bound for New Zealand."

"Deydie called and told us the news. She knew our flight was delayed. We had to come. We piled in Graham's auto and here we are."

Cait and Pippa walked arm in arm toward the waiting room, which was filled with their people.

Well, *his people* now, too.

Mattie pulled the movie star over to Max and spoke quietly. "Grandda, this is Max McKinley."

Graham stuck out his hand. "Nice to meet you. Pippa's beau, I presume?"

"Aye," Ross said from behind them, clamping a hand down on Max's shoulder. "I think she chose well for herself."

"Welcome to Gandiegow. Ye're going to love it." Graham turned to the boy. "Mattie, do ye think we need to find yere mama before we lose her for good and miss the next plane out?"

"Aye," Mattie said, smiling up at his famous grandfather.

Max followed them down the hallway, but when he looked in the waiting room, he had the sinking feeling he wouldn't be able to get Pippa alone any time soon. Miranda didn't look as though she was going anywhere either. The way Kit had her tucked in the corner, engaged in deep conversation, it looked as if Miranda would need to reschedule her flight.

There was so much Max needed to say to Pippa. He needed to tell her about the MTech deal for one, but it could wait. He felt in his pocket for the last page of the contract and knew it was safe with him.

More important, he had to tell her that he loved her with all his heart. But with Pippa occupied, it might take some time to get her to himself. In the meantime, he could take care of business. And after he acquired what he needed, and as soon as it was at all possible, Max would ask the McDonnell for Pippa's hand in marriage.

Chapter Twenty-one

Pippa saw Max standing in the waiting room doorway, watching her. Everyone in Gandiegow wanted to bend her ear, but just having Max nearby helped, his presence such a comfort. He made his way over, leaned down, and kissed her cheek—in front of the whole town. Sure, she'd jumped into his arms earlier, but this was different.

"I have to head out," he said.

Her heart sank and she sucked in a deep breath. *So this is it. He's leaving for good.* Of course, it couldn't last forever. There was no way Max could stand to live in a tiny town like Gandiegow. He had a life to get back to in the States.

He shook his head and laughed nervously, reaching for and squeezing her hand. "No, no. Just an errand." As if he'd read her mind. "I'll be back."

"Then you won't be gone long?" Everyone was listening to every word she said and she didn't care. She didn't even care how vulnerable she sounded.

"I'll be back before you know it."

"Miss McDonnell?" A nurse stood in the doorway, peering around the crowded room.

"Yes?" Pippa said, standing.

"Yere father wants to see you."

Max pulled her in and kissed her hair this time. "I'll see you soon. Tell Lachlan hello for me."

He walked with her to the hall, but then they parted ways. Pippa followed the nurse through a set of double doors that led into a sterile-looking hallway. Now that her da was going to be okay, Christmas Eve in the hospital seemed surprisingly cheery. For the first time, it registered with her how the nurses and doctors wore Santa caps, and that carolers roamed the hallways. They seemed to be making the rounds, spreading holiday spirit through song, and handing out small gifts of stockings and Christmas candy.

The nurse pointed to the third room on the left. "Yere mother is already in there."

Pippa started to question her, but then noticed Freda sitting inside, holding her da's hand, and gazing upon him with love.

"Dearest?" Freda said. "She's here."

Da's eyes eased open. "Pippa?"

She ran to his bed. There was so much she wanted to say. She wanted to apologize for everything. For running off to Edinburgh. For not coming home sooner to help with the factory. For not being honest where Ross was concerned. But mostly, she wanted to ask for forgiveness ... for not being the daughter she ought to have been.

"Pippa, I'm sorry," her da said, surprising her. His voice was raspy. "Freda's told me that I've been railroading ye into marrying Ross."

"Aw, Da. It's okay." She gave him a gentle hug. "I'm the one who's sorry, for not speaking up and telling ye the truth about not wanting to get married." *Without love.* She took a deep breath, ready to really lay it on the line. "I'll always be your daughter—"

He cut her off. "But ye're not a little girl anymore. Ye have to live yere own life, the way ye see fit."

"Aye." She kissed his forehead.

He smiled up at her. "I'm getting married, though."

Pippa laughed—*oh, how good it felt.* "To who?" she teased.

The McDonnell pulled Freda's hand up and kissed it. "To the woman I've cared about for many, many years."

The nurse leaned in the room. "I need a minute alone to check his incision."

"We'll step out." But Pippa had one message to relay before she left. "Da? Max said to tell you hello."

Her father nodded and she kissed him on the forehead.

Pippa smiled at Freda and took her arm. The two of them left together, united, with the world feeling nearly righted. Except for one thing.

Pippa glanced down at her purse, knowing what lay at the bottom under her wallet. When they arrived in the waiting room, she let go of Freda. "I'll be back." Feeling determined, she bravely went in search of the restroom.

It took two minutes to read the directions, less than one to do the deed, and five to find out if her life was changed forever. After it was done, Pippa stared in the mirror for a long time, trying to glimpse any difference in her reflection.

She was still the same lass, the one who would remain in Gandiegow to run the factory. But she was different from when she moved back home, because now she knew this was the life she wanted. *If Freda can stretch and grow in our small town, then so can I.* Pippa wouldn't be alone. She'd have her da, once he got over the shock of it, and Freda would be as wonderful to the babe as she'd been with her.

And she wouldn't think any more on Max leaving. It was enough that he was in Scotland now, when she needed him most.

She wet a paper towel, laid it to her cheeks, and calmed her red face. "Sufficient unto the day," she said to the mirror. "Sufficient unto the day."

Deydie didn't necessarily like the big city, but she sure had to hand it to their grocery stores. It took several hours, but she and Bethia finally found everything they needed. Now that the McDonnell was out of danger, many had returned home for their own Christmas Eve festivities. Deydie still couldn't believe Miranda had left with Ailsa and Aileen to have dinner with them.

"Hurry up and get the food unloaded," Deydie ordered. "It's late." And the others would be there soon. They were going to have a feast in the waiting room. And if the McDonnell was up to it, they'd roll him down to join them whether the bossy nurses would allow it or not. She'd vowed not to miss her Caitie, Graham, and Mattie, and would think of them only when she drank a toast to their good health.

By the time they made their way back upstairs to the entrance of the waiting room, Deydie was winded. Bethia, too. And Pippa was the only one in sight, sitting alone, staring off at nothing with a foolish look on her face.

Deydie marched up to her and handed over her armload. "Make yereself useful and set these things out over there."

Pippa glanced up at her as if seeing her for the first time. "Oh. Sure." She stood.

Deydie harrumphed. "So, now, do ye believe me?" She didn't need to say the word "pregnant" for the lass to know what she was about.

Pippa only smiled.

Deydie picked up a package of napkins and tore them open. "Have ye talked to the lads about yere predicament?" She nodded to the room down the hall, meaning the Yank and the McDonnell.

Pippa spun away, fiddling with a container of figgy pudding, not answering her, as if she didn't hear.

Before Deydie could light into her, Max appeared.

"I'm back." He crossed the room quickly and kissed the lass on the cheek. "Is everything all right? How's the McDonnell?"

"Doing well," Pippa said. "He's awake. I just peeked in on him."

"Are ye gonna tell him now?" Deydie said to Pippa pointedly.

The stubborn lass glared at her and shook her head. Deydie wished she had her broom to knock some sense into the girl. Keeping secrets could only lead to trouble.

Max must've had something else on his mind, because he didn't seem to notice. "I'm going to see if I can speak with your father." The Yank seemed nervous. He smiled once more at Pippa, then walked away determinedly.

Deydie shook her finger at Pippa. "I'm tired of nagging ye." She latched onto Bethia's arm. "Come on." Christmas Eve or no—it was time for at least the Mc-

Donnell to know the truth. Deydie dragged her old friend from the waiting room with her.

Once in the hallway, Bethia tried to pull back. "Haven't we intervened enough?"

"Nay." But when they rounded the corner, the Yank stood outside the McDonnell's door, talking to himself and pacing.

Deydie dropped Bethia's arm, rushed to the room, and pushed past the Yank. She put her hand out. "You wait. I need a moment with the McDonnell first."

The lad acted as if he wanted to argue.

"Ye're no match for me. Now go help Pippa with the food," Deydie said.

He looked frustrated as hell, but she didn't care. She had real business with the McDonnell. *Baby business.* When Max didn't budge, she left him standing in the hall.

Bethia followed her in and grabbed her arm. "Deydie, let things take their natural course. Please. For once."

Freda glanced up from her conversation with the Mc-Donnell. "Deydie and Bethia have come to see ye, Lachlan. I'll get you propped up." She pushed a button on the side of the bed and the top half rose.

He waited a moment while she adjusted his pillows for him. When he was settled, he looked toward them. "How's my two favorite ladies?"

Deydie huffed, knowing he thought them a couple of busybodies. "I'm not going to beat around the bush. I know ye've had a tough go of it, but I've something to say. And since no one else will do it, then I will. Ye need to make the Yank stay in Gandiegow, come hell or high water."

The McDonnell's brows pulled together. "What's this about?"

"Max," Bethia provided.

"Stop frowning at me that way," Deydie said. "I'm not the one who got Pippa pregnant."

"What?" The McDonnell leaned forward, stopped suddenly, and winced. "Bethia, is it true?"

Bethia sighed. "Deydie says it is, and ye know she's never wrong on that count."

Deydie tried again. "Max'll have to stay and help Pippa care for the bairn. Ye can't let him skip town."

The McDonnell slammed his hand on the tray. "Send McKinley to me."

Deydie felt like they'd done this before.

"Ye should take a minute to calm down," Bethia said.

The McDonnell pushed away the tray. "I said send Max McKinley to me now!"

Pippa heard her father yell Max's name. She ran down the hall, knowing exactly what was going on. As she rounded the corner, she saw Deydie drag Max inside.

"Shit," Pippa hissed. "Those two are up to it again."

When she got to her da's door, Freda was just leaving. "I was coming to get you."

Pippa crossed the threshold. Her father was much more awake than earlier, now propped in his bed, glaring at Max who stood by the window. Deydie hovered next to Da, acting like a sentinel to the proceedings. Poor Bethia cowered behind her.

"Pippa's here, too," Freda said.

The McDonnell waved his good arm. "Pippa, go stand next to Max so I won't have to crank my head around. I'll speak to ye both."

"Sir, I wanted to talk to you, too. About a couple of things. The MTech deal—"

Pippa grabbed his arm. "The deal is done. I only need to sign the final contract."

Max shook his head. "No."

"I don't want to talk about the MTech deal," the McDonnell growled.

Max put his hand up. "Don't let her sign. I'm your new investor."

"What?" both she and her da said together.

Max turned to her and took her hand. "MTech won't give up until they have everything—your patents, and the doors to NSV closed for good. I know you made a concession to make the deal. You can't sign, Pippa." She stared into his eyes and drank in the honesty and sincerity there. She could gaze upon him forever.

Max turned back to her da. "This next part is trickier. I wanted to speak with you in private, but if I don't get this out soon . . ."

"I already know," the McDonnell ground out. He motioned to Deydie and Bethia. "They told me."

Max's expression was a puzzled mixture of a frown and curiousness. "How did they know I wanted to ask your permission to marry your daughter?"

Pippa couldn't breathe. And her da cocked his head to the side as if he was letting Max's words roll in so he could process them. Pippa needed to cock her head to the side, too.

"I love her, sir. Heart and soul."

Bethia exhaled.

Deydie smacked her knee. "Best news I've heard all day."

Freda only smiled.

Max turned back to Pippa. "I should've realized from the beginning that I'd fallen in love with you. But I was bullheaded enough to think I didn't need love and marriage. You've given me everything, Pippa, everything that was missing. You gave me back the spirit of Christmas. You made me part of the community that I now feel is my own." He kissed her hands. "But most of all, you've shown me I can love beyond measure. Marry me, Pippa. Say you'll be mine forever."

Pippa leaned over and kissed him as proof of what was in her heart, also. "I love ye, too, Yank."

Her da cleared his throat. "Can I get my two pence in? I haven't replied to Max's request yet, so ye two are getting the cart before the draft horse."

"Aye. They got it all arse-backward," Deydie said with a hearty laugh.

"They did indeed." Da looked intently at Max. "To whether I'll give permission or not, this is my answer . . . the only way I'll bless this union between the two of you is if ye promise to raise my grandchild—"

"Granddaughter," Deydie corrected.

Da gawked at Deydie. "Really? A granddaughter?"

"Aye."

Pippa didn't dare look in Max's direction. What if he was upset, or angry, or he didn't want their baby. She couldn't bear it.

Da continued on. "As I was saying, the only way I'll bless this union is if ye raise my granddaughter in Gandiegow." Her father stared at Max, waiting for an answer.

Pippa was waiting, too, terrified Max would want to catch the first flight out of Scotland.

Max spun and grabbed her arms, gazing into her eyes, searching. "God, Pippa! Is it true? Are we going to have a baby?"

"Nay," Pippa said, trying to hide her joy. "Ye're going to sit by and watch me while I grow large, and then I'm going to have the bairn."

Max kissed her hard and quick, leaving her breathless. But not breathless enough not to tease. "I'll let ye change the nappies though."

"This is great news!" Max hugged her and twirled her around, which wasn't an easy feat considering the tight quarters.

Her da cleared his throat louder this time. "Ye've not answered me, son."

Max put Pippa down and gave her da his full attention. "Yes. Of course, we'll raise our child in Gandiegow."

Max's phone rang then. The familiar twinge of jealousy was gone. Kit said she was going to find Miranda a good man to call her own—either in Scotland, or Alaska, or someone back in the States. It didn't matter. Pippa had her man.

"Take it," she said. She leaned down and kissed her father on the cheek. "Thank you, Da."

"Mom?" Max beamed at Pippa with his phone to his ear. "Merry Christmas Eve to you, too. I've got big news." He gazed over at Pippa with love in his eyes. "You know how you've always wanted to come to Scotland? Well, pack your bags."

He smiled at them then. "I'm going to book you and Bitsy into the Kilts and Quilts retreat."

He held the phone away from his ear as they all heard

his mother squeal. Deydie clapped her hands with delight.

"But I'll need the whole family here, too—Jake, Little Max, Hannah, everyone. Bring nice clothes." He paused and listened. "Because you'll be coming to the wedding."

Pippa took his hand and squeezed.

His eyes twinkled. "Whose wedding?" he repeated back into the phone. "Mine."

His glee vanished and worry took its place. He shifted away from them. "I know . . . I know, Mom . . . Don't cry."

He listened for a second. "You're going to love her, Mom. Her name is Pippa."

Suddenly a nurse appeared behind the quilting ladies. "What's going on in here?"

Good ole Bethia was on it. She spun around and touched a frail hand to the nurse's arm. "Would ye like to join us for our Christmas Eve feast in the waiting room? We bought plenty. Maybe all the nurses on the floor would like to stop in."

No one could deny Bethia when she was at her sweetest, but the nurse gave it a weak try.

"But I've got to take Mr. McDonnell's vitals."

"Right. Right." Bethia patted her. "Can we have another moment?"

The nurse nodded in agreement.

Bethia ushered her out.

Max still held the phone to his ear. "The ring?" He smiled down at Pippa and pulled out a box.

That smile always did make her breath catch.

"Hold on a second, Mom." Max put the phone on speaker and laid it on the floor. While he was down there, he dropped to one knee and held out the opened ring box. "Pippa, I didn't get your answer before. Will you be my wife and make me the happiest man in the world?"

A sob escaped from Pippa. *Engineers don't cry.* But maybe this one did, especially since her heart was so full.

"Aw, Yank, of course, I'll marry ye." She looked over to see her da, who wiped the mist from his eyes as well. Cheering resounded on the other side of the phone. She helped Max to his feet, took the ring from the box, and slipped it on her finger. "It's beautiful."

"It's the reason for my errand earlier," he said.

The design was perfect, a simple wide gold band with a single diamond. Her man understood her so well. She wrapped her arms around him and kissed him soundly, sealing the deal for all time.

Deydie pushed past them. "Stop accosting him and get yere arses down the hall. I'm hungry and the food will be too cold to eat. Or the nurses will've reived it all before we get any, or the rest who are coming."

"The rest?" Pippa asked.

Freda touched Pippa's arm. "Those from Gandiegow who don't have family close by. We were planning a Christmas Eve feast at Quilting Central, but we moved it to the hospital. Abraham is driving a van full here right now."

"Aye. So hurry it along," Deydie said.

It didn't take long to finish setting up the waiting room into a buffet. In the end, Pippa, Max, and Freda made their plates and took them back to her da's room.

Love was definitely in the air. Neither she nor Max could keep from gazing at each other, and Da and Freda couldn't keep from staring at each other either.

Freda left for a few moments and came back with

Deydie, Bethia, and a bag of presents. "I had Abraham stop by my cottage and yeres to pick them up."

Pippa was glad she'd had the foresight to wrap her packages days ago and slip them under the tree. She dug in the sack and pulled out the first one to give to her da.

"For me?" But before she could answer, Da ripped off the paper and a dozen engineer notebooks spilled out.

She picked them up and set them in his lap. "I'm a practical lass. I expect yere help with the factory. I need ye to fill those up with new ideas for us to try."

Her father beamed at her, but it was Freda who spoke up.

"Not until after the honeymoon. Do ye hear me, Lachlan?"

"Aye," her da agreed.

They all laughed.

Pippa dug out Freda's present next. She could see the question in her future mama's eyes as she sized up the package with her hands.

"No. It's not a cookbook," Pippa said. "Go on. Open it."

Freda carefully undid each tape strip as if to savor the moment. When she pulled out the pillow and flipped it to the front, she gasped. "Oh, Pippa, it's beautiful."

"Better than a cookbook?" Pippa was pretty happy with how the quilted house block pillow had turned out.

Tears ran down Freda's face. "I love it."

Bethia handed Freda a tissue, but Deydie pounded her on the back. "It's not truly Christmas until someone cries."

Everyone laughed again.

Freda grabbed a box and handed it over to Pippa. "I've got yere present right here."

"What is it?"

Freda smiled at her warmly. "I had a feeling I needed to hurry it along. And I was right."

Pippa pulled off the ribbon and opened the box. Inside was the English paper piecing quilt top that Freda had been laboring over—on and off—for years. Pippa held the unfinished quilt up, the perfect size for a baby. "But how did ye know?"

Deydie grabbed the quilt top and checked the stitching. "I might've let it slip."

Pippa carefully took the quilt from Deydie and held it to her chest. "Does that mean the whole town knows that I'm pregnant?"

"Nay," Deydie said. "I just didn't see any harm in letting Freda know as she's going to be yere mama."

Pippa wrapped an arm around Freda's shoulders. "Thank you. It's perfect. And I am so happy about you and Da. Ye deserve all the happiness in the world."

Freda glanced over at him. "I know. And now I have it in ye two." She glanced down at Pippa's belly. "Well, three." Then she looked at Max and laughed through her tears. "Our family is growing quickly."

There was more laughter as other presents were handed out. Pippa went to sit beside Max. She took his hand and squeezed it. "I got ye a present, too."

"Oh?"

"It's not something ye can unwrap here." She raised her eyebrows, giving him a knowing gaze. "But maybe we can steal away later and I can show ye."

He kissed her. "I'm going to love being married to you."

"Aye. I'll do my best to keep it interesting."

"Pippa?" Da said, interrupting them from making bedroom eyes at each other. "Lass, it's time for me to give ye my Christmas present."

Pippa looked around, but all the gifts had been unwrapped.

Her da noticed. "It's not here. It's back in Gandiegow."

Freda stood beside Da with her hand on his shoulder. He looked up at her and smiled.

"Freda and I talked about it, and we're giving ye and Max the house."

Pippa stood, maybe a little too quickly, because she felt woozy. Max steadied her, standing, too, wrapping an arm around her waist.

It took a second, but Pippa finally found her voice. "Where are you going to live?"

"I'll move in with Freda."

"After we're married, of course," Freda clarified.

"Which will be soon," her da added.

Pippa still couldn't believe it. "But why? It's yere home. Why give us the house?"

Her da smiled playfully. "To fill it with grandbabies."

Max hugged her, squeezing her middle and whispering into her hair. "That we can do."

Epilogue

Pippa lay on the cold table as Max stood beside her. They both stared at the screen in disbelief. It had been a crazy couple of months. Their double wedding with her da and Freda had been quite the undertaking, especially with Deydie as the head wedding planner. At the end of the day, though, she and Max, Da and Freda were married. How happy everyone was now, and the best news of all was that her father was responding well to his new treatment. But this . . .

"Deydie was wrong." Max's voice held wonder.

"Sort of." Pippa couldn't quite wrap her brain around what she was seeing, and what the technician had said. She thought about their bedroom back in Gandiegow, with the quilt from the auction hanging on the wall behind their bed, and the cradle sitting at the foot, the cradle that had been hers as a baby.

Max gazed down at her with complete love and devotion in his eyes. "Deydie was right about one thing; we are having a girl."

"Aye." Pippa tugged Max's hand until he got the

hint and gave her a quick kiss. "But we're having a boy, too."

"Sonograms never lie," Max said.

Pippa smiled up at the love of her life. "We're going to need another cradle."

Continue reading for a preview
of the next book in
Patience Griffin's Kilts and Quilts series,

The Trouble with Scotland

Coming from Signet Eclipse in April 2016.

Chapter One

A light Scottish summer breeze deposited a leaf on the hood of Ross Armstrong's red truck. He brushed it aside, dropped the rag he'd been using into a bucket, and stepped back, admiring his masterpiece—a newly restored 1956 Ford F-1. Ross hadn't done it all by himself, not by a long shot. His brothers, John and Ramsay, had helped, and Doc MacGregor had been invaluable, from rebuilding the engine to the new paint job. But Ross felt a sense of accomplishment anyway.

As if the wind had dropped something heavier than a leaf—perhaps an anchor—a thought hit him, crushing his good mood. *Now what am I going to do?*

For the last seven months he'd spent every spare second on his truck when he wasn't working on the family commercial fishing boat or helping out at NSV, the North Sea Valve Company. He'd filled his time, hoping to keep the women, *and men*, of Gandiegow from bugging him, trying to set him up with their daughters and granddaughters. Now that Pippa—his ex-long-intended—was married, the town thought he should be hitched, too.

But Ross had other plans. With Robert and Samuel

out of school for the summer, the teens could take his place on the family fishing boat while Ross did something else.

He just didn't know what.

"There you are."

Ross groaned as he glanced back at Kit, the town matchmaker, barreling toward him. She might be his sister-in-law, but it didn't give her the right to meddle in his nonexistent love life. Sure as shite, she held her damned matchmaking notebook to her chest, and right beside her was Harry Dunn looking intently at him, too.

Ross tossed the bucket into the bed of the pickup, pulled his keys from his pocket, and hopped into the front. "Gotta run."

"Wait up," Harry hollered. "My niece is coming in today for the quilt retreat. She wants to meet you."

Ross turned the key and revved the engine. "Sorry, Harry. Can't hear ye over the noise." He cranked the window up as fast as he could and pulled out.

"That was a close call," Ross said to the refurbished gray interior of the truck.

He wasn't being rude, only preserving what little sanity he had left. He'd done what the town had wanted. He'd waited years for Pippa to return so they could marry. She'd returned, all right, but instead of marrying him, she'd met and married her true love, Max. Max was a hell of guy, and Ross wholeheartedly gave his blessing to their quick wedding. That should've been enough to satisfy Gandiegow. *But no.* The second Pippa was married, Kit started pestering Ross to take out the new schoolteacher. Against his better judgment, and to get Kit and everyone else off his back, he'd gone to dinner a time or two with

Kirsty. She was okay—nice-looking and everything—but his time would've been better spent chopping bait for the family fishing boat.

As he drove from the community parking lot and up the bluff, he caught a glimpse in the rearview mirror of Kit with her hands on her hips. There'd be hell to pay for foiling her plans. He was going to have to talk to his brother Ramsay about setting his wife straight. Ross couldn't be tied down right now. This was his time to play the field. Hell, he wanted to wear it out!

Maybe he should drive to Lios or Fairge to do just that. But first he had to pick up some goat cheese at Spalding Farm for Dominic and Claire, Gandiegow's restaurateurs.

Farther up the road over the bluff, just past NSV, a coach bus came into view. Ross eased his truck to the side to let them pass. Harry's niece was most certainly on that bus headed for the quilt retreat. He pulled back into the road and kept going.

But going where? *Have I wasted my life up until now?* His little brother Ramsay, for gawd's sake, owned his own business! Ross had always worked on the family fishing boat. And that was fine, but shouldn't he want more? What did he own besides this truck and a few shares in NSV? He'd wasted his life doing what was expected.

As if a thick fog had lifted, everything became clear. He was done doing what everyone else wanted, and he wasn't going to do what was expected anymore!

He glanced over at the quilted grocery bags beside him. *Except today*. He would run errands for the village. But later ...

Later he would make a stand and take back his life.

*   *   *

Sadie Middleton didn't like zombie movies, but as she stepped off the bus a mile out of Gandiegow, Scotland, she felt like the lead in her own dreadful film. *Sadie of the Dead.* Not some glamorous zombie, either, but a plain zombie who wanted to vanish. The other women around her were excited, giddy about their first evening at the quilt retreat. Sadie only felt waylaid. Shell-shocked. Miserable. If she were still at home in North Carolina, she would have been sitting on the porch with her grandmother Gigi, drinking sweet tea and waiting for the July Fourth fireworks to begin.

Except they weren't in the U.S.

And Gigi was dead.

The gravel crunched under Sadie's feet as she made her way, along with the other quilters, to the North Sea Valve Company's factory door. Their bus had died and coasted into the parking lot, and they were to wait here until she and the others could be transported into the small town. She leaned against the building, unfolded the printed e-mail, and read it again:

Dear Sadie and Gigi,

Pack your bags! Your team has won the grand prize in the quilt block challenge. Congratulations! You are coming to Gandiegow! For complete information regarding your free Kilts and Quilts Retreat and all-expense-paid trip to Scotland, please e-mail us back.

Sincerely,
Cait Buchanan
Owner, Kilts and Quilts Retreat

Having read the note a hundred times, Sadie shoved it back in her pocket. It seemed a cruel joke from the universe—to receive this letter only hours after Gigi's funeral.

At hearing the news about the retreat, her brother, Oliver, had gone into hyperdrive, using his grief to propel him into action. Insisting Gigi would have wanted Sadie to fulfill their dream of a quilt retreat abroad, Oliver had made all the arrangements and had brought her to Scotland—packing her bags and having her out the door before Sadie had known what had happened. His bullying made the trip feel more like a kidnapping than a respite.

Sadie's grief had the opposite effect, immobilizing her, making her want to crawl under a quilt and never come out. She waffled between feeling despondent and angry. But the one constant was her guilt for the part she'd played in her grandmother's death.

Her quilted Mondo bag slipped from her shoulder . . . She and Gigi had made matching bags at their last quilting retreat together. Memories of that glorious weekend were stitched into Sadie, the moments long and meaningful. She pulled the bag up, held it close, and squeezed her eyes shut.

The last twenty-four hours were wearing on her. Sadie was exhausted, depleted. But she had to keep it hidden at all costs. She glanced over at her ever-helpful brother as he assisted the rest of the women off the bus. *Good.* He was being kept busy. She was sick to death of Oliver's fussing over her and telling her what to do.

At that moment, two vans pulled up. A tall nice-looking man got out of one and a clearly pregnant strawberry blonde got out of the other. As they spoke to the bus driver, the woman handed over her keys to him.

Oliver, who had only just finished unloading the last quilter from the bus, hurried to the couple who'd brought the vans. "Excuse me."

"Yes?" answered the man. He clearly had an American accent.

Oliver pointed to Sadie. "My sister needs to be in the first group into town."

Embarrassment radiated from her toes to her scalp. *Dammit, Oliver.* Sadie ducked behind another woman as the two newcomers turned in her direction.

"Sure," the man said. "We can take her in first. I'm Max, by the way."

Oliver introduced himself, too, and unfortunately felt the need to explain further. "My sister is ill."

The couple's curious gaze transformed into compassion. The women around Sadie spun on her with pity as well, staring at her as if they hadn't just spent the last couple of hours with her on the bus in quasinormal companionship. To them, Sadie had been just another quilter, a fellow retreat-goer. Now she wasn't. She was to be flooded with sympathy and compassion. No longer included. On the outside because of her disease.

Oliver spoke to Sadie but pointed to the vans. "Get in. They'll get you to town." He'd said it as if Sadie's problem was with her ears and not her kidneys.

Without a word and anxious to hide her red face, Sadie walked with a compliant exterior to the van. On the inside, though, she was raging. She climbed in and took a seat in the back. A minute later, others were climbing in as well. No one sat next to her, leaving her alone to look out the window at her overly responsible brother.

The couple climbed into the front seat of the van and

began chatting with the other quilters. Sadie found out the couple's names and their connection to Gandiegow— Max and Pippa were engineers at the North Sea Valve Company and were recently married. They kept up a steady conversation, asking the quilters about themselves, but thankfully left Sadie alone.

A few minutes later, when they reached Gandiegow's parking lot, a group of men and women were waiting for them.

"We're a closed community," Pippa explained. "No cars within the village. Everyone is here to help carry yere things to the quilting dorms." Sure enough, many of the women had wagons beside them, while the men had their muscles. "Deydie will want everyone at Quilting Central as soon as possible. She's the head quilter and town matriarch." Pippa made it sound as if they'd better do as Deydie bid or there might be trouble.

One by one, they disembarked from the van. When Sadie got out, a young woman in a plum-colored dress moved forward.

"I'm Moira. I'll help ye get settled into the quilting dorm."

Sadie followed her, quite pleased with her handler. Moira was blessedly quiet and shy.

Even though it was early evening, the sun was in the sky, probably due to how far north they were. They walked through the minuscule town along a concrete path that served as a wall against the ocean. Moira pointed to where Oliver was to stay and then took Sadie next door to the quilting dorm Thistle Glen Lodge. It was nothing more than a bungalow set against the green bluffs of summer, which rose nearly straight up at the back of the town. The young woman led Sadie inside to the way too cheery interior and down the hall to a room with three beds. The decorations were plaid and floral—a little French country on the northeast coast of Scotland— and too optimistic and exuberant for Sadie. Two of the beds had personal items on them, from her roommates for the next week.

Moira watched Sadie and nodded. "Aye. The Sisters MacCrumb from Perth—Polly and Paddie." Her voice was quiet but lilting. "This is their second retreat with us. Nice women. Arrived an hour ago. Ye'll like them ... friendly but not overly."

Perfect.

Moira motioned for Sadie to go on in. "You can store yere clothes in the armoire. The kitchen is stocked with tea, coffee, and snacks. But all yere meals are provided either at Quilting Central or the restaurant. If ye like, though, I can bring ye scones and tea in the morns."

Sadie set her Mondo bag on the bed. Moira was nice, but Sadie wanted only to be left alone to crawl under the quilt and hibernate until life wasn't so crushing. And she was so very tired. People didn't understand that though she looked fine, she was often exhausted and run-down. Patients with chronic kidney disease usually weren't di- agnosed until it was too late, already in stage four like herself, and in need of a kidney transplant.

She'd found out only last month, and Gigi had prom- ised to be with Sadie every step of the way. But Gigi was gone, leaving Sadie to deal with everything alone. Oliver couldn't; he had his own life. He didn't have time to sit with her while she had her blood drawn week after week. He couldn't put his life on hold while Sadie waited for the day to come when the doctors would move her to the active transplant list.

Sadie looked up, realizing she'd slipped into herself again, something she'd been doing a lot since her diagnosis.

Moira, though, seemed to understand and went to the door. "I'll give ye a few minutes to settle in. Then Deydie expects all the quilters at Quilting Central for introductions and the quilting stories." It was another warning that Sadie shouldn't dawdle.

A sound rang out, a hard knocking at the front door that made her jump.

Moira put her hand up, either to calm Sadie's frazzled nerves or to stop her from going for the door herself. "I'll see who it is."

Sadie dropped down beside her bag and smoothed her hand over the pinwheel quilt that covered the bed. A minute later she heard her brother's exasperating voice at the entrance. Heavy footsteps came down the hall. She thought seriously about crawling out the window to escape what was sure to be more nagging.

She didn't turn to greet him. "What do you want, Oliver?"

"I came to walk you to the retreat. We have to hurry, though. One of my clients needs me to hop online and check for a bug."

If only Gandiegow didn't have high-speed Internet, then Oliver wouldn't have been hell-bent on coming to Scotland to keep an eye on her! But her brother's IT business was portable.

Moira saved Sadie. "Don't worry. I'll get her to Quilting Central safely."

He remained where he was. Sadie could feel his gaze boring into her back.

"Go on, Oliver. Your customer is waiting."

She still didn't hear him leave. Sadie rolled her eyes heavenward and heaved herself off the bed. She plastered on a fake smile and faced him. "I'm fine. Really."

"Okay. But if you need me, I'll be next door at Duncan's Den." The other quilting dorm, only a few steps from this one.

Sadie nodded.

Oliver held his phone up as if to show her he was only a call away.

"Come," Moira said. "It's time to meet Deydie and the other quilting ladies."

Oliver gave Sadie one more worried glance, then left. She grabbed her Mondo bag and a sweater.

Outside, Sadie trudged along, and for the first time, really looked around. The village arced like a smile facing the ocean, the little stone cottages an array of mismatched teeth that somehow seemed to fit together. The rounded green bluff loomed at the backs of the houses, a town blocked in, but cozy. Yes, the village was *quaint* with its oceanfront views from nearly every house. But sadness swept over Sadie once again. Gigi would've loved it here, as she often reminisced fondly of the small town in Montana along the Bitterroot River where she'd grown up.

Moira stopped in front of a building with a sign that read QUILTING CENTRAL. "This is it."

Sadie opened the door and stepped in. And a tidal wave of emotion hit her.

The smell of starch.

White- and gray-headed women.

Fabric stacked and stashed everywhere.

All the things that reminded her of Gigi. If that wasn't enough to have her bolting for the door, a crowd of women scuttled toward her. She backed up.

One tall, thin elderly woman clasped her arm, stilling her. "We're so glad ye're here. I'm Bethia."

A short battle-ax of a woman barreled through to get to Sadie, grabbing her other arm. "I'm Deydie. We've been waiting on ye."

Sadie was short of oxygen. She desperately wanted to disappear.

Gray-haired twins, wearing matching plaid dresses of different colors, stepped in her path. The red-plaid one spoke first.

"Sister and I were distraught when we lost our gran."

They knew. Sadie looked at the faces around the room. *They all knew.*

The green-plaid one bobbed her head up and down. "That was many years ago. We've all experienced loss." She gestured toward the crowd. "We understand what ye're going through."

The other whispered loudly to her sister, "But not about the kidney disease."

Oh, crap! Sadie wasn't the all-out swearing type, but internally she formed a string of obscenities to sling at her brother that made her cringe.

"Back," Deydie said to the twins. "Give the lass room to breathe. She's not well."

Well enough to scream!

A thirty-something woman carrying a baby made her way to Sadie. "I'm Emma. And this is Angus." She had a

British accent, not a Scots one like the others. She turned to Deydie. "I should take over—don't you think?"

Deydie nodded vigorously. "Right. Right. It should be ye." The old woman cleared the others away.

"Come sit down," Emma said. "The town can be a bit overbearing. But they mean well." She led Sadie to a sofa.

Deydie called everyone's attention to the front and began welcoming all the quilters.

Emma leaned over. "I'm a therapist. It can be helpful to talk to someone when you're grieving. I wanted to let you know that I'm available if you need me."

A moment ago, Sadie had thought the woman had her best interests at heart, but she was just like the others, trying to suffocate her, trying to tell her how to deal with her grief. Sadie didn't deserve their attention. Her selfishness had killed her grandmother. She opened her mouth to set the well-meaning therapist straight, but the woman's baby fortuitously spewed down his mother's blouse.

"Excuse me." Emma stood with the little one. "We'll talk later."

Or not.

Emma's leaving should've given Sadie's senses a reprieve, but in some respects, all the women smothering her had been a distraction. The room, this place, was too much, and she couldn't sit here with a huge group of women reminding her of her grandmother. Sadie had to get out of here . . . escape!

She looked longingly toward the door, only ten feet away. Everyone was listening to Deydie, finally not focused on her. She stood nonchalantly and walked toward the exit, slowly and with purpose, like she'd left her curling iron on back at the dorm.

Two more steps. She eased the door open so carefully that the bell above the door barely jingled.

She slipped out, gulping in the cool summer air like it was water and she'd been stuck in the desert. But it wasn't enough. The town still felt claustrophobic. She'd do anything to get out of here!

The tide was up and the ocean was slapping itself against the walkway with increasing ferocity and passion. The sea was alive, the waves crashing, telling her to run.

And on the breeze, she heard the strangest thing . . . male voices singing. It was surreal. She followed the sound, heading back in the direction of the parking lot where the van had dropped them off. She stopped when she discovered the music was coming from the first building in town, the pub The Fisherman. The song pulled her up the steps and had her opening the door. As she crossed the threshold, the song came to an end.

The room was mostly filled with men, all sizes. The vast majority looked as if they could've done a magazine shoot for *Fishermen Now.* A few looked her way, but being plain, she didn't have to worry about anyone hitting on her or even approaching.

She put her head down, made her way to the bar, and sat on the only open stool at the far end. Next to her was a particularly large, rugged, all-muscle—and from what she could see of his profile—handsome man, undoubtedly one of the fishermen, too. Another man, short and squat, stepped between them, partially blocking her view of Handsome.

Squat clamped a hand on Handsome's shoulder. "Ye'd like my niece, Euna. She's not a pretty lass, but she can cook and sew. She'd make ye a good wife—I promise she will. At least meet her while she's here for the retreat."

The way Handsome was scowling over his drink, Sadie was certain he hadn't been one of the men singing moments ago. He looked as if he'd given up singing permanently.

The bartender waved to Sadie. "What can I get ye?"

"Water," she said automatically. Cola and alcohol were now out-of-bounds. She would do everything she could to keep off the active transplant list for as long as possible.

Handsome glanced her way and, damn, he was good-looking. Not that a guy like him would notice someone like her. Sure enough, he went back to his drink without a word.

Squat was fidgeting, beginning to look desperate. "What do ye say? I told Euna ye'd see her. Take her to dinner. Or maybe have a stroll to the top of the bluff." He chewed the inside of his cheek. "The exercise would do her good."

Sadie felt sorry for Handsome. Couldn't Squat see that he didn't want to do it? The bartender set her glass in front of her and left to help a patron at the other end.

"Dammit, Harry," Handsome growled. "Ye're putting me in a hell of a spot."

Sadie made a snap decision. She reached for her glass and clumsily knocked it over, spilling water all over Harry.

He jumped back. "What'd'ya do that for?"

She reached for the towel at the end of the bar and began blotting at the water on Harry's shirt. "So sorry. I guess I wasn't paying attention."

When Harry wasn't looking, she tilted her head at Handsome for him to make a run for it. This fisherman was no dummy. He was out the door before she could order Harry a drink to make up for the drenching she'd given him.

Once Harry was settled and complaining to the barkeep about her clumsiness, Sadie decided to leave before she brought any more attention to herself. She headed for the door, no closer to finding a way out of Gandiegow.

Outside, she paused on the top step and spoke to the vast ocean in front of her. "I have to get out of here!" That's when she realized she wasn't alone.

Leaning against the edge of the building a few feet away stood Handsome. He walked toward her and stuck out his hand to help her down the last few steps. "I owe you, lass. Tell me where you want to go. I've got a truck."

Ross couldn't believe the lass had not only saved him from Harry and his dreadful niece, but the American lass had read his mind, too. *I want out of here as well.* Her hand was warm in his and she held on tight. He glanced down at them linked together, and though it felt strange, it felt right, too.

Yeah, so earlier Ross had skipped out when Kit had tried to set him up. And here he was now with a stranger . . . headed off to God-only-knew-where.

He looked down at the lass again. "Were ye serious about getting out of town?"

"You have no idea."

He cocked an eyebrow at her. "And ye'd run off with a man you don't know?"

She didn't hesitate, as if she already had his number. "I figured you for a nice guy from the get-go."

"How so?"

She shrugged. "If I hadn't rescued you, you would've agreed to go out with Harry-there's niece."

Ross shook his head. "Ye can't go around hopping into anyone's vehicle who offers."

She put her hands on her hips. "You don't know how badly I want out of here."

The lass was determined, he'd give her that. "Fair enough."

He really looked at her. She was shorter than him by at least a foot, with bangs framing an innocent face with her bobbed brown hair setting off her deep brown eyes. She had a birthmark above her mouth that reminded him of a heart. She seemed sweet, but her full-of-wisdom eyes seemed to contest her age, and at the same time they spoke of sadness and distress, too.

A wave of protectiveness came over him. "Do ye want to tell me what's going on?"

She shook her head no, as if that was all the answer he was going to get. She glanced back at the rest of the town and then pointed to the parking lot. "Can we get going?"

"Aye. This way."

She walked beside him the forty-some steps it took to get there.

"Is that your truck? The red pickup?" She walked toward it with purpose.

It was the only truck in the lot.

She opened the passenger side. "I like it. It has character." She slid in and shut the door.

He did the same on the driver's side. "Where to?"

"Away."